The Devil's Bones

ALSO BY CAROLYN HAINES

SARAH BOOTH DELANEY MYSTERIES

Game of Bones

A Gift of Bones

Charmed Bones

Sticks and Bones

Rock-a-Bye Bones

Bone to Be Wild

Booty Bones

Smarty Bones

Bonefire of the Vanities

Bones of a Feather

Bone Appetit

Greedy Bones

Wishbones

Ham Bones

Bones to Pick

Hallowed Bones

Crossed Bones

Splintered Bones

Buried Bones

Them Bones

NOVELS

A Visitation of Angels

The Specter of Seduction

The House of Memory

The Book of Beloved

Familiar Trouble

Revenant

Fever Moon

Penumbra

Judas Burning

Touched

Summer of the Redeemers

Summer of Fear

The Darkling

The Seeker

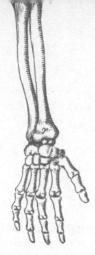

The Devil's
Bones

CAROLYN HAINES

MINOTAUR BOOKS
NEW YORK

First published in the United States by Minotaur Books,
an imprint of St. Martin's Publishing Group

THE DEVIL'S BONES. Copyright © 2020 by Carolyn Haines. All rights reserved. Printed in the United States of America. For information, address St. Martin's Publishing Group, 120 Broadway, New York, NY 10271.

www.minotaurbooks.com

Library of Congress Cataloging-in-Publication Data

Names: Haines, Carolyn, author.
Title: The devil's bones / Carolyn Haines.
Description: First edition. | New York : Minotaur Books, 2020. |
    Series: A Sarah Booth Delaney mystery ; 21
Identifiers: LCCN 2020006759 | ISBN 9781250257864 (hardcover) |
    ISBN 9781250257857 (ebook)
Subjects: LCSH: Delaney, Sarah Booth (Fictitious character)—Fiction. |
    Women private investigators—Mississippi—Fiction. |
    Murder—Investigation—Fiction. | GSAFD: Mystery fiction.
Classification: LCC PS3558.A329 D49 2020 | DDC 813/.54—dc23
LC record available at https://lccn.loc.gov/2020006759

Our books may be purchased in bulk for promotional, educational, or business use. Please contact your local bookseller or the Macmillan Corporate and Premium Sales Department at 1-800-221-7945, extension 5442, or by email at MacmillanSpecialMarkets@macmillan.com.

First Edition: 2020

10 9 8 7 6 5 4 3 2 1

For my wonderful Lucedale friends
and the golden years and grand adventures that we shared

The Devil's Bones

1

There's nothing like springtime in the Deep South, especially lower Mississippi. The counties warmed by the coastal breezes off the Gulf of Mexico spring to life with a palette that takes my breath away. When it comes to the season of showy flowers, the southernmost counties are floozies with a celebrated taste for riotous blooms.

The Delta, in the center and northern part of the state, has a vastness, a sense of eternity, that is a special beauty. But down in George County, the landscape is alive with those gay and frivolous blossoms. The azaleas, wisteria, Chinese fringe trees, mimosas, bottlebrush, tulip trees, and the first windings of coral crossover vines put on a show. Color pops in a range from vivid purple to orange, coral, pink, lavender, carmine, and white.

At the super exclusive and isolated Bexley B&B, where I am spending the weekend, towering banks of shrubs scale over eight feet tall. "Fancy ladies" was the term Aunt Loulane used to describe the riot of azaleas. Landscaped with bridal wreath, dogwoods, and amaryllis blooms, this is a magical place. I could easily imagine fairies hiding about the grounds. I think of the Easters of my childhood with a bittersweet pang. Vivid memories of egg hunts, chocolate bunnies, and Easter dresses.

It's almost dusk as I wander through the gardens of the B&B near the small town of Lucedale in the southeast corner of my state. I inhale the fragrance of wisteria and nostalgia floods me. What I wouldn't give to be a child again, safe in my parents' care, excited that while I sleep the Easter bunny will visit and gift me with colorful eggs and candy.

I leave the sweet scent of the flowers behind and walk under the spreading live oaks that drip with Spanish moss. There is so much to love and cherish in my home state. So much beauty. And somehow Tinkie, who has arranged this very special and celebratory girls' weekend, has found the perfect spot.

The Bexley B&B is built on the grounds of what had been a settlement structure that housed a general store, post office, doctor's office, and railway ticket station. Constructed from heart of pine lumber cut from virgin timber and taken to the local sawmill, the B&B has defied more than a hundred years of humidity, hurricanes, and hapless renovations. Now that Donna and Frank Dickerson have taken it over, the grand old lady is back—and vibrantly so. I turn around to glance at the inn as the lights begin to wink on. Surrounded by the graceful limbs of the oak trees wrapped in white fairy lights, I half expect Tinker Bell to show.

"Pray, hide me from the god who desires to take me underground and ravage me."

I spin around to face a beautiful woman in a toga and sandals. A crown of dahlias rests on her head and long blond hair streams down her back. Fear animates her lovely features and heightens her agitated breathing.

"Who are you?"

"My name matters not. If you do not act, I will be a live woman swept into the realm of the night lord, the ruler of the dead, and there I will be forced to live for the six long, dark months of the year. Please, help me. I cannot allow him to catch me."

I don't know who this guest is, but I'm pretty sure she's lost her rudder. This mini-vacation was too good to be true. Now I discover we're lodging in a lunatic asylum that Tinkie has booked under the pretense of being a spa.

"Good luck." I start walking, as fast as I can, back to the inn that glitters in the distance.

"Please, kind stranger. Protect me. Pluto comes when the final light dies, and he will make me his bride to sit at his side in Hades. I cannot endure another season as his queen, ruling over the dead. I am young and wish to live above."

My cat's name is Pluto, a beautiful black beast that's smarter than most people. He is indeed named for the god the ancient Greeks believed ruled the land of the dead. I slow. I know this woman—or I know of her. "Persephone?" I'm not surprised that the maiden who returns to Earth every spring after spending fall and winter in the land of the dead should appear at Easter. Hers is also a resurrection story.

"Yes, can you find my mother to protect me? Please, I am begging you."

I'm a pretty good private investigator, but I'm not up to the task of tracking down a goddess from the Greek pantheon. And this was no lowly demigod but a full-blown goddess. Persephone is the daughter of Zeus and Demeter. In other words, she's no one to mess with.

"Look, I have my own mother issues," I tell her. "I wish I could help but I can't."

"You mighty quick to run away from a challenge." She gives me the stink eye.

That stops me in my tracks. For all of her toga, sandals, and noble bearing, she raises a red alert. I smell a rat! Jitty, the resident haint of my family home in Sunflower County, has hitchhiked all the way down to Lucedale with me. And she was having some kind of fun at my expense.

"Jitty! What are you up to? Better yet, what are you doing here?"

"I'm here making sure you're an honest woman. You and that pack of divas you run with could be looking for trouble."

Jitty adores Tinkie and Cece, so she is definitely up to something else. "I'm on vacation. You're always telling me to relax, unwind. Remember, stress is a real ovary killer, and god knows if my ovaries croak I'll be of no use to you." Jitty has two goals in life—to torment the snot out of me and to get me with child so she has a Delaney heir to haunt.

"Your ovaries are dying all on their own. It's called Spinsterhood! You can't blame that on me. You're humping it hard toward thirty-five, still unwed and unbred. You'd think you were some high-strung Thoroughbred the way your body rejects pregnancy."

I held up a hand to stop that talk in its tracks. "Watch yourself."

Her grin told me how unafraid she was of my threats. "You left that hot man all alone in a town filled with hungry, single women. Not a smart move, cupcake."

"Coleman is grown. And besides, he needs some time on his own, too." I truly had no worries about Coleman Peters, my lover. He was true blue and a law-and-order man. He was also the sheriff of Sunflower County. "If Coleman gets up to no good, I'll get phone calls from at least a dozen people."

She didn't argue that fact and moved on. "Spring is the renewal, Sarah Booth. For you and everyone. In the natural world, this is the time for pregnancies, and you are wasting it here by yourself on an evening so beautiful it's a cryin' shame Coleman isn't here to share it."

I wouldn't mind a rendezvous with Coleman, but I would never admit it to Jitty. I remained stubbornly silent.

"That partner of yours is glowing. Think about that. If you had a baby, the little Toscar, or maybe Tinkos, as I'm going to call it, would practically be cousins with your little Deters! Even better, they could grow up to marry and then there would be plenty of money to restore Dahlia House."

"Back off!" Jitty was getting way over her skis on this. "Besides, if they're raised as cousins, marriage would be kind of icky."

"You're too literal, girl. Just too literal."

"Let Tinkie have this time of joy without interference or interruption. She's wanted this for so long."

Tinkie, after years of being told she was medically unable to have a child, was finally pregnant. She was aglow with her baby potential. Her husband, Oscar, walked around town like a preening peacock. I couldn't say if her unlikely pregnancy was actually the result of a spell cast by the Harrington sister witches or if rescuing her pregnant cousin and delivering the child had kicked her Fallopian tubes into action. Maybe it was simply a very strong and lucky little swimmer that made it past the scar tissue and landed on her egg. It didn't matter. The reason for our girls' weekend was to celebrate this joyful beginning to new life, something I'd wished for Tinkie for a long time.

"Jitty, why are you running around as Persephone?"

Jitty waved a hand around her. "Look at this beauty, this renewal, this celebration of life returning. Easter is the perfect resurrection story, but so is Persephone. We all long for redemption and resurrection."

She was right about that.

She looked pensive. "You know I came here to go to the sunrise service over at the miniature Holy Land. Sarah Booth, do you realize the responsibility that goes with bringing a child into this world and teaching her values?"

"Her? Tinkie is going to have a girl?" I did a little dance. Jitty had let it slip! She'd given me an answer from the Great Beyond that was top secret. "She wants a girl. She doesn't say that out loud, but I know it. Oh, this is wonderful!"

"Hush!" She leaned in and looked around as she began to morph slowly into the mocha-skinned ghost that was my nemesis and savior. "Keep your lips zipped, Sarah Booth. I shouldn't have said that. It's against the rules."

I had a real impulse to make hay with Jitty's indiscretion, but I didn't. She was my anchor to the past and the future, and the rules of the Great Beyond were strictly enforced. I would never risk having her get in trouble. The celestial power brokers might take her away from me.

I hit upon a sensible solution. "Tinkie could have an ultrasound to determine the sex, but she won't. She and Oscar want to wait."

"Then don't breathe a word." Jitty frowned with great concentration, like she was going to intimidate me into silence.

"I won't tell her because she doesn't want to know. And because I don't want you to get in trouble."

She sighed. "Okay. Then it's no big secret for you to know that I'm here to help Tinkie find the right path for her baby. She's afraid she'll pick wrong and not give the baby the proper religious instruction. I'll just prod her along the path."

I'd been a regular Sunday School girl until my parents died. After that, I refused to go to church for any reason and Aunt Loulane didn't make me. She had enough battles to fight and she let that one slide. My approach to life had come not from a specific religion but from watching the ethical way my parents lived their lives. They'd instilled a set of values in me that functioned as my day-to-day manual of conduct. Tinkie had her Daddy's Girl rule book, and I had my memories.

"Tinkie will figure this out. She feels like this baby is a special gift. She only wants to be sure she does everything she can to give her baby a happy foundation. And she will. No matter if the child decides on Buddhism, Christianity, Judaism, Islam, Zoroastrianism, Hinduism,

Jainism, Shinto, Confucianism, Taoism, or Sikhism."
I named off the great religions of the world. I'd done
my final literature research paper on this subject at Ole
Miss, and I'd been astounded at the similarities among
most of the great religions. The loss of my parents had
shaken my entire belief system, and I was searching,
even then, for something to grasp onto.

"I just don't want to see her go nuts and join some
kind of cult." Jitty no longer wore a toga. Instead she
sported a colorful sarong that was a fine complement to
the bank of fuchsia azaleas she stood beside.

"Tinkie? Join a cult? Who are you kidding? What
cult do you know that serves all organic, gourmet food
with no pesticides or toxins, gives foot massages, rubs
her belly, and talks baby talk to it? She has the Order of
Oscar Who Waits on Her Hand and Foot! That's all she
needs." I had to smile. Oscar was adorable in his role as
father-to-be.

"Just sayin', I'm keepin' an eye on things."

When Jitty started to get folksy with her language, I
knew something was up. "What do you know?"

"There's danger in the most unlikely places, Sarah
Booth. Just keep your eyes open for people who don't
seem authentic."

"Will do." The only people I hoped to meet this
weekend were masseuses, personal trainers, nutrition-
ists, and my two best friends. I figured I was pretty safe
from negative influences. "Hey, Jitty, are you going to
bring me an Easter basket in the morning? You know I
love dark chocolate and nuts. Maybe some of those robin
eggs. Reese's eggs are good, too. None of that nougat
stuff." I made a face.

"I remember how you used to steal little Tommy Atkins's chocolate bunny at the school Easter egg hunts. You would wait for him to get distracted, then run over, grab the big bunny out of his basket, and bite the head off."

I couldn't help but laugh. I had done that. "Yeah, those were good times. He cried every single time I did it."

Jitty shook her head. "It was also mean."

"Not really." Tommy Atkins was the biggest bully in the school. I was the only person who could bring him low, and I did it every single Easter at the class egg hunt. He never believed I'd do it again after the pounding he gave me. But I did it anyway. "Some people never learn," I said.

"Yeah, and you are one of them!"

There was the melodious clinking of wind chimes and the back door of the B&B opened. Tinkie stepped out on the porch, her body backlit by the porch lights. Dusk had slipped into darkness. "Sarah Booth, it's time for the meditation session! Are you out here?"

"Headed your way," I said as I stepped out of the trees and onto the path where she could see me. It was going to be a fun evening.

2

"I cannot believe we're on vacation and have to get up at five o'clock." Cece held a cup of hot coffee as she drilled both me and Tinkie with her gaze. Outside the dining room windows at the inn, night still lingered. "Why don't we cancel attending the service and just go back to bed?"

"Not on your life. It's a sunrise service. That means we have to be at the gardens at sunrise," Tinkie said. "You knew this when you signed on."

Cece gulped some coffee and sighed. "Yes, I did. I must have been delusional at the time. It's Easter Sunday and I'm going to hear a religious sermon at the butt-crack of dawn." She shook her head.

"Come on, hot diggity. We'll take the Roadster. The air is cool and it should wake you up." The truth was,

I loved driving my mother's old car at dawn on a warm spring morning. The pine woods around the inn were lovely, and at some of the old home sites, the scent of wisteria wafted to me.

"Maybe I should stay here and book another massage," Cece said, but she winked at me. She was just trying to get Tinkie's goat.

"You are *not* staying behind!"

Cece cackled gleefully and I aimed her at the door of our suite and gave her a gentle kick in the pants. "Tinkie is pregnant and you should not torment her."

"I know, but she's taking this whole child-rearing thing so seriously. Tinkie, you're a good person. You and Oscar both. You will raise a good child. Of all the people in the world, you shouldn't worry."

Tinkie nodded quickly. "Thank you, but I just want to know what's available. I do think some type of religious or spiritual instruction is important. Faith can be an anchor in times of crisis."

I wasn't going to dispute that. Besides, what I believed wasn't the issue at all. Tinkie had to find her own path. My job, as her friend, was simply to keep her company as she searched.

"Donna Dickerson said she'd have breakfast ready for us." I pointed to the door. "Let's grab a quick bite before we head out."

We bantered and teased each other as we took a seat at a window table with a view of a meditation maze. It was filled with spring bulbs and so beautiful.

The sound of rattling dishes and pots came from the kitchen so it was no surprise when Donna came out with fresh coffee. She was filling our cups when I heard a male voice.

"Ladies, are you attending the sunrise service?"

I looked up into the face of a very handsome man about our age. "We are."

"I'm Hans O'Shea, a traveling correspondent for *Places Off the Beaten Path* and *Globe Trotters*. I'd like to get some quotes from you after the service. Ladies as beautiful as you three will increase my viewership."

Hans was tall and well built, and he had the ease that came with being in front of a camera. Charm was his middle name, and while all three of us were totally committed to our men, we could enjoy a little masculine attention. Hans was not above shameless flattery and we ate it up with a spoon.

"*Globe Trotters* is that show about semi-famous people who travel to exotic locations," Cece explained. As a journalist herself, she knew a lot about the subject, even entertainment journalism. "You were nominated for an Emmy last year."

"You've heard of me?" Hans was thrilled at the recognition. His blue eyes lit up with merriment. "Let me compliment you yet again on your discerning viewing choices."

The man was full of himself, but he was also self-mocking. It was a fun combination.

"Millie is going to be really upset she missed this trip," Tinkie whispered to me.

Millie Roberts ran the local café in Zinnia and she was a fiend for celebrity gossip and scandal. If the Kardashian family was hosting an event she knew all about it. She knew who wore who on the red carpet for the Oscars, who was borrowing jewels and who was lending them, and who was making moon eyes at whom. She would be heartbroken at missing a chat with Hans. In fact, she and Cece were collaborating on a website that would replace the dying *National Enquirer* and also allow Millie to expound on her favorite topics, such as the ghost of Elvis and aliens landing in the Delta. Millie's stories were tongue-in-cheek with one exception. Princess Diana was serious business. Some bond had formed between the restaurateur and royalty. Millie had championed Diana in life, and in death she guarded her reputation. No one made fun of Princess Di around Millie and lived to tell about it.

"I know," I whispered back. "I hate she had to stay at the café, but her head cook was in the hospital. Next time." I tuned back in to the conversation Cece was having with the handsome television host.

"Are you doing a story on the miniature Holy Land and the surrounding gardens?" Tinkie asked Hans. "The exotic plants in the gardens rival any locale in the Deep South. And the curator of the gardens, aside from being a master of miniature construction, is a respected biblical scholar."

"That's exactly why I'm here. I'm curious about all of the above. The plantings of natural flora in the Garden of Bones is one of the best kept secrets of the state of Mississippi. Because the proprietor has also included even poisonous plants that are native, the local nickname for the gardens is the Devil's Bones."

"You have gotten the scoop, haven't you, Hans? I'm looking forward to seeing it all in a couple of hours." Cece motioned for Hans to take a seat at our table.

Donna Dickerson arrived with a platter of hot croissants filled with scrambled eggs and bacon. We each grabbed one. I wasn't particularly hungry, but the flaky crust called to me.

"Have you ladies heard that Bruce Springsteen is going to play a concert in Mississippi?" Hans had the latest celebrity scoop and it would be fun to listen to his gossip and stories.

"No." We all spoke in unison. "Tell us," I said.

"He's teamed up with several other stars. It's going to be a mega fundraiser for hurricane victims."

"We haven't had a really bad hurricane in a while." Cece was quick to point out the obvious. "It would be terrific if they could build up a fund and have something to fall back on when disaster does strike, because we all know it's an inevitability. And the hurricanes are so big and destructive now."

"That's the plan," Hans said. "The fund will be used for future storms, and not just in Mississippi but all over the nation. The casinos along the Mississippi Gulf Coast are hosting the event and offering a lot of incentives to performers. The tentative lineup is pretty impressive. It's going to be really, really big." He tilted his head and studied Cece. "I could get backstage passes for you and your friends if you'd help me do some interviews." He tsk-tsked. "Your reputation as a fine journalist precedes you, Cece. I know all about the work you do."

"She'll do it!" Tinkie said. "And we'll need four passes. We can't leave Millie out."

"For sure," Cece said. "Thank you, Hans."

I tapped my watch—it was time to go. I wanted to get to the destination with some time to learn the lay of the land. I'd heard about the miniature Holy Land for most of my life but had never had a chance to explore the area. From the brochure I'd read, the key cities and events portrayed in the New Testament of the Bible had been crafted in miniature by several biblical scholars.

The Holy Land was built to scale; one yard equaled a mile. A walking tour gave attendees a chance to see the geography of the Middle East and the travels of Jesus of Nazareth. I was eager to take the tour.

Cece chose to ride with Hans—they had a lot to discuss. If he was offering her a chance to interview for a television show, it was an opportunity she needed to explore. Tinkie settled in the front seat and strapped on her seat belt without me nagging at her. She had become very conscious of protecting her baby.

"Hans is very handsome," she said.

"And a good stepping-stone for Cece to get into TV. Not that she wants to leave Zinnia or the *Dispatch*. It could be good for Millie, too. Maybe Hans can use her on camera. She would love that."

"She'd die." Tinkie shook her head and laughed at the thought. "She would die *and* love it at the same time."

Hans and Cece took off before us, and I was in no hurry to catch up. The crisp Easter morning, without humidity, felt like silk sliding over my skin as I drove with the top down. It was one of life's simple pleasures. "We turn here to the right," I said as we topped a hill. I almost slammed on the brakes. Some neon monstrosity blinked gold, green, and purple at the top of the next hill.

"What is that?" Tinkie asked.

"Mardi Gras is over. I have no idea. It's an advertisement of some sort."

As we drew closer, it was clear that it was, indeed, an advertisement that had been programmed with blinking, zipping, dancing lights.

"Oh my goodness. I've never seen a billboard that big," Tinkie said. "Ewww. Look at that tacky thing."

It was pretty tacky. I slowed so I could read the copy.

THE MISSISSIPPI MALLET GETS THINGS DONE. ACCIDENT, DIVORCE, THE SWEET TASTE OF REVENGE—CALL PERRY SLAY, SOUTH MISSISSIPPI'S FOREMOST INJURY LAWYER. IF WE DON'T GET YOU MONEY, YOU DON'T PAY.

"This lawyer advertising is getting out of hand," Tinkie said.

I pressed the gas pedal to move along. No point causing an accident because we were staring at a god-awful sign.

"Drive faster. It looks like a pawn shop advertisement, not a lawyer. Your daddy would spin in his grave, Sarah Booth."

That was true. James Franklin Delaney had viewed the right to practice law as sacred. Those in the legal profession were called upon to act with ethics and integrity, always. Advertising for personal injury was not my daddy's style, though he had certainly had clients who'd been injured by accidents or corporations. Getting justice for those without power was a big part of who he'd been.

We made the turn and left the sign behind. The first tinge of dawn peeked on the eastern horizon and I increased our speed. While it was called sunrise, the service started at six o'clock. We had twenty minutes to make it.

Jitty's nocturnal visit came back to me. I never mentioned Jitty to anyone, not even my partner and best friend. Jitty was private, and I didn't want to jinx her continued residency at Dahlia House. But I could relay Jitty's message—as my own.

"Tinkie, don't ever worry that you and Oscar won't be great parents."

"This is such a privilege, Sarah Booth. We have been entrusted with caring for and teaching a new soul. Our child might cure cancer or save the planet."

"Or he or she may be a soybean farmer and marry the person he or she loves and raise a passel of children that you can pamper and adore." I didn't want her to put that kind of pressure on herself or her child. "The only thing that matters is that the child is whole, happy, and lives in joy. That's the only important lesson to teach."

"Do you think I shouldn't explore religions?"

"I think you should do whatever makes you happy. Just don't overburden yourself with expectations one way or the other."

"Good advice." She pointed to a big sign—this one tasteful—that marked the entrance to the Garden of Bones.

"Why do they call it a garden of bones?" I asked Tinkie.

"The literature says that the land was originally bought for a Confederate cemetery. That's how the gardens were started. There were plans to make a national cemetery, like they have in Vicksburg, but it never happened. Native and exotic plants from all over the South were brought in to create the gardens, paid for by donations from people who wanted to honor the dead. This was long before the concept of the miniature Holy Land was created. When Dr. Daniel Reynolds, theologian and Ph.D., saw the gardens and the lay of the land, he had a dream where he envisioned the entire concept. He and his wife started work, building first the City of Bethlehem and laying out the travels that Jesus made, according to the record of his life."

"That's some undertaking." I couldn't help but be impressed with just the idea, not to mention the execution.

"I want my child to know people who are dedicated to principles and values. People who believe in something bigger than themselves. I thought this would be a good place to start." She grinned. "And I really wanted to see the miniature Holy Land for myself. I've heard about it all my life."

"I'm on board for all of the above." We'd arrived at a parking lot that was beginning to fill up. I found a place beside Hans's SUV and Tinkie and I made our way to an outdoor amphitheater just as the sun broke through the morning mist. Golden light filled the area. No matter what happened after that, I would feel like something special had been sent to me.

A tall man with a huge one-eyed dog at his side stepped to the center of the stage. "Welcome to the Garden of Bones and the replica of the Holy Land. We're here to celebrate the resurrection of Jesus Christ on this Easter Sunday. When the service is over, you're welcome to tour the gardens and the grounds. I'll be leading a tour, as will my wife, Paulette." He pointed to a young woman who stood at the edge of the amphitheater. "Or you can go on your own. For those familiar with the travels of Jesus through the Middle East, the tour is self-explanatory. Some of you come every year. We thank you for your support."

"That's Daniel Reynolds," Tinkie said. "He has a doctorate in history but he never tells anyone that."

I nodded. Reynolds was a fit and strong man. His daily hours of toiling in the gardens had sculpted him to sinew and bone. The dog who'd taken the stage with him sat lovingly at his feet. I settled into my seat and simply enjoyed the familiar story I'd heard all of my childhood.

3

Reynolds focused his talk on the crucifixion and resurrection as the sun moved higher in the sky. It glittered through the thick pine boughs, warming the wooden benches and my body. A deep peace settled over me, and I looked from Tinkie to Cece and said thanks for the wonderful friends I'd been given. This was not the Easter of my childhood, the days I longed to recover, even briefly. This was my grown-up life, with friends who would show up for me no matter what.

Lulled into a place of real contentment as Dr. Reynolds moved into the benediction, I sat bolt upright in shock when a handsome man in a T-shirt, jeans, and work boots stepped onto the stage. "You have to stop this!" He stormed up onto the platform, sending a gasp

through the audience. "For the sake of future generations, you have to stop this madness."

Reynolds frowned, but kept talking.

"Who is that man?" Tinkie asked. "He is very rude."
She was pissed. She had no use for interlopers spoiling a
perfectly good Easter sermon.

"I don't know," Cece said, "but I smell a story." She
nodded at Hans, who'd taken a seat two rows behind us.
They both slipped from their seats and headed around
the edge of the amphitheater toward the stage.

"Cosmo, you should leave." Reynolds was calm and
collected. In fact, there was a hint of sadness in his stance
and voice. "You're only going to get in trouble again.
Now go take a seat for me, please."

I watched as Cosmo squared his shoulders and lifted
his chin. He was prepared to hold his ground, whatever
that was. He reminded me a bit of the underdog hero in
a movie.

"You have to stop people from tromping all over the
woods," Cosmo said. "The egg hunt! Those screaming
children running all over the place. The damage they'll
do to an already precarious ecosystem. Please, I'm begging you to stop it." He turned to the audience. "Get
out of here. Leave. This has to stop."

Cosmo was passionate in what he was saying, but I
took note of the crowd. Most people were ignoring him.
I leaned over to a woman who heaved a heavy sigh and
rolled her eyes.

"Who is that?"

"Cosmo Constantine. He's an entomologist. He says
humans are killing all the beneficial insects. He's been
writing letters to the editor of the local paper for months
now about how the gardens here are dangerous to the

future of the planet. He's always been a little . . . different, but lately he's looking deranged. Daniel is going to have to press charges, though he doesn't want to."

A very handsome man in a tailored suit stepped up on the stage. He spoke quietly to the bug boy, and with a nod at Dr. Reynolds, the new man led Cosmo away.

"Thank goodness someone is able to get that Cosmo fellow off the stage," I said to our talkative neighbor. I was relieved that an altercation had been avoided. Sparring at a sunrise service was not what we'd come to the area to see.

"That's Erik Ward." The woman sighed, but this time with satisfaction. "He's a dreamboat. And he's single. Never married. He's going to be a catch for someone."

Clearly she hoped it would be her. "He must be friends with Cosmo."

"I think Cosmo and Erik went to high school together. Erik runs the local pharmacy, Best Buy Drugs. He's a good guy and kind of like Cosmo's guardian angel. He tries to keep him out of trouble. Erik loves cats and old people. When some of his older clients can't afford to pay for their medicine, Erik just lowers the charge. He eats the loss."

He did sound like a nice guy, and he was certainly handsome enough to draw the attention of the ladies, young and old.

With a little maneuvering, Erik moved Cosmo away from the amphitheater and the two men disappeared down the trail and into the miniature Holy Land.

Reynolds picked up where he left off and continued with a history lesson, some geography, and a fascinating recounting of the political situation that led to the strong resistance to Christianity.

Reynolds's lecture ran long, but I was enthralled. When the service was over, most of the congregation went to sign up for the tours with Dr. Reynolds or his wife. We got in line and another half hour passed as I listened to the gossip around me. A lot of people didn't hold back on their opinion that Cosmo was half a bubble off plumb. The talk, though, was not malicious. Whatever his mental state, he was part of the community and folks seemed to suggest that ignoring him was the best route for Dr. Reynolds to take.

Finally, the younger children, wild with excitement, were led to another part of the gardens where eggs had been hidden for them to find. I gathered this had become Easter tradition for many locals. We went to watch for a few minutes as the little hellions scoured the area like locusts. There were squeals of delight when an egg or chocolate was found. The acreage for the hunt was vast, and the field had been broken down by age groups so all the kids had a fair chance.

"Let's get ahead of the crowd and tour the Holy Land by ourselves," I said to Tinkie and Cece. They both nodded, and we slipped away from the festivities and found a cart trail through the woods. I was selfish, but I wanted to view the miniature cities without the hubbub of lots of other people. There were wonderful plaques that detailed the biblical significance of each place.

"Look at the River Jordan!" Tinkie exclaimed as we came upon a winding stream that had been carefully engineered to traverse the sites. The locations of so many Bible stories I'd been told as a child came to life.

"Oh, look at those little houses and that temple, and that looks like a plaza!" Tinkie was beside herself.

We were talking when we came upon the first miniature town. I was stunned by the amazing detail as the city of Bethlehem spread out before me. Dr. Reynolds had created a detailed city, complete with temples and plazas and walls with little plastic centurions and foot soldiers. The buildings ranged from the more modest six-inch adobes to palatial luxury homes with a series of levels, mosaic-tile courtyards, wells, and stables where livestock looked out from tiny stalls. Some buildings were designed on terraces, as I'd seen in photos of the Middle East. The affluent adobe houses, temples, and other buildings of the wealthy had domed roofs. The entire city of Jerusalem spread across an area the size of a very large backyard. The care that had gone into the making of this world had me awestruck.

"This is wonderful." Cece was busy snapping photos. "This will make a great spread for the Sunday section. So many people have never heard of this place."

"Look! Look at the little donkey and the sheep. And there's a manger! This is the stable where Jesus was born." Tinkie was thrilled.

"How did you think to come here for Easter, Tinkie?" I asked.

"A friend of mine in the garden club grew up down here and she said she loved this place. She promised that the Easter service was the most special of the year. And she was right."

Far in the distance I heard the squeals and screams of young children as they continued to scour the land for prizes. They were closing in on the last moments of the egg hunt. I looked over at Tinkie's abdomen in sudden sympathy. Her life was about to change forever. And possibly her hearing, too. Jitty was all over me to have a little one, but I wasn't certain that was the path for me. I'd see how it went with Tinkie. Godmother might fit me better.

"I can't wait to get back to the B and B for one of those Bloody Marys," Cece said. "Breakfast was delicious, but it's time for a libation, don't you think?"

"Sounds great."

"Coffee is fine for me." Tinkie was being really stalwart about the fact she could no longer drink. Bad for the baby.

"And we can have another massage," Cece said. "That won't hurt the baby."

"Right." We walked across the dam of a pond that was bordered by an incredible wall of bamboo. There were plants I'd never seen, vibrant lilies and azaleas. The Garden of Bones was a beautiful place, even without the exquisite work of the miniature towns and villages.

None of us knew the order of the travels of Jesus, but we could enjoy the scope of this creation and the care for detail. We came upon Jerusalem as the sun topped the pine trees and brought the entire area into sharp focus. I put a hand out and stopped my friends in their tracks.

"What?" Tinkie asked.

"Is that a . . . body?" I pointed to the far side of Jerusalem, where what appeared to be a body was flung across the Garden of Gethsemane.

"A body?" Cece stepped forward. "It couldn't be. It has to be sand or something."

I knew better. "It's a body." Dread touched my neck. This could not be happening on our Easter vacation. I eased a little closer. I could make out what looked like one arm, outstretched. Legs were partially on the path.

"Don't be ridiculous." Tinkie was impatient and I could tell by the way she tapped her toe that she needed a facility. She'd always had a tiny bladder, but now she went every thirty minutes. "Let's head back to the office. I have to use the restroom."

She turned around to leave but Cece and I remained, staring at what could be a misplaced mannequin or scarecrow. Or a dead person. We were all reluctant to go close enough to check it out.

"Tinkie, hold up a minute." I took matters into my own hands and advanced on the pink-and-khaki lump. The closer I got, the bigger the sense of dread I felt. When I was within about twenty feet, I stopped. "Guys, it really is a body." There was no doubt, and the reality settled on all of us like a shroud. The man wore neatly pressed slacks and what had once been a crisp, starched shirt.

"Are you sure he's dead?" Cece asked.

"He looks dead." I moved closer. Whoever it was, he was on his stomach, his arms flung across the Garden of Gethsemane and almost touching the walls of Bethlehem, his face in the shallow river, really a two-foot-wide stream, that wound through the region. Had the River Jordan been at flood stage, he might have drowned.

Tinkie had slipped up beside me as I picked up a hand to check for a pulse. He wore a very expensive Rolex watch and a pinky ring. His dark hair was longish and when I looked closer I saw that it was dyed. His body was still warm. He'd died recently.

"Wait a minute," Tinkie said. "Wait a hot minute. I know who he is."

"You do?" How would Tinkie know a dead man in a garden of miniature cities of the Holy Land?

"It's that guy on the billboard. The lawyer. Perry Slay."
I looked more closely at his profile. "She's right."

"Don't touch him anymore, Sarah Booth." Cece pulled
Tinkie back. "It's a crime scene."

"What if he just had a heart attack?" Tinkie was
clearly hoping for the most reasonable explanation.

"Tinkie, hurry back and find Dr. Reynolds. Get him
here fast, before they start bringing those walking tours
through. It'd be best for everyone if this is kept quiet."

Tinkie didn't need a second urging. She headed off
toward the offices as fast as she could go. Cece and I
looked at each other.

"You don't think he had a heart attack, do you?" she
asked.

"No. The foam at the corner of his mouth is kind of
a dead giveaway. I think he may have been poisoned."

4

Thirty minutes later, Tinkie had returned and I was startled to hear the sound of horse hooves coming my way. I was sitting on a bench by a stone pillar that had once been Lot's wife. She should never have looked back at Sodom and Gomorrah. Pillar of salt and all of that.

"Is that a horse?" Tinkie asked. "Someone is riding a horse to a crime scene?" Pregnancy was making her just a tad short-tempered. But even Cece and I were sick of sitting on the bench waiting for the law to get there so we could give our statements.

"Wouldn't a donkey or burro be more appropriate to the region?" Cece asked.

I only rolled my eyes but stopped when a very handsome red bay horse came into view. The dark-haired woman sitting on the horse was a born equestrian. Her position in the saddle was perfect, and she rode up to us and hopped off with great agility.

"Sheriff Glory J. Howard," she said. "Folks just call me Glory."

Okay, so first it had been an entomologist trying to take over a sermon, then a dead body in the miniature Holy Land, and now a horse-riding sheriff. This was one of the coolest girlfriends' weekends I'd ever participated in. While Cece and Tinkie made introductions with Sheriff Glory, I examined the horse. He was a fine creature, perfect conformation, striking black stockings, black mane and tail, and an alert yet calm disposition. I was about to fall in love.

"His name is Raylee," Glory said. "He's the best deputy a sheriff could have, and a good thing, too, since the county supervisors don't really provide a budget for more than two human law officers. I hear you ladies found the dead lawyer?"

Tinkie explained how we'd come upon Perry Slay, flung out in the garden.

"Did you see anyone suspicious when you came up here?" Glory asked.

"No." I said. "There wasn't anyone around. At first we didn't believe it was a body. When I checked, he hadn't been dead long. He was still warm to the touch."

"You touched him?" she asked, nodding to a woman who arrived and began to kneel beside the body. "That's the coroner."

"I touched him to check for a pulse."

"We told her not to," Tinkie said. She had returned to the bench to sit. The growing baby was really pulling on her energy supply. She looked ready for a nap.

"No harm done," Sheriff Glory said. "I'll be right back." She left to speak with the coroner and I followed to see what I might overhear. This wasn't my case, but murder always piqued my interest. When I looked back, Tinkie was almost dozing, and Cece was in a huddle with Hans, who'd just arrived and was in near shock. Coming up the hill was Dr. Reynolds.

"I've canceled the tours," he told Glory. "The children are finishing their egg hunt then everyone is packing up. What can I do to help?"

"Did you notice Mr. Slay in the congregation?" Glory asked.

"I didn't," Reynolds said. "But I wasn't paying particular attention to everyone who was here. It was a big crowd."

He was telling the truth about that. Nearly two hundred people had appeared for the service.

"Mr. Slay was known for his litigious behavior," Glory said. "Had he filed any suits about you or the gardens?"

This was an interesting angle. I tried as subtly as possible to read Daniel Reynolds's response.

"Not with me," Reynolds said. "Slay was always threatening people, though. He'd sue if he thought he could wring even a small payment out of someone just to avoid the trouble of court."

"Was he any good as a lawyer?" I asked. I realized too late that I'd interjected myself into a conversation I had no part in.

"He was . . . prolific in filing suits," Glory said. "You and your friends need to stay in the county. You did discover the body, so, at this time, it's a request."

"We had planned on going home tomorrow," I said.

Tinkie and I could stay, but Cece had a demanding job at the newspaper. "Mrs. Richmond and I will be happy to stay, but my reporter friend may need to leave."

"I'll do my best to get through this quickly and release you all," Glory said, but it was clear she meant for all three of us to remain in the area. It looked like we'd be forced to endure the luxury of the B&B for another night or two. Oh, how cruel was fate.

I had one thing to tell the sheriff, and I pulled her aside. "There was a man who interrupted the service. Cosmo Something. He's upset with Dr. Reynolds and what's going on here at the gardens. I just wanted to mention it, since the body was found here. With that foam at the victim's mouth, it does look like foul play."

"Are you implying that Cosmo might have killed Slay to throw a crimp in Dr. Reynolds's plans to expand the gardens?"

"There's a plan to expand the gardens?" This was the first I'd heard.

"There is," Reynolds said. "Cosmo has been upset by my ideas for expansion."

"You think he'd kill someone because of that?" It did sound like a wacko scheme, but I'd learned that motives for murder never made sense to sane people.

"Cosmo is passionate about his beliefs, as misguided as they are," Daniel Reynolds said.

Glory gave him a long look. "Thanks. I've never considered Cosmo as dangerous, but he's let this whole thing eat at him."

"What's his beef? Who could get angry about gardens? Even gardens with miniature buildings?" I asked.

Glory answered, indicating Cosmo's issue was long standing and known to the law. "Reynolds diverted water from a ground spring to create the River Jordan. The spring once fed a natural habitat for different insects, reptiles, and small fish. Cosmo sees the gardens as a commercial tourist trap that is destroying the balance of nature."

"How long has he been fighting Reynolds?"

"A couple of years, but he seems to have intensified his objections lately. I heard he'd been put on some medication, but that could just be a cruel rumor. This is a small county with a small population. Sometimes that's a good thing, but sometimes it's a really bad thing where unfounded gossip is concerned."

I looked around and pointed at the handsome man who'd gotten Cosmo off the stage. He'd been sitting quietly in the back of the audience before he'd gone to help. "He seems to be a friend of Cosmo. He was helping him. Maybe he has some answers for you."

"I'll check with Erik. He has his own beef with Slay," the sheriff said to me.

"If you find out Slay was murdered, do you have any serious suspects?" I could already list at least three, but the sheriff would know the potential seriousness far better than I would.

"A lot of people hated Slay. He filed lawsuits against most of the elected officials. Believe me, some of them deserved it, but some didn't. The pay for supervisor or alderman isn't really worth the trouble to me. Folks expect a miracle. The residents want paved roads, clean ditches, water services, great schools, and they don't want to pay a dime in taxes. The ones who benefit the most and can best afford to pay are the ones who whine and moan the most."

"It's not always the pay that matters. It's the power."

I didn't mention that kickbacks and under-the-table payments could also be a juicy enticement for folks to go into "public service." "How did you end up being sheriff here?"

"Got too old to rodeo, and I grew a conscience. Couldn't stand the way the animals were hauled around, never getting to be animals. I like my horse better than most people, and I just didn't care to put him through the stress any longer."

"I get leaving that life, but why a law officer?"

"My dad was the sheriff back in the seventies. Folks loved him. They offered me the job after the last sheriff went to prison." She laughed at my startled expression. "Tampering with evidence, intimidating witnesses. The sheriff was deep into bad behavior. I'd just come home and they hired me to fill out his term. Then I ran for office and here I am."

I didn't ask but I wondered if Glory J. Howard had any of the necessary skills to be an effective lawman. This little county couldn't afford a showpiece lawman. They needed someone who could actually investigate a case. But thank goodness that wasn't my concern. In a day or two I'd be home in Sunflower County with Coleman Peters, the lawman who'd won my heart.

"Excuse me, looks like the coroner is ready to move the body. Ladies." Glory tipped her hat. "I'll be in touch."

"Sure thing," Tinkie and I chorused.

Cece was still gabbing enthusiastically with Hans the TV reporter, and we watched her for a moment. "They've really hit it off," Tinkie said. "If Cece got a chance to work for a national TV show do you think she'd leave Zinnia? I mean Jaytee's career is there with the band. He can't just go off and leave."

"She could travel and always come home to Zinnia.

People have a lot more freedom now than they did fifty years ago. She could make it work."

Tinkie sighed. "I don't know, Sarah Booth. Maybe this baby is just sucking all of my energy, but I think about how much work a relationship is and I don't know how it can really work if one partner is always on the road."

I didn't want to be on the road away from Coleman, and I doubted Cece wanted to leave Jaytee alone too much. "We have to trust Cece to know how far she can stretch that connection, and how much she wants. She may not want to be on TV at all. She's got her own following in the Delta and she has lots of social power there. She seems content enough to me."

"I'm just borrowing trouble," Tinkie said. "You're right. Now let's stroll back to the office. I want to head back to the B and B. I do need a nap, and I want to talk to Oscar. I know you're missing Coleman, too."

"Some food first."

She nodded. "After all—"

"You're eating for two," I finished for her.

Hans decided to join us, and we drove to the quaint town of Lucedale for a late second breakfast in the Coffeepot Café.

"I've been told the coconut cream pie is the best in the nation," Hans said. "That's what I'm having."

It was pie all around, and I had a chance to compare this diner with Zinnia's own Millie's Café. What I discovered was that they were both very similar—right down to the woman who owned the Coffeepot and came to talk to us to personally assess the service we'd received. And the coconut pie was to die for.

We shoveled the delicious concoction of meringue, custard, and flaky crust into our pieholes as Hans regaled us with hysterical tales of his filming around the South. His mission was to discover little-known attractions—hidden gems such as the Garden of Bones and the miniature Holy Land. I interjected, "It's possible that dead lawyer was poisoned. Just something to keep in mind for your potential story."

"That place is exquisite," Hans said. "Despite the dead body. Man, what was that all about?"

"You aren't really going to use that in your piece, are you?" Tinkie asked.

"Not certain yet. You have to admit, it's a bit of drama for a travel writer. I got some great footage of the dead man's hand, flung in the River Jordan and near the walls of Jerusalem." He leaned toward us, his eyes dancing. "I always wanted to be a crime reporter. I love entertainment and travel news, but there are so many instances where an innocent man is railroaded into prison, don't you think?"

"It can happen," I said. "We're lucky in Sunflower County to have a sheriff who cares about catching the bad guys, not just improving his statistics. Sheriff Glory seems pretty dedicated to justice."

"She does at that," Hans said.

"Did she mention if she had any suspects yet? I asked, but she didn't answer me directly." I couldn't help myself. We'd found the body of a man I was 99 percent sure had been murdered, likely poisoned. Though I had no reason to involve myself in this case, I couldn't forget the way the body had been sprawled across the Garden of Gethsemane, crushing the painstaking work of Dr. Reynolds. The symbolism of killing a personal-injury lawyer at a religious site on Easter Sunday was not lost on me.

"Not really. She plays her cards close to her vest," Hans said. "I did a little digging on Glory J. Howard." He held up his smartphone and waggled it. "Want me to dish the dirt?"

"Yes!" Tinkie and Cece couldn't wait.

"She rode on the U.S. Olympic equestrian team in 2000, but after the Olympics she took her horse and began to follow in the footsteps of Annie Oakley as a trick rider in various rodeos. She can ride and shoot and hit the target—it's amazing. And she can do rope tricks and she also does tumbling tricks off her horse. She's a world-class athlete."

So far the dirt he was dishing was only topsoil. No muck or slime, yet. "Nothing scandalous?" I asked.

"She was married once, to a farrier. He was kicked in the head by a horse he was shoeing and died." Hans leaned in. "It happened at their ranch. It was her horse. There was more than a little talk that she wanted him dead."

"Kind of hard to train a horse to kick someone in the head, don't you think?"

"Maybe, maybe not," Hans said with a twinkle in his eyes. "I did a little checking, and Sheriff Howard is big on raising money for the Boys and Girls Ranch and other charities that involve kids."

The wicked glint in his eyes told me he was about to dish the subsoil now. "Go on."

"One of the events used in the fundraiser is Glory setting up a target with a photo of a person on the head. For twenty dollars, she would get her horse to kick the photo. The horse hits the person's head ninety-nine out of one hundred times." He arched his eyebrows three times to emphasize his point.

Glory Howard could have trained her horse to kill her husband. And it sounded like a murder that could never be hung around her neck. Trick horse taught to kick a target on command—right. Except I knew horses and how incredibly smart they were. A target-kicking horse could be a lethal weapon. It was absolutely brilliant! And based on the fact she publicly displayed the horse's skill in front of the entire community, no one would believe she'd deliberately used that as a means of murder.

"Do you really believe Sheriff Howard is corrupt?" Cece asked Hans.

"Oh, no, I'm just telling you the gossip. Unproven gossip. The husband's death was investigated by a sheriff in another county and she was never implicated. Accidental death. Dangers of the farrier trade. But gossip is my specialty, you know." He laughed and looked around the restaurant. "Too bad we can't get a good Bloody Mary here."

"Let's head back to the B and B," Tinkie said. Her pie was long since gone. The spurt of sugary energy she'd received from it had peaked and dissipated. She needed a nap.

The bell over the café door jangled and Erik Ward walked in. He looked around and nodded to us. "I saw you at the sunrise service. You found Slay's body, didn't you? Good riddance."

Tinkie stood up abruptly and waved him over. "Join us. We aren't staying much longer, but we'd like to ask some questions."

I nodded approval at Tinkie. She might be baby-fuddled, but she was working the case, even though it wasn't our case.

Erik pulled up a chair and joined us, also ordering a slice of coconut pie and some coffee. We made introductions, explaining we were private investigators and journalists. Hans picked up the job of interrogator. He was very good at sliding a pointed question into a conversation.

"What's going on between you and Slay?" Hans asked Erik.

Tinkie, Cece, and I perked right up at this sudden shift in conversation.

"I was suing him," Erik said. "I'm just glad that worthless skunk is dead."

Not the smartest thing to be saying about a murder victim. "May I ask why you were suing Mr. Slay?" I asked.

"He was a common thief," Erik said, not bothering to hide his ire. "The man was a menace. He sued everyone all the time about nothing, but that's not the worst. He preyed on old people who thought he was someone they could trust. He all but hung a sign around his neck calling himself Atticus Finch, the lawyer who would stand up for the innocent. He was a fraud."

Erik still hadn't given us the reason he was at odds with Slay, but I could see Tinkie working it out in her head as to how to get that information. She put a hand on Erik's biceps and gave a little squeeze. "What did Slay steal from you?" she asked.

"A section of timberland," Erik said. "Over in Butler County, Alabama. He tricked my father into signing it over to him as payment for writing his will."

I swallowed. A section of land was 640 acres. That land, if it had harvestable timber, was worth over a million just in timber, not to mention the value of the land itself. "That's a helluva price to pay for writing up a will." I could see why Erik was hot under the collar.

"I don't believe it will hold up in court. My dad was sick and in the hospital when he signed that agreement. He was dying, and he wanted to be sure he took care of everything. Perry Slay went in the hospital room. Dad was drugged and Perry got him to sign that document. It won't hold up. Anyone can see that my dad didn't realize what he was doing then." He lowered his voice. "Only a snake would take advantage of a sick man. I'm glad Slay is dead. I'd like to shake the hand of the person who made it happen."

"If only I had my camera rolling," Hans said. "That would have been a quote."

Erik sighed. "Of course I don't mean that I'm literally glad he's dead." He paused. "I'm glad his ability to create mischief and strife for a lot of people is done. *That* I'm happy about."

"Who else hated Slay?" I asked.

"Just about everyone who ever had any dealings with him," Erik said.

"What about your friend Cosmo?" I asked.

"He's not all that much of a friend, I just feel sorry for him," Erik said. "That area where he lives is everything to him. He knows every plant, beetle, or butterfly. He loves it, even the snakes."

"And he was upset with Dr. Reynolds about . . . ?"

"Reynolds diverted the water from a natural spring that once flowed onto Cosmo's property. It was vital in creating a wetlands where so many insects thrived."

"Can you legally divert water like that?" Cece asked. "In the Delta, water is frequently a property issue."

"It was a natural spring on the land that Dr. Reynolds

owns." Erik seemed to know the whole story. "To his credit, Reynolds had no idea when he dug a channel and diverted most of the water into his Dead Sea and Jordan River that it would have any impact on anyone else."

"But he won't undo it?" Tinkie asked.

"He can't. The way he added on to and modified the Holy Land there, he needs that water, too. The little spring is abundant in the warm, wet months, but during the drier months, there's barely enough water for Reynolds's purposes."

"Who else would like to see Slay dead?" Cece asked. "Let's make a list." She whipped out a little pad and pen from her purse. She was a reporter—she was always prepared to take down information.

"I heard he had a couple of girlfriends that he pissed off," Erik said. "He sued some drug companies. They could have sent a hit man after him. Look, the man had a personality like a porcupine. He could needle anyone, even those who tried to be friendly." Erik took the last bite of his pie. "Now if you'll excuse me, ladies and gentleman, I need to get busy."

"Thanks for chatting with us," Tinkie said. "You do stay fit, don't you?" She was taking in his physique. "Are you a runner?"

"Not hardly," Erik said, but he flushed a little.

"A gymnast?" She squeezed his muscle a little more.

"Tinkie!" I was shocked. "That's almost assault, girlfriend."

Tinkie and Cece howled.

"I just stay on my feet a lot," Erik explained. "I do a lot of gardening, too."

"Ignore them," I told him. "Tinkie is pregnant and

suffering from baby hormones and Cece is just plain wicked."

"I can handle that," Erik said as he put money down to pay his check.

We followed suit and filed out of the café. Hans excused himself, saying he had an interview to conduct. We stopped by the scratching post on Main Street, where back in the 1960s and '70s movie stars had paused to scratch their backs. We all had to give it a try. It was a beautiful afternoon, and the little town was bustling with activity. Several car horns honked as Cece put a little more hip action into her back scratching than was really necessary.

Erik grinned. "You ladies are going to set Lucedale on its ear."

"Might be fun," Cece said with a wink. "We enjoy a little upset on occasion."

"If you need any aspirin or such, come on down to Best Buy Drugs. That's my business." He pointed down the block. "We even have an old-fashioned soda fountain."

He was about to walk away when I called out to him. "Erik, do you think Cosmo killed that lawyer?"

Erik laughed. "Cosmo can't kill a fire ant when it's biting him. Highly unlikely that he'd kill a man. He's the most peaceful man I know. He's happy to stay out in those woods if others will just leave him alone."

"Who would kill Perry Slay?" Tinkie asked.

"I'd be the most likely suspect." He spoke without hesitation. "I hated his guts and made no bones about it."

"Did you do it?" Cece asked.

"No. I hated him, but I didn't kill him. Though, truthfully, it wouldn't be any worse than stepping on a cockroach." He gave a cheerful wave and headed down the street.

"Stay out of it." Cece looked at me. "You're on vacation. You aren't getting paid to poke into this. Let's go for a massage."

"Right on," I said and led the way to the parked cars.

5

Bonita, the masseuse, had hands of steel, and she knew how to use elbows and knees to work the deep kinks out of my muscles. I sighed with contentment as she pummeled, punched, and unknotted the long months of tension. Cece and Tinkie were also on tables getting a good working over. We would be useless for the rest of the day. A wheelbarrow would be required to get us back to our rooms. If we ever got a chance to go there. Tinkie was making sure we had every bit of pampering we could stand.

"I've booked us for those special clay masks. The clay comes from a gully here in the county and it's being called a miracle antiaging mask."

"Oh, Tinkie." All I really wanted to do was sink into bed and conk out.

"I'm the pregnant one, so stop acting like you're about to run out of steam."

She was right. I needed to buck up and slither my way down the hall to the clay-mask session. I took some satisfaction in Cece groaning a little as Tinkie herded us to our next appointment.

An hour later, we were sitting in chairs with our feet soaking for a pedicure while our faces were pulled and contorted by the drying clay. It was a creepy feeling, but also pleasant. The pedicurists brought shades of nail polish and we each picked one.

"Hhwwts hor hinner?" Tinkie asked.

She couldn't actually move her lips to speak. It was kind of delightful. But I could interpret Tinkie speak—she wanted to know what was on the menu for dinner. She was hungry all the time.

"Ladies, let's wash those masks off," the clinician said and slapped a hot wet towel over my face. In just a few moments, the clay softened and was removed. I could talk.

"Some kind of grilled vegetable delight. If I stayed here a couple of weeks, I could lose all the weight I put on over Christmas and it wouldn't be a chore to do it. The food is delicious."

"And mostly plant based," Cece threw in approvingly. She was admiring her newly painted toenails—purple passion. It was a color that suited her nature.

"What's next?" I asked, hoping Tinkie would say it was nap time.

"A hike in the woods."

"Yay!" I tried not to sound sarcastic.

There was a light rap on the door and the B&B owner stepped into the room. "Sorry to interrupt your relaxation, ladies, but there's someone here to see you. Erik Ward."

"Please tell him we'll be right there," Tinkie said. She always had the best manners. "What does he want?"

Donna's mouth twisted into a lopsided grin. She knew something we didn't and she was about to spill it. "I'd hazard a guess that he's here to hire Delaney Detective Agency to prove he isn't guilty of murder."

"What?" we all three said as we sat up.

"Erik was charged with murder?" Tinkie asked.

"He was." Donna enjoyed sharing the nugget of gossip.

"For killing that lawyer?"

"Exactly." Donna nodded. "Heck, everyone in town wanted Perry dead. I don't see why Glory wants to go and pin it on Erik. Even if he did do it, he should get a medal and a stinking parade. Slay was a blight on the community."

I hadn't met a single soul who wanted to shed a tear for poor, dead Perry Slay.

I was about to start to the parlor where Erik waited when Donna put a hand on my shoulder. "Maybe take a look?" She gave me a hand mirror.

I glanced at my reflection and then gave a yelp of horror. My face was beet red. As in cooked. I glanced at Cece and Tinkie, who were also an unattractive shade of carmine.

"Not to worry. In about an hour, the red will fade and you'll be left with the skin of a twenty-year-old." Donna was trying hard not to laugh at our distress. "Normally our guests take a nap after a clay facial."

"Which is exactly what I'd like to do," I said.

Tinkie looped my hand through her arm. "Come on, ladies, time's a'wasting."

Erik stood at the large window looking out over the beautiful gardens where fallen bridal wreath petals had coated the ground like fairy snow. When he heard us enter the room, he faced us. He was a handsome man, and one who was worried. "They've charged me with Slay's murder. Lucky I could make bail."

He gave us the rundown, clearly too upset to comment on our beacon-red faces. Erik had been overheard Saturday night having an argument with Perry Slay. The two had almost gotten into a fistfight, and Erik had loudly declared, "You conniving bastard. I'll put you in your grave for tricking my father."

We listened to Erik's story, but all I heard was a threat, certainly not evidence of murder. I couldn't believe Sheriff Howard had actually arrested Erik on such flimsy evidence. "The charge is murder?"

"Yes. The coroner's findings are preliminary, but it looks like a classic case of poisoning." Erik paced in front of the window. "You said you were private investigators. I did some checking around and you have a good reputation. Will you take the case? I didn't do this."

"Of course we will," Tinkie said. She looked at me and I nodded in approval. "Coleman and Oscar can do without us if we need to stay."

"Okay," I said. Coleman would be very eager to see me when I finally got home, and I intended to take full advantage of that. "Other than making threats against

Slay's life and filing a lawsuit against him, what's the evidence against you?"

"The sheriff suspects poisoning. I have loads of different poisons at my fingertips in the drugstore. I'm educated in drug interaction. That, coupled with the threat on Saturday night . . ." Erik heaved a sigh. "And I was the last known person to see him alive."

"Can someone alibi you?" Tinkie asked.

"I live alone, though I date a number of women out of town. I enjoy the single life. Maybe too much." He sighed again and then drew out a checkbook and wrote out a check for our retainer.

He hadn't actually answered Tinkie's question, but I let that go for the moment. "Who do you think killed Slay?"

He scoffed. "Top of my suspect list is Dr. Mike Snaith."

"A medical doctor?" Cece asked.

"Used to be—until Slay sued him for malpractice. Snaith either lost or gave up his license, not sure which. Now he concocts herbal remedies and snake oil that he sells on the internet. He's a caricature of what he used to be."

Now *that* sounded like a motive for murder. "Where does Snaith have his business?"

Erik frowned. "He has that old Victorian house with all the levels and balconies and turrets at the dead end on Ratliff Street. You can't miss it."

I gave him my blank look. I didn't know much about the town.

"I did a lot of research on the area before I came. I know where it is." Hans O'Shea had popped into the parlor without making a sound. For a big guy, he could move fluidly. "I'd be happy to show you, ladies."

"You'll have to go on your own," Erik said. "My presence will just excite Snaith into name-calling and threats. He hates me. Besides, I'm needed at my pharmacy. I have a terrific staff, but I need to be there. My customers expect personal attention."

"We're on the case," Tinkie assured him. "We'll check out Snaith. Please get in touch with us when you close the pharmacy for the day."

"Sure thing." Erik said his goodbyes and headed back to town.

"Shall we boogie into town to talk to Snaith?" Cece asked. She was ready for an adventure. I noticed that most of the redness was gone from her face, and Tinkie's, too. Which meant I should also be back to my paler shade of pale.

"Road trip!" Hans called out. He was such a big kid that I couldn't help but smile, and I didn't see the harm in him tagging along.

"I do need to talk to Dr. Snaith." I was curious to meet the good doctor. If he was concocting herbal cures, it wouldn't be a far stretch to think he might also be well versed in poisons. "And we need to get a copy of the coroner's report. I believe Sheriff Howard will cooperate with us."

"Saddle up," Tinkie said as she grabbed her purse. "Hans, are you coming with us?"

"Wouldn't miss it for all the tea in China. Would it be okay if I film the investigation? It could make an interesting segment on traveling private eyes."

"I don't know—" I started, but Tinkie cut me off.

"That would be great fun. Have mystery, will travel. Kind of a modern-day paladin. Brave and heroic knights, or private detectives, as the case may be, on the road solving mysteries and bringing justice to all."

"You've been watching way too much daytime TV," I whispered to her.

"Nonsense! She's right," Hans said. "It even has the potential for a series. I can pitch this to my producers."

"We can't solve a case a week," I warned him. That kind of schedule for a weekly TV show was quicksand and I was the only one smart enough to see we were sinking fast.

Hans laughed out loud. "We film year-round, but we only air eighteen shows a year. You can handle it."

I did sigh in relief. "Maybe." I still wasn't ready to commit.

Hans had been in the area for several days, and he had mapped out the high points of interest, including Snaith's Apothecary, as the doctor's business was called. It was a quaint, two-story Victorian with big windows that gave a glimpse of a beautifully tiled floor and walls with murals of plants and gardens that contained fairies and elves tucked among the leaves. It didn't strike me as the kind of décor that a former doctor/current herbalist would select.

When we opened the door, a bell jangled and Mike Snaith came from the back to greet us. He took in Hans and his video camera, Cece with her newspaper camera, Tinkie with her baby bump, and me. "How can I help you?" he asked.

Hans took the lead, which surprised me but I was happy to go with the flow. "I'm filming a travel show on the Garden of Bones. I'm sure you've heard a body was discovered there."

"Oh, indeed I have." He almost rocked forward on his toes in glee. "Couldn't happen to a nicer guy."

Was everyone in this little town so open about their dislike of each other?

"So you knew the deceased?" Tinkie asked. She put on her signature charm that could melt a man all the way down to his shoes. She sidled up to Snaith and batted her big blue eyes up at him. Men fell for this every single time.

"Everyone knew Perry Slay," Snaith said. "Everyone hated him. May I get you a chair, Mrs. . . . ?"

"Richmond." Tinkie made all the introductions. "Hans is filming his TV show on the gardens and we're interested in the murder of Mr. Slay."

"Interested? Why?" Snaith was almost the perfect Oil Can Harry. His dark hair was sleeked back, his mustache waxed on the very ends. He wore loose-fitting dun-colored pants with a high-collar shirt and wide braces. He could have stepped out of 1900.

I didn't want to give away that we were working for Erik—at least not yet. Thank goodness Hans seemed capable of carrying the whole conversation.

"The murder is the perfect conclusion for my piece on the gardens," he said. "I mean it's not every day that a Gulliver is found dead amongst the religious Lilliputians."

"I adore Jonathan Swift," Snaith said. "A man of great wit and political acuity. But your analogy has flaws. Gulliver was not a bad man. Slay was a vile miscreant."

"We've heard as much about Slay," Cece said. She had her notebook and pen in hand. "Why did you hate him so much?"

"He sued me for malpractice in a case that had nothing to do with my work as a doctor. He won and bank-rupted me. I lost my license and means of making a living. Slay never had the evidence to win his case. What he had was a jury he could pay off."

That was a serious charge. "Can you prove that?" I asked.

"I could have until the foreman on the jury died last year. There went my hope for appealing the judgment. I wouldn't be surprised if Slay was the one who bumped her off."

"Aren't you even a little worried about speaking ill of the dead?" Cece asked. "Especially someone who's been murdered."

Snaith laughed, and I expected him to twirl his mus-tache. "Haven't you heard? Erik Ward has been charged with the murder. Dear goodness, life doesn't get any better than this."

"I take it you don't like Erik either?" I said.

"He is my nemesis. He thinks that just because he has a pharmacy license he can imply I'm selling fake medici-nal cures. He wants to support the drug companies and hook the local residents on chemical medications. I offer natural solutions. He maligns me all the time. I'm happy to see him on his way to Parchman prison."

Snaith referred to the state penitentiary that hap-pened to be in the Delta. It was a pretty harsh place. I'd come to conclude that I didn't want to get on the bad side of anyone in this town.

"Were you aware that Slay was poisoned?" I asked.

Snaith shrugged. "I always figured he'd catch a bullet from a jealous husband, but poison works for me, too."

"You aren't curious about what kind of poison?" I pressed.

"Nope," Snaith said. "You say tomato, I say to-mah-to. You say dead by poison, I say no matter the method as long as he's stone-cold dead."

"You aren't worried that you could become a suspect?"

"Me? Heavens no. They've already snared Erik." He laughed out loud and actually rubbed his hands. "He's obviously the murderer and he's on his way to his just rewards."

Either he was really innocent or he'd somehow engineered the frame of Erik. Now, that was an interesting direction to pursue. "Why are you so sure Erik is guilty?" I asked.

"He hated Slay. Maybe more than I do. Er . . . did."

"Tell me about that feud between Erik and Slay." I wanted to hear his take.

"Delicious!" His eyes sparked with amusement. "Erik's father was a very smart man and acquired thousands of timber acres. He paid a fair price and folks liked him. That's in contrast to some of the scoundrels who come in here and buy up land at tax sales. Sure, it's legal. Sure, they have a network where they can rush in and scoop up the best land at the best price. But the folks who lose the land never forgive them."

"So Erik's dad was a good guy," Cece prompted. We were all enthralled with the details of this land deal.

"He was a good man and a smart businessman. But he was fair. People respect that. Or they used to."

"Slay bamboozled Ward senior, is that the jist?" Tinkie asked.

"Just before Ward senior died."

"Surely that kind of deathbed shenanigan won't hold up in court," Hans said.

"Depends on the judge." Snaith shrugged. "I feel for Erik on this. I do. Slay was a slimy bastard. There wasn't an underhanded deal going that he didn't want in on. Erik took this especially hard because it made his dying father feel incapacitated, as if he'd been duped."

Probably because he had been. I had several older friends who were simply tired. And many older-generation folks had a real respect for lawyers, ministers, and police. I myself had come to question all three professions. No profession was free of crooks and cheats. Those who presented themselves as honorable because of their job were often the best at deception.

"I can see where that would scald Erik. He seems to be very fond of his family."

"To his credit, he was and is."

Snaith had actually said something nice about someone. I saw Cece write that down.

"It doesn't make sense that Erik would kill Slay, especially if his case is going to the courts. It's likely he'll win and the property will be returned," Hans said. "I don't think Erik did it. But what about you?"

Hans didn't pull any punches. He put it right out there.

"Me?" Snaith laughed. "Oh, I am glad he's dead but I'm a doctor, not a killer. I heal the sick and wounded."

Hans picked up a bottle of liver cleanse. "This works?"

"You have to try it to believe it. All-natural products such as milk thistle and my secret ingredients, of course. It really helps those who've overindulged in alcohol."

"What're the special things you include?" Hans held it up to the light coming in from the front door as if he could ascertain the ingredients by viewing the bottle.

"The ingredients are my secret formulation. If you

Carolyn Haines

want to try a bottle, take that one for free. Judging from your profession, I'd guess you've done your fair share of heavy drinking. Give it a try." Snaith squared his shoulders. "Now, I have work to do."

As did we. First stop, the county courthouse to talk with Sheriff Glory about the autopsy report.

6

The day was absolutely stunning. Flowers were in bloom everywhere around the small town, and the heady scent of wisteria was on the spring breeze. If heaven had a scent, it would be wisteria.

We pulled up at the courthouse under a big white oak that was budding out in bright green finery. Cece and Tinkie followed Hans to the steps of the old courthouse. The building was redbrick with a dome, the original structure very symmetrical and uniform, double doors opening to the four directions. Not elaborate, but graceful. As my friends hurried toward the wing where the sheriff's office was located, I lingered in the central hallway. Stairs led up to the second floor, where there would be a courtroom. The design of the building was standard for a lot of rural counties. Time had forced the addition of more office space for chancery and circuit courts as the population had grown, but the basic purpose of the building was easy to see and the symmetry was appreciated.

My own Sunflower County courthouse wasn't much different in design, and I hurried up the stairs to take a look at the courtroom. I'd spent hours after school sitting in the Sunflower County courthouse balcony watching my father defend clients. Though he'd never, to my knowledge, set foot in this courthouse, I could sense him with me. For a moment the present faded away, and I was once again a secret spectator of my father standing before the witness box questioning a man about his whereabouts on the night in question. My father was never loud or aggressive. Theatrics weren't his style. But he could drill down on a man with intensity if he thought he was lying. I knew how that felt on the rare occasions I'd been hauled before his bar. A full confession was the only way to make it stop.

He turned from the witness to catch sight of me standing in the aisle. His smile reminded me how easily he gave his love.

"Daddy?" I didn't expect an answer, but I whirled around when a blond woman wearing red lipstick entered the empty courtroom. Her pale hair was curly and short, and her dark eyebrows arched with playfulness. She wore a 1960s-style dress belted at her small waist with a skirt that flared out and a pair of high heels that showed her legs to advantage.

"Give a girl the right pair of shoes and she'll conquer the world." She gave a coquettish giggle that made me smile.

For a moment, I was stunned. This woman exuded a sweet sex appeal that came from another era. She'd stepped out of the 1950s, whoever she was.

"Can I help you?" I asked, because I didn't have another opening gambit and I wanted to talk to her.

"I don't know. Can you?" She winked. "A wise girl knows her limits. A smart girl knows that she has none."

I knew her then. Marilyn Monroe, a woman my mother had always admired and mourned. My mother, Libby Delaney, said that Marilyn had never gotten a chance to prove what she could really do. She'd been crushed by the Hollywood machine that wanted to squeeze the sex appeal out of her like toothpaste but wanted nothing to do with her intelligence and emotional depth. Marilyn was a tragic figure to my mom, and therefore to me.

"What's shaking, Jitty?" I knew who was behind this vision of sex appeal.

"It's all make-believe, isn't it?"

Another great Marilyn quote that almost broke my heart. "Give it a rest, Jitty. Marilyn had a tragic life. I can't change that."

"No, you can't." She sighed. "You're on a new case. I thought I'd stick around and see if you needed my help."

Jitty never, ever helped me with a case. Not directly. Sometimes I could put two and two together, based on her disguise or something she said, but not very often. Mostly she showed up to bedevil and torment me—because she could and she liked it.

"Who killed Perry Slay?" If she was going to pretend to help, I was going to force the issue.

"Look at the clues, Sarah Booth. Killed in a miniature

biblical Holy Land, with poison, on Easter Sunday. What does that add up to?"

"A religious madman?" I could devil her, too.

"No! You are just being deliberately dense."

"Oh, I know. The Easter bunny did it."

She put her hands on her hips and her red lips drew into a pout. "I'm going back to Zinnia if you're going to be so mean."

I really didn't want to send her packing—I just wanted to get equal aggravation time. "Okay, sorry. Help me out."

"What strikes me is the timing. Easter Sunday. To get the biggest crowd possible at the gardens."

She actually had an excellent point. "Someone looking to make a point about this murder."

"I would think so. But I'm not the big-reputation private investigator! I'm just a lowly haint."

"A haint I love." I pulled her up short before she could continue the pity party. She'd actually given me something to think about. "Thanks for the tip. Now I've got to find my crew."

"I've got my eye on you, Missy." The body was Marilyn, but the voice was my ghost. She disappeared on the sound of a loud air kiss.

"Who are you talking to?" Hans stood at the door to the courtroom.

"My better self," I said breezily. "Did Sheriff Glory give you the autopsy report?"

"She did. It's very informative."

"Great." I joined him at the door and we walked down the stairs together. "My father was a lawyer and he practiced in a courtroom much like that one. Lots of great memories." I thought I'd throw him a bone of explanation before he asked more questions about the invisible conversationalist I was talking to.

"Tinkie told me how you kind of fell into becoming a private investigator by finding and returning her dog that had been dognapped. That moment was a life changer for her. And apparently for you. It sounds like she'll never forget what you did in saving Chablis. From how she told the story, it seems that dog is like a child to her."

This was a sore spot with me. In a moment of abject desperation, I had actually stolen Tinkie's little dust mop, Chablis—and returned her safely for the ransom money. I'd almost confessed to Tinkie a million times, but I knew it would be the end of our partnership and our friendship. Had there ever been a time for unburdening my evil deed to her, it was when it first happened. Too much time had passed. Too much water under the bridge. Too many long days of such wonderful friendship. No, I would suffer alone with the knowledge of my horrid action for the rest of my life.

We moved to the central hallway, and I followed Hans to the sheriff's office. Tinkie and Cece were leaning on the counter sipping coffee provided by Sheriff Glory, who was on the opposite side of the counter. Even seated on a stool she had the perfect posture of a high-level equestrian. Her motions were contained, deliberate— the way people learned to move around horses that were excitable.

"Erik's in a holding cell," Tinkie said. "He wasn't supposed to leave town and he went out to the B and B."

"To hire us," I explained to the sheriff.

"He needs to learn to respect the law."

I knew the drill. "Can I talk to him?"

"Sure." She nodded to the door behind her. "Deputy

Mixon, would you walk her back?" As I passed by she handed me a copy of the autopsy report. "Your client is a pharmacist with a serious knowledge of poisons. Keep that in mind."

The tall, slender deputy nodded at me to follow him. It was a short walk to a cell where Erik sat on a bunk. The red spots in his cheeks let me know his temper was short, and I didn't really blame him.

"We've got some good leads," I told him. I looked down at the report. "Slay died of a poison that he could have gotten into by himself. Spotted water hemlock."

Erik nodded. "It grows wild. The local veterinarian has had some dealings with it with livestock. I wouldn't be surprised if Slay somehow poisoned himself. He wasn't terribly bright."

"Okay. Who would know the spotted water hemlock was easily accessible and would also want Slay dead?"

"Snaith. That snake-oil salesman. No telling what he's cooking up in the back of his house. He's capable of anything. Look, he concocts all kinds of things. Some of it just gives people indigestion or gas. Some of it, though, there've been a few incidents of folks having their stomachs pumped because of his fake products."

"Why isn't he in jail if he's even mildly poisoned people?"

"His victims won't come forward and press charges." Erik leaned closer. "I think they're afraid of him. And I've heard rumors he still practices medicine—without a license. But a lot of people feel like he's really devoted to helping them get well. He is the consummate con."

"It's possible if Slay poisoned himself then the charges against you will be dropped, but just in case this doesn't pan out, tell me where you were Saturday evening and night."

Erik's jaw set. "No. I don't need an alibi because I'm innocent."

"If you have one, it's the quickest way to end this mess."

"Not going to happen."

This was an unexpected roadblock. "Erik, please. It's a simple thing if someone can vouch for you."

"I told you. I was home alone."

He was lying, but I didn't know why. Right now, though, it was pointless to push him. "Okay, I'll just have to find out on my own, then."

The door to the cells opened and Sheriff Glory walked toward me.

"Come on, Erik. You're free to go. Now, don't test me again. Honor the restrictions, okay? Stay in town."

Erik shot me a dour look. "Saints preserve me. This is going to be hard to take."

I laughed out loud. "You're lucky to have a sheriff who cuts you some slack."

"I'm going back to the pharmacy for a few hours," Erik said. "I'm sure there's plenty to do."

"It would be better if you stayed at work," Glory told him.

Erik started to snap back, but he only nodded. "Good thinking. I'll be sure to keep that in mind. There are plenty of customers at the pharmacy who will vouch for me today."

We all left the jail. We offered to drive Erik the few blocks to work, but he decided to walk. "I need to move around. Being in a cell even for a little while has made me feel . . . cramped."

"Don't go disappearing," Tinkie said. "Don't make us waste our time keeping track of you."

Erik didn't rise to the bait. "If you decided to tail me, you'd have more fun than you've ever had." He flashed a smile that made me think of Patrick Swayze. "But I will behave."

"What's next on the agenda?" I asked Tinkie.

"I'm thinking we should talk to Cosmo."

"Hans has asked me to interview Donna at the B and B for his travel show," Cece said. "Would you mind if I begged off talking to Cosmo?"

"Absolutely beg off," Tinkie said. She hugged Cece. "This is a wonderful opportunity for you." She hugged Hans. "Thank you! Cece is one of the best interviewers on the planet. You're going to see that the camera loves her, too. Just keep in mind you can't steal her from us in Zinnia."

"Cece has already made it clear she could only work special assignments for me," Hans said. "Even a little bit of Cece is better than no Cece at all."

We waved them to Hans's vehicle, and Tinkie and I headed for the naturalist's abode deep in the woods.

7

On the drive out, Tinkie mulled over possible suspects in Slay's murder. The problem was that so many people wanted the lawyer dead. When we finally arrived at Cosmo's house, I stopped the car and took in the rammed earth cottage. The wilderness encroached up to the front door. Had we not known the address, we would never have found this place. Whatever else Cosmo might be, he wasn't a fraud. He walked the walk of environmental responsibility. The solar panels told the tale of a man who was dedicated to his belief system.

We'd just gotten out of the car when Cosmo appeared at Tinkie's elbow, almost like a wraith. She jumped backward and knocked into me, which made me bite my tongue, which then made me curse. I tried not to do that in front of strangers.

"I like a woman who can talk dirty," Cosmo said.

I wanted to pop him, but I didn't.

Tinkie laughed. "Oh, Sarah Booth can be very, very naughty. I have to keep a tight leash on her."

Since I was standing behind Tinkie, I pinched her hard on the behind. She squealed like a little piggy and jumped forward, knocking into Cosmo.

"You look too old to be in sixth grade, but you sure act like middle school kids. What brings you two out here? Grilling me about Perry Slay's fortuitous murder?"

"Yes, that's why we're here." I didn't see a reason to lie to the man. He was plenty smart, if a little eccentric. "Did you have anything to do with the murder of Perry Slay?"

"Murder? Are you sure that's what it was?"

It was possible Slay had accidentally ingested some spotted water hemlock. Maybe. "I've heard you have a lot of that hemlock growing around your place," I said.

"Yeah, here and all over any of the marshy areas. But Slay was a turkey hunter. He would know to stay away from that plant."

"Unless he was drinking heavily," Tinkie said. She was making a guess at Slay's personal habits, but chances were she was right.

"Slay liked to tipple the bottle, that's for sure," Cosmo said. "But he wasn't so stupid he'd eat hemlock. He was too damned mean to off himself."

"It seems almost everyone in the area had a reason to want Slay dead. Did you?" Tinkie asked.

"Sure I did. That lowlife filed a nuisance lawsuit against me. He claimed I was breeding fire ants or termites or some such ridiculous thing. He had half the county ready to come out here and burn me out because I was infesting their homes. Moron."

"Were you?" Fire ants and termites were ugly insects. I believed all things had a right to live—just not around me.

"I wouldn't have brought the fire ants here for any amount of money. They're smart, industrious insects, but they aren't native to this land. You know they came in on a ship at the Port of Mobile. But the ecosystem is delicate. So many species have been badly damaged by herbicides, poisons, development, and the flooding of natural habitat. It has to end. Without insects, all life on this planet will die."

"But the Garden of Bones is a garden, a place where insects and wildlife can thrive," Tinkie pointed out. "Why do you have such a burn on for Daniel Reynolds and his project?"

"Oh, the gardens are lovely and he does an excellent job of promoting natural species. Have you seen his wild azaleas—the orange is so vibrant. And he has a native holly that the birds love. He does remarkable work with the plants."

"And yet you interrupted his service to make a point that you wanted him gone." Tinkie wasn't going to let it go.

"He brings all those people here. That's the problem. They climb around, disturbing the natural barriers to flooding, stomping tender young plants. Those little hellion kids scream and run around hunting eggs. Do you know how much litter they throw on the ground? They have no upbringing."

Tinkie put a hand on her stomach. "Children need

space to run and play. Do they really do permanent damage?"

He'd apparently guessed at her condition and was smart enough to back off. "Well, they could be quieter and less destructive."

"Does Reynolds have a reason to want Slay dead?"

He shrugged. "Ask him."

"And Erik Ward? Would he kill Slay?"

"Erik has a reason to hate Slay, but I can't see him killing a man over something that will eventually be sorted out in a court of law. I mean what Slay did wasn't just unethical, it was illegal. It likely contributed to Erik's dad's death, too. Still, Erik knew he'd win that land case in court. He didn't have a need to kill Slay. And certainly not on Easter Sunday."

"Who would you put your money on?" Tinkie asked.

"That Snaith. Man, he hated Slay. But it could be anyone. Think about who might be setting Erik up as a killer. Or even Reynolds, for that matter. I mean the body was found in the middle of his miniature Holy Land. Maybe someone left Slay's body there to implicate Reynolds, not Erik."

"You're implying that Slay was collateral damage in an attempt to frame Erik or Dr. Reynolds for murder," Tinkie said.

"Reynolds knows as much about poisonous plants as Erik or Snaith. The man has researched all the native plants. I don't know when the coroner deduced that Slay died, but I'll bet there's a window of time when Reynolds *could* have done it. So he could be the killer, or, as I first posed, perhaps he was the intended victim of a frame."

Cosmo was right. Reynolds had means and opportunity. "Would Reynolds have a motive to kill Slay?" I asked.

"I don't know any specifics, but everyone in the region has a motive to want Slay dead. A man like Slay made a lot of enemies."

"It would seem Dr. Reynolds has made some enemies, too." And I was talking to one of them. "I mean why kill Slay here?"

"That's a good question," Cosmo said. "If Reynolds did it, I don't have an answer. And frankly, I don't care. Slay's dead and that's a good thing. Now if you'll excuse me, I have some water quality testing to finish."

"Cosmo, Erik has been a friend to you. He's being cagey about an alibi for the early-morning hours on Easter Sunday. Do you have any idea where he might have been?" If the two men were good friends, Cosmo might know more about Erik's habits. It wasn't crucial—yet—to provide that alibi, but it would be once Sheriff Glory truly began to investigate.

"Erik has always been smart enough to keep his personal life to himself. In a small town, it's the only way for a bachelor to survive. Erik's business requires that he not be the center of gossip. I could maybe hazard a guess what he was doing, but I won't. He'll talk when he's ready."

"Is he involved with a married woman?" Tinkie asked. She'd gone to the logical conclusion.

"Ask Erik," Cosmo said.

I was frustrated. "You don't think being charged with murder is going to put him in the middle of controversy?" I asked.

"In a small town, there are things worse than murder

to be accused of." He scoffed. "If Erik wants to tell you, he will."

He walked past us and disappeared in the pine woods that surrounded his house.

"What do you think Erik is into that he would have to keep so secret?" I asked.

"I don't know, but we're going to have to find out." Tinkie brushed a few blond curls from her face.

"Do you think Cosmo could kill Perry Slay?" I asked Tinkie as we loaded up in the car to drive back to the main office of the gardens.

"He doesn't strike me as a man with enough fire in his belly to kill a man, or even an insect." She grinned. "Erik said he was gentle and that's my reading."

"So Snaith is still our primary suspect."

"If we discount Erik and Reynolds, we're left with Snaith."

"What shall we do?" I asked Tinkie. "Are you tired? Do you need to rest? What about a vitamin shake?" I'd been preparing power shakes with spinach, kale, tomatoes, and protein powder for her to drink.

"If you push one more of those awful drinks at me, I'm going to vomit on your shoes."

That was a very unladylike Tinkie threat. Daddy's Girls did not vomit in public. "I thought you liked them."

"Like a teenager likes an STD."

"Tinkie!" I was shocked. She never talked like this. She was always the proper Daddy's Girl and she knew every rule in that handbook.

"I'm hormonal. So sue me. I can't drink alcohol. I can't smoke cigarettes."

"Wait, you never smoked."

"Like I said, sue me. I want a cigarette now. And some fried dill pickles. And a foot massage."

"Okay, I can get you the pickles and the foot massage. For sure. No cigarettes and no alcohol." I was dealing with a Tinkie I didn't know.

I pulled up in front of the B&B and asked Donna to borrow some supplies while Tinkie waited in the car. It didn't take long to gather what we'd need, and then we drove back to the miniature Holy Land. We pulled up at the office of the gardens and got out.

Tinkie had already forgotten her list of demands and was off on improving her garden at Hilltop. "Let's get some cuttings of some of these plants. I think my gardener might be able to make a lot of them grow with proper placement in sunny areas. I realize Zinnia has colder winters than here, but the gardener works magic with plants, and I'd love some of these exotics to show to the baby as she's growing up. Also we need to look for that spotted water hemlock stuff. If we can find it growing wild here, it will make a good case for accidental poisoning." She was off on another tangent. Hormone brain! And Jitty wanted me to conceive? Coleman would lock me in a cell and Jitty would throw away the key if I was all over the place like Tinkie.

"Sure, we can forget all about a murder and go look for plant cuttings." It was easier to go along with her than to argue. Besides, we'd soon have to go in. The soft dusk wasn't far away and a bit of a walk would do us both good. When we opened the trunk to search for something to collect plants, I heard what sounded like two men arguing. Curious, Tinkie and I crept closer to the small office where Dr. Reynolds worked.

"You can't expand!" I recognized the voice as belonging to Cosmo Constantine. We'd left his house earlier and here he was, back at the scene of the crime.

"These gardens and the miniature Holy Land are my life's work," Reynolds said calmly. "I promise you, Cosmo, that I will take the utmost care with the natural world. I don't put out any poisons or toxins. I don't even kill off the poisonous plants. You know this. And you also knew the expansion was inevitable. This isn't a new conversation."

Tinkie and I moved closer and closer to the office until we could peek in the window. Cosmo was talking.

"It isn't enough to *be careful*. Humans foul everything they touch. Besides, you diverted the water from the spring that fed my marsh. It's all drying up. The turtles, snakes, and water birds are hurting."

"I'm sorry. I had to have the water to fill the Dead Sea."

"What do you need a lake for? Why can't you reduce the size of your Dead Sea? No one will know the difference."

Reynolds sighed heavily. "The sea is part of the biblical landscape. But I will reroute the spillover back to your property. That's the best I can do."

"I'm not sure it's enough," Cosmo said, leaning forward. "I'm onto you, Reynolds. I don't know how Erik Ward was arrested for killing Slay when I know it was you who killed him."

"I wouldn't kill anyone. I detested Slay, but I'm not the kind of man who resorts to violence."

"You can sound all holier than thou, but I know what you did last summer. I won't forget it either."

"What did he do?" Tinkie whispered.

"I don't know." We were both shamelessly eavesdropping. "Hush so we can hear."

Her response was a stomach growl loud enough to wake the dead. She made an O with her mouth and clapped a hand over her face, as if that was where the noise had come from.

"You can't be hungry again. Can you?"

She nodded. "Starving."

The door of the office opened and Cosmo came out. He threw a wave at us as he headed into the woods and disappeared among the thick pine trunks. Daniel Reynolds came out next. He took in the gloves and trowel we held.

"I remember Tinkie admired some of my native plants. I'll help you gather some cuttings, and I have some potted plants you're welcome to," he said.

"Great." Tinkie looked behind his back at me and mouthed the words, "Ask him."

I wasn't about to. If we wanted that information we were going to have to trick it out of him.

The three of us walked abreast as we traveled through the stories of the Old and New Testaments. We came to the Garden of Gethsemane where we'd found Perry Slay's warm corpse. Reynolds had been busy repairing the damage to the area. There was cement mixed in a wheelbarrow where he was repairing the buildings, and new sprigs of plants to make up for the flora that Slay had crushed.

"Hard to believe Slay was here," he said, looking around. "I've found a lot of wild creatures here, from snakes to turtles to lizards and frogs. I never anticipated finding a dead body."

"Do you think the murder will harm the tourist

trade?" It occurred to me that killing Slay here might be directed toward running the gardens out of business. Cosmo had suggested that perhaps Reynolds was the intended victim of a plot.

"Maybe," Reynolds said. "On the other hand, people can be ghoulish. It might help draw more tourists."

He was right about that—and Reynolds had a pretty good understanding of human nature.

We wandered along the trail, taking in the magic of a land so meticulously crafted in miniature detail. I marveled at the tomb where Jesus was buried. At the large stone that was rolled away from the opening. At the sad hill with three crosses. I was completely caught up in the adventure that Reynolds was leading us on when I heard a dog barking.

"Brutus!"

Reynolds picked up his leisurely pace and hurried up a hill. Tinkie and I chugged along behind him. We didn't move as fast as he did.

"Brutus!" he called his dog. "Come on, boy." He looked back at us. "He looks fierce but he wouldn't harm a fly."

I'd seen the dog and he looked as if he could fit a whole human head in his jaws if he decided to give it a try. We ran up on Reynolds at a sign that declared THE DEAD SEA.

This was the body of water Cosmo had been complaining about. Brutus stood at the edge of the lake, barking at something in the water. The sun was setting, and the glare made it hard to see, but I shielded my eyes with my hand and squinted. Something white floated on the water. Floated very still. Floated very much like a dead body.

"It's a person!" I kicked off my shoes but Reynolds was faster. He dove in the water and took off with the stroke of an Olympic champion. In a moment he had the body in a fireman's carry and was pulling it toward the shore. I waded into the chill water to help him bring the body of a once-beautiful woman ashore.

8

"It's Patrice Pepperdine," Reynolds said as he sat on the edge of the Dead Sea, shivering and gasping for air. We were both winded and freezing. "I know her from town."

"What would she be doing out here at dusk?" Tinkie asked the logical question even as she was dialing the sheriff's office.

"I don't know."

"Was she a regular at the gardens?" I asked. Finally I stood and started jumping around to warm up.

Tinkie held up a hand for quiet as she spoke with Sheriff Glory. She described how we'd found Patrice in the water, dragged her to shore, and were waiting for Sheriff Glory, an ambulance, and a coroner. Maybe not in that order.

"She's safely out of the water, meaning she can't float off or sink." Tinkie was giving the details.

The Dead Sea wasn't that big, but in the growing dark we could have lost the body had Brutus not alerted us. I didn't want to look at her, but I did. I was no judge of dead people in water but my guess was that she'd been dead less than a few hours. The wear and tear of water decomposition weren't yet visible to my eye. The coroner would be able to determine a more accurate time of death.

"Do you know this woman well enough to say if she may have been depressed?" It was possible this was a suicide.

"She never struck me as someone likely to . . . drown herself. Even if she chose to take her own life, why here? The gardens have no meaning to her as far as I know." He hesitated. "What do you think happened?" Reynolds was pretty shaken.

"I was going to ask you the same thing. Who is Patrice Pepperdine? What's her story?"

Reynolds rolled his eyes. "You aren't going to like this at all. She's Erik Ward's neighbor, and they've been in a violent feud."

"What kind of feud?" Erik didn't need this new connection, but if there was something here, I wanted to know all the details.

"Oh, it's not good. Erik had the oldest camellia bush in the Southeast in his yard. It was a magnificent version. In fact, he's given me several cuttings and I have them here in the gardens, which is a good thing because I can make sure Erik at least has a part of that magnificent plant."

"Okay, okay, so he had an old bush. How does this relate to Patrice?"

"Someone poisoned the bush. Poured enough herbicide on it to take it down to the root despite all that Erik did to save it. He accused Patrice, who denied it, but the consensus of opinion in town is that Patrice did it. Erik and Patrice had some kind of vendetta going."

"And Erik would kill her over a bush?"

"Those heritage camellias are better than gold. They've endured all kinds of weather changes and attacks by insects and fungus." Reynolds gave me a look that let me know he realized I had a black thumb instead of a green one. "A non-plant-lover can never understand how some of the magnificent plant creations are like our children. Equally beloved."

I could grasp that. I loved my cat, dog, and horses as much as most people loved their children. It didn't seem too far-fetched to extend that sentiment to plants. I loved the sycamore trees that lined the driveway to Dahlia House. They were my sentinels. Sometimes the wind sang a lullaby in their leafy branches. Who was I to judge another person's love?

"Maybe Erik and Patrice had a war going on between them, but this is also the second murder here at the gardens." I wasn't really defending Erik, because he didn't need defending. I was only pointing out the facts. "Maybe it's someone with a burn on for you."

Reynolds looked truly taken aback. "No one hates me enough to kill two people just to . . . to . . ." He threw up his hands. Brutus came over to make sure his master was not in distress.

"To put you out of business? To ultimately frame you for murder? Like it or not, if the gardens get a reputation for being the grounds for a serial killer, it will put off the tourist trade. If they suspect you of being the killer, that's the end of your business no matter how innocent you are."

"I was talking to my congregation when the first body was found," he said.

"When the body was found. Not when the murder occurred." It was an important distinction.

Tinkie finally got off the phone. "You'd better call Coleman, Sarah Booth."

I was reluctant to tell him about the murders. He'd be justifiably upset. And five hours away, which would only make him fret. "He can't do anything here. We aren't in any danger."

"You need to call him and keep him abreast, just the way I do Oscar. It's what caring people do."

I felt like a bug pinned to a page. "Right." I'd thrown my phone on the bank of the lake before I jumped in, so I searched around until I found it. I walked down the trail toward Jerusalem as I called my lover. Coleman answered on the first ring. "What's wrong?" he asked.

"Nothing. A lawyer was murdered during the sunrise service. The man suspected of killing him, Erik Ward, wants me and Tinkie to prove his innocence.

"There's a small complication. There's been another death. A drowning, it appears. Tinkie and I should wrap this up quickly."

"What the heck is going on there, Sarah Booth?"

"This is normally a quiet little community. I don't really know anything about this victim, except that her name is Patrice Pepperdine. She's Erik Ward's neighbor. They were at odds."

"Is Erik still charged with the first murder?"

"He's out on bail." How much better it would have

been if he'd stayed in jail. "But he was going to his pharmacy so he should have a good alibi. I don't think this woman's been dead very long."

"It worries me that a killer is on the loose down there. You haven't seen anything strange, have you?"

"Other than two dead bodies at a religious site, you mean?"

"Other than that. Anyone following you or acting suspicious?"

"No. Is there a reason you're asking that question?"

"You and Tinkie have a knack for finding trouble, or sometimes it just finds you."

I had a sense that he wasn't telling me exactly what was on his mind, but since he was right about what he said, I didn't press it. "I just wanted to keep you posted and to let you know I'll be home as soon as I can. I miss you."

"Maybe I should drive down."

There was a wistful note in Coleman's voice that made me realize just how *much* I missed him. "Can you leave work?" The plan had been for a girls' weekend, but with two murders, that had spiraled out of control and it would be nice if our men could join us.

"Yes. I've got two burglaries in town. DeWayne and Budgie can handle it, but I need to make some calls to neighboring law enforcement. I'll check in at Dahlia House, make sure the animals are good, and see what tomorrow brings. I hope I can get an early start. I'll give Oscar a call and see if he wants to come. Jaytee, too. Maybe he can find a backup harmonica player for the band."

I loved the idea that I'd see my man by lunchtime the next day. "Perfect." I caught movement down the trail.

People with flashlights were coming toward us. "Here's the sheriff. I need to go. And I need to get back to the B and B and change into some dry clothes." I'd warmed up considerably, but it was still chilly.

"Give Tinkie and Cece my best."

"Give the critters a smooch for me. And one for you."

Coleman hung up and I turned to face Sheriff Glory. She sighed heavily. "Before you came to visit, we didn't have bodies all over the place," she said.

"Before I came to visit, I'd never seen a dead person in the Dead Sea."

Glory grinned. "I take your point." She motioned for me to wait before I rejoined Tinkie and Dr. Reynolds. "I have some bad news. I checked on Erik Ward right after I hung up with Tinkie. You should know Erik never showed up at work and now he's completely disappeared."

9

Once the body had been removed and was on its way to the coroner's examining table, Tinkie and I repaired to the B&B where Cece was waiting, sans Hans. The video reporter had left her to track down a Lucedalian he needed to interview for a story on the history of train lines in Southern Mississippi. Hans had learned the key to success was to maximize every location.

Donna must have sensed we were in distress, because she found an alcove in the glassed and heated sunroom and brought a bottle of tequila, lime slices, salt, and shot glasses. For Tinkie, she brewed a cup of herbal tea. Boy, was I glad I wasn't the pregnant one.

"You look like you could use a drink," she said as she pushed the shot glasses toward me and Cece. "To paraphrase William Hurt in one of my favorite movies, 'Some days the crap comes down so hard you have to wear a hat.' Drink up, ladies, as long as you don't plan to drive anywhere."

I poured a shot for Cece and one for me, then handed her a slice of lime. We salted the junction of thumb and forefinger, licked the salt, threw back the tequila, and bit the lime. The rush of heat through my body was more than welcome. We each had another for good measure. And I hadn't even told them Erik was out of pocket.

I started with the good news. "Coleman is coming tomorrow, if he can. He said he'd bring Oscar and Jaytee if they can get away from work." I thought that might cheer them up—before I revealed the lack of Erik Ward or an alibi.

"Oscar has to go to Memphis tomorrow," Tinkie said. "He'd dig seeing the miniature Holy Land, but we'll have to come back after the baby is born."

"Jaytee is auditioning potential band members. You know, for those instances when someone wants to take a vacation. Like that's ever going to happen for Jaytee and me at the same time." Cece made a face. "I do have to get back to work soon. Ed has been pretty tolerant of my absence."

Ed Oakes was a reasonable boss, but Cece was his prime asset and he needed her on the job.

"Can you send him some photos of the gardens? You know, kind of a society story?"

"Two steps ahead of you. He ran an Easter story on the web about the gardens."

"Maybe Millie could do a guest column about Hollywood scandals."

"She's already on the case." Cece grinned. "Great

minds think alike. She's hot on the trail of a haunted mansion over in Greenwood. The house is up for sale, and I think she's going with a team of paranormal investigators to check it out. Elvis's ghost has been reported there. If she gets some shots with orbs or anything the least bit paranormal, it will be terrific."

It was fun to see Millie coming into her own with the newspaper. Millie's Café was still her primary focus, but she loved investigating entertainment and odd stories for the *Zinnia Dispatch*. "Terrific."

Tinkie offered to pour another shot, but I passed. I had a small buzz going, and that was perfect. By all rights, I should have gone into town to look for Erik, but I was aggravated with our client. He'd been told to go to work where he would have had an alibi. Now we had a second body, no Erik, and no alibi. If he was arrested again, he could stay behind bars. If he'd done what he was supposed to do, he would have been off the hook for both murders.

I finally told Cece and Tinkie about Erik's wayward behavior.

"That man won't help himself," Tinkie said, with more than a little aggravation. "He promised to stay at the pharmacy."

"Yep." I sighed. "I'm exhausted just thinking about him."

"What about another massage?" Tinkie suggested.

I could tell she was getting antsy to go home, but we were stuck. At least for another day. "Sure, let's go get pummeled." As we were about to head to the spa area, Hans returned.

"I had a terrific interview," he said. "How did the rest of your day go?"

"Another dead body," Tinkie said. "Erik is a suspect because he took off from the drugstore. Again."

"Let's give him a chance," I said.

Tinkie only glared at me. Pregnancy made her short-tempered, and her feet weren't even swelling today. Oscar was going to be in for some fun times as she got further along.

"Should we look for him?" Hans asked.

"He has our phone numbers. We're going for a massage," Tinkie said.

"Maybe Hans and I will go into town and check him out," Cece suggested. Hans nodded enthusiastically. It seemed he liked hanging around detective women and talented print journalists.

"Suit yourself." I needed to stay close to Tinkie. Her energy went up and down erratically. And she was emotional.

"We'll be back in an hour or two," Cece said. Hans picked up his camera and they hustled out into the night.

Tinkie and I went to the spa to see if it was too late to request a massage. The spa was dark and empty. The weekend was over and most of the people staying at the quaint inn had left. The only guests were the three of us and Hans. A whole new batch of guests would start arriving Thursday, but if we could resolve our case, we'd be long gone.

It seemed the spa staff had also gone home, and I was just as glad. The tequila had made me a little lethargic, and I wanted to curl up in the comfy bed with a good mystery and go to sleep. Tomorrow I'd find Erik—if Sheriff Glory didn't beat me to it. Maybe I'd have more patience with the dawn. I was pretty aggravated at the moment.

I went to my room and opened my laptop. I looked up Patrice Pepperdine plus Erik Ward, just out of curiosity. The first thing that popped up was a story in the local newspaper. Erik and Patrice had gotten into a heated confrontation on his back lawn. Patrice had called the law and both had been warned that any further misbehavior would result in a disturbing-the-peace charge.

There was a photo of Patrice—with her lawn shears in hand, standing by a beautiful old camellia bush. All around her feet were branches filled with huge blooms. She'd attacked the bush when the flowers were the most beautiful, slashing away at any limbs that stretched even near a line of pink plastic tape she'd strung to mark her property.

I started reading the story. "That stupid bush was growing across the line and into my yard," she declared. "I hate camellias. I hate azaleas. I hate them all."

The shrub had been planted at least ten feet from the property line, but it was huge. It had spread out over the decades. But why in the world would anyone object to those beautiful flowers?

I continued reading. "She's a dingbat from Hell," Erik said of her. "She's anti-plant and poorly educated. She's butchered a beautiful heritage plant that's an important part of the town history, and because that wonderful foliage is destroyed, I'm left with an eye-bleeding image of her coming out of her house every morning in her bathrobe with these ratty pink foam curlers in her hair. She's fodder for a horror movie. Trust me, she gives me nightmares."

Wow. That was a slam I hadn't heard in quite a while. But the news reporter had done due diligence and had plenty of quotes from both sides of the story. Patrice shot back, "Erik Ward is a property thief. He tried to buy my place at the tax sale. He was sneaky about it, too. He didn't even come over and tell me he was trying to buy it."

That was a claim I'd have to check out. Even if true, it wasn't illegal to buy property that the current owner failed to pay taxes on for several years. But it could put a bad taste in someone's mouth, especially if Patrice was having financial issues. Nearly losing one's home stung—I knew that from personal experience.

I looked up from my reading when Tinkie came down the hall. "I'm not waiting up for Cece," she said. "We can try for a massage tomorrow."

"Me either, and it's just as well because the spa is closed. I'm about to sack out." We were tired. Cece, of the three of us, was truly capable of handling almost any situation. She'd be perfectly fine. We said our goodnights, and I closed and locked my door and hit the sack.

I awoke to a tap, tap, tap on the window of my room. "If you make me get up, Jitty, I will kill you twice." I was in no mood for the shenanigans of my nemesis.

The tap, tap, tap came again. I rolled over and stood up. I was going to kick some butt. When I went to the window, though, I dashed back to the bed and grabbed the comforter to wrap around myself. It wasn't Jitty at the window—it was Erik.

I unlocked the window and lifted it up. These were the old-fashioned windows with weights and sashes. "What are you doing standing outside in the middle of the night? Where have you been? Sheriff Glory is looking for you and she's charging you with a second murder." I was a little agitato, to quote my old friend Kinky Friedman.

"I can't go home. Glory has my house staked out. They'll arrest me if I try to get in."

"And this is my problem why?" I was angry.

"I know I should have stayed at the drugstore, but I had an appointment I couldn't miss."

"Good. Then you have an alibi. That's all that really matters." If he had a solid alibi I would forgive him for worrying me.

"I do have an alibi, but I can't say what."

"Erik, do you have a death wish?" I said it very slowly.

"No, why?"

"Because I am going to kill you, right on that spot where you're standing outside my window."

"Can I come in to talk?"

"Sure." I checked my watch and it was nearly five o'clock. I'd slept the whole night away and it felt like only fifteen minutes. Dawn would soon be breaking. "I'll go get us some coffee."

10

Donna Dickerson was always up early, and she put on a pot of coffee first thing. In fact, I could hear her stirring around, getting the day started.

"I take mine with cream and sugar," Erik said as he climbed in the window. "One spoon and about an ounce of heavy cream, if she has it."

I could tell by his unrepentant grin that he was having sport with me. He didn't care that I was annoyed. "However you like it," I said sweetly and grabbed my robe before I walked down the hall to the kitchen. I almost woke Tinkie up, but she needed her sleep. She wasn't just eating for two, she was sleeping for two, too. Cece, on the other hand, was an early bird like me. I tapped on her door. It wasn't locked and I looked in the room. No Cece.

I had a lot of questions about that, but no time to pursue them. Whatever Cece and Hans were up to, they'd apparently hit a hot lead for a story. She'd either be back soon or would give us a call. I wasn't worried about her and I had to wring an alibi out of Erik.

I greeted Donna, who was in the kitchen and humming golden oldies. I poured two cups of coffee, putting in the fixings that Erik liked. When I got back to my room, he was on the sofa with my comforter around him. "It's chilly outside."

"Boy, your mama must have raised a fool."

He just laughed out loud. "She raised a man with irresistible charm. Admit it, you know I'm dashing and . . . exciting."

The bad thing is that he was. No matter how outdone I was with him, I couldn't stay mad. I took the chair across from him and we sipped our coffee. It was good on a chilly morning. "So where have you been?"

"You don't know what it's like living in a small town," he said. "I can't buy groceries unless someone has a comment about the bread or fruit or vegetables."

"Yes, I do know what small towns are like." And I did. Zinnia wasn't much bigger, if at all, than Lucedale. "Everyone knows your business. Everyone makes your business their business. It's a blessing and a curse."

"The Delta is different than here," Erik said. "I have friends in the Delta. The parties are incredible. People know how to have some fun, and they don't judge every little thing. Here, there are so many things that people find immoral or indecent or even illegal. Harmless little things anywhere else in the world, but here, it's a capital offense."

I knew it was true that the Delta was more wide open. The rural areas of the state were far more constricted than the Delta or the Gulf Coast, where casinos had blossomed in the nineties and gambling was big business. "I don't care what kind of pressure you're under to conform, you need to tell me where you were and what you were doing."

"I didn't kill Patrice, though I would have stuck her foot in a fire-ant bed if I'd gotten the chance."

There was no point asking Erik how he knew Patrice Pepperdine was the second body. "Tell me what you know about Patrice. There's been no coroner's ruling. Yet. It could have been a suicide." That was cold comfort, but still a possibility.

"I heard you found her in the Dead Sea. Kind of ironic."

He wasn't going to get me to laugh about a death, no matter how hard he tried. "Brutus actually saw her. Dr. Reynolds dragged her in and I helped get her on shore."

"Did she drown?"

That was the question. "I don't know. We're waiting on the report."

"What was Patrice doing out at the gardens? She hated plants and I never thought she was all that religious."

"I don't know that either. No one seems to know why she was there." I had a terrible thought. "You don't know, do you?"

Erik stretched. "I told you, I was out of town. Since

I got a court order making Patrice stay out of my yard and leave my camellias alone, I haven't spoken to her. Now I think I'm going to take a nap, if that's okay with you. I'm exhausted."

It didn't appear that I had a choice. Erik had already pulled the comforter over his head and was snuggled in. I would have liked to go back to sleep, but I had things to do. I was tempted to see if there was a room at the B&B where I could lock Erik up—a prison of luxury, as it were. The fallout from that would be dragging the Dickersons into a series of murder cases that could impact their business.

And to top it all off, Cece still wasn't back. She'd likely run off on an assignment with Hans, but it wasn't like Cece to leave without a text or call. The hot pursuit of a story was no excuse. Hans had said something about the barrier islands off the coast of Mississippi and Alabama. Cece might be doing that—and it was possible there was no cell reception on a barrier island. She and Hans seemed to be thick as thieves. I had to admit that he was giving her a wonderful opportunity. Cece was not only a terrific reporter, she was also beautiful and photogenic. She'd be a hit on his show, and it might lead to a real television contract. Not that I wanted Cece to leave the Delta, but Memphis was close enough that she could do a weekly show and still work at the *Zinnia Dispatch*. At least to my way of thinking.

I turned to tell Erik to get up, but he was sound asleep. Happy and content. Even though I wanted to kick him, I didn't have the heart to wake him. He could stay in my room until we figured out a plan. He would have to report to Sheriff Glory, but we needed to turn him in with the best defense we could muster. Which meant as soon as Tinkie was up, I'd send her in to work her magic on him. Erik was a charmer, a real rascal who got away with . . . murder? Because people wanted to give him the benefit of the doubt. But Tinkie had her own skill set of man-manipulation tools. He would be putty in her hands.

To give Erik a little private snooze time, I went back to the kitchen. Donna Dickerson was singing "Mustang Sally" and doing a little chair dancing as she sat at the kitchen table stirring up a batch of batter for French toast. She was crumbling up pralines in the batter. "How does French toast sound?" she asked.

"Delicious. But I'll wait for Tinkie to wake up. I should tell you Erik Ward is asleep on the sofa in my room. He's a fugitive from the law."

"You know Sheriff Glory has her ranch not far from here. I could give her a call and she'd ride over on Raylee and lasso that naughty rascal." Obviously, Donna didn't take Erik seriously as a suspect for murder.

"I'll drive him to town when he gets up." I sighed. "What's going on here, Donna? You've lived here all your life. Why is someone suddenly killing people in those lovely gardens?"

"Perry Slay was a gnat in the eye of mankind. Patrice, well, the most charitable thing I can say is that they should skip the funeral because no one is going to mourn her passing."

"I read an article where she attacked a heritage camellia in Erik's yard. It just doesn't make any sense."

"Oh, she did worse than just chop off a few limbs. She poisoned that poor shrub."

"That's just awful." Why would anyone carry out a vendetta on a plant?

"It sure is. Glory could never prove it, but she knew it was Patrice. We all knew it. There are still people in town who cross the street when they see her because they have such hard feelings. That camellia bush was part of the town's history. It was planted there when Erik's house was the first Methodist church. It was a sign of God's beauty put there for all to witness as they entered."

"And Patrice hated it because it touched her property line?" I wasn't getting something.

"She hated everything about Erik. His handsome good looks, his easy charm, the way people flocked to be around him. He had qualities she'd never aspire to because her personality was just like biting into a green persimmon. She'd make your mouth pucker and your eyes water and put you in a place where you might consider inducing vomiting just to get rid of the taste."

"Okay, then. Did anyone else really hate Patrice?"

"How much time do you have? She'd pissed off everyone in the county one way or the other. She tried to stop trick-or-treating, 'cause she said it worshipped evil. She stood in the middle of Main Street and blocked the Christmas parade because she said it was unholy. She tried to get the area churches to boycott the Garden of Bones because of the children's Easter egg hunt, which she said was pagan. She was against everything that gave anyone a smidgen of pleasure. Which is probably why she hated Erik so much. Folks love him. There's always a cluster of customers in his drugstore, just hanging out. It's become a gathering place to talk about ideas and solutions for some of the things that need fixing around here. Erik's been trying to find investors to bring in a bowling alley or movie theater or Putt-Putt golf. Something for the young people to do. But there's big opposition to that, too, and Patrice was the loudest voice. She felt like she'd had nothing coming up, and that young people should just suffer like she did. Then again, she didn't have a single idea in her head, so I've always kind of thought someone was egging her on to be so disagreeable."

This was an interesting avenue. "You mean using her to block progress in town?"

"Exactly."

"Who would do that?" What kind of person would be against movies or Putt-Putt?

"Who would it harm to have some entertainment for teens? And grown-ups, too. Frankly I think there were interests across the state line paying the churches to rail against these things."

I didn't know the community well enough to make a guess. "Do you have any ideas who these people might be?"

"I have some theories but no facts. Is it possible, though, that Patrice finally realized she was being used and was going to do something about it? Like blow the whistle on the people who want to keep everything exactly the way it is in town."

"And since Erik is already charged with the murder of Perry Slay, why not pin this one on him, too?" It was another fascinating possibility. "Do you know anyone who had a beef with Erik, Patrice, and Slay?" The location of the Garden of Bones as a body dump seemed to connect both murders and Erik.

"Perry and Patrice were despised. Not Erik, though. Maybe it's just someone killing off warts on society. Could be they want to put Dr. Reynolds out of business."

Yowza. Donna Dickerson didn't hold back. I liked her a lot. "Can you name someone—just a lead. Someone I could talk to, not an accusation."

"The sheriff has had her problems with both Perry and Patrice. She might not tell you, but she didn't love either of them. You might talk to Leda Sellers at the local newspaper. Perry was always going on and on and on about suing the newspaper for a story he didn't like. He never had a leg to stand on, but that didn't stop him from being a total pain in the keister."

"Thanks, Donna."

The phone rang and Donna answered. "Sure thing," she said and hung up. "Glory is stopping by for some of my special praline French toast this morning." She looked at the big clock in the kitchen. "She should be here any minute. Just so you know."

It was time to rise and shine. "Thanks. Let me shake my crew out of bed. This is the perfect chance for me to talk to the sheriff. My boyfriend, who is also a sheriff, is headed this way today. I think he and Glory would see eye to eye."

"She's the best law officer around. Now you'd better hurry if you don't want Erik and Glory running into each other."

I took off for my room and roused Erik. He'd wisely parked his car down a trail near the B&B and he slipped out the window he'd come in. "See you in town," he said as he took off running across the back lawn of the inn.

I got Tinkie up with the promise of French toast, and went to see if Cece had returned. She hadn't. I was worried, but if she was working on a break in her career, I had to back off. I did text her just in case.

Where are you? I'm concerned.

Cece replied: *I'm perfectly fine. Have some big news. Headed back to the B&B. Don't tell Tinkie, please. She doesn't need to worry.*

OK. See you soon. I wanted to grill her on the spot, but I'd wait to talk to her in person. I knew Cece well enough to know she wasn't flirting with Hans. Whatever they were up to was strictly business. Cece loved Jaytee, and the bond they shared was powerful. Hans was certainly attractive and fun, but Cece's heart was in Jaytee's pocket. She was not the kind of person to betray her love. So what were Cece and Hans up to? My curiosity was an itch that would ultimately have to be scratched.

When I went back by Tinkie's room, she was coming out. She'd thrown on some clothes and made a pass at her hair, but this was not the normally coiffed and classy Tinkie Bellcase Richmond, Queen Bee of the Daddy's Girls. Man, if pregnancy could knock Tinkie from that throne, I was going to run from it like the plague.

"You okay?" I linked her arm through mine.

"I'm exhausted." She looked at me. "I want this baby so much, Sarah Booth, but I feel like a parasite is devouring me."

I couldn't help it. I laughed out loud. "And oh, what a special and remarkable parasite it will be."

"Don't mock me. I can barely put one foot in front of the other. She's draining my energy supply and my brain."

I took pity because she did look exhausted. I didn't point out that she and Oscar had made it very clear they didn't want to know the gender of their baby. It could as easily be a he. "This is the worst stage for being tired." I'd read a few books. "At least you don't have morning sickness."

"Oh, don't even mention such a thing. I'm tired and hungry all the time."

"It might not be pregnancy, Tinkie." I hugged her. "And if it is, remember, this is what you've always wanted. Nothing we really want is easy. You've sacrificed so much for this, and now you just have to relax, accept that the next few months you're going to yield your physical body to grow the baby you've always wanted. Think about that. You are going to bring a new life into this crazy old world."

"That terrifies me. What if I'm not a good mother?"

My snort of laughter was sincere. Tinkie would be the best mother. She was tender and kind and giving. She was generous with her money, but she was even more generous with her heart. "This will be the luckiest child ever born."

"I'm really scared." Her blue eyes were wide with emotion.

I was, too, but I wasn't going to say it. "Your baby will be surrounded by people who love him or her unconditionally. Your baby is going to have a marvelous life."

Tinkie stopped and stepped in front of me. She pulled me close. "I love you, Sarah Booth. More than if you were my sister. Thank you."

11

We entered the kitchen just as Glory Howard stepped in the back door. She was all business in her brown uniform with the gold star pinned to her chest. She joined us in the dining area and took a seat at the table with me and Tinkie.

The front door opened and I heard Cece's distinctive laugh. She came in with Hans and an armload of stargazer lilies. Once the flowers were in water, they joined us just as Donna put a platter of French toast and bacon on the table. Maple syrup and butter were already there.

We helped ourselves, and I felt Glory's gaze on me. The chatter around the table was light as Cece and Tinkie asked questions about the town and its history. Glory and Donna gave the facts and a few yarns. When the dishes were cleared and we were sipping a final cup of coffee, Glory turned to business.

"I got the autopsy report on Patrice Pepperdine. They're not through running the complete tox screen, but we have cause of death."

This was not going to be good. I could tell from her expression. "How did she die?"

"She didn't drown."

Which meant someone had hauled a body to the Dead Sea and dumped it. "So then . . . what did kill her?" I asked my question again.

"Another case of poisoning."

"More hemlock?"

She shook her head. "Herbicide. It's allegedly the same poison she used to kill Erik Ward's camellias. Not so easy to buy and highly toxic. You almost have to get it from a professional landscaper or nursery."

"She was poisoned with her own killer potion?" Tinkie asked.

"I don't think so. Meaning I don't think it was hers. We found a partially used container of the herbicide in Erik Ward's garden shed."

"Are his prints on it?"

"The container was wiped clean."

This was not good at all.

Glory focused in on me. "Where did Erik go this morning when he left here?"

I took a deep breath. No point denying it. Glory knew Erik had been here and it wasn't Donna who told her. I'd been with Donna the entire time. "I don't know where he is. Last time I saw him he was asleep in my room."

Cece's and Tinkie's heads swiveled around to look at me. "Say what?" Cece said.

"He showed up early this morning. He said he couldn't go home because there were deputies watching his house. I let him stay so we could decide how to turn him in. Last I saw him he was napping on the sofa." This wasn't the complete truth, but I didn't see the point in admitting that I'd watched him make his getaway.

"Did he tell you where he'd been?" Glory asked.

"He said he had an alibi for the time of Patrice's murder, but he wouldn't tell me where he was."

"If he really had an alibi, don't you think he'd come forward with it?" Glory asked matter-of-factly.

I had to admit, I saw her point. But I still couldn't believe Erik was a cold-blooded killer. "I just don't believe he killed anyone."

"Me either," Tinkie and Cece said in chorus.

Glory shrugged. "Bring him to the courthouse and let him turn himself in. That's the best thing. There's talk in town and it's ugly."

That unnerved me. "What kind of talk?"

"Erik is well liked, but folks are getting spooked with rumors of a serial killer at work. Now, if you know where he is, get him up to the courthouse pronto."

"If we see him, we'll strongly urge him to go to the sheriff's office," I promised.

"Could I have a word with you?" Glory asked.

I followed her out onto the lovely porch where lemon trees, with all their heady fragrance, were budded out. Honeybees buzzed all around the citrus plants. I inhaled. "This is so wonderful."

"You need to bring Erik in. And don't let him come back to Donna's. That puts her in a bad position."

"I'm sorry. I had no idea he'd come here. If he shows up, I'll bring him to the courthouse."

She nodded. "I could charge you, but I honestly doubt that Erik killed anyone. Still, he has to answer the charges and he is violating his bail. He needs to turn himself in ASAP."

"When I see him, I'll make sure."

Glory started to turn away, but I caught her arm. "Has anyone recently filed a complaint against Snaith for any of his concoctions?"

"Not recently."

"I'd like a copy of the autopsy on Pepperdine."

"When it's official, I'll share that with you."

"This herbicide that was used to kill her. How does one go about buying it?"

"That's exactly what I intend to find out," Glory said. "You might ask your client. He did have some in his gardening shed."

Oh, I intended to squeeze some truth out of Erik as soon as I found him. That or drop him as a client. If I couldn't trust him to do the smart thing, it was crazy of me and Tinkie to try to defend him.

"I think the common link to the murders is the gardens, not Erik." I put that theory out to Glory.

"Both Slay and Pepperdine had a large number of enemies. Most folks love Dr. Reynolds, but there are those who are disgruntled by the popularity of the gardens. Jealousy is such an ugly human emotion. And some people actually think the gardens are a bad idea, even though Dr. Reynolds is so careful to plant native species."

"Cosmo Constantine would be one such person."

"He's one of them, but Cosmo has always struck me as a gentle soul."

"Does he have an alibi for the murders?" I knew Glory had checked it out. She was a professional.

"He doesn't. But he's alone most of the time. That's just who he is. But I haven't cleared him of all suspicions."

"And he hates the gardens. Maybe killing people there is his way of putting Dr. Reynolds out of business."

"Maybe, but that's a far stretch, don't you think?"

I did, but I didn't say so. "Who else are you looking at? Tinkie, Cece, and I could help. We mainly want to clear Erik but we can also check out some leads. You're pretty shorthanded. You have a big county and not a lot of help."

"There's not enough funding for more deputies. You're right about that. Sure, I'd appreciate the help."

"Great." I told her Coleman would be arriving after lunch and would be happy to consult with her if she wanted him to.

"Sheriff Coleman Peters," she said. "I met him at a law officers conference once. Sure, I'd love to bend his ear about this case."

"One more question. Do you know where Patrice was killed?"

"We haven't found the original crime scene. Her house hasn't been disturbed. There didn't appear to be any altercations around Erik's yard or garden shed. We're still looking."

"How would the killer get the body to the Dead Sea, and why leave it there?"

"That's a question that needs an answer," Glory said. "My guess is that the killer rolled the body there in some kind of cart." She gave me a steady stare. "Dr. Reynolds has a cart in the shed by his office. I've spoken with him and he said he doesn't keep the shed locked. We searched the premises and he doesn't have any of that herbicide. Nor did Cosmo, who nearly flipped out at the thought of herbicide being used in that 'delicate ecosystem.' Reynolds's house is about a quarter of a mile deeper in the woods from the parking lot and sheds, so it's possible that someone could have driven up, gotten the cart, unloaded a body, and pushed it to the Dead Sea."

"That's an awful lot of work."

She nodded. "Which means that the garden location is worth a lot of effort to the killer, for whatever his or her reasons. It's not a body dump site of convenience."

"Her?" No one had mentioned anything about a female killer.

"Poison is typically a woman's method of murder. It's just a possibility. I looked at the cart in Dr. Reynolds's shed. It wouldn't take too much strength to haul a body around the gardens if the woman was physically fit. Like you."

"Am I a suspect?" I was a little surprised.

"No. I was just making a point. We don't know enough to rule anyone out." She put her hat on. "Now get Erik back in my office before I have to hunt for him. That would make me annoyed. He's going to like me a lot better when I'm not annoyed."

"I'll do what I can." Her attitude was more than reasonable; Erik would do well to obey her orders. From the looks of it, he was safer in jail than out. At least if the killer kept racking up a body count, Erik couldn't be blamed if he was behind bars.

"When you get the full tox screen on Pepperdine, don't forget to let me know." As a pharmacist, Erik could explain how the herbicide worked, and that might prove helpful.

"I will. Just a heads-up, I'm going to have to put Erik in jail when I find him. And the bail bondsman is pretty upset. Erik lost his bail money and will have to come up with more if the judge considers letting him out and the bail bondsman is even willing to work with him. These are facts I can't change." Glory gave a wave as she headed to her pickup truck.

I hadn't really considered the implications of Erik violating the terms of his bail. It was not going to be pretty, for sure. I didn't know the specifics, but bail on a murder charge would likely be high. And since Erik disappeared and couldn't be found—while another murder was committed—he'd lost a lot of money.

Back in the dining room, I paused in the doorway to watch Cece and Tinkie in an animated conversation. When they caught sight of me they waved me over.

"Cece did some legwork for us yesterday," Tinkie said.

"Well, for you and also for Hans," Cece clarified. "He's got several story angles going."

"What did you discover?"

"We talked with the judge who was supposed to hear Erik's case against Slay over the property matter."

"And?" I poured another cup of coffee and eased into a chair. I wasn't keen on including Hans in my investigation, but I couldn't help but be grateful that this was one step Tinkie and I wouldn't have to take.

"The judge said the contract Ward Senior signed was nothing less than highway robbery. He said the contract wouldn't have stood up in court, as it was clear the elder Ward hadn't understood what he was signing."

"This is in Erik's favor," Tinkie said. "He would likely have won the court case. He had no reason to kill Slay."

She was right about that, but I could see Cece wasn't finished. "And?" I pressed.

"And Slay has done a number of those land swaps for legal services in the past. He's ripped a lot of people off from tracts of timberland."

"Why hadn't someone stopped him?"

"I suspect because the elderly people didn't complain. There was a time when people held lawyers in great respect. You know that. Your daddy's word was law to a lot of people in Sunflower County." Tinkie motioned at the coffeepot for me to pour her another cup.

"My daddy wasn't a crook," I pointed out.

"True, but people don't know that these days. It's like a lot of people want to be bamboozled. They've forgotten how to research and make their own decisions. Hive brain. They fall for anything."

She was right about that.

"Things are more complex now, too. That's why they hire lawyers, because the entanglements are dense, the language deliberately obtuse. Lawyers are officers of the court and a lot of people think that means they're honest and decent. A lot of them are, but someone like Slay: rotten apple."

"Did you get any names of people Slay had duped out of land?" Tinkie asked.

"We did. We're going to talk to them this morning, if that's okay?"

Cece, I trusted with my life. Hans seemed fine, and I was sure he was rolling footage of the interviews in case this turned into something worthy of his TV show. That wouldn't interfere with the Delaney Detective Agency agenda, and it might be that he was letting Cece interview so he could assess her skills or offer her tips. "That would be a big help. But just keep us posted where you are. I was a little worried when you didn't show up last night."

"Will do. Hans was saying how he has an idea for a hot music competition, like a reality TV show, centered around the blues and juke joints."

Tinkie's blue eyes widened in excitement, an expression that had brought many a man to his knees. "This could be great. If this came to Zinnia and Sunflower County, what a boon for the economy it would be. And Delta State has that great music component—we already have the trained talent. That's a great idea, Cece."

Tinkie, more than anyone else I knew, had one finger on the pulse of the community. New businesses helped the bank her daddy owned and Oscar operated, but it was more than just monetary motivation. Tinkie wanted everyone to have a good job, to have warm housing, and healthy food. She wanted prosperity for all.

"Where is Hans?" He'd completely missed breakfast and there wasn't even a slice of French toast left for him.

"He dropped me off and went back to town. He's also getting some footage on the history of Lucedale. He's going to make several shows about his visit here. Smart move budget-wise. Last night we took some footage at the casinos on the Gulf Coast. Lots of potential there."

I had to agree with that. "Okay, then let's get going."

"Do you have any idea where Erik might be?" Cece asked.

I shook my head. "I don't. But the town is only about five thousand people. How hard could it be to find a pharmacist?"

Cece and Tinkie both laughed. "Girl, there may not be a lot of people here, but there sure are a lot of woods," Cece said.

"I hope Coleman brings Sweetie Pie and Chablis. We could use a pup with sniffing skills." I almost texted him, but I didn't want him to turn around and go back for them if he was already on his way.

"And Pluto?" Tinkie's eyes sparked mischief. "I wouldn't leave that cat behind. You know he'll pee in your shoes for revenge."

Pluto didn't do those things, but I'd known felines who had incredible powers of revenge. Pluto had other methods of making his wishes known, and I grinned at the idea of seeing him. I'd missed the black devil.

12

Cece took off for town to interview more people who'd been snookered out of land or money by Perry Slay. The problem was not that we couldn't find other suspects in Slay's murder, but that we had too many. Patrice Pepperdine also had an enemies list a mile long, but most of the names on it belonged to bridge club partners or civic organization members who'd had a run-in with her. From all accounts, she had not been a pleasant woman.

Tinkie and I loaded into my car and headed out to follow two leads. One was the purchase of the herbicide and the other was Leda Sellers, publisher of the local newspaper. I had high hopes that Leda knew the undercurrents of life in the little town, and that she might have an idea how Erik Ward spent his free time away from the drugstore he owned and ran.

"Who is working for Erik at the pharmacy?" I asked. "Does he have a fill-in pharmacist?"

"There's an older man who retired but fills in."

"And there's no other pharmacy in town?"

Tinkie shook her head. "Only Erik's. I'm coming up with crazy theories at this point. Do you think another person might want to drive Erik out of business so a new pharmacy could be opened? Having the only drugstore in town sounds pretty lucrative to me."

She was right and it was something else to check into. "But why dump the bodies at a miniature Holy Land? That's the part that's really getting to me. It just doesn't fit in with an ordinary scenario of greed or revenge. Why not just leave the bodies in Erik's garden shed or on the side of the road?"

"That would be far less shocking." Tinkie bit her bottom lip as we got in the car and drove toward town. "It's obvious the killer enjoys shock value."

"And doesn't care that he's violating a place a lot of people think is sacred."

"That's true." Tinkie stretched. "I can't seem to get enough sleep. All I want to do is eat and sleep."

I patted her shoulder. "So let's solve this case and get back to Sunflower County. You may be pregnant but I think Oscar would like some more practice at making a baby." We'd come to the turnoff at the main highway that led into Lucedale proper, and I took a right just as my phone began to ring. The Roadster was an antique, without the newfangled phone technology that allowed for hands-free driving, so Tinkie answered my phone.

"Hello, Coleman. Are you near? Is Sarah Booth going to be a happy woman in a few short hours? Could Oscar get away?" She was like a Gatling gun of questions.

She put the phone on speaker, and I pulled off the road near a stand of pines so I could talk to him without distraction. "Give Tinkie some chill pills," he said, amusement in his voice. "She's way, way too tightly strung."

"She needs more sleep." I grinned at her. "Is Oscar with you?"

"Couldn't get away. Neither could Jaytee, and I hate to say it, but I can't come either."

"What?" Tinkie and I said in chorus. "Why not?" We were echoes of each other.

"I've got my own murder to solve, Sarah Booth."

"Who died?" I asked.

"The guy wasn't from Sunflower County. He was with a traveling card game. Looks like someone cheated on a hand of poker and things got too hot. He was shot in the chest."

"I'm sorry to hear that. Any idea who shot him?"

"An idea. And an eyewitness. DeWayne, Budgie, and I are headed to roust a suspect now."

"Be careful."

"You do the same. When do you think you're coming home?"

"Day after tomorrow. I hope."

"I miss you, Sarah Booth. I miss sleeping with your leg thrown over me like I'm an old horse."

Tinkie and I both laughed. Coleman had to remember that Tinkie was right there, listening. To compound matters, she chimed in, "I've heard you've given Sarah Booth many a good ride, Coleman."

Coleman was more than ready for this game. "She's

quite the equestrian. She has me high stepping and cutting caprioles, courbettes, mezairs, the croupade, and the levade."

"I don't have a clue what that might be, but it sure sounds kinky," Tinkie said.

Tinkie could think what she liked, I wasn't going to tell her Coleman had listed high-level dressage movements. And where had he learned about those? Coleman was a fine horseman, but his focus had always been riding on the farm and trail riding. He was a constant and delightful mystery.

"Tinkie, if I were to teach Oscar some of those moves, you'd be pregnant with triplets." Coleman could give as good as he got.

"So why isn't Sarah Booth with child?"

"We are working on it. Hard," Coleman said. "Just ask Sarah Booth how much she likes it when we apply ourselves."

"So, you two think you can embarrass me?" We were near the outskirts of Lucedale and I wanted to focus on the case, but there was still time for a little fun. "Just so you know, Coleman, I miss the way your shirt smells like sunshine and starch and home. I miss the security of lying in your arms. I miss the way you wake my body up with your touch. I miss the way your lips move down my—"

"That's enough!" Tinkie pulled the plug as I knew she would. She liked to torment but she got flustered at any real details. "You two are giving me a hot flash." She fanned herself with her hand even though the air blowing in the convertible was still cool.

Coleman and I both laughed. Tinkie had stuck her hand too close to the fire.

"Sarah Booth has given me a hot flash, too," Coleman said, still chuckling. "Now you two get busy and solve that case so you can come home."

"When you see them, give Oscar and Chablis my love," Tinkie said before I hung up.

"Will do." Coleman promised. "You look out for my girl, okay?"

"At the top of my to-do list," Tinkie said. When the connection was broken, she turned to me. "I'm sorry he's not coming, Sarah Booth."

"Yeah, me, too." It was crazy how sad I was because I wouldn't see Coleman for another day or two. I'd known him since grammar school and there were many years we hadn't spoken a word to each other. But that was before. Before we finally accepted that we had an itch we had to scratch. "Let's focus on the case." Because doing anything else was only going to make me miss Coleman more.

The local feed and seed, G&D Farms, was the place to be on weekday mornings in the spring. When we pulled up in the lot, there had to be at least ten farmers getting fertilizer, grass and crop seeds, equipment, and herbicides. Sociable groups of men and women stood around talking weather, crops, and politics.

"Welcome to G and D," a pretty brunette behind the counter said. "What can we help you with?" I took in the big, new store with all kinds of horse and grooming supplies as well as a huge warehouse behind with feed, seed, and fertilizers. This was a place I could wander around in for hours, finding all kinds of things I needed for the horses.

I introduced myself and Tinkie and explained that we were private investigators. Hardly anyone ever asked to see our license, but this woman, who said her name was Starla, did. She was nobody's fool. She was plenty friendly, but she wanted verification. We both showed her our certifications.

"We're working for Erik Ward," Tinkie explained.

"Damn shame how he's being railroaded," Starla said. "Erik's a cutup and a charmer, and he wouldn't hurt anyone."

"I'm glad you feel that way. Did Erik ever buy an herbicide from you called MoBlast?"

"Not from me," Starla said, "and not here. We don't carry it." She motioned to a customer in the supplement aisle who was obviously looking for something. "The probiotics are down and on the right."

"Thanks," the young woman said and went back to her shopping.

"Where would someone get this MoBlast herbicide?" I asked. "Is it easily available?"

She hesitated. "Erik would know where to get it. He's a pharmacist, so he knows a lot more about those things than most people. Farmers generally just use what their daddies used or what the county agent recommends. But the biggest user of that particular type of herbicide around here are the commercial lawn companies. They give their clients a perfect lawn—no weeds, edged sidewalks, grass so green it looks to be plastic. But that all comes at a price. Probably a good thing their kids don't ever go outside to play because they'd be exposed to god knows what kind of chemicals."

"Are there lawn companies that spray MoBlast in this county?"

"Sure. There are new subdivisions outside of town with big homes and lovely landscaped lawns. It's not like the farm I grew up on anymore. We mowed the grass and kept things neat, but there wasn't an obsession over a dang dandelion on the lawn. I have to tell you, I'd take my childhood over anything available today. Swimming in the river or creeks. It was carefree and available for me and all my friends whenever we had time."

She was right about that. Dahlia House and the many different areas on the property were a fantasy land of fun and imagination for me growing up. "Can you give me some names of people who use MoBlast?"

Again, she hesitated. "I don't want to accuse anyone, and keep in mind that a lot of those landscapers park their vehicles and trailers on the side of the road. While they're working, anyone could come up and steal herbicides off their trucks."

I hadn't thought of that, but she was dead right.

"A name?" Tinkie flashed her award-winning smile. "We aren't accusing anyone, but we are trying to clear Erik. That chemical was found in his garden shed. The prints had been wiped off it, so it's pretty obvious it was put there to frame him. Now we need to know if any of these landscapers with access to MoBlast had a reason to want to see Erik in trouble."

"Fair enough," Starla said. "There are a number of small operators, just basically lawn services with mowing, raking, weeding, and fertilizing the lawns. Rory Palente runs Forever Lawn. He puts in the lawns at the exclusive subdivisions and maintains a lot of high-end businesses. Rory is a good guy, but he and Erik didn't click. I don't know why. Rory considers himself something of a ladies' man and the women preferred Erik. I suspect that's at the heart of their issues."

"Thanks, Starla."

"Rory runs about ten trucks, so it could have come off any of them. I know he uses that product to kill persistent problems."

"How dangerous is it?"

"Depends on who you ask. Label says it's safe, but caution is needed in fields that run off into live streams." She scoffed. "That's just about every field around here. I hate to think that stuff's getting into the water supply, but it's legal to buy and use."

"Could you tell us where we might find Rory Palente?"

"Since he's not here gabbing with the other men, try one of the diners. If he isn't working, and he works hard, he's shooting the breeze with some of his friends."

"Thanks, Starla."

"Tell Erik that no one believes he's guilty."

"Will do."

Starla caught my sleeve as I walked by. "Be careful. All of you, including Erik. I heard—" She stepped back from me.

"Heard what?"

Starla looked around. "I heard someone intends to pin this on Erik and anyone who gets in the way is going to be hurt."

"Who said that?"

"It's only gossip. Some of the men were talking about the murders. No one had anything specific, except that this was dangerous and everyone knows you're in town working on Erik's behalf. There are people who'd run you off, by means fair or foul."

"How about some names?" Tinkie said, handing her

a card. Her hand went protectively to her stomach, even though she only had the tiniest bump—and that might merely have been from overeating.

"I don't have any proof," Starla said. "You've already talked to Snaith. I promise if I hear anything specific, I'll give you a call."

She was going out of her way to help us. That was a good thing. "Thanks, Starla."

"Just be careful."

13

We found Rory Palente mowing a rolling, two-acre lawn at a French provincial two-story house. The place was perfectly landscaped, including a garden that mimicked the one at the French palace at Versailles. Rory had a four-man crew that was busy trimming hedges, weeding flower beds vibrant with daffodils, lilies, and even a few early tulips. A man on a golf cart spread fertilizer, and another had a pole chain saw and was trimming low-lying limbs. They worked with a precision that made me tired. When Rory stopped the massive mower beside his big pickup truck, Tinkie and I walked over to introduce ourselves.

"You're the detectives helping Erik out, aren't you?"

"We are." He was a good-looking man. His face was

tanned a beautiful bronze that only added sparkle to his blue eyes. Close-cropped hair, a trim waist, and nice shoulders added to the all-American package. I could see where he and Erik might be in competition for the ladies in the area. Rory was the rugged outdoorsman and Erik was the devil-may-care bringer of fun.

"You're here to ask about MoBlast, right?" He didn't beat around the bush, and his knowledge of Patrice Pepperdine's death told me how quickly gossip spread around the small town.

"We are," I said. "I understand you use MoBlast in your lawn work."

"Sure, I use it." He waved around the yard. "This climate is a license for weeds to grow, and grow aggressively. With the hot temperatures and high humidity, if you're sitting still, you're losing ground to the weeds."

The subtropical temperatures aided the undesirable plants as well as the foliage that people valued. He was right about that. "People are okay with all these chemicals?" I'd read too much lately on the dangers of herbicides, pesticides, and genetically engineered crops. Billy Watson leased the land around Dahlia House, and we'd come to an agreement about cutting way, way back on all those things. It was a gamble, but one Billy and I both were willing to take for the good of the planet. "Don't your clients worry about their children and their pets?"

"Basic economics, Ms. Delaney. Good lawn workers require a decent salary, and not a lot of people can or want to pay for someone to go around digging up weeds. A worker can spray an acre in the time it would take him to hand-weed a single flower bed. I don't like using a herbicide like MoBlast, but my clients demand it. They want a perfect lawn." He laughed and shook his head. "I don't know why. They never set foot outside of their homes to enjoy the outdoors. I guess it's for the annual Christmas card—the house and lawn look great."

I wasn't going to get diverted by talking about the craziness of people and their pretensions. That was a well-worn rabbit trail. "Has any of that chemical gone missing from your business?"

He shook his head. "I can't answer that question. Not completely. What I can tell you is that none of the workers have reported any chemicals missing. Of course that doesn't mean it didn't happen. You know how it is. Stuff disappears, and no one tells the boss because it looks like maybe the person reporting it is guilty of theft." He shrugged. "I pay these guys a lot more than minimum wage. They don't want to lose their jobs. Even if they didn't steal it themselves, they'll think I want to hold them responsible, even though I wouldn't." He gave Tinkie an *I'm a nice guy* grin.

"You're aware that MoBlast was used to kill Patrice Pepperdine?" I wanted to nip his charm in the bud. "The local feed-and-seed store doesn't carry it. Where do you buy yours?"

"Yep, I'm aware. I buy my supplies online. Like every other lawn service that works with a large number of clients." He leaned on the fender of his truck so that he was just a little closer to Tinkie. "I also heard a container of the herbicide was found in Erik's garden shed. I like Erik, but it's true that he hated that old bat. She poisoned his heritage plants and he sued her. To be honest, I don't blame him. Those old stock camellias are tough plants, and a lot of the newer varieties don't hold up nearly as well. I've been getting cuttings from Erik's plants since I started my lawn business. I could have gladly bopped Patrice on the head for killing those shrubs." He shrugged. "Folks get emotional about their gardens."

"How emotional?" Tinkie was doing her wide-eyed routine and it was having an effect on Rory. He'd forgotten I was standing there.

"Oh, very emotional. They nurture and care for them. It's a huge blow if something untoward happens to them."

"I can see that," Tinkie said. "My grandmother had a rosebush that she brought over from the old country. It was the most precious thing to her. When she passed, she bequeathed a cutting from the plant to all of her children, and I have the one she gave my mother. It's my most prized possession. Smells like it should be growing at the gates of heaven."

I did my best not to look shocked. Tinkie didn't have a family heritage rosebush—she wouldn't know a rosebush from a prickly pear if it was growing in the wild. And she certainly didn't have a grandmother from "the old country." She'd kissed the Blarney Stone for sure to come up with that lie.

"Then you know exactly how this goes," he said. "When Patrice poisoned Erik's heritage plants, I think it sent him around the bend a little bit."

"Did he publicly threaten Patrice?" Tinkie asked. I leaned against the hood of the Roadster and pretended not to be there. Rory only had eyes for Tinkie. I was completely extraneous, but not for long. Tinkie had softened the ground for me to sweep in for the kill.

"Do you really think Erik killed Patrice?" I stepped

into the conversation, and my reward was a glare from Rory.

"It's possible," Rory said. "Honestly, I had some dealings with Patrice. Most everyone in the county has had a run-in with her. I promise you, I could have bashed her brains out with a shovel she was so aggravating, and I'm not the only one who felt that way."

I was shocked again at that revelation—and the violence behind it—but I didn't say anything. Tinkie pressed on with her questions while flirting with Rory with her eyes.

"Do you know anyone who hated Patrice who also hated Perry Slay?"

Rory wasn't shy with his answers. "You know, it could be anyone. The saying around town was that if Perry and Patrice ever got together it would be Lucedale's Kim Kardashian and Kanye West couple. Neither one of them ever walked away from making a spectacle of himself or herself."

"Were they romantically involved?" I finally had to ask.

Rory made the universal shrug for "I don't know."

"There's a difference between being a social pain in the batookus and being someone that people hate enough to kill." I floated it past Rory to see how he'd react.

"I deal with a lot of people who aren't so nice," he said. "Homeowners forget that I don't control the weather or pest infestations. They get mad and arrogant about things I can't help. You just have to learn to shake it off. I never cut Patrice's yard, so I didn't hate her as intensely as some. I think she'd been through every lawn service in this county and was finally hiring folks to come up from Pascagoula because no one local would work for her. Perry Slay was a con man, but he never filed suit against me. I believe in the old 'live and let live' motto."

"If you had to name three people who might want both of them dead, who would it be?" Tinkie asked.

He thought a minute and then laughed. "Probably Erik Ward, top of the list. Snaith, the former doctor, would be second." He looked around the yard, checking on the crew he had working. "I don't know a third name."

"How about Rory Palente?" I asked.

"Hardly. If I killed off every aggravating client, I'd be out of business. Besides, I've never worked for Patrice or Erik or Slay," he said. "Now let's conclude the business about the MoBlast. It's possible someone stole it off one of my employees' trucks. I don't carry it on my truck." He pointed at the lawn he was working on. "This is the Calhoun lawn. They're chemical and herbicide free. The people I take care of are antiherbicides. Won't even poison fire ants. They're totally nematode users. I handle these clients because they're so techy. Check with the other crews. And now I have to get back to work."

He was already walking away when I called out to him. "Where were you Saturday night and last night?" I asked.

"Saturday night I was in bed with Marcus Jenning's wife, and last night I was at a dart competition at Popeye's Bar in Mobile. Ask the bartender. I won the competition." He sauntered back to his mower, hopped on, and cranked it up wide open. He tore off with leaves and grass clippings flying behind him.

Tinkie and I had no choice but to leave. Rory hadn't given us anything much, except that anyone could have gotten the MoBlast. Anyone. It didn't help us narrow our suspect list.

"Let's head to the newspaper," I said. "Maybe Leda Sellers can help us out."

The weekly newspaper office was going great guns to meet the Tuesday night deadline for printing the paper and getting it in the mail on Wednesday. When we got to the *Lucedale Gazette,* we found Leda in her office going over the page proofs for one section. She looked up expectantly.

When we introduced ourselves, her eyes lit up. "How about an interview?" she asked. "I can get a reporter in here and have it done in fifteen minutes. You're working for Erik Ward, and we'd love a statement."

I shook my head. "We're private investigators, not spokespeople for Mr. Ward."

She shrugged. "Can't blame a girl for trying." She picked up the front page proof again, ignoring us.

"Could we buy you a cup of coffee?" Tinkie asked. "We need to ask a few questions, but we'll be quick."

Leda sighed. "I do need some coffee." She motioned us to follow her into the back of the newspaper office, where a pretty redheaded woman was busy setting headlines on a machine.

"Jojo, would you have time to read over these proofs?" Leda asked.

"Sure thing." The redhead took the proofs and Leda waved us out the back door for the short walk to the local diner. The day was sunny and warm and the short walk felt good. We found an empty booth in the diner and the waitress brought three steaming cups of coffee without even being asked.

"Your friend Cece Dee Falcon came by earlier," Leda said. "She was with that TV guy, Hans."

"Cece is helping us out and she's helping Hans out, too," Tinkie said.

"She's a good reporter and a smart cookie. A video presence will move her career along. Hans produces some really good stories and he maximizes his time. But you aren't interested in my opinion of Hans. What do you want?"

"We need some viable suspects who might have wanted Patrice Pepperdine and Perry Slay dead." Tinkie ordered three slices of lemon meringue pie when the waitress stopped by to fill our cups. When I looked at her, she made a face. "If you don't want yours, I'll eat it. I'll eat them all. If this is anything like the coconut custard, then this will be the best lemon meringue pie I've ever put in my mouth."

With the pie issue settled, Leda returned to possible suspects for the two murders. "Look, a lot of people disliked them both. I always suspected Slay was up to his ears bribing juries and intimidating witnesses, but I could never prove it. He was a smarmy attorney, but he won a lot of cases for his clients. While the opposition hated him because his tactics were . . . questionable, those who hired him loved him. He won for them. For some people, that's all that matters, and those are the kind of people who hired Slay." She chuckled. "I should probably be on the suspect list. I can't count the number of times he threatened to sue the paper."

"Did he ever file suit?" Tinkie asked.

"He didn't. Not because he didn't want to. We're just extremely cautious about printing stories. We have the

facts to back everything up. Like your friend, Cece."
Leda continued, her blond curls bobbing. "I did have
an interesting visitor this morning. About an ad, not a
news story."

Tinkie leaned forward. "Tell us," I said to Leda.

"A woman came into the paper today and bought a
display ad."

I waited.

"The ad contains copy that makes the claim that
Erik Ward poisoned a man named Johnny Braun on a
Caribbean cruise."

Tinkie put down her fork. "What?"

"That's what the ad says. It was a "payment for more
information leading to the arrest of Erik Ward for poisoning Johnny Braun" ad. There's a photo of Erik, like
a wanted poster."

"You aren't going to run that, are you?" I asked.

"Not this week. But if I check with the Miami police
and they confirm that Erik was suspected in a murder
on a cruise ship, I'll have to go with it. In a story if not
an ad."

"How long ago was this alleged murder?"

Leda thought for a minute. "I'm not certain. It was
one of those cruise tours around the island hot spots.
Shouldn't be too hard to track down."

"Thanks!" This wasn't the information I'd hoped to
obtain, but it was another step in the development of
our case. I liked Erik, but there certainly were a lot of
dead bodies piling up around him.

Leda dug into her pie as Tinkie finished my piece.
"Good to see your appetite doesn't suffer from bad news,"
I said dryly.

Tinkie pushed back from the table. "Do you remember the name of the woman who wanted to buy the ad?"

"Sure do. Betsy Dell. Said she grew up here but moved to Mobile. I haven't had a chance to run down the facts about her."

"We could stop at the local high school," Tinkie suggested. "If she went to school here in the county, someone will remember."

She was right about that. In rural high schools, memories were long. Football heroes and popular cheerleaders were big deals and that sometimes lasted their entire lives.

"Check at the local library, too. Those librarians are pretty good detectives themselves." Leda stood up from the table. "Thanks for the pie and coffee. Now I've got deadlines to meet."

14

George County High School, located about two miles from the city limits, served the entire county. We met with the high school principal, Hank Chisholm, who said he remembered Betsy Dell as a pretty high schooler who was "more timid than most."

Hank walked us down the main hallway to a display of photographs and pointed out a slender young woman with a sweet smile who was secretary of the Home Economics Club. "The Dell family moved away years back." He thought a minute. "Betsy followed the rules. I can't imagine her ever being in trouble."

"She isn't in trouble, but one of her classmates, Erik Ward, is having some difficulties."

"Yeah, I heard about the murders. Erik likes to carry on a lot of foolishness, but I don't see him harming anyone. Let me tell you what I know." The principal, who'd gone to high school with all of the parties involved, painted Erik as a very bright student who could solve chemistry and math problems in his sleep. "He could have worked for NASA or any other big concern, but he loves being a pharmacist," Hank said. "We play golf together about once a month. Erik is social, and he enjoys fun and having a good time. He has a wicked sense of humor and a little bit of the devil in him, which adds to his charm. But there is a secretive side to Erik. There's a part of him he holds back. I just never thought it was a dark side." Hank had a pretty accurate handle on our client. "How does Betsy figure into the situation?"

"Betsy has made a pretty harsh accusation against Erik. Would you know why she might do that?"

He shrugged. "Look, I'm a little older than Erik or Betsy. I knew who she was, but she disappeared right after high school graduation. Someone said she'd moved to the West Coast, or maybe Idaho. I can't remember. She was never really part of our county clique, not that it's like an exclusive thing. She just wasn't around. Those of us who got an education and then returned to Lucedale, well, we enjoy socializing and doing things together. She wasn't living here, so she's kind of slipped from the collective memory. I don't even remember who she hung out with. But she never struck me as someone who would levy accusations at anyone. For any reason. She's a follower, not a leader." He snapped his fingers. "The library has some yearbooks. You might check there. See what groups she belonged to. She's likely got friends still living around here and if you can find them, you'll get a lead on her. If you want to find her, that would be the best way."

"Thanks, Hank," Tinkie said.

"Not a problem, ladies." He turned and started down the hallway to the front door. "If you need anything else, just give a call."

We were off to the next location. Over the past cases Tinkie and I had resolved, we'd both learned one valuable lesson—PI work included a lot of legging it around to different places and people. We had to turn over a lot of rocks to find a diamond.

When we returned to town, we located the library with ease. Ten minutes after we arrived we were sitting at a table with a computer and three George County High School yearbooks. We found Betsy Dell's senior year and began searching for her face in group and organization photos. She was a pretty girl with dark hair and a heart-shaped face. In the photos her shoulders were slumped. She always took a position on the end of the back row in any group, seeming to stand a few inches farther back from the photographer than anyone else, as if she might be trying to get away before the shutter snapped.

"If she stood up straight and had a little confidence, she'd be a lovely girl," Tinkie said.

She was right. Betsy had belonged to a few different high school organizations, but she was never in the front row smiling. If she held an elected post, it was one that did all the work. After another twenty minutes, I identified several other women who were in photographs with her. I took the yearbook and the names up to the front desk.

"Do you know any of these women?" I asked.

The librarian looked them over. "Sure. And I know Betsy, too."

This was a stroke of luck. I noted the librarian's name tag. "Thank you, Polly Jean. Do you know where we could find her?"

The librarian shook her head. "We weren't close friends in high school, but I liked her. Betsy left for Hollywood the day of graduation. She wanted to act. She said she was tired of being a nobody. She kept all of that to herself until the day we were supposed to show up for the graduation ceremony. She had a bus ticket to Los Angeles."

"She just hopped a bus and went on her own?" That was impressive.

"I sat in the bus station with her until she left. She didn't have anyone else. No one from her family was there to see her off."

That made my heart ache. I'd had my aunt Loulane, who was the best second mother a girl could ask for.

"We understand Betsy was terribly shy. That seems like it would be hard to be in the movie business. In the limelight, as it were," Tinkie said.

Polly Jean's smile was tinged wth sadness. "I think Betsy believed that she could slip into different roles, become someone different. She was shy, but she was really smart, and she was also driven to get out of this county."

"Was she successful as an actress?" I couldn't help but hope she'd found some triumphs.

"I don't know. Her parents moved about a week after she left. As far as I know, no one has seen or heard from Betsy or any of the Dell family. I have to say, it came as a shock to me that Betsy aspired to be a movie star.

She was always so . . . mousy in high school. Quiet. Shy. Who knew she harbored those big dreams, but she had more courage than a lot of us. She took action to manifest her dream." She tidied a stack of books. "I honestly haven't thought of her in a long time."

Sometimes, big dreams were just a way to escape the tedium of everyday life. But if she'd gone out to Hollywood, at least, as Polly Jean noted, she'd made an effort to reach for her ambitions. Maybe she hadn't been totally successful, but she'd been brave enough to try. I knew what that felt like.

"Did Erik and Betsy ever date?" Tinkie asked.

Polly Jean rolled her eyes. "Heavens no. Erik was the most popular boy in his class. He just knew how to have fun and all the girls dated him, casually. He made sure they understood it was casual and just for fun. Erik was in it for the fun, but he was emotionally elusive. He loved life, and it was contagious."

"You haven't heard from Betsy recently?" I asked.

Polly Jean shook her head. "I wish I'd stayed in touch. I got married, had a couple of kids, just got swept up into the daily grind."

"I know how that goes," Tinkie said without a smidgen of irony.

"You wouldn't know anything about cruise lines out of Miami, would you?" I asked. "Maybe a trip that's especially popular with local folks here?"

She frowned. "Some of the churches sponsor bus vacations to Branson, Missouri, or winter trips to Dollywood to see Pigeon Forge and if they're lucky, they run into some Christmas snow. The garden clubs sometimes take tours of places like Calloway Gardens, but I don't know of any group that goes on cruise ships. Sorry.

There's a cruise line that runs out of Mobile down to Miami and then into the Caribbean. Gulf Voyager, I think is the name. That's all I know."

"That's okay, and thanks for the help," I said. "I need to make some copies of these yearbook photos." I had them on my phone, but I needed print copies in case I had to leave them somewhere. We desperately needed a line on Betsy.

The librarian pointed me toward a copy machine that was for the public to use. Five dollars later, I had pretty good prints of every photo with every person we'd been able to identify. The hunt was on.

Tinkie and I decided to stay in town for some food. I loved Donna's cooking at the B&B and also her smart-aleck remarks, but we had a lot of ground to cover if we were going to find Betsy Dell before the day was over.

We stopped at the local diner and the same waitress came over with a grin. "You look like you could use some fried catfish, turnips, sweet potato casserole, and how about some praline pound cake for dessert."

She had Tinkie pegged for a big eater. In the South, being a big eater is a high compliment to the cook. Every child I'd grown up with had been taught to "clean their plates" because there were hungry children doing without. Tinkie had never belonged to the clean plate club until her pregnancy. Now she could clean her plate, my plate, and anyone else's plate at the table.

"That sounds like a lovely lunch!" Tinkie was all in. "Could we also have a side of fried dill pickles?"

"Absolutely." The waitress turned to me. "And for you?"

"Vegetable plate with turnips, butter beans, fried okra,

and cornbread. And one question: Do you know this woman?" I thrust a photo of Betsy at her.

"Sure. Betsy Dell is her maiden name. She married a Bastid out in California."

"What's her married name?" I had my pen out.

"Bastid. Are you hard of hearing?"

Tinkie giggled, and I couldn't help but smile. "No, no . . . I thought you were saying something else," I explained.

"Yeah, like my general description of men. Because they're all bastards, one way or another." The waitress poked through the other photocopies I had. "If you're looking for Betsy, she lives over in Mobile. About forty minutes from here, but she seems to have left Lucedale behind. She had such big dreams about going out to Hollywood. I guess it's hard to come home."

My failed career as a Broadway actress had given me a taste of coming home with my tail between my legs, but in the long run, it had been a wonderful decision. I'd saved my family home, learned to deal with a bossy and aggravating haint, and fallen in with the best bunch of friends a girl could have. And then there was Coleman.

"You wouldn't know how to get in touch with her, would you?"

The waitress pulled an order pad from her pocket and wrote down something. "Here's her email. Drop her a line."

When she went to put our orders in, I looked at Tinkie. "I'm going to ask if we can meet with her. In person."

She nodded. "But first, I think after this meal I'm going to need a nap. Could we make the appointment for a little later?"

"Sure thing, partner."

I sent Betsy Dell an email while we were waiting for the food, and by the time we finished eating, I saw that Betsy had replied and agreed to a chat later in the afternoon.

We arrived back at the B&B and Tinkie went straight to her room. I checked in with Donna, who said Cece had called to let her know she wouldn't be back for dinner. She and Hans were covering some territory, it seemed. In the quiet of my room, I called the number Betsy had given me.

On the phone, Betsy sounded older and more self-assured than I expected. Looking at photos of someone in her teens can be misleading. Turned out Betsy was a nurse at a Mobile hospital and the mother of two children. Whatever dreams of being an actress she'd once held on to, she'd set them aside for the satisfaction of motherhood and a regular paycheck.

"I understand you paid for an ad regarding Erik Ward," I said. I'd already explained that I was a private investigator hired to prove Erik was innocent of killing Slay or Pepperdine.

"That's right. And I know the libel laws." She might have the law on her side but she sounded super stressed, like maybe there was more to the story. "Truth is a defense."

"Hold up, I'm not accusing you of anything. I just wonder why you think Erik is guilty of—"

"Of murder? Because I have good reason to believe he is. He and Patrice . . . look, you can search for all the evidence that shows Erik to be innocent that you want, but Erik is guilty."

"Do you have proof?" I wished I was talking to Betsy

in person, but a phone call was as good as it was going to get for now.

"Did Erik tell you about the cruise?" she asked.

"No." This was exactly where I wanted to go, though. "It appears there are more than a few things Erik hasn't told me."

"That's because he's guilty."

"Of what? Patrice died here in George County. She wasn't on a cruise. I don't have a clue who this Johnny Braun you mentioned in your ad might be."

"He died, and Erik is guilty of killing him."

Either she really believed that or she was stuck in some alternate-reality delusion. "How does that relate to Patrice Pepperdine's death?"

"It all goes back to the dance competition. Johnny was Erik's number-one competition for the Caribbean Cruise International Dance King competition title."

"What?" Now I was really bumfuzzled.

She laughed. "Erik didn't tell you about his secret life? Why am I not surprised? Erik is a professional ballroom dancer. Not just a professional, but a highly ranked dancer. He specializes in the shag and the tango. It's all a big, hush-hush secret because a lot of people think dance professionals like Erik are gigolos and also that little thing of a murder accusation hanging over his head. Erik was convinced his drugstore would suffer if people knew about Johnny Braun and that Erik was paid to dance with lonely women."

This was sounding worse and worse, not because there was anything wrong with dance competitions but because our client had been lying—if not lying outright then withholding the truth. "No one has told me anything about any of this. Why don't you enlighten me?"

"Gladly. Maybe then you'll stop trying to save him. Erik is one of the top ballroom dance competitors in the Southeast. He's highly sought after for competitions and as a partner. Patrice was his dance partner, up until he threw her over for some Latin lady from New Orleans. You'll want her name, Ana Arguello. A real fiery Latin beauty. That's why Patrice poisoned his shrubs, not because she hated his plants. He hurt her and she wanted to hurt him back. And that's why he killed her—because she was filing suit with Perry Slay for breach of promise."

"Wait! Breach of promise?" That could mean only one thing. "As in marriage?"

"Exactly. He told her he was going to marry her and then he backed out. Then she threatened to tell everyone in town about his secret life as a dance master, the murder accusation, and that he was a cad who didn't honor his word."

"So?" I loved dancing. Great exercise. No crime there. And engagements were called off all the time. It happened. None of this amounted to a valid reason to commit murder.

"There was a national chain of drugstores looking to come into the Lucedale area. Erik has a lock on most of the local business, because he's well-liked and popular with everyone. His store is a community gathering place. Some folks would disapprove if it had gotten out that he was a dance master and someone who broke his word, but the real problem, as I see it, is the deception. Folks don't like to believe a person is one thing and then find out he's something else. Especially not a murderer. His business would have suffered and the chain pharmacy would have come in."

I felt my stomach drop to my feet as I listened. This shed a whole new light on his possible involvement in Patrice Pepperdine's murder.

"How has Erik kept his whole secret life so . . . secret?" I asked.

"Patrice was the only person in the county who knew about his passion for dance. He had another dance partner before Patrice, but . . . Claudia Brooks moved away. She didn't really have any option. You should ask him about her. See what he says."

"How did you stumble on Erik's passion for dance? His whole involvement in this world?"

"Johnny Braun was my dance partner. We were in the running for the win, which had a fifty-thousand-dollar purse attached. More than the money, though, I would have been a star. Finally. Then Johnny was murdered just before the competition was to begin."

"This was on a cruise ship?" I had to be certain I understood.

"It was. The Gulf Voyager Cruise Line, which hosts the Christmas Dance Extravaganza each year. This is the biggest competition in this part of the world. The dancers are given a free two-week cruise, and we perform every evening in different dances for the entertainment of the passengers. Erik had the shag sewn up, but Johnny and I took top honors with the waltz and cha-cha. We still had the tango, the rumba, and the salsa left to dance. Johnny had the hip action for the salsa and everyone knew it. We were going to win."

"What happened?" I had to know.

"Someone poisoned Johnny. He was fine one minute and sick the next. We were at dinner, just before the final dances. Johnny turned kind of green and went outside.

He was going to be sick and he was embarrassed. I tried to go with him, but he told me to stay and talk to the cruise employee who was taking care of the music. There was a live orchestra because this was such a big event."

"And what happened?"

"Johnny fell overboard. He was throwing up and lost his balance and went over."

"You saw this?"

She shook her head. "No, I didn't. But that's what had to have happened. Johnny was leaning over the rail—another passenger saw him—and then he was gone. He disappeared without a trace. They searched the ship high and low. That's the only thing that could have happened."

"Surely there was an investigation."

"Of course. His death was ruled accidental. But I know it was Erik. He poisoned Johnny and it's his fault. He ruined my life and my chance to be someone."

15

We talked for another half hour before I circled back to a point I couldn't let go of. "Betsy, you need to come forward with this information. Sheriff Glory Howard will want to hear this from you."

"I thought you were working for Erik?"

"I am, but I am first and foremost working for justice. I haven't found any evidence yet that Erik hurt anyone, but the sheriff needs all the facts." The best thing for Erik, and everyone else, was to put the facts in front of Glory and let her investigate. I trusted her not to rush to judgment.

"Are you going to tell her all of this? This makes Erik look really bad."

Suddenly she was shy about calling Erik a murderer?

"You're trying to buy an ad in the newspaper to destroy Erik's reputation. I'd much rather see this put before the sheriff and have an investigation rather than assassinate him in print."

She sighed loudly. "I'll think about it. Now I have to go."

"Where can I get in touch with this Claudia Brooks?"

"I have no idea. She went home to her family, as far as I know. Good luck tracking her down."

The line went dead and she was gone. I drew in a deep breath and put in a call to Coleman. Tinkie was asleep and Cece was running the roads. I could have a little dirty phone talk with my favorite lawman.

He answered on the second ring with tension in his voice. "Are you okay?"

That wasn't the response I'd expected. "Yeah, I'm fine. Why? Is something wrong?"

Coleman quickly got a handle on his tone. "Nope. Things here are fine. I was just thinking about you and when you called, it hit a nerve."

"The critters all good?"

"I took Lucifer out for a ride early this morning. He was feeling his oats in this fine spring weather. Sweetie Pie was delighted for a run. Pluto is really, really pissed at you. He sits in the parlor window and watches the driveway. He was also sniffing your shoes, like maybe he was going to let you know how aggravated he is."

"Pluto wouldn't do that."

"Wouldn't he?"

I heard the teasing note in Coleman's voice. He was pulling my leg. Pluto was far too dignified to do such a thing. I hoped.

"What's really going on?" I asked. There was something up with Coleman.

"I just keep trying to get away from here, but the lawbreakers are working overtime."

I wanted desperately to see Coleman, but I respected how seriously he took his responsibilities in Sunflower County. He would never leave if there was a hint that he was needed.

"What about tomorrow?" I asked, trying to keep the plaintive note out of my voice. The Bexley B&B would be so much more fun with a hunk of burning love beside me.

"Maybe. DeWayne, Budgie, and I are busting it. You know I'll be there when I can. Or you could come home."

I told him about the recent discoveries of my dance master client and the mysterious death of one Johnny Braun—something I needed to talk to Sheriff Glory about when Tinkie woke up.

"Why would anyone care that Erik is a dance champion?" Coleman was puzzled. "Dancing is good, healthy fun."

"I think it's perception."

"You have got to be kidding me?"

"Not kidding. Accused of offing a competitor, and maybe it's the breach of promise thing. If he really walked out on Patrice Pepperdine, that would explain her vindictiveness. If folks around here take that kind of thing seriously, it could affect Erik's business. Remember old Lenny Lucas and how everyone stopped going to his hardware store after he got Sula pregnant and wouldn't marry her? They ran him out of business and then out of town. People who breach community standards can suffer."

"Good point."

"As sheriff, folks hold you to a higher standard, too." Now was my chance for a little fun. "I mean, if you were to betray me or hurt me, I don't think folks would stand for it."

He chuckled. "I don't know, Sarah Booth. I might get more votes. Folks think you're on the nosy side."

I laughed, too. "Go ahead, just try to wiggle out of loving me. Bad things will happen." I thought of Jitty. Lord, she'd have a conniption and maybe bring down the wrath of the Great Beyond on his head. Jitty adored Coleman, but if he ever hurt me, she'd be singing a different tune.

"It might take some serious convincing to keep me on the hook." There was a playful note in his voice.

"Oh, I get the picture. You see yourself as some kind of big rainbow-colored trout, all sleek and cagey. And I'm the worm, that little brown nugget of temptation."

Coleman's laughter made me feel closer to him. "I didn't exactly picture it that way in my head, but now I don't think I'll ever get that out of my brain."

"Oh, I have some images I need to put in your brain." I had a hot-flash memory of Coleman sweeping me into his arms and carrying me upstairs. He put me on the bed and began kissing me. When Coleman kissed me, there was no time at all to think. My body responded and desire pushed out all rational thought.

"Yeah, I have plenty of my own, like you in front of a Christmas tree in a sexy red bit of fluff and lace."

I pulled myself out of memory lane with my breath short and my heart pounding. That little outfit had been a Christmas present, and it had worked very effectively to leave Coleman haunted by ghosts of Christmas past.

But May Day was coming, and I intended to make some new memories with my man. I'd missed the Easter bunny, even though I still had a sexy little bunny suit I intended to surprise Coleman with when I got home.

"Coleman, I need to be serious. Do people really kill each other over a breach of promise?" It sounded archaic. Like something a nineteenth-century woman might do if her honor and reputation had been destroyed.

"People value things differently, Sarah Booth. You know that. You've always been your own woman. Your parents taught you that, and Aunt Loulane polished it off. It doesn't mean you don't get hurt, but a man will never be able to crush you, no matter what he might do. Other women see their only value as the wife of the man they're married to. If that man leaves or betrays them, it could push that type of person into murder."

There was a mighty big compliment in his words. And also a deeper understanding of who Coleman was as a man and as a lover. He'd never been drawn to the vulnerable girls, the ones who wanted a man to shape and complete their world. Plenty of those had chased him because he was strong and able to bring a sense of safety and stability. In the South, and maybe a lot of other places, a certain type of woman had been raised to hunt for the alpha male, the breadwinner and responsibility shoulderer. It wasn't that I didn't crave those things. It was just that I realized after my parents died that it was up to me to create my own safety net, my own stability. No one could truly give me that—because when it came from anyone else, they could also take it away. It wasn't a fair burden to put on another person. The era of women being taken care of by their men had died back in the 1950s. Some people just hadn't snapped on that fact yet.

"I guess I need to understand Patrice Pepperdine a lot better if I'm going to understand Erik."

"It's possible that she *assumed* they were going to marry. If she was a little unhinged or a tad narcissistic, she'd believe her fantasy was reality, and she'd blame Erik for tearing it apart."

He was talking about another whole kettle of fish. "You sound like that comes from personal experience."

"When you were in New York I dated a woman from Jackson for over a year. We had a lot of fun. I wasn't the sheriff yet and I had a lot more freedom to travel and enjoy the pleasure life offers."

I couldn't help the instant jealousy that swept over me, even though this was the past and I'd been intricately involved with an actor, Graf Milieu, while Coleman had been busy with his female friend. I didn't ask her name—I didn't want to know. Because then I'd be tempted to look her up, to judge her as a competitor, and that was not the way I wanted to spend the coming days and weeks. "Obviously, this took a bad turn. As you know, I'm no stranger to bad romantic turns."

Coleman's laugh was more poignant than merry. "How well we both know this. I cared for her. I enjoyed her company, but I didn't love her. Not in the way that I hoped to one day love a partner."

The jealousy faded as quickly as it had come. "There are so many different ways to love people, aren't there?"

"Maybe this Patrice really, truly gave Erik her heart, and he didn't recognize it. That would tend to make a woman very angry."

"Again, talking from experience?"

"Yes, and rueful experience at that. I hurt someone badly. I never meant for that to happen. I was so thick-skulled I didn't even know it was happening. I just assumed she felt exactly as I felt—that we were having a whale of a good time but that it really was just for a time. Not forever. I think back and I should have seen the signs, Sarah Booth. And that makes me worry that I'm misreading you, too."

It was fish or cut bait time. Part of being a grown-up was stepping up to the plate when the pitcher threw a ball. "I want more than just a passing good time. I want a shot at something permanent. Is that the reading you're getting from me?"

"It is," Coleman said, "and boy am I relieved, because that's exactly what I want, too."

I looked out the window of my B&B room at the beautiful gardens and thought of Snow White for some crazy reason. I could hear the birds outside chirping, going about their business of building nests and preparing for the cycle of new life. Any minute now the blue-bird of happiness would perch on the windowsill and the Seven Dwarfs would come marching down the garden trail singing "Heigh-Ho."

"When are you coming home?" Coleman asked, this time with real longing in his voice.

"As soon as I can, Big Guy."

"Stop it."

"How about Big Mon, like Cletus calls Dave Robicheaux." The James Lee Burke mysteries were some of his favorite books.

"Don't call me that. It's a sacrilege."

"Dead-Eye Pete?"

"When I get my hands on you, I'm going to make you pay."

"Marshal Dillon?" That would get him going.

"Should I call you Festus or Miss Kitty?"

"Okay, let me think." It was a nickname for him I was after. "Okay, I've got the perfect nickname. Mr. Law and Order."

"That's worse, Sarah Booth."

"Walking Tall."

"That's the worst one yet. Don't dare call me that. Or I'll call you My Little Private Instigator."

I laughed. "I don't mind that. I'd like to instigate some changes in your blood flow."

"Sarah Booth, you are a naughty minx."

Now that was one step too far. "No. No Naughty Minx." I searched for a new label. "How about I call you My Sweet Little Six-Shooter. People can draw the implication they choose."

"No." But he was laughing. "Keep it up and I'll have to come down there and handcuff you."

"And that's when the fun would begin. Just remember, turnabout is fair play."

I heard someone outside my door in the hall, and it was past time to wake Tinkie. We still had some ground to cover. "Call me tonight, please." We were as bad as teenagers.

"Will do, Miss Snoop."

"Now I like that one. Keep it." I severed the connection before he could come up with something worse.

The noise came at the door again. This time with a creepy footstep, kind of a step and shuffle. Step and shuffle. I instantly thought of someone dragging a dead body. It's just the way my mind works.

I popped out of the chair and picked up a heavy candlestick from a small desk. It had heft and would be easy to swing. My gun was in the trunk of my car. I'd never considered that while I was on a girls' weekend I might need protection.

The step, shuffle came again, and then a bang on my door. I grasped the knob and prepared to open it.

16

I took a gulp of air, twisted the knob, and threw the door open. A young woman stood in the hallway. I took in her mohawk haircut, the black Goth makeup, the ring in her nose, the heavy boots, and her black clothing. Her sleeveless tank top revealed a lot of ink. What really caught my attention was the tattoo needle in her hand and the little generator she was dragging.

"Who are you and what do you want?"

"I want justice. And revenge. And I want to make cheating, lying men suffer." She had a slight accent I couldn't place.

That set me back on my heels. "There's not a man in my room."

She rolled her eyes. "Like that comes as a surprise to me." She brushed past me and stepped into my room. She looked around, finally taking in my T-shirt and sweat shorts that I usually slept in. "In that getup, if a man showed up he'd run for the hills."

I knew her, of course. "Jitty, dammit, you scared me."

"You think you didn't give me a start? Girl, look in the mirror. You look like you just got evicted from skid row."

"I didn't realize I was going to have to try to impress Lisbeth Salander in the middle of a beautiful spring afternoon." I'd finally figured out who Jitty was pretending to be. "Have *you* looked in the mirror? You'd scare the pants off a man—and not in a good way."

"The better to ink him up good. Did that lawman you're playing hot sheets with happen to leave any handcuffs? I might need them for an apprehension. I heard there was a marriage-contract breaker on the loose."

"If you're referring to Erik, we don't know that he proposed to Patrice Pepperdine and then reneged. She could have lied to her friends. Keep in mind, we don't *know* anything."

Jitty made a little gesture of dismissal with her hand, as if she were flicking off a fly. "He's a man. He's guilty."

This was certainly a different song than Jitty normally sang. Most often she was throwing shade at me for any number of things. I was the problem; Coleman was her golden boy.

"Okay, Lisbeth, what brings you to Lucedale, Mississippi?" Since I was the only person who could see her, I didn't have to worry that the residents of George County would stroke out if they saw her outfit.

"I'm here to protect you and the girls."

Now that was an interesting twist. "Do we need protection?"

Her features morphed from the pale Goth of the main character of the novel *The Girl with the Dragon Tattoo*, back to the beautiful and healthier-looking ghost of Dahlia House. "You need to be careful. Your mama would skin me if I let anything happen to you."

I knew that Jitty, my parents, Aunt Loulane, and even Great-great-great Grandma Alice all conspired to torment me—but also to keep me safe. They were busy in the Great Beyond. "Why is my mama worried about me?" There was something else going on with Jitty. She never told me anything about what happened to people after they died. There were rules. Plenty of rules. I was a rule-breaker for the most part, but not when it came to the Great Beyond and Jitty. If I lost her, I would have no family at all. So I played by the rules.

"Libby is looking out for you. James Franklin, too. All of them. You better not disappoint them."

When she threw the whole thing back on me, I felt a lot better. This was how our conversations usually went. I was always the one at fault. "Not my circus, not my monkeys."

"What tidbits of wisdom you spout. Try this one on for size. 'The past is never dead. It's not even past.'"

I recognized the William Faulkner quote. It troubled me as much now as it had when I first heard it in a literature class at Ole Miss. Faulkner had loved his bottle but the man had a lot of wisdom and could turn a phrase. "Is something bad about to happen?" She wouldn't tell me but I had to try.

"Something bad is always about to happen, Sarah Booth. It's the nature of life."

She was suddenly back to Lisbeth, and her words were so sad and poignant that I stepped closer to her. "What is it? Tell me."

She shook her head. "Keep an eye on your friends."

I nodded. "Are they in danger from the killer?" Tinkie was asleep, but Cece was out of pocket. "Should I be worried?"

"Stay alert. And do what you have to do to stay safe."

With that, she spun around so I could see her back, and the dragon's tail winding down her left arm. The design seemed to take life. The figure of the dragon circled her, looking over her shoulder and puffing out a long, hot lick of flame and a belch of smoke. And then she was gone.

The door to my bedroom opened and Tinkie stood there. "Are you okay?"

I didn't want to say anything because I didn't trust my voice. I nodded.

"Who were you talking to?" She looked around the room, searching for my conversational companion.

I was tired of lying to Tinkie. "Lisbeth Salander. She stopped by to warn me that danger was around us."

Tinkie made a sour face and gave me a look. "You're always talking to someone and when I ask, you blow me off with crazy things like you're talking to characters out of a book. One day I'm going to find out who it is you chitchat with when you're alone."

"I hope you do." I meant it, too. I would give a lot to share Jitty with Tinkie. They would hit it off and probably gang up on me, but it would be so worth it. The fly in this particular ointment was the possibility that if I told anyone about Jitty, she would be recalled by those who ran the Great Beyond. I might never see her again. That I couldn't risk.

"You look kind of sad, Sarah Booth. What's wrong?" Tinkie put her hand on my arm. "I worry about you sometimes. You take on a lot of burdens for your friends."

"I'm fine. I was just thinking of that famous Faulkner quote about the past not being dead."

Her hand slipped up my arm and over my shoulders as she pulled me into a hug. "I do believe you'll see all your family members again. Since I found out I was pregnant, I've really been thinking about what I believe and don't believe. Humans need something to believe in, Sarah Booth. Which is why we're here at the miniature Holy Land. I love the stories and parables about Jesus. There are so many wonderful belief systems. I want my child to have a connection to something bigger than herself. Or himself." She grinned because she knew I was dying to figure out the gender of her baby.

"If you teach her—or him—to be curious, the child will find his own path."

She kissed my cheek. "You're smarter than you give yourself credit for." She yawned and stretched. "I'm hungry."

"That's just not possible." At lunch she'd eaten the amount of food she generally consumed in three days.

"It is possible. Let's see if Donna has any coffee and something sweet. Maybe she'll have some of those egg custard mini-pies. They are so good."

"Oscar is going to have to put a lock on the refrigerator, Tink. You seem to have lost your willpower."

"I've got cells multiplying at a rate of speed that would

make your head spin. You realize that in months, I'll give birth to a unique human being. I think about that and I am gobsmacked. This baby, I can feel it growing. I imagine how it's developing, cell by cell, and I want it to have plenty of fuel so that he or she comes out big and fine and healthy."

"You never do anything by half measures, Tinkie. Let's see what Donna has to snack on." Arm in arm we walked down to the dining area where Donna already had a pot of coffee on. Donna Dickerson was just the person to ask about Erik's tangled romantic past.

She brought us steaming cups of java and ramekins of apricot custard. Tinkie was growing a child, but I was merely growing a spare tire. If I didn't get her home to Oscar, I was not going to fit behind the wheel of the Roadster. Still, the custard was so delicious, I couldn't pass it up.

"Sit with us," I invited Donna. "I have a few questions."

She took a seat. She pushed a second ramekin toward Tinkie, but didn't offer a comment.

"Was Erik ever engaged to Patrice Pepperdine?" I asked.

Donna tilted back in her chair. "Now that's a question I don't know the answer to. There were some rumors that Patrice was up at the drugstore a lot, taking Erik special dishes she cooked. She was . . . hovering. I only know this because a few of my friends commented. Erik is quite a catch, and folks could see that Patrice was spreading her net for him. How far it got, I don't know."

"What's the gossip?" Tinkie asked. She sipped her coffee.

"Gossip is that he dumped her. But I'm not sure I believe that."

"Why not?" I ate another mouthful of the custard and let it melt in my mouth. Delicious.

"I don't see Patrice as someone Erik would be interested in. She was after him, but that doesn't mean it was reciprocated."

"They were dance partners, but it could have been more. It's possible he led her to think he would marry her."

Donna shook her head. "Engagements are broken all the time. That's life. Would she have been vindictive enough to try to ruin his reputation?"

"Patrice was not a nice person. You would think someone who was as physically beautiful as she was would have been happier." She frowned. "I can't remember a time when she seemed to take pleasure in the day. She was always a sour person. Remember, though, I wasn't around her a lot. Maybe she had reason to be sour. There's something else you should know. Maybe twenty years ago, a man set up a dance studio in town. You know, lessons with his skilled employees. Some of the churches opposed it, but the studio opened. Except the whole setup was a con, and several people were played for a lot of money. Several people were humiliated by being duped by the dance master. People have long memories, and I can see why Erik would simply prefer to keep his private life private." Donna shook her head. "I don't know if any of that applies to what's going on with Erik. I stay out here at the inn and mind my own business. I've got plenty to do here with the cooking and gardening. And this makes me happy."

"Donna, what do you know about Snaith?" Tinkie asked.

"I know enough to steer clear of him. Those remedies he concocts and sells—I wouldn't touch them with a ten-foot pole. The shame of it was that I heard he was a good doctor, but Slay ruined him financially and he lost his license. Snaith, like any doctor in a small community, was looked up to, so this has been a hard fall for him. He had cause to kill Slay but that doesn't mean he did it."

My only other suspect, so far, was Cosmo, but mainly because he was so close to the site where the bodies had been dumped and he had expertise in poisons and herbicides. "Do you think Cosmo Constantine is capable of murder?"

"I don't know anything for a fact, but I will tell you that I saw Cosmo and Patrice get into an argument in the local grocery store. I mentioned it to Glory when she was here. The incident occurred right after Erik's camellia bush was poisoned. Cosmo is weird, especially about plants, and I heard him threaten Patrice. He said she was a murderer and that she deserved to die just like that bush."

Tinkie and I exchanged looks. Patrice had died of the same herbicide. And Cosmo did have a beef with Daniel Reynolds.

"Thanks, Donna. For the wonderful stay and your help."

"I'm just an innkeeper," Donna said.

"You're a smart lady," Tinkie said. "And a dynamite cook." She pushed back from the table. "Let's get to work, Sarah Booth, before I need another nap. Where are we headed?"

"I think our client owes us an explanation."

17

Erik's pharmacy was located in the middle of Main Street and was a step back in time—even further back in time than when I was a kid. We pushed through the plate-glass door that had a sticker of a penguin with a KOOL INSIDE notice of air-conditioning. We stepped from current times back to the 1960s and into a pharmacy that was part gift shop, part café, part soda fountain, and part drugstore. The hottest hits of the '50s and '60s were piped in.

"I love this place," Tinkie said. "A soda fountain. Man, I haven't had a Coke float in years. When we're finished talking to Erik we can have one." She pointed to the back of the spacious store where Erik stood on a small platform so he could see throughout the area.

Behind him were shelves of pills. I was a little surprised to see him there since I figured the sheriff would still be looking for him.

He waved us back to join him and a cluster of pretty women. They obviously didn't think he was a killer because they were flirting to beat the band. They all giggled on cue at something he said.

"Erik, the Joe Jefferson Players in Mobile are staging *Cabaret*. Would you like to go with me? I've read the reviews and it's a fine staging of the show," a pretty brunette asked.

"No, he can't do that. He's going with me to the picnic over in Fairhope," a honey-blonde said. "I'm making my famous chicken salad. Erik loves it. And some walnut brownies to die for."

"I'll check my calendar for both events," Erik said. "Now, if you ladies will excuse me, I need to speak with Sarah Booth and Tinkie."

The young women turned to face us. "You must be the private investigators," one said. "That's a cool job. If you need help, I'm available. I'm very good at prying into other people's business. Some say it's a real talent."

"Jessica, let it go." Erik came around the counter and shook his head at her. "Go tell Adam to make you a banana split or whatever you want." He shooed them all away. "All of you. The treats are on me."

Laughing and teasing each other, the young women went over to the soda fountain and perched on stools as they gave the soda jerk their orders. Were it not for their modern attire—shorts, jeans, and leggings—it could have been a scene out of the 1950s.

When we finally had Erik to ourselves, I asked, "Why aren't you in jail?"

"I went by and talked to Glory. She gave me a pass, just this once."

"Did you tell her where you were?" I was curious.

"I answered all of her questions until she was satisfied. She understood."

It would seem that Erik could talk his way out of a lot of serious trouble. Well, he wasn't going to bamboozle me. Not this time. "Does the name Ana Arguello mean anything to you?" I asked.

Erik went pale. He swallowed hard and motioned for Tinkie and me to follow him through the door that separated the pharmacy area from the rest of the store. Behind that was a storeroom. When we were inside, he closed the door. "Where did you hear about Ana?"

"Oh, we got an earful from Betsy Dell. Remember her? She's saying you threw Patrice Pepperdine over for a hot Latin dancer and also that you killed a dancer named Johnny Braun." I was a little hot under the collar about his failure to tell us the truth. It made me wonder what else he might be lying about.

Erik had the decency to look stricken. "I didn't kill Johnny. Why does she think I killed him?"

"To win the dance title and fifty thousand dollars."

"That's a nice motive," Tinkie threw in.

"That's ridiculous. I could beat him dancing with one foot in a cast. And Betsy always thought she was far better than she was."

"How about Patrice? How good was she?"

He looked down at the floor. "She was an excellent dancer. For a woman who never cracked a smile, she could turn it on for a dance competition. Those minutes she was on the dance floor she was fully alive."

"But this Ana was better?"

"Patrice was skilled at the dances I also excel at. Ana," he drew in a breath, "she was like dancing with fire. She sizzled, and sometimes she burned. I love dancing with Ana. I love being with her."

I had a very clear picture why Patrice hated Erik. I didn't believe he was cruel, but in some ways he'd treated Patrice like an old shoe.

"Did you ask Patrice to marry you?" Tinkie asked.

He shook his head. "Never. But I probably didn't discourage her thoughts from going in that direction. Until it was too late."

A sin of omission. "Why didn't you tell us this before?" Tinkie asked.

Erik finally met her gaze. "I was ashamed. Because I knew I should have been firm when she kept talking about getting married. I never asked and never promised, but I also didn't state firmly that it wasn't going to happen. She was my dance partner, and it made us shine that she was a little bit in love with me."

"A little bit?"

He had the decency to look remorseful. "A lot more than I knew. I thought it was a crush. You know dancers get crushes on each other all the time. It's part of the competitions. When you're on the dance floor you become part of the story that the music tells and you share that with your partner. It's magic for those three or four minutes. Then the music stops, folks go home, and the crush fades."

"It obviously didn't fade for Patrice. I heard she was suing you for breach of promise."

"She said she was. She threatened it, but I never knew for certain if she really talked to Slay. I never got legal notification. I hoped if I ignored it, she'd let it slide, too. Surely she had to see that a court battle would only bring more humiliation on her. I didn't want that for Patrice. I really didn't."

"So this is why she killed your shrubs?"

"The bad thing was that Patrice lived right next door to me. I caught her more than once watching me from the windows. If I had a woman over, or did anything in my yard, she was right there. Like a stalker. I think she killed my bushes so she could spy on me more easily."

"You should have told us," I said. "And you have to tell Glory. If she doesn't already know." I told him about Betsy's ad that was waiting to be published at the local paper. "Betsy means business. She wants you to pay for killing Johnny."

"Betsy is a crackpot, and I didn't kill anybody. You have to believe me. Not Johnny and certainly not Slay or Patrice."

"There's a wake of misunderstanding behind you, Erik. Especially with women—Betsy, Patrice. And a lot of dead bodies. This doesn't look good, and I'm not certain I trust you anymore."

He looked down. "I deserve that."

"Who else do we need to talk to? We need to have all the facts before Sheriff Glory gathers them. And then we need to go to her and put it all on the table."

"Ana Arguello. You might want to speak to her."

"What about those young ladies who were all over you? Are you involved with any of them?"

"I like them, too. Look, I love having fun. There's no crime in that, and that's why I keep my business to myself. Some people hate it when anyone else has a good time. They resent a person having joy in his life. When Patrice and I first started dancing, I didn't realize she was like that. Then the more I got to know her, the less I liked her. To give the devil his due, she was a remarkable dancer. When the music began, her entire personality changed. We had that Ginger-Fred timing, which is hard to find."

"So how'd it all go sour?" I asked.

"Last fall, she went off the deep end. She proposed to me and I told her I wasn't going to marry anyone. After that, she was horrible. Spiteful and vindictive. We'd signed up for the dance championship competition on the Gulf Voyager, and neither of us wanted to back out. I thought I could get through it, maybe remain friends with Patrice. She did a lot of crazy things that I never told anyone, because I didn't want her to get in trouble. Maybe I should have. If she'd gotten help for her mental problems, she might be alive today."

I didn't doubt a word Erik was saying, and Tinkie seemed to believe him, too.

"Why didn't you just tell us the truth?" I asked.

"This is a small town. It's best to keep private business private, and it had nothing to do with Slay or really with Patrice. Look, I didn't kill her. I wouldn't. No matter how crazy she became. Once you've danced the tango with someone, there's a bond."

"Is there anything else you're not telling us?" Tinkie asked.

He sighed. "No. There isn't. And please, just keep my dancing life on the QT if you can."

"Sure," we said in chorus. We had no reason to discuss Erik's hobbies with anyone—except the sheriff.

"How can we get in touch with Ana?"

He led us back to the pharmacy area and got a business card. He wrote a number on the back. The area code was Alabama. "Call her. She'll tell you about Johnny."

"Okay."

I was about to leave when Sheriff Glory came into the business. The women at the soda fountain completely ignored her, but Erik nodded a greeting. "Can I help you, Sheriff?"

"Have you heard from Cosmo Constantine?"

Erik glanced at me, which made me realize he was about to lie. "I haven't. Cosmo doesn't come into town but about once a month, to get his prescriptions filled. He was in here before Easter, so I won't see him again for several weeks."

"Really?" Glory held her ground. She was nobody's fool.

Erik seemed protective of Cosmo. Even when maybe he shouldn't be. Even when Cosmo had threatened Patrice.

"Why are you looking for Cosmo?" Erik asked.

"One of Rory Palente's yard crews pulled into the Chicken Shack last week. The crew went inside to eat, and while they were inside, Cosmo stole some chemicals off their truck."

"Are you sure?" Erik was surprised. "Cosmo is opposed to chemicals."

"I'm very sure. The Chicken Shack has surveillance cameras. We have him in black and white stealing herbicide. He wasn't parked in the lot, but he comes out of the back of the business, heads straight to the parked lawn service truck, and he lifts the pesticide right off the trailer and leaves with it."

"The herbicide that killed Patrice?" Erik asked.

"That's the one." Glory waited.

"Cosmo wouldn't kill her," Erik insisted. "He had no reason to kill her. Or Perry Slay. He may have stolen herbicide, but he isn't a killer."

I couldn't help but wonder why Erik was sticking up for Cosmo. The man had means and opportunity, and possibly motive, based on Donna's information. More importantly, he was the person who could take some of the heat of suspicion off Erik. Certainly Erik shouldn't throw him under the bus, but he didn't have to be so vocal in declaring his innocence. At least not right now. Unless there was more to Cosmo's actions and they involved Erik.

"Why don't you leave it up to me to decide who's a killer and who isn't?" Glory asked with a broad hint of sarcasm in her tone. "If you see him, call me. Tell him to turn himself in. If he's got a logical explanation for stealing that herbicide, I need to hear it."

Glory sauntered out of the drugstore in the same low-key way she'd arrived. I faced Erik. "What is he doing with herbicide?"

"I hope my suspicions aren't real, but I'm afraid he may be trying to damage the gardens at the miniature Holy Land. He hates what Dr. Reynolds is doing out there. Everything Reynolds adds is another inducement for a boatload of tourists to stomp through the area. Cosmo really believes the flood of tourists is destroying the delicate ecosystem and that a lot of vulnerable insects and plants will suffer."

"He would poison the gardens? That seems . . . counterproductive." I remembered the beautiful plants and the exquisite landscaping that Daniel Reynolds had worked so hard to build.

"He might. I can't think of any other reason he'd steal

that kind of potent herbicide. He knows it killed my prize camellias." He sighed. "Look, Cosmo hasn't been himself lately. It all came to a head this past weekend with the sunrise service and the Easter egg hunt. He kind of flipped his wig. I need to go out there and see if I can find him and talk him into coming back to town with me."

"Why do you care so much?"

Erik thought about it. "Cosmo is a loner. Afghanistan veteran. He wasn't always so antisocial. I remember him when he was young and fun. He doesn't have anyone else to care what happens to him."

"PTSD?"

"I don't know. Cosmo never talked about what happened over there. Ever."

"He never got help?"

Erik snorted. "Right. Because there's so much help available for our veterans."

He was right about that. Help was in short supply for the troops that fought to protect us. "Do you think you can bring him back to town?"

"Maybe. I have to try. I'll go when I close the store."

"Tinkie and I are going to get in touch with Ana Arguello."

"Knock yourself out," Erik said, but with a hint of good humor. "She's a little firecracker. Don't let her take you out drinking. She can put you under the table and still dance a rumba like you've never seen. Tell her I'll be in touch about our next practice session. By the way, I was with Ana the Saturday night before Easter Sunday."

"When Slay was killed."

"Yes. I just didn't want to drag Ana into it. She's got a crazy ex. She doesn't need to be pulled into a murder investigation."

"Gallant but stupid," Tinkie said. "We'll talk to her about alibiing you for the time Slay was murdered. Then you'll be off the suspect list, Erik. Tinkie and I can go home."

"But not before you see me dance." He did a fancy cha-cha step.

I suddenly wanted to see Erik dance. "When is your next performance?"

"Ana and I have a competition in New Orleans soon. I'll get tickets for you and your fellows. I know I should have been more forthcoming with you and Tinkie, too. I'll do better."

"I'm going to hold you to that."

18

As soon as I walked to the soda fountain, Erik got on the phone and I presumed he was calling the stand-in pharmacist. I took a stool beside Tinkie. The young women had already left and the only person near us was Adam, the soda jerk, a young man with an easy smile who went out of his way to give us some privacy.

Tinkie had ordered some Coke floats. I dug into mine with a long spoon. It had been many years since I'd had the fizzy ice-cream concoction and it was even better than I remembered. The carbonated soda did something magical to the ice cream. I wasn't even hungry but I couldn't stop eating it.

My cell phone rang, and I anticipated seeing Coleman's name on the caller ID, but it was Ed Oakes instead.

Cece's boss. He was likely looking for his wayward reporter, and to be honest, I needed to track her down myself. Whatever she was up to with Hans O'Shea, she needed to get her focus back on her work at the *Zinnia Dispatch*. And on her friends. I was all about career advancement, but she needed some balance.

"Hello, Ed." I glanced at Tinkie, who stopped eating to listen in. I put the phone on speaker. There was no one else around us that we would disturb.

"Where's Cece?" Ed was always no nonsense and today he was irritated.

Technically, I didn't know. She'd been gone all day with Hans, presumably doing interviews and scouting locations and videoing for his show. That was information I wasn't willing to divulge. Not my business. "Have you called her?"

"No, Sarah Booth. I thought I'd call every one of her friends first, just to see if they were up to speed on her whereabouts."

Ed was a master of sarcasm, and he made me smile. "She's here in Lucedale. Maybe she's working on a story for the paper. Seems like there may be a serial killer on the loose here."

"We don't have a lot of readership in Lucedale."

Again, the sarcasm. "I'll track her down and tell her to give you a call, but I have to warn you, the sheriff has asked all three of us to stay in town. We've been finding bodies like Easter eggs."

"She might have called to tell me that."

"I'm hoping we're cleared to leave by tomorrow." If Ana alibied Erik for the first murder, I believed he might be off the hook for Patrice's death, too. Especially since

Cosmo had moved up to first suspect on the list, and Snaith was also a viable suspect.

"Tell her to call me, pronto. Better yet, tell her to get her butt back up here. We're getting ready to launch that column she and Millie Roberts cooked up. I'm a newsman, not an expert on celebrity frivolity. This thing could go off the rails if she isn't here to shepherd it along."

He was right about that. Cece and Millie were the perfect blend of straight news and what had once been the fun elements of grocery-store tabloids. Cece brought the weight of a serious journalist to the column. Millie had the dead Elvis sightings and the alien-baby births or abductions down pat. Point and counterpoint, all done with good humor and a saucy writing style. It was a brilliant plan to showcase fun stories and also professional questioning of those stories by a top-drawer journalist.

"First I have to find her, then I'll have her call."

"Thanks," Ed said.

I hung up and looked at my partner.

"Call Millie," Tinkie said.

It was an excellent suggestion. In a matter of minutes I had Millie on the phone. Afternoon was a slow time for her in Millie's Café, so she was able to talk freely. "Have you heard from Cece? Ed is looking for her and he's not a happy man."

"I spoke with Cece this morning," she said. "She promised to be home tomorrow."

That was good to know. It would have to do for Ed Oakes. The day was concluding here, and it was a long drive home. Cece could get up early and be in Zinnia by eleven o'clock. That was better than driving at night and having an accident. There were a lot of deer crossing the road between here and there.

"Did she mention what she was working on with Hans?" I was curious, I had to admit.

"She didn't, but I've made my own deductions."

"And they are?" Millie probably knew me, Tinkie, and Cece better than we knew ourselves. She wasn't that much older, but she mother-henned us, which we all loved.

"Hans has all but offered her a job, but she won't leave Zinnia. She'll take special assignments and work it out with Ed. She's proving herself on camera to Hans, and she deserves this chance, ladies. So don't give her any grief."

That was a big relief. I wanted my friend to do well in her career and to fulfill all her dreams—but I wanted her to stay in Zinnia to do it. "We're excited about the big launch of your column," Tinkie threw in. "Tell me the name again?"

"The Truth Is Out There."

Tinkie and I both laughed. The reference to *The X-Files* was truly delicious.

Millie's voice danced with excitement. "Harold is hosting a big launch party on Sunday for the column. He's invited hundreds of people. You have to promise to be back for that, both of you."

Harold Erkwell worked at the bank that Tinkie's husband ran. He was one of our running buddies. "I can't wait," Tinkie and I said in unison. Sometimes we did have a twin moment.

"Neither can I," Millie said. "He and Roscoe have been very, very busy."

"Roscoe?" That was Harold's evil little dog. I'd got-

ten him during a case in Natchez, Mississippi, before
he was put down, shot, or thrown in the river because he
was truly, truly incorrigible. Harold had taken him in,
and they were the perfect team. "What's Roscoe been
doing?"

"He's back to his old ways. He's been running around
town tearing into people's garbage and dragging it back
to Harold to give to me for a little local focus on the
gossip angle. I tell you, Sarah Booth, I can't reveal any
names, but did you know there was such a thing as devil
head condoms?"

"What?" Tinkie and I were in sync. "Holy crap," I
said, and Tinkie said something a little more profane.

"It's true, and I know who they belong to and it isn't
some cult person. You would laugh and laugh."

"You aren't going to use that in your column, are
you?" I could see why Ed Oakes was going nuts.

"Of course not, at least not with the person's name."

"Someone is going to shoot that dog and then Harold and then you, Millie." Tinkie was concerned.

"Roscoe is smarter than you think. He only hits
places when the people are gone to work or out of town.
It's amazing the things you can learn about a person by
going through their garbage."

"Does Coleman know about this?" I had a sudden
suspicion.

"Maybe," Millie said.

I couldn't hold back the laughter. "If the voters get
wind that he knows what Roscoe is up to and did nothing, he won't get reelected."

"Maybe," Millie said, and then she laughed. "Hurry
home. We have plans to make."

"Sure thing."

"Home soon," Tinkie said before I hung up.

I returned to my float, but I couldn't force down another bite. When Tinkie's glass was empty, I stood up. "Let's get busy."

"I don't know if I can walk," Tinkie said, putting a hand on my arm. She actually looked distressed.

"What do you mean you can't walk?"

"The waistband of my pants is so tight I think it shut off the flow of blood to my legs. I can't feel them."

"Are you messing with me?"

Tinkie pushed her empty glass away. She was serious. "I am not kidding. I've gained about ten pounds and I just can't bring myself to buy a larger size."

"You're having a baby, Tinkie. You're going to gain weight."

"Some people don't."

"Some people don't eat two slices of lemon pie, ramekins of custard, Coke floats, and all kinds of food."

She bit her bottom lip in an old gesture that made me smile. "I have gone hog wild, haven't I?"

She sounded so sad and remorseful that I couldn't be stern. "Your body is doing a lot of crazy things. Cut yourself some slack."

"It's not my body I'm concerned about, it's my mouth. It's working overtime. This is it. I'm going to find my willpower and zip my lips."

"Uh-huh." I didn't believe it for a minute, but I loved Tinkie too much to devil her about her sugar addiction—at least not any more than I already had. "Let's call Ana." I punched in the number Erik had given me and helped Tinkie out to the car. We'd parked on Main Street and I couldn't help but admire the Chinese red of the old Roadster with the dove-gray interior against the backdrop of a small-town street. It make me think that I'd stepped back into the 1970s.

The phone rang and rang, but no one answered, so I hung up and refocused on my partner. "Can you feel your feet yet?"

"Yes, but I wish I couldn't. Even my shoes are getting too tight."

I managed not to chuckle as she abandoned my arm and slipped into the passenger side. I stepped behind the car, waiting for a truck to pass, when I noticed a dark car speeding toward us. Lucedale was a sleepy little town with a twenty-five-mile-per-hour speed limit. This car was going at least sixty, coming from the west. This driver was cruising for a six-hundred-dollar ticket and loss of insurance. I had plenty of room to get into the Roadster, and I stepped into the street and opened the door.

Because I was watching the fast-approaching car and not what I was doing, I snagged the toe of my shoe on the doorframe. With the forward momentum of my body, I pitched headfirst into the front seat, knocking Tinkie into the passenger door and out onto the sidewalk just as a gunshot blasted. The drugstore's plate-glass window on the other side of the Roadster splintered and glass rained down.

The black car tore down Main Street, traveling now at a very high speed. Merchants and customers poured out of the stores nearby, and the soda jerk came out of the pharmacy, looking at the broken window with awe and fear.

"Tinkie! Tinkie!" I climbed over the console and out the passenger door to where my partner lay in the gutter. "Call an ambulance!" I yelled at the soda jerk. "Hurry."

There was a spatter of blood on Tinkie's face and she was pale, too pale. "Tinkie." I almost couldn't speak. "Where are you hit?"

She didn't respond. I looked up and down the street, hoping by some miracle a doctor would arrive. Or someone who could help my partner. I brushed the blood from her face and realized it came from a tiny cut made when the glass shattered and fell on her. I looked her over and didn't see any serious bleeding.

"Tinkie?"

"Get off me," she said. "I can't breathe."

I rolled off her and got to my feet. Her eyes were open and I offered her my hand. With a groan she got to her feet, shedding shards of glass everywhere. "Who was that trying to kill us?"

I shook my head. I was so relieved she was okay that I honestly couldn't frame a sentence.

"When I catch whoever it was, I'm going to hurt them bad." She shook her clothes and turned to the pharmacy where Adam stood with an open mouth. The plate-glass window was completely destroyed.

"Why was someone trying to kill you?" Adam asked.

"I don't know." I hadn't gotten a look at the driver or the license plate. All I'd seen was a black, sleek car. "Tinkie, did you see the make and model?"

"Trans Am, newer year. That's all I got. I wasn't paying attention either."

"You both could have been killed," Adam said.

"Had my partner not knocked me out of the car, I really might be dead." Tinkie looked at me. "Thank you."

"Are you sure you're both okay?" he asked as he pulled out a cell phone and called the authorities. "Sheriff Glory isn't going to like this. She takes it kind of personal when people shoot up her streets."

"Shall we try to go over to Mobile and interview Ana Arguello?" I asked Tinkie. We'd finished at the sheriff's office and stepped outside to stand in the sunshine on the courthouse steps. Neither of us were hurt, and if we could solidify Erik's alibi, we might be able to get out of town and get home. Glory had taken down the very sparse information we could give her on the Trans Am. She'd engaged the authorities in Alabama, which was only sixteen miles away, to be on the lookout for a car of that description. The bullet lodged in the drugstore wall had been collected, and she'd helped the store employees call a glass service since Erik wasn't around or answering his phone. She'd done what she could.

She'd questioned us as witnesses, prying a little too hard to see if we'd made anyone in town mad enough to kill us. Then she'd cut us loose to walk back to the Roadster, which was remarkably unscathed. I needed some physical exercise; it would allow me to clear my mind. I was still a bit shocked that someone had tried to kill us. It didn't make a lot of sense. At the back of my mind was the real concern about telling Coleman and Oscar about this latest event. Both men would press us to come home—and they had every right to. But something was going on in Lucedale that I didn't understand, and I wasn't ready to walk away. Now that someone had tried to murder me and my partner, I had a dog in this fight. I had a real burn on to find the driver of that black Trans Am.

"There's a lot of violence here for such a pretty little town," Tinkie commented.

"Yeah, you're right about that." She still hadn't answered my question about tracking down Ana Arguello and I sensed that Tinkie was exhausted. It had been a helluva day. "Maybe we should call it quits and head back to the inn."

It was a little surreal to stand in the silence and sunshine after such a violent event. Down the street I could hear children playing. School was out and the afternoon light was slanted, casting long shadows. Tinkie hadn't been hurt, but she didn't look 100 percent.

"We really should talk to this Ana. We need to conclude this case. I'm ready to get back to Zinnia. I wanted this baby more than anything, and I'm not complaining, Sarah Booth, but I never expected to be tired and hungry all the time. I feel like I don't own my body anymore."

I put an arm around her and gave her a hug. "You don't. But it will be worth all of this when you hold that baby in your arms."

That pleased her and she nodded. "You're right. Thanks for knocking me out of the car." She kicked some glass off the sidewalk. "Do you think someone local really tried to kill us?"

The attack had come from out of the blue. "Why? Because we're working for Erik?"

She shrugged. "Why else?"

"I have no idea."

"It was the killer, wasn't it?" Tinkie looked more tired than upset. "He must think we're getting closer and closer to the truth. But what truth?"

"I don't know. It could have been the killer, you're

right, but why shoot at us? Why not shoot Erik?" I didn't say it, but Erik had, once again, been absent. I didn't like the direction my thoughts were taking. Every time anything untoward happened in this town, Erik was nowhere to be found. He might, of course, be bringing Cosmo Constantine in to talk to the sheriff, but in my heart of hearts, I didn't believe that. And as evidence against Cosmo stacked higher and higher, I had to question Erik's continued attempts to protect him from the consequences of his actions.

"You're looking pensive. What are you thinking?"

I didn't want to further upset Tinkie with my suspicions about our client. Not yet. "Shall we head to Mobile?" That was where Ana lived. It was also where Betsy Dell lived, and I wondered if it might be beneficial to drop in on Betsy unannounced. Glory had been so busy getting APBs and volunteers to look for the car with the person who'd shot at us that I hadn't bothered her with the details of Erik's dance history. I really wanted him to tell her. It would look better coming from him, especially if what Betsy had said about Johnny Braun being murdered proved to be true.

"We need to go to Mobile, but I'd rather go back to the B and B and have a nice foot massage. My feet are swelling. I've heard some pregnant women go up a shoe size or two."

I'd heard that, too, but I wasn't going to say it. Tinkie had a small fortune invested in shoes. Especially stilettos. She loved a sexy high heel and she could run as fast in five-inch heels as I could in sneakers. If her feet grew, she'd be inconsolable—until the baby arrived. "It's probably just that you've been standing on them too much."

"You're probably right. Let's find Ana and get this behind us."

We were about to leave when the soda jerk hurried out to us. "There was a call for you."

"In the drugstore?"

He nodded. "On the business phone. It was a woman. She asked me to tell you, 'I have information that can ex . . . exon . . . exonerate your client.' Those were the exact words. She made me repeat them."

"Did she leave a number or a way to get in touch?"

"She said she'd meet you in forty minutes on the Escatawpa River."

"You have got to be kidding me," Tinkie said. "Where is that?"

"No, ma'am, I'm not kidding. That's what she said. There's a swimming hole on the east side, the Alabama side of the river. She said to take that little dirt road and go down to the water. It's about a mile off Highway 98. She'll be there waiting for you."

"You're certain it was a woman?" I asked.

"Yes, ma'am, it was a lady. An older lady, I think." He shrugged. "Maybe not."

"Thank you." I offered him a tip but he refused. "Mr. Erik pays me real good." He went back into the drugstore and got a broom and dustpan and began sweeping up the broken glass on the sidewalk.

19

"We shouldn't go running off into the woods," Tinkie said. "We were almost killed, Sarah Booth. This could be an ambush."

She was right about that. More than anything I wished Coleman was around. I'd feel a lot safer. Not that Glory wasn't an exceptional lawman; she was. I just knew Coleman inside out. The wise decision would be to ignore this anonymous tipster, but that was hard to do. "What if the caller really has proof that Erik is innocent?"

"Erik hasn't been one hundred percent honest with us the whole time," Tinkie said, a little more hotly than I expected. "Let *him* go off in the woods and get the proof that he's innocent."

She might be angry, but she was also thinking clearly. "You're right. He should be the one, but he isn't here." My intuition gave a nasty little pulse. As we'd begun probing into Erik's background, maybe there was something there to hide. Something worth hurting us for— or at least making us believe we would be hurt. And yet again, Erik was off on his own when tragedy struck. "This might be a good lead, but someone wants to meet us in the woods an hour after a shooter tries to blow our heads off. I don't think so."

She pulled out her cell phone and dialed. "Erik, when you get this message, call me right away. Someone says they can prove your innocence. If you want the evidence, you'll need to go over to the Alabama side of the Escatawpa River. There's a woman there waiting to meet us at . . ." She looked at her watch. "Five thirty. You'd better hurry."

She hung up and looked at me as I backed up to avoid any scattered glass in preparation to ease out into the street. "Where are we going?" she asked.

"To the B and B. The streets are going to roll up in this town any minute. Call Ana again."

She did and held out the ringing telephone so I could hear. No answer. "Damn. We're blocked at every turn." Tinkie turned in the seat and looked east, toward Alabama. The road was empty. The few cars that had been parked on Main Street were long gone. "Dammit, let's go to the river."

I looked at her. "I don't think that's smart, Tinkie."

"I know it isn't smart, but whoever made that call lives here in town. Let's take the meeting and get it over with."

"How do you know the caller lives in town?" I asked.

"That older woman could be someone Erik put up to

calling us. Or Snaith." Cosmo was still a prime suspect, but somehow I didn't see him having the charm to con an older lady into making calls for him. "Maybe they're just trying to divert our focus, or maybe it's a setup where we get hurt."

Tinkie's brow furrowed and her lips drew down. "I don't like thinking our client may be trying to kill us."

"Neither do I. But Erik is a chronic liar. He's loaded with charm. He's able to talk his way out of trouble easily enough."

"And he has means, motive, and opportunity. Unless we find Ana Arguello and prove that he was indeed with her in a public place the night Slay was killed. And where the heck was he when Patrice was poisoned?"

"Missing in action."

"But why dump the bodies at the Garden of Bones?" Tinkie seemed as perplexed as I was.

"That's one thing we need to investigate. I don't want to believe it's Erik, but things just keep happening that point the finger of guilt directly at him. Think about it. This strange woman, offering an alibi for Erik, who isn't around to get the collaborating evidence himself, calls just when we arrived back at the drugstore. That's a little more than a tad convenient unless she was watching us arrive here."

"The caller couldn't be the person who tried to kill us," Tinkie continued. "But it could be a confederate, if you believe there's a ring of assassins after us." She gave me a wry look.

I didn't believe a gaggle of assassins was after us, but the shooting didn't feel like a warning. Someone meant to hurt one or both of us. Tinkie had good instincts and she'd made a good point. "You believe the shooter and the caller who has information for us are two separate people?"

"I do. If the caller meant to kill us earlier today, wouldn't she have first tried to lure us into the woods so we were easy and convenient targets without a townful of potential witnesses? I mean, taking someone out on Main Street is pretty . . . hard-core criminal. It's two separate people. I hate to say it, but that's why we need to go to the river and meet with this informant. I want to go home. I miss Oscar. I miss Chablis. I know my emotions are all over the place."

I gave her a one-armed hug, which was the best I could do in the car. "You have a right to be emotional." I waited until she was looking into my eyes. "Cece is going back to Zinnia tomorrow or Ed's going to scalp her. You can ride back with her. I'll finish here."

"No." She had her jaw set and her lips in a pout.

"I can finish up this case. The most important thing you can do is take care of that baby."

"And that is exactly why I'm not leaving. If I can't pull my share of the duties, I'll quit the agency."

"Oh, no you won't." The very idea that she might quit upset me. There wouldn't be a PI agency without Tinkie. If she quit, I wouldn't be able to carry on alone, not even with all the help from Coleman and the deputies. Tinkie and I were a team.

"I don't want to be deadweight on you." Tinkie was about to cry.

"Yes. Especially not now that you're soon going to weigh as much as a whale." I said it very seriously. It took her a moment before she burst into laughter.

"You are awful."

"Of course I am. That's why you love me."

"Let's go to the river. If there's evidence to exonerate Erik, let's get it and then we can both go home. Or there is another possibility. Maybe someone is going to meet us to give us evidence *against* Erik. We just have to be prepared for anything."

I eased the car into the sparse traffic. I had one more thing on my mind. "Listen, Tinkie, before you talk to Oscar, think about this. Oscar and Coleman are going to have a lot of questions for us when we get home. If they find out we were almost shot on the street, they'll be determined to keep us safe."

"Right. Coleman may need his handcuffs."

I laughed, too, and we were off. We'd just make the deadline if I put the pedal to the metal.

The dirt road that led down the east side of the Escatawpa River was easy to spot and looked well traveled. I'd grown up swimming in creeks with my friends and our mothers. We didn't consider it old-fashioned to take a hand-crank ice cream maker and take turns churning the custard my mother had cooked, or sinking watermelons in the cold creek water so that when it was time to cut them, they were sweet and icy. Those memories flooded back to me as we drove along the side of the amber river that was filled with beautiful white sandbars. The Escatawpa was one of the most beautiful small rivers I'd ever seen.

It was a little early for swimmers—the days were turning warm and sunny, but not enough to make a dip in the river tempting. In another month, the sandbars would be filled with people who'd come to enjoy the water.

The trees along the bank were pine and scrub oak, not the beautiful live oaks that had grown up in some places. Palmettos were scattered about in clumps. We rode with the top down, and the sunlight filtering through the trees was golden. From somewhere nearby the lemony scent of a magnolia in bloom came to me.

Around us was the chatter of small animals and birds. Squirrels darted across the road in front of the car, apparently on a suicide mission. Luckily I was going slow enough to easily dodge them.

"How much farther?" Tinkie asked.

The odometer showed we'd traveled a mile on the dirt road. We were exactly where we'd been told to be. I slowed to a stop. The woods seemed to be empty, except for us.

"I think we've been had," I said. "This was a practical joke."

"Let's give it a minute. Maybe turn around so we're headed out."

I did as Tinkie instructed. When the Roadster was pointed toward the highway, I cut the engine and we settled into the seats to enjoy the serenity of the woods that surrounded us. It was a perfect spring day, too soon for the mosquitos or yellow flies that would hide in the woods during summer.

I turned the radio on and picked up a country station that was playing some oldies, tunes that dated back to my childhood, when I would watch my parents dance. They weren't ballroom dancers, like Erik, but they were perfectly in tune with each other. They'd danced close, seeming to lose themselves in the music and each other.

After three songs, Tinkie had slumped in her seat, the sunshine falling softly across her face. In that instant, she looked so much like a child she almost broke my heart. She was about to give birth to her own child, and in the golden light of a spring day, she looked no older than fourteen.

The crackle of a stick made me turn my attention from Tinkie to the woods. The undergrowth beneath a large oak tree began to move and quiver. Someone was hiding under the tree, and he had a clear line of sight on us.

"Tinkie." I'd slipped my gun under the front seat. I slowly reached down and grabbed it. "Tinkie." She was sound asleep and I hated to disturb her, but I had to. "Tinkie, wake up but don't move too fast."

She slowly came awake and focused on my face. "What's wrong?"

"There's someone under that big oak." As if to emphasize my words, the underbrush began to move again, and there was the crackle of another dead branch. "I can't get a view of whoever it is."

Tinkie played it cool and sat up straighter, using the side mirror to check for the intruder. She saw him. "I see the movement, but I don't see who's making it. They're well hidden and have the advantage. We're sitting ducks."

We were. Yet I was loath to run away if someone was there to deliver evidence of Erik's innocence to us. We'd agreed to the meetup place, but I hadn't anticipated that the person we were to meet would be in hiding, watching us.

"It's like one of those horror movies you watch. *The Hills Have Eyes* or *Texas Chainsaw Massacre*. You know, the deranged backwoods family is hiding in the woods, ready to take us hostage to cut us up with a saw."

I liked horror, but not that kind of mayhem. "Stop

it." She was giving me the willies. Tinkie had thrown me into a movie set where I didn't see a part I wanted to play. "We're waiting another two minutes. If someone has something for us, he can approach so we can watch him. Otherwise, we're leaving."

"Okay."

We were both still staring at the bushes around the big oak when something crashed through the underbrush.

"Holy hell," I said as a giant black boar came rushing out. It stood about four feet tall and had tusks that could gut a man. We were both so shocked that we didn't move, and the hog bolted in the opposite direction.

"Damn," Tinkie said. She hardly ever cursed, but we were both shaken. I was still holding the gun with one hand and my keys in the other when my cell phone rang. It was so loud in the quiet of the woods that I jumped clean out of the car seat, bumped the phone, and sent it flying under the front seat. Tinkie and I leaned down simultaneously, knocking heads with a definite bang.

"Damn," we said in unison as a shot rang out and slammed into a tree on Tinkie's side of the car. Had she been sitting up, her head would have been obliterated.

My reactions were swift and instinctive. I jammed the keys in, turned the car on, and hit the gas pedal. The little Roadster flew down the sandy road. "Where the hell did that shot come from?" Tinkie asked as I put everything I had into driving.

"I think it came from across the river. Someone was on the other side."

"They ambushed us."

"They did," Tinkie said. She put a hand on my arm. "Only a few people knew we were coming here, to the river."

She was right. The caller, whoever that was. Adam in the drugstore, who could have overheard our conversation. And no one else. Adam was a kid, completely clueless. But he worked for Erik and would never think twice about Erik questioning him. "We're going to find Erik, and we're going to get some answers."

"What the hell is going on with this case?"

"I don't know, but we're going to find out." Being shot at twice in one day was way over the top.

20

Tinkie recovered the phone to discover that Cece had finally called us back. She'd saved our lives with her call, but I wasn't about to tell her that. Not until after I'd kicked her butt for disappearing on us.

"Where have you been?" Tinkie made the call and she was as peeved as I was.

"Hans and I have been doing interviews, but I found some time to work on your case for you."

"Really?" I wanted to hear what she had to say more than tell her about nearly getting shot . . . twice. When we made it to the highway, I turned west, toward Lucedale. When I was sure we'd evaded the shooter, I pulled over. "Tell Cece we'll call her back in a minute." I had to report the shooting to Sheriff Glory instantly. When

Tinkie handed me her phone—mine was still under the car seat—I dialed Glory, put the phone on speaker, and filled her in on what had happened.

"You girls have stirred a hornet's nest," she said. "Any idea why?"

"No." That was an honest answer.

"From what you say, the shooter had to be across the river on the Mississippi side, so it's my jurisdiction. I'll call the Mobile County sheriff's department to take a look on the Alabama side to see if they can find any evidence."

"Thanks, but I'm pretty sure there was nothing there but the boar."

"No matter, we'll check it out."

I liked the way Glory thought. She and Coleman were on the same law-enforcement page. "Thanks."

"I'll give you a call if I find anything. Sarah Booth, I like you. I think you're good at your job. But maybe you should consider going home and letting me handle these murders. I'm not out to get Erik. You have to know that, but he is the most viable suspect. The man can't seem to help himself by staying put and having an alibi no matter how many times I warn him."

She was right about that, and I was beginning to have some doubts of my own. Where Erik was concerned, Tinkie and I were no longer positive he was as innocent as we'd once thought. I wasn't yet ready to confess to the sheriff that I thought my partner and I had been played, but it was a consideration I was entertaining. "We'll think about it."

"I'd rather see you home safe instead of bleeding on the side of the road. I get the sense this case has become . . . personal for you. It might also become fatal."

She had a rather graphic way of making me see her point. And she'd hit the nail on the head. Two attempts at gunning me and Tinkie down made it seem mighty personal. But that didn't make a lot of sense since neither one of us had ever met or known anyone from Lucedale until this weekend.

When I didn't say anything, Glory continued. "I don't normally share information with anyone outside my department, but you should know that Snaith came to me with video documentation of Erik prowling around his shop. Snaith said he was afraid for his life. I found Erik's fingerprints on a window that someone tried to jimmy."

Tinkie put a hand on my arm. Her face registered real alarm. "When was this video taken?" Tinkie asked.

"The night Patrice Pepperdine was poisoned." She gave it a beat. "Does Erik have an alibi?"

"Erik hasn't confirmed it, but I believe he was practicing with his dance partner, Ana Arguello, in Mobile."

"Dance partner." She chuckled. "Why didn't he just say so?"

Because maybe it wasn't true. That's what I thought and Tinkie seemed to be on the same page, judging by her expression. "I'll ask him. Maybe you should ask Ana. Tinkie and I plan on tracking her down." I gave her the contact information Erik had given me.

"When I find Erik, he's going to park it in jail."

That might prove to be to Erik's advantage since he couldn't stay out of trouble. "Thanks, Glory. Gotta go," I said. "Call if you need us."

I hung up and glanced at Tinkie before I pulled back onto the four-lane highway. "I think we seriously have to consider our client may be guilty," she said. "We've been looking for proof that he's innocent. Now we just need to look for proof of the person who killed two people."

I nodded. "Call Cece back and find out where she's been."

She got our friend back on the phone and put the question of her whereabouts to her. In a moment she hung up and turned to me. "She's been with Hans. She has something important to tell us. She's waiting at the B and B for us."

"She couldn't spill it over the phone?"

"She wouldn't." Tinkie's frown spoke volumes.

"What's wrong?"

"Cece didn't sound right."

"We're about twenty minutes from the B and B. We'll weasel the information out of her and find out what's wrong." If that Hans had done something to hurt my friend, I'd make him pay.

"Sarah Booth, I have a big favor to ask of you."

Tinkie knew I'd do anything in my power that she asked. "Okay."

"We can't tell Oscar or Coleman that someone has tried to shoot us. Twice. Not until we're safely home."

"I kind of think we have to." I had made a promise to myself that I would not lie, by commission or omission, to Coleman. In the past, I'd skirted the truth about the dangers Tinkie and I faced. The consequences had been grave. He knew my work could be dangerous, as was his. Lying wouldn't change that fact but it would destroy the trust between us.

"No, we don't." Tinkie didn't wait for me to respond. "Oscar is crazy protective since I got pregnant. Honestly, he barely lets me walk to the mailbox without him. If he finds out someone has shot at us twice, he's going to blow a gasket. He'll hire bodyguards and security and he'll never let me leave the house."

She wasn't exaggerating. "Maybe, but at least you would be safe. I'm worried about you, too, Tinkie. In either of these incidents, you could have been killed, or the baby could have been hurt. Maybe it's time for you to be swaddled in protective layers for the remainder of your pregnancy."

"Don't say that. Not even teasing me."

One look at her face and I could tell she wasn't kidding. "What is it?"

"For the last decade or so I've had to live with the knowledge that my body wasn't capable of doing the basic act of reproduction."

"Tinkie, you had a medical issue. You've always had all the right plumbing, but your Fallopian tubes were scarred. It's not—"

"My body was scarred because of a decision I made. Oscar and I together. It almost ended my marriage, because I went along with him when it truly wasn't what I wanted. I wanted that child. More than anything. But because of the way I was raised, I let him make the decision. The man ruled. That's how I was taught."

I knew how she'd been raised and she was right. Patriarchal to the core.

"For a long time I dreamed about my child, the one that I aborted. I would dream she was in the house or the yard. I would hear her singing and playing, always just out of sight. For a long time I stayed home alone each day, just to spend time with her. And I began to hate Oscar. Remember back to the time I hired you to check into Hamilton Garrett?"

I remembered. Her retainer for my services had saved

Dahlia House and set me on the path of becoming a PI. "I do." I'd also been a little shocked that Tinkie had a big enough interest in Hamilton's past to pay me to vet him for her.

"I was going to have an affair with him. I'd given up on Oscar. I almost couldn't stand to be in his presence."

"Why didn't you? Sleep with Hamilton?"

"It was so evident he was smitten by you. And in seeing that, I realized what a dangerous game I was playing. I had to accept what had happened and forgive Oscar. But mostly I had to forgive myself."

Tinkie had told me about the abortion and how hard it was for her not to be able to have children. She had viewed it as God's punishment, which I certainly didn't believe in. But I'd never realized how close to the rocks her marriage to Oscar had come. "The important thing is that you're going to have a baby now. Your very own. And Oscar is more excited than you are, I think."

"He's ready now for a family. When it seemed we couldn't have one, he really began to think about what that meant and what we'd never have. He matured a lot, and so have I."

"Okay, but none of this has anything to do with keeping you safe."

"Of course it does. Oscar has to trust me to keep myself and this baby safe. If he doesn't, we'll end up divorced. I can't be smothered, and I know he's going to try. Once the baby is here, it will ease up a lot. So I'm asking you, if you value my marriage, please don't tell Coleman what happened. Not until we get home and you can make him understand that he can't tell Oscar anything right now."

She had amazing belief in my ability to convince

Coleman to do anything. He was about as hardheaded as a Rocky Mountain boulder. But I had to try. My friend had asked for something that would cost me, but not to give it to her would cost her a whole lot more. "Okay. I won't tell him. Until we get home."

"Great!" Her whole demeanor changed. She pointed down the highway to the garish sign that touted the skills of Perry Slay, Esquire. A man now dead. "They should take that down."

"For a whole lot of reasons," I agreed.

21

Cece was waiting for us in the garden, which had just sprung to life with twinkle lights. She'd ordered a martini for me and a Virgin Mary for Tinkie. I was glad for the drink, and even more glad to see my friend. The glow she wore so well told me things were going great with Hans. Tinkie's worries seemed unfounded.

"Ed wants you back in Zinnia," I told her.

"I'm heading out tomorrow, early."

"Tinkie, you should go with her." I didn't look at my partner. We'd agreed not to tell anyone about the gunshots. I could have asked Cece to simply not tell, but I realized the burden that placed on people. To be loyal to me and Tinkie, she'd have to be disloyal to Jaytee and

Coleman. That was a place that rubbed me raw, and I didn't want to do it to Cece if I could avoid it.

"I'm not going anywhere." Tinkie edged her stiletto closer to my toes with the intention of punishing me for persisting with a topic she'd already given her final word on. I moved my foot. She turned to Cece. "What did you find out? You were excited on the phone."

"It's Snaith," Cece said.

"What's Snaith?" I asked.

"Snaith is the killer." Cece spoke with utter confidence.

"How do you know?" This was an interesting twist, especially since Sheriff Glory believed that Snaith was a potential victim.

"Hans and I have been doing some investigating—"

"What did you find out?" Tinkie interrupted.

"The nights before the bodies were discovered, Cosmo Constantine saw Snaith slipping around the gardens."

"What?" Tinkie and I sat up and paid attention. This was interesting since Snaith was accusing Erik of slipping around his place.

"I know." Cece almost clapped her hands. "Cosmo saw it, and he's willing to go to Glory and tell her what he saw."

"Why hasn't he come forward before now?" Tinkie asked.

"He thought that Glory would close the investigation if she had proof Snaith was the killer. Cosmo didn't want that. He believed that if there was enough stink about the murders at the gardens, Reynolds would have to shut the place down. He'd accomplish his fondest dream—to get rid of Reynolds and his miniature Holy Land."

"Talk about self-interest," Tinkie said, rolling her eyes. "Had he come forward with this information after the first murder, Glory might have put a tail on Snaith and saved Patrice Pepperdine."

"I know," Cece said. "Hans is going to talk to Sheriff Glory, but she wasn't in her office. She was out at the site of a shooting, the dispatcher said."

I held my breath to see what Tinkie would do. It was up to her, and now was the time if she was going to spill the beans to Cece.

"Has Hans offered you a job?" Tinkie turned the conversation to another topic.

"He has, as a correspondent. I'll work on a contract basis for a certain number of stories a year. But first I have to clear this with Ed. You know I wouldn't go behind his back and take another job, not even a part-time one."

I was relieved, but not surprised to hear that. "So this is for the internet?"

"Yes, Hans says there's tremendous opportunity there for this kind of semi-news, semi-entertainment story. Exploring the back roads, looking up the history of forgotten places. At first it would be regional to the Southeast, but then it could expand, if we decide to do that."

"We?" I asked. Cece was excited, and I didn't blame her. When she'd first transitioned from Cecil to Cece, she'd been shunned in Sunflower County. No one understood—or even wanted to try to understand—why she'd taken the path she'd taken. She'd been given a reporting job at the local newspaper because Ed Oakes, the managing editor and owner of the paper, had recognized a great reporter when he met Cece. From there, she'd risen to society editor. Now she was accepted and embraced by the community. But she would never forget those early, hard years when it seemed everything was against her, especially her own family.

"Yes, Hans is hinting that if the show goes national, I would be head of the Southeastern region. I told him I'd never leave the *Dispatch*. He understands."

Tinkie beamed her approval. "Cece, that is so great. I'm really happy for you."

"Ed is a little concerned that the celebrity column you and Millie hatched is going to launch Sunday and you aren't there to shepherd it along," I reminded her.

"I'll be home in plenty of time," Cece said. "Besides, Millie has this in hand. Did she tell you Harold is hosting a big party Sunday when the paper is out? It's going to be Hollywood themed, so be thinking of which celebrity you're going to come as."

This was a fresh hell. I had no inkling of who I might pretend to be.

"I'm going as Reese Witherspoon," Tinkie said. "She's short, blond, cute, and from the South. It's a natural for me."

Now the heat was really on me. I shrugged. "I'll think of something."

"Vivien Leigh," Tinkie said instantly. "You've got the whole Tara thing going and I know your mama had plenty of those old antebellum costumes up in the attic. Coleman could dye his hair and go as Rhett Butler."

I didn't know if Coleman would go for hair dye, but I'd learned not to argue with Tinkie when she had the bit between her teeth. "We'll see."

"When you get home, ask Coleman to take you to the attic so you can find one of those dresses. You need to hang it in the bathroom, steam it, and then let it air in the sun. Although mothballs may be appropriate since Sarah Booth is far over the age of belledom."

I tried to glare at Tinkie, but we all ended up laughing. It was wonderful to see my two friends so happy and excited over something as small as a party. And a bright future for both of them. I, too, had no complaints. Coleman as Rhett was not a bad future.

"This is my last night here at the B and B," Cece said. "What shall we do?"

"Where's Hans?" I asked.

"He was going to a local studio to go over some of the footage we got today, but he should be back any minute. He knows someone with the software that he can use to put together a two-minute package to send to some of the cable executives—just a quick example of what we've done so far. He wants to stay streaming, but he'd like some financial backing."

"Let's have dinner here and just relax and talk," Tinkie said.

Cece took pity on her. "I know you're exhausted all the time. Let's do just that."

"Call Erik," Tinkie said. "Invite him. That way we can keep an eye on him and also make sure he's telling us the complete truth. If Glory doesn't have him in the pokey by then."

"Did you see Erik with Cosmo today?" I asked.

Cece shook her head. "I didn't. We weren't with Cosmo but a couple of hours, though. I think Hans and I convinced him to see Sheriff Glory early in the morning. Cosmo said he had more details that would prove Snaith was the murderer, but he wouldn't tell me and Hans. Hopefully that will wrap up this case and you and Tinkie can hightail it home."

"An excellent plan," I agreed just as Hans joined us. He couldn't look at Cece without beaming, and I realized that he'd fully recognized her talents and abilities. Cece's career as a journalist was on the brink of big change. "What's your pleasure, Hans?"

"Scotch on the rocks, please."

"I'll get us all another round of drinks. Tinkie, you call Erik. Tell him we need some dance lessons." The truth was, I needed an opportunity to talk—face-to-face—with Erik about his nocturnal wanderings on Snaith's property. I didn't know what evidence Cosmo had—or claimed to have—or if this was something Erik and Cosmo had cooked up together, but I intended to find out. One way or the other, this was going to be resolved. I was almost at the door when Hans spoke up.

"I can dance."

We all whipped our heads around to stare at him. He was graceful and looked to be in terrific shape. "Can you waltz?" I asked.

"It's my second favorite. Right behind the shag."

"The shag!" Cece was up and on her feet. "I love to shag. No one knows how to do it anymore except for Harold, one of our Delta friends. He's always got a dance card filled a mile long whenever there are dances at home."

"How did you fall into dancing?" I asked. How strange that both Erik and Hans were into the world of ballroom dancing.

"My mother was a dance instructor in Chicago." Hans held out his hand to Cece. "My father was often gone, and my sister and I would accompany my mother to the studio where she taught. The older ladies there loved me, and I realized I enjoyed dancing and I could make good money. I paid for my college education teaching dance lessons."

"I took cotillion at Ole Miss." Tinkie gave me a sad face. "You were learning jazz and modern dance and tap for your acting career. I was doing the rumba and the cha-cha. Oh, and I know it isn't really a dance, but I did love the conga lines in the sorority house."

Tinkie put some music on her phone, turned up the volume, and watched as Hans and Cece performed a dance where their upper bodies seemed to float while their feet were Snoopy dancing. Amazing.

Tinkie and I applauded when they finished.

"I'm impressed," Tinkie said. "Rumba?" She held out her hand to Hans. "Dance with me."

He pulled her from her chair in one swift move as Cece put the right music on, and I watched in amazement at the things Tinkie's hips could do. No wonder she'd defied scar tissue in her Fallopian tubes. Those hips just tossed those little swimmers right on up past the blockage and to the egg.

After the dance, Tinkie placed a call to Erik. Of course he didn't answer, but she left him a message asking him to come dance with us. I doubted we'd see him before I tracked his butt down at the drugstore tomorrow—if Glory didn't get him first. Tinkie and I had been shot at twice, and I found it difficult to believe he hadn't heard about what happened. Yet he'd failed to even call to check on us.

I went to the bar and fixed drinks for all. I tapped lightly on Donna's door to invite her down for the dance. She declined, citing a need for sleep, but she told me where to find some snacks to help absorb the alcohol she seemed certain we'd consume.

"Donna, we may be leaving tomorrow. I can't say for certain. Cece is going home for sure."

"She told me," Donna said. "Hans is also leaving. You and Mrs. Richmond stay as long as you like or if you need to go, that's fine, too. It's been a pleasure having you here as guests."

"Thanks." I took my tray of drinks, stopped for the snacks, and headed back to the dance-a-thon. I arrived just in time to see Hans, Tinkie, and Cece going to town doing the twist. I put the goodies down and jumped to the dance floor. I didn't have a lot of grace, but I sure did have a heart for dancing.

When we finished the twist, Cece put on a waltz and I accepted Hans's invitation. Coleman was a good dancer, but he lacked the polish and skill that Hans displayed. A strong lead could make even a mediocre dancer like me feel like Ginger Rogers. I gave myself to the flow of the music and Hans's talent. We ended the dance with a flourish. From the waltz, he went to the salsa with Cece and on to the bolero. Cece jumped back for a paso doble and she took on the role of the bull with great vigor. I was exhausted by the time they were done. We all sat down laughing as we sipped our drinks.

Watching Hans and Cece together, I clearly saw the chemistry that would make them a dynamic duo on the small screen if their show took off. Hans said he would be happy to film in Memphis so Cece could keep her job in Zinnia. I wondered how much she'd told him about her reporter job. It had been—and still was—her lifeline. When she was transitioning, that job had given her a purpose and also forced the town to confront her. She was the society editor, and nothing would go in the paper without her say-so. Either Cece had told Hans, or he was intuitively astute enough not to try to steal her away from the newspaper. My friend's life had hit one of those happy plateaus that sometimes happened.

"It's bedtime for me," I said. I had one more thing to do before I called it quits for the night. I wanted to look up any news stories about the death of a dancer on a cruise ship in the Caribbean. Snaith might be the villain in this story, as Cece thought, but my client had a past that needed some explanations. I wanted all the facts at my fingertips when I confronted him. That cruise-ship death still hung over Erik's head.

22

I took a tray of dirty glasses and a stack of empty snack bowls to the kitchen. The sink and counters were spotless. Donna had cleaned everything up before she went to bed. I was tired, but not sleepy, so I decided to wash the dishes. It wasn't expected, but Donna had been a terrific host, catering to our every whim. I knew how aggravating it was to get up in the morning, prepared to cook breakfast, and find the counters filled with dirty dishes. And I was the only one to blame at my house.

I ran the sink full of soapy water and immersed my hands. Truth be told, I enjoyed washing dishes when I had a spacious drainboard, which Donna had. She had one of the old farm sinks with a long, funneled ceramic slab. A huge bamboo rack held the clean dishes so they could air dry. I had a sudden memory of Aunt Loulane washing dishes in Dahlia House. She had never complained, not one time, about all the work she did for me.

Wind chimes outside the open kitchen window made me smile. Aunt Loulane's favorite scent, a light eau de cologne that smelled of magnolias, drifted in the window and I inhaled, closing my eyes as I let the memories slide over me. A pang of loss hit me hard below the ribs. I missed my family.

A voice came from the kitchen doorway. It sounded like a young person. "When he was nearly thirteen, my brother Jem got his arm badly broken at the elbow."

I whirled around to find a young girl standing behind me. She wore overalls and a cotton shirt, and her hair was cut with bangs straight across. I knew her instantly. Jean Louise Finch, better known as Scout. She'd lost her innocence one summer in a small Southern town when she'd run into the true ugliness of racism. I'd read the book, *To Kill a Mockingbird,* when I was a girl, and it had marked me in ways that still reverberated today. Scout was my North Star, a tomboy who was book smart and determined to be valued for her own worth. She demanded to be taken seriously as a person, not as a woman. She had a pure heart that didn't recognize skin color or socioeconomic class. That was the code I'd been raised on.

"Well, well, Jean Louise, did you bring Jem with you?" Scout hated to be called by her given name.

"Don't call me that."

"Sorry, Scout." But I couldn't help but grin. I knew Scout wasn't real. This illusion was my very own haint come a'calling as a literary character who'd had a profound effect on me. I'd give my eyeteeth for a chance to talk with Scout, Jem, Dill, and Atticus—people, perhaps fictional, but so real to me. They'd shaped my own childhood, my view of right and wrong, and taught me to value my father because he was a man who stood up for principle.

"I came alone," Scout said in that straightforward Southern voice I heard in my head whenever I read *To Kill a Mockingbird*.

"Why are you here?" Jitty always had her reasons for the presentation she brought me. I almost never understood them until too late, but I would always try to decipher her puzzles. Even when she drove me to drink.

"It's about the truth, Sarah Booth."

"What about the truth?" Even though I knew it was Jitty, I was softer, more tender in addressing Scout. She was, after all, a young girl who was about to lose her innocence in a brutal way.

"Not everyone is a good person," Scout said, hooking her fingers in the straps of her overalls. "Your daddy knew that, like mine did, but Atticus chose to believe in people anyway."

There was no doubt my father, James Franklin Delaney, had met the bottom-feeders of humankind in his law practice. He'd shielded me from the worst of people as much as he could. "Sometimes it only takes one good person to stand up for what's right."

That was the lesson of Atticus Finch. He had not saved Tom Robinson. That was never even a possibility—and he knew that. What he had done, though, was stand against the corruption of the justice system. He'd demonstrated courage against a mob.

"Standing up for what's right is dangerous." Scout rubbed her nose as if she could scrub the freckles off.

"It's always dangerous. You're right about that." I wondered where she was going with this. Scout was so serious and earnest. "What truth have you come to tell me?"

"I don't have anything to tell. Or anything that I *can* tell," she said, "but I wanted to be sure you still believed in the truth. The importance of facts stacked atop one another to come to the truth."

"I do." How could I not? It was the way I was raised.

"Be careful, Sarah Booth. Speaking out against lies and corruption comes at a price. Just be sure you and your friends are willing to pay it."

"My friends?" I hated warnings about my loved ones. The last time a series of Native American female warriors had brought me a warning about danger to those I loved, Coleman had been shot—twice—and nearly killed. It didn't escape my notice that Tinkie and I had only hours ago escaped being shot—also twice. The parallel was not pleasant.

"Atticus always said that caring about other people was a vul-ner-a-bil-ity." She got the word out with pride. "Bad people see a weakness and they stab right at it. Like Jem takin' care of me. That's how he hurt his arm."

"You're scaring me." She was. Her words sounded ominous.

"Good. You're always more alert when you're scared."

"Who's in danger? Is it Tinkie or Cece?" Jitty, no matter what guise she wore, never really told me any answers. It was against the rules of the Great Beyond. But I had to ask anyway. "Do you know who shot at me?"

She looked down, scuffing the toe of her shoe on the rug. "You know I can't tell you facts. Just don't forget to ask for help when you need it. That's a big, important lesson."

"Scout . . . Jitty, if you know something, please tell me. I'm asking for help. Your help." If my friends were in danger, I'd grovel.

"In your heart, you know it already. You just haven't put it together yet, but you know." She went to the door. "Calpurnia is calling me to dinner. I have to get home. She's making fried chicken." She was gone on the sweet scent of magnolias that fluttered into the kitchen on a spring breeze.

When I went down the hall to my room, I heard my friends still laughing and cutting up. I was tempted to rejoin them, just to be sure they were safe. Jitty had upset me. Scout had called it. My most vulnerable spot was the people I loved. Jitty tormented me about my dying eggs, Coleman's jumping sperm, and a host of sexual matters, but she would never scare me about the safety of the people I loved without reason.

She'd also left me with a riddle. She said I knew the danger. But, truly, I didn't know anyone in Lucedale who would want to hurt us. Actually, I didn't really know anyone in town at all. Even if Erik was guilty, all he had to do was fire us. He didn't have to shoot us. Jitty had urged me to stay alert, and that I could do.

I left a message on Erik's phone, letting him know I was more than a little upset with his constant disappearing act. Bitching at an answering machine was not very satisfying. When I hung up, I powered up my laptop and began the process of searching the web for information on Johnny Braun, a dancer who'd died at sea.

It took several tries with specific wording, but at last I found an article where a man had fallen overboard from a Gulf Voyager cruise ship off the coast of Mexico. The article was brief, naming Johnny Braun as the deceased. The article quoted the captain of the ship, who said that Braun had appeared unwell at dinner. The dancer had left the table to go outside for some fresh air. When he didn't return, his dance partner, Betsy Dell, had gone outside to check on him. There was no trace. The alarm had been sounded and the ship searched. The presumption was that he'd leaned over the rail to vomit—a trace of throw-up had been found—and that he'd accidentally lost his balance and gone over the rail.

The Mexican authorities had investigated but had not found any signs of foul play. The ship's captain said the incident was, sadly, an accident and charges would likely not be filed.

When I checked deeper into the reputation of the cruise line, I saw the incident listed as an accident. There appeared to be complete transparency on the part of the cruise line. They'd dotted all i's and crossed all t's. The ship had been searched again at the port in Cozumel. The dancer was simply gone. All of his possessions remained untouched in his room.

If there were any criminal charges filed against Erik or anyone else, I couldn't find them. In the morning I'd let Leda, the local newspaper publisher, know what I'd discovered. If the paper ran the ad Betsy had left them, it would clearly be libel against Erik, and I suspected the editor wanted to avoid that.

That put that issue to bed—for the moment. Erik needed to go to Sheriff Glory and this accusation about Braun was something he had to tell her himself, if he expected her to believe him. Glory might be able to find out more information through law enforcement channels. I could call Coleman, but I was reluctant to do so. This case had spread in a multitude of directions. And while I really wanted to hear Coleman's voice, I didn't want to lie to him about the shootings. A lie of omission was just as bad as an outright lie, and I hated to lie to Coleman.

I poked around on the web a little more and found the obit for Johnny Braun. A memorial service for him was held in Mobile at a local funeral chapel. He had no family, according to the obit, but was a "beloved" entertainer. Since there was no body, there was no interment. It was just a sad conclusion to a life cut short too soon.

Weariness touched me and I shut down the computer and crawled into bed. Tomorrow I'd find Erik—and Cosmo—and I'd take them to talk to the sheriff myself. I'd had enough of this dodgy business from both of them.

My cell phone rang and I was a little surprised to see the call was from Sheriff Glory. I answered and she got right to the point.

"Don't you drive an old Mercedes Roadster?"

I did. She'd seen it multiple times.

"I have a puzzler for you. My deputies and some volunteers combed the woods on the west side of the river. We found an abandoned Mercedes that looks a lot like yours. It wouldn't start so I had it towed into town. The mechanic said the alternator had gone bad."

It wasn't anything Glory had said, but my stomach clenched with dread. "Who does the car belong to?"

"It's a rental out of Mobile. I'm going over tomorrow to check out the signature on the lease. I just find it coincidental that two antique cars looking so much alike would appear in Lucedale at the same time. I'm not a big believer in coincidences. I could handle it over the phone but something tells me to check this out in person."

"Sheriff, if this car was rented by the person I think it was, that's going to explain who was shooting at me and Tinkie."

"You brought your own set of troubles to town, didn't you?"

"Maybe." I didn't want to say the name of the person I suspected. I didn't want to believe she was still alive and still trying to harm me and my friends. I could feel my heart running like a crazy locomotive.

"So who is this mystery shooter?"

Even though I hated conjuring her up by saying her name, I had to. "Her name is Gertrude Strom. She's tried to kill me before."

23

I got off the phone with the sheriff and took a moment to think back to my first encounter with Gertrude at her bed and breakfast, The Gardens, in Sunflower County. It was an old plantation with truly exquisite gardens. Gertrude, along with a persecution complex and unchecked homicidal tendencies, had been a terrific gardener. She could make anything grow and blossom—except sanity.

She'd gotten it into her head that my mother had betrayed her by repeating gossip that had scalded Gertrude with shame and that began a chain of events that could only end in terrible tragedy. Gertrude blamed my mother for an action—revealing that she'd had an illegitimate child—that my mother had not done. And since my mother was dead, Gertrude had targeted me for what she viewed as her rightful revenge.

She'd tried more than once to kill me, and she'd shot my fiancé, Graf Milieu, in the leg. That wound had almost crippled him and caused him to lose out on a movie deal he'd just negotiated. Worse than that, it had broken the bond between Graf and me in the way that only something horrible can come between two people. He didn't blame me, but I blamed myself. He'd had to confront what it might mean to him if he lost the physical ability to walk and be the action-movie actor that he'd viewed as his future. That had shaken the foundation of who he knew himself to be.

Gertrude Strom had done a number on both of us.

And now she was back. She'd followed me to the bottom of the state and tried twice to kill me or Tinkie or both. She had to be stopped. Jitty had tried, in her own way, to prepare me for the news that Gertrude was hunting me again. I'd understood she was warning me of impending danger. I just hadn't realized it was Gertrude that was on Jitty's radar. Gertrude was more dangerous than most because she was completely insane. Her reasoning was flawed, and the conclusions she drew were ridiculous. Even if my mother had gossiped— which she had not—why would Gertrude want to kill me? I'd been twelve when my mother died. Whatever Gertrude had made up about my mother, why would she put that over onto me, a child when this supposedly took place?

Gertrude's misbehavior had cost her dearly, too. She'd lost everything, including her own son, who'd died of poisoning Gertrude had intended for someone else. But

I couldn't afford to feel sorry for her, because she truly meant to kill me.

I went to alert Tinkie and Cece, but when I went down to their rooms, they were both sound asleep. Cece was heading back to Zinnia in the morning, first thing. We'd be up early and I could share this unfortunate news then, so Cece could report to Coleman. If Cece would carry the weight of telling Coleman about the two shooting incidents *and* Gertrude Strom's reappearance in my life, Tinkie and I could try to close this case and get out of Dodge. Nothing would make me happier than to find myself safe in Coleman's arms tomorrow evening.

I just wouldn't think about how pissed he was going to be that I hadn't called him right after the shots were taken at me and Tinkie.

I tossed and turned in the bed, going over Gertrude's influence in my life. I'd hoped she'd simply taken off for a place without extradition and had begun to build her own life. I'd been wrong.

I finally drifted into sleep and almost levitated out of bed when there was a sharp rap on the bedroom window. I picked up one of my shoes, ready to do battle. Too bad I didn't have a stiletto, like Tinkie. Flats weren't nearly as deadly.

"Sarah Booth! It's Erik. Let me in."

I didn't know if Erik viewed himself as some kind of midnight batboy or what, but I was ready to give him a good kabonk. He'd scared half a year off my life by pounding on the window. I unlatched it and let him climb into my room.

"Where the hell have you been?" I asked, not bothering to hide my cranky nature.

"Cosmo and I were supposed to meet up. He didn't show. He said he could clear my name."

I heard the inflection—worry mingled with aggravation—in his voice. "And?"

He shook his head. "Sarah Booth, I'm very concerned."

"Erik, I hate to say it, but I'm about done with you. You're like a magician with a bad disappearing act. When you could give yourself a reasonable alibi if you just did what the sheriff asked, you don't. Tinkie and I have risked—" I stopped myself. It wasn't Erik's fault that Gertrude was in George County. She would have found me wherever I was, so it was silly to blame this on him. "Someone tried to kill me and Tinkie. We were shot at twice today. Once in front of your drugstore and once in the woods beside the Escatawpa River when we went to gather evidence to try to save you."

"I'm so sorry, Sarah Booth. Damn. Did the sheriff catch the shooter?"

"No. And once again, you were nowhere to be found." I let that lay out there.

"I was on the other side of the county, looking for Cosmo."

"So you say. Can anyone verify that?"

He looked aghast. "You don't think I took a shot at you, do you?"

"No, I don't. In fact I think I know who did, but that doesn't relieve you of the responsibility for looking out for yourself and your interests. Every time something bad happens, you're off God knows where and no alibi. You need to go to work, stay there, and make sure someone the sheriff trusts is with you 24/7. Or you may no longer have that option. Sheriff Glory said she was going to put you in jail, and I don't blame her."

"Who shot at you?"

"A crazy woman. She blew out the window in your pharmacy and shot at us again in the woods when Tinkie and I were trying to help you."

"I do apologize. I would have come back had I known." He held up a hand. "I know. I should have answered my phone. No wonder I had twenty calls from the drugstore." Erik was glum. "I'm so sorry, Sarah Booth. Who was trying to kill you?"

I gave him the condensed version of Gertrude Strom and her vendetta. "This has nothing to do with you and I'm sorry I snapped at you."

"Except you wouldn't have been in the woods or in front of the drugstore unless you were trying to help me."

"I could have been home at Dahlia House or walking out of Millie's Café in Zinnia and she would have targeted me there. This wasn't your fault in any way."

"Can Sheriff Glory catch her?"

Coleman had been trying for months. Without success. Gertrude had evaded roadblocks and dragnets across at least eight counties. She knew the Delta backroads better than anyone I'd ever met. And she obviously knew her way around George County to set up an ambush.

"Glory is going to try. I'm leaving it in her hands. So where is Cosmo?" I changed the subject. It only made me antsier to talk about Gertrude.

"Someone had turned his cottage upside down. Looking for what? He disdains valuables. There's nothing there to steal. The only thing he cares about are the wetlands and the insects that he feels he's been sent by God to care for."

"He's on videotape stealing MoBlast off a lawn-service truck. That's the herbicide Patrice was killed with."

"I know." Erik shook his head. "I know it looks bad."

"What was he planning to do with the herbicide?"

"He was going to poison Dr. Reynolds's gardens. That's why I had MoBlast in my shed. I took it away from Cosmo and put it in the shed. I was going to put it back on the lawn-care truck, but I didn't get a chance. Patrice was poisoned and they found it in my shed."

"Did Cosmo poison her?"

"No. I don't think he would have gone through with damaging Reynolds's place. He gets angry and does rash things, but killing plants is just not in his nature. He certainly couldn't kill someone, and he really had no cause to kill Patrice. Still, this doesn't look good. Someone was looking for something at his house."

I had to agree with Erik. This didn't look good. "Maybe he's visiting a relative?"

"As far as I know, he doesn't have any, and the way his place was torn up . . . it worries me."

Erik was right. This case was only getting deeper. "You didn't touch anything, did you?" I had a terrible feeling that Erik had been framed yet again. If something had happened to Cosmo, and Erik was on the scene as he'd indicated, he would be the perfect fall guy.

"I had to pick up some things."

I closed my eyes as a sudden weariness overtook me. "Were you wearing gloves?"

He shook his head. "No. Why would I have gloves? I was there to help a friend."

His point was well taken, but common sense wouldn't matter once Glory found his fingerprints at the site of another missing person somehow connected with the miniature Holy Land. "Why were you snooping around Snaith's place?"

"He's a danger to the community. Some of that nonsense he sells as miracle cures is harmless, but I had reason to believe he was selling a very dangerous compound. I was trying to get some proof."

"That's not your job." This was certainly the pot calling the kettle black. I had a history of poking into things that weren't my business.

"It's my job when I find people I have known for years getting sicker and sicker instead of better. I had to do something."

Once again, Erik was convincing, but this time I was not so easily swayed to his favor. "You can explain that to Glory when I take you in. And don't even think you're going to slip out of here." Another thought occurred to me. "When you were over at Cosmo's place did you stop by the gardens and see Dr. Reynolds?" Reynolds might be able to corroborate Erik's story.

"No, but I saw that big one-eyed dog. He was nosing around Cosmo's place howling like he'd just escaped Sherlock Holmes on the moors."

"But you didn't see Daniel Reynolds?"

"No."

My observation had been that wherever Daniel went, Brutus followed. The dog was Daniel's guardian angel. And if Brutus was on the loose and howling, maybe he was on the trail of whoever had trashed Cosmo's place. And I wondered if that person might be Dr. Reynolds. Cosmo was certainly a thorn in his side. "There was no indication of where Cosmo might have gone?"

"That's why I was plundering through his stuff. I hoped I could find a clue as to where to look for him."

The problem with Erik was that everything he did made logical sense—and every single bit of it put him directly in the top slot as prime suspect. "And you didn't find anything?"

"Catalogues for ordering plants and insects. Soil samples. Worms and funguses in the refrigerator. He was obsessed with what he called the biosphere of that small part of the county. I wouldn't be surprised if he hadn't counted the pine needles in his domain. I'm afraid he's in trouble." Erik stood up quickly and then sat back down. "He never leaves home. Never. And that one-eyed dog was clawing at the garden shed door where Cosmo keeps some of his tools and supplies."

"Did you look there?"

"I did, but there wasn't a trace of Cosmo. His old Karmann Ghia was in the garage behind his cabin. I don't even know if it still runs. Cosmo hardly ever leaves his place unless I pick him up to take him to town for a haircut or something."

As I'd gotten over my frustration with Erik, I had more room for real worry about Cosmo. He didn't strike me as a man who did a lot of running around. His world was right outside his back door. Where could he have gone?

"Look, you're welcome to sack out on the sofa. I need to get some rest. Tomorrow morning we'll talk with the sheriff and then I'll head out to look for Cosmo bright and early."

"Thank you." Erik toppled over onto the sofa as if his bones had melted. "I'm exhausted."

"If you snore I'll smother you with a pillow," I warned him.

"I don't snore." He chuckled. "But you do."

"Only when I'm trying to aggravate the other person in the room with me." I got under the covers and rolled over, pulling the sheet over my head. It would be daybreak before long, and I needed at least a few hours of sleep.

24

Tinkie was up at first light, tapping at my door like a freaking raven pecking at a treasure chest.

Tap, tap, tap. "Sarah Booth, let me in." Tap, tap, tap. "Open the door, Sarah Booth." Tap, tap, tap.

"Nevermore!" I yelled at her.

"What?" She wasn't up on her Poe, apparently.

"Quoth the raven, nevermore," Erik supplied.

"Do you have a man in your room?" Tinkie asked, hammering on the door with her tiny little fists.

"She does," Erik said with great delight. "And oh what a man he is!"

"Let me in!" Tinkie pummeled the door some more.

I got out of bed since Erik wasn't moving from the

sofa and let her in. She sailed to the bed and jumped into my spot. "Sarah Booth, could you get us some coffee?"

She was mighty frisky and bossy after dancing all night with Hans O'Shea. But I would have my revenge for her waking me.

"Man, Tinkie, all that dancing, look at your cankles. They're bigger than your knees."

She threw the covers over her feet. "You're cruel, Sarah Booth."

"Cruel to a bed thief who wakes me up at the butt-crack of dawn? I think not!"

We all laughed and I scuttled down the hall to get coffee for the three of us. When I ran into Donna in the kitchen, she asked what we wanted for breakfast.

"We're good with whatever. I think I should wake Cece and Hans. I'll ask if they have a preference."

She pointed to the clean dishes in the drainboard. "Thanks for doing that, but it wasn't necessary. And your friend Cece already checked out. She said she had to get on the road early. She sure was focused on getting out of here, too. She was in too big of a hurry to even let me fix her something to eat."

"Her boss wants to chew her out for being gone." Cece hadn't said a thing last night about cutting out this morning before breakfast. "I'll wake Hans."

"He left, too. Same time as your friend. Said he was going to Memphis to search for office space. He was going to follow Cece part of the way home."

That made perfect sense. "Okay, thanks. Don't make breakfast a problem. Tinkie will be hungry, I know, but at the rate she's going, she'd eat an old shoe. We'll have whatever you're making. And Erik Ward is here again."

"That man needs to rent a room or stay home," she said, though she didn't actually sound upset.

"Yes, he does. I honestly think he may need to spend a night or two in jail to reset his priorities."

"Most men need a night or two in jail." She pulled a dozen eggs out of the refrigerator. "I'm thinking sweet pepper, fresh asparagus, and soy sausage frittatas. In about forty minutes?"

"Perfect."

Erik took his coffee to the porch and Tinkie took hers back to her room so we could get dressed and ready for the day. As the hot spray of the shower washed over me, I thought about Cosmo. Erik was right to be worried. Where would Cosmo go? His car was still at his place. He didn't have any friends that I knew of. So where was he? And was he hiding from someone who wanted to hurt him or hiding from the consequences of his actions?

I went to the porch to talk to Erik while we waited for Tinkie. I was torn between taking Erik to the sheriff and thereby washing my hands of delivering him or of checking to see what I could glean about Cosmo's disappearance. I might need Erik for that. "Let's head over to the gardens first thing."

"You think something has happened to Cosmo, don't you?" Erik seemed really worried.

"I hope not, but I think we can't rule anything out. We'll eat fast and get over there. Should I call Daniel Reynolds to check around the area?"

Erik shook his head. "Think about this. How is the killer getting past that one-eyed dog to dump the bodies?"

He had a point. An excellent point. "Good thinking."

I liked Daniel Reynolds, but that didn't preclude him from being a psychopathic killer. And while Erik didn't have an alibi, I wondered if Reynolds did. He was married, but wouldn't a wife back up her husband's alibi?

"Do you know if Reynolds was being sued by Perry Slay for any reason?"

Erik's eyebrows jumped up. "There was some talk last year that Slay had turned his ankle on a tour of the gardens. He was telling everyone in town that it was from Reynolds's neglect."

"Very interesting."

"What's interesting?" Tinkie had joined us.

I filled her in on the latest revelation about Slay's possible suit against the miniature Holy Land.

"That's bull," Tinkie said. "Reynolds would never be held responsible for someone turning an ankle on a nature trail. No jury in the world would view that as Reynolds's fault or responsibility. They would see that Slay was just a scammer. He'd pinch a penny until Abe Lincoln screamed."

It was a nuisance suit for sure, but sometimes, getting rid of a nuisance might be worth a little poison.

"Time for breakfast, Tinkie. Then we have to get busy." I followed her to the kitchen, and Erik followed me. We had a lot to do before the sun set.

Daniel Reynolds was in his office when we arrived at the gardens. Brutus lay on a soft mat outside his door. The windows were open and I could hear Reynolds typing away.

Brutus raised his head and looked at us, and then went back to sleep. He wasn't the best watchdog I'd ever met. Brutus looked fearsome, but he was a pussy-cat.

I knocked on the door and entered. "We're going to take a look around the gardens again, if that's okay."

"Help yourself. I got a nibble from a publisher about my book." Daniel Reynolds pointed at his computer screen. "I think it's because of the murders."

Now that was a benefit of being a body farm that I hadn't anticipated. "What's the book about?"

"History, geography, and fiction. It's actually a murder mystery."

"Based on the murders here?"

"Oh, no. I've been working on this book for several years. It's actually set in the 1900s, when the railroad first came through this area."

That was a relief. I'd heard authors might do crazy things to get a book published. "Have you seen Cosmo?" I looked out the door to see Tinkie and Erik heading down the trail. They'd obviously gotten tired of waiting for me.

"Now that you mention it, I haven't." He grinned. "Which is a relief. He's always ragging on me about something I've done that's environmentally damaging."

"Tinkie, Erik, and I are going to scout around the gardens looking for him. It seems someone broke into his place and tore it up. You wouldn't know anything about that, would you?"

He searched my face as if to read my intention. "No."

"Cosmo may have pertinent information to the murders, too. We need to talk to him."

"If I see him, I'll be sure and let him know, though he doesn't take too kindly to anything I try to tell him."

I had one other question. "You haven't seen a woman

in her late fifties or early sixties. Wiry red hair. Glasses." That was the last description of Gertrude Strom that I had. Since I'd last seen her, she could have had plastic surgery for all I knew.

"My wife said some woman stopped by yesterday morning. I was in town, so I didn't see her."

"Did your wife say what this woman wanted?"

"She was asking about you. Said she wanted to hire your PI agency for a case."

Not likely. She wanted a chance to take another shot at splattering my brains across the highway. "If you see that woman again, call Sheriff Glory, please."

"Why?"

"She's trying to kill me."

Reynolds slowly got out of his chair. "Wow. That's one bold would-be assassin." He realized what he'd said. "I'm sorry. My wife told her where you were staying."

Gertrude probably knew all of that anyway. She was nothing if not thorough. "If you see her again, call the sheriff and try to keep her distracted until Glory can arrest her."

"Why does she want to kill you?"

"Long story, but the short version is that she's not mentally right. Did she say where she was going?"

"I'll talk to my better half and see if she can remember any of the specifics. We see a lot of people here at the gardens, you know. But check back here when you come by the office. And if you don't mind, I'd like to hear the long version of why she wants to kill you. You know, motive is everything in fiction."

"Sure." I had to catch up with Tinkie and let her know Gertrude had been here. I should have done that sooner. We had to use extra caution now that we knew she was stalking us. I had no doubt Gertrude would kill Tinkie to hurt me or just out of sheer damn meanness.

I found Erik and Tinkie at Golgotha, looking at the miniature tomb with the stone rolled away.

"Life is very hard," Tinkie was saying. "Without the hope of the resurrection, some people might quit trying."

"All religions have a resurrection story at their heart," Erik agreed. "The Greek and Roman theology is rife with gods and demigods that return to life. One of my favorites is Persephone, who brings spring when she returns to Earth from Hades."

Jitty came quickly to my mind. Her appearances always had a purpose. Always. Resurrection. I had to put my thinking cap on about that. I stopped down the trail where I could see and hear Tinkie and Erik. They were chatting like old friends, and I paused to enjoy how open they were with each other as they explored their own beliefs. Why did some people find it so hard to hear about a different belief system?

"Sarah Booth!" Erik spotted me. "While we've been waiting for you, we searched the area around the Dead Sea and there's no sign of Cosmo. I thought if he were in the gardens, he'd be here because of the water issue he's been having with Reynolds. I've called him several times and he still doesn't answer."

That didn't bode well for Cosmo, but I kept my lips zipped. "Let's get busy."

We decided not to split up, even though we would cover more ground that way. With three of us searching for footprints, cart tracks, and any disturbed areas, we could search more thoroughly. While we walked, I told them both about Gertrude.

"Why can no one catch her?" Tinkie asked. "It's almost like she's a ghost."

"She's no ghost." I sighed. "She's devoted her life to harming me. Time is slipping away from her. She could change her name, settle somewhere with a great climate, and have a decent life. Why doesn't she? I've never hated anyone enough to destroy my life trying to make them suffer."

"And that's the difference between you and a psycho would-be serial killer," Tinkie said, grabbing my hand. She laced her fingers through mine and we swung our hands in time with our steps just like we'd done when we were ten.

We'd just rounded a turn in the trail and I saw a sign that read SODOM AND GOMORRAH. The story of Lot's wife turning into a pillar of salt was one of my all-time favorite Old Testament tales. God did have a sense of humor in that story. It was also a reminder of the danger of living in the past, of clinging to what has already slipped through your fingers.

"Why did Lot's wife look back?" I asked Tinkie.

She shrugged. "Curiosity?"

I had a sudden sense that we were being followed. It came over me as quickly as a cloud can cover the sun. "Get down!" I grabbed Tinkie and pulled her into my arms as I rolled to the ground and into an azalea bush. Erik did the same on the other side of the path.

"What the hell?" Tinkie was indignant. "We're not schoolkids, Sarah Booth. I'm pregnant."

As if I didn't know that already. She said it about fifty times a day. "Someone was following us."

I'd used my body as a soft landing for her and she eased off me and crept out from under the azalea to scan the path. "I don't see anyone."

"Maybe I'm just unnerved by Gertrude's reappearance." I'd been certain that someone was behind us, following slowly, watching. But I was edgy.

"Better safe than sorry." She started to get to her feet when she stopped. "There is someone!"

I reached to pull her back down into the cover of the bush but she dodged me. "It's only Brutus, Reynolds's dog. He's guarding us."

I got to my knees and then my feet as Erik did the same. The big dog came up to us, tail wagging and tongue lolling. He flopped over for a belly rub, which Tinkie gave him.

The dog then hopped to his feet and took off down the sloped grassy hill to another body of water, which I assumed was the Mediterranean Sea. Geography was not my strong suit.

"Brutus! Brutus!" Tinkie went after him and I smiled as she ran through the wildflowers that nodded yellow, pink, lavender, and blue in the spring sunshine. Daniel Reynolds had created a small slice of paradise on the property.

I started after her when I saw something lying in the grassy wildflowers. Something deep coral and turquoise. Something that, on closer observation, looked a lot like a dead body.

25

I knelt beside the body of a young woman that had been dumped in the sloping field that eased downhill to the Mediterranean Sea and automatically felt for a pulse. To my surprise, there was one. "She's not dead! Call an ambulance! Call Reynolds! Call Glory!" I erupted in a series of orders because I didn't know what to do to help the woman.

Erik knelt on her other side and checked if she was breathing. Tinkie was immediately on the phone, calling the necessary help.

The woman's color is ghastly, and her features are badly swollen. "Do you know this woman?" I asked Erik. I figured she was another local. I could only hope she had no connection to Erik.

"I do. It's Betsy Dell, and she's barely breathing."

He began administering rescue breaths, and I rocked back on my heels. "The woman who is accusing you of murdering Johnny Braun?" She was so badly bloated I wouldn't have recognized her.

"That would be her."

"I thought she lived in Mobile."

"She does, as far as I know."

"What in the hell is she doing here, off in the middle of the woods?"

"I don't know. If we can keep her alive, you can ask her." He kept giving rescue breaths every few seconds. "Check her pulse."

I did as he asked. "I don't feel a pulse!" I listened for the sound of help arriving. Betsy looked dead already. Her skin was a bluish tint, and white foam had begun to form at the corners of her mouth. Watching Erik work on her to keep her from dying, I felt my opinion of Erik changing yet again. If he'd meant to kill her, why work so hard to keep her alive?

"I think she's been poisoned." I wasn't a doctor, and it was just a guess. One that followed the pattern of other deaths in the miniature Holy Land. Erik seemed to agree.

He pushed his hair out of his eyes and started chest compressions. "She needs immediate medical attention. I'm worried that she won't make it 'fore the paramedics get here. I'm going to be accused of another murder I didn't commit."

"What can we do to help?" I asked.

"Get the cart from the garden shed and get Daniel. We need to move her now. If we can get her to the office area, the ambulance can get her to the hospital quicker."

He was right about that. "Tinkie, let's go get the cart and Daniel."

Brutus had returned to watch over Betsy, while Erik continued chest compressions. Tinkie and I took off through the woods like scalded dogs. I was in paddock boots and Tinkie wore only three-inch heels, a concession to her swollen feet and the baby weight. But she could still keep up with me.

"Don't slow down," Tinkie said. "I don't want to run up your back."

I went to the garden shed for the cart and Tinkie went for Reynolds. We'd need his strength to load Betsy into the cart and then haul her back here. The path was sandy and up and down hills. It was going to take some muscle.

The shed probably had a light switch, but I didn't know where it might be. And I didn't have time to look. I stumbled into the small, dark enclosure and tripped on something on the floor. "Dang it!" I wanted to say worse, but I was too close to the miniature Holy Land to risk cursing. I fumbled at the wall until I found a switch. Light flooded the small room and I saw what had nearly broken my neck. Legs. Two legs in worn jeans and tied around the ankles with a rope, to be exact.

I stepped around a generator and felt the throb of a wicked headache begin. Cosmo Constantine lay on the floor, trussed up, and in a pool of blood.

It seemed an eternity passed before the ambulance and Sheriff Glory arrived. I checked Cosmo's pulse, which was thready and irregular. I didn't try chest compressions because I didn't know how that would impact his head injury, which looked as if he'd been whacked with a ball-peen hammer. Confirming my assessment, Tinkie found a hammer with blood on it tossed behind some cardboard boxes full of gardening supplies.

I took photographs of Cosmo, because I realized that under the circumstances, we weren't likely to get copies of the same from Sheriff Glory. Erik was her number-one suspect, and we were his agents. He'd been in the area last night—again without an alibi until he'd shown up in my room. The evidence continued to pile up against him.

At last the medical experts arrived and Tinkie and I cleared out of the little shed to wait. We didn't discuss what had happened, but we were both keenly aware that Cosmo might have brain damage from the blow he'd sustained. Sheriff Glory was photographing the shed. When she finished, she came over to us.

"Show me what you touched," she said to us. We pointed out the exact places we'd been and what we might have left trace evidence on. "We came in here to get the cart to transport Betsy Dell for easier ambulance pickup," I explained.

"I get it." Glory was not happy. "How many bodies does this make that you've 'stumbled' on?" She used air quotes to emphasize her sarcasm.

"These two aren't technically dead." I was pointing out the obvious, not trying to be a smart-ass, but Tinkie put her blunt little heel onto my big toe and shifted her weight until I squealed. At last, Glory gave Tinkie a nod of approval. My toe had been sacrificed to regain a civil relationship with the sheriff. I wondered if it would be worth it, down the road.

The paramedics brought Cosmo out of the shed on a

stretcher. He was pale and unconscious, but he was still breathing regularly on his own.

"He needs an immediate scan," one paramedic said. "We have a specialist on the way. We'll meet them at the hospital."

I was shell-shocked by the unexpected carnage and the swift turn of events. My head was throbbing. The discovery of two bodies—though both were alive, as far as I knew—had sent me into a fight-or-flight state. I didn't want to talk to Glory, I wanted to find the person responsible for this mayhem and end it. On top of all this, I wanted Gertrude Strom behind bars or in a grave. I didn't care which.

The paramedics loaded Cosmo into one ambulance and tore off with lights and sirens blaring.

"Do you think he's going to live?" Tinkie asked.

"I don't know." There had been a lot of blood around his head. Aunt Loulane always told me that head wounds bled a lot. But how much blood could a body lose and still remain alive? I was never going to ask that question because the answer would haunt me. Ignorance was sometimes bliss.

Tinkie put her arm around my waist. "Let's see if Dr. Reynolds has some coffee or something. You look a little pale."

My head was throbbing. I pointed to the trail where the paramedics were returning with Betsy on another gurney. They were making great time on the rough path. They loaded her in the ambulance and after a private word with Sheriff Glory, they hauled it to the hospital.

"The EMTs think they'll both live," Glory said as Daniel and Erik joined us.

"Erik, they said you probably saved Betsy's life with your CPR."

"I hope she's okay," Erik said. "I think she was poisoned. Did they say that's what happened?"

"We'll know more once the doctors examine her." Glory watched us closely to gauge our reaction. "Cosmo may have bleeding on his brain. If they can relieve the swelling and there's no damage . . ."

"Who did this?" Erik asked.

"A good question. Where were you last night about ten o'clock?" Glory asked him.

When Erik looked at me, he knew he was in serious trouble. I wouldn't lie for him. I couldn't. He was my client, but Tinkie and I had a code of ethics. "He was with me part of the night," I said, hoping she wouldn't ask me to specify.

"When to when?"

"From about three until now." Erik didn't wait for me to lie. "Is there a way to know when Betsy and Cosmo were attacked?"

Glory countered with a question of her own. "Do you think Cosmo poisoned Betsy?"

"Why would he?" Erik asked. "I doubt he even knew her. I can't figure what she was doing in this neck of the woods. She never comes to Lucedale. Never. Why would she be in the gardens in the dead of night? It doesn't make any sense."

"Unless she was lured here," Glory said quietly.

"Is that what happened?" Erik asked.

"We'll know more when the doctor finishes with her. Let's hope she regains consciousness and can tell us why she was here and who hurt her." She turned to Erik.

"I'm going to let you turn yourself in. I need to get to the hospital. But I'm warning you, if you aren't at the courthouse when I get there, it's going to go harder on you."

In other words, Glory didn't want to tell us any details, and I didn't blame her. Erik was her prime suspect. I had the sense she was pretty much done with sharing information with us, and while this would make it harder on us, Erik had brought her reluctance to trust us on himself.

Glory left us for a brief consultation with Daniel and Mrs. Reynolds. Erik blew out his breath. "She is really torqued with me."

And I didn't blame her. "Erik, you've lied to us more than once. And the victims—alive and dead—are always in your vicinity. Count yourself lucky she's letting you turn yourself in."

"I should go to work now, just for a while. To get things settled at the drugstore before I turn myself in," Erik said.

"Until you're in that cell, I'm telling you for your own good, always have someone with you. Don't go anywhere alone. Not even the bathroom if you're going to be longer than ten minutes. I'm dead serious about this. If there are more murders and you don't have a solid alibi, the judge will set the bail so high you won't be getting out again."

"Yes, ma'am," Erik said, and he didn't seem to be pretending to be contrite. Glory had finally penetrated his hard head with the utter necessity of having an alibi. I only hoped it wasn't too late.

When Glory returned, she had a few questions. "What was Betsy Dell doing at the gardens? If you have any inkling, now is the time to spill it."

"I don't know," Erik said. "I really don't. Betsy hates me, and I understand she was trying to buy an ad accusing me of killing Johnny Braun on a Christmas cruise, but I never spoke with her."

"What?" Glory's forehead was a thundercloud. "Erik, you need to tell me all about this. The complete truth. Who is this Johnny Braun and where was he murdered?"

I let Erik tell the story, and once again, he told Glory the same thing he'd told me. His consistency with the details spoke in his favor regarding the dancer's death, but it didn't remove him as a suspect in two other deaths and two attacks.

"Braun's body was never found," I told her. "The supposition that he was poisoned came from Betsy, not any officials, as far as I can tell. You'll have better access to records from Cozumel."

"I'll get on that right away." She rounded on me and Tinkie. "You knew this?"

We both nodded. "I wanted Erik to tell you. And he was going to."

"When were you expecting him to come clean? Sometime this decade?"

"ASAP," I said. "He was going by the office to tell you this morning, but he decided to come with me and Tinkie to look for Cosmo. He was worried about his friend."

"Did it occur to any of you that you should have reported Cosmo missing?"

"I wasn't certain anything was wrong. Sometimes he goes off in the woods to sleep under the stars," Erik said. "I figured he'd turn up, but I wanted to be sure that he was safely home before I went back to town to talk to you. I would have called you had we not found Miss Dell, and then Cosmo."

"You have a lot of woulda, coulda, shoulda stories going, Erik." Glory stared at him, arms akimbo.

"I'm not in the habit of thinking someone will be murdered. Or attempted to be murdered. Call it one of my character flaws." He was a little prickly.

Glory gave him a cold look. "You take the cake. You're up on two counts of murder, two attempted murders and you want to snark at the person who can help you."

"Chalk that up to another character flaw," Tinkie said.

"What are your plans for the rest of the day?" Glory asked Tinkie and me.

"We'd planned to visit Betsy Dell in Mobile today, but I guess we'll check at the hospital to see if she can talk. Did you have a chance to talk with Erik's dance partner, Ana Arguello?"

Glory shook her head. "It's on my to-do list."

"Tinkie and I will check that out. I'll also tell her to get in touch with you ASAP." But I had something else to tell her. "I did some basic research on Johnny Braun. His death was officially ruled accidental. He was a top dance competitor on the cruise line, a regular in the dance world throughout the Southeast, and he was popular with the ladies."

"I can't tell you the number of women who were after his scalp," Erik said. "He was caught dealing from the top and bottom of the deck too many times. Most of the women took a fling with him as what it was— temporary and just for fun. But Johnny led a few of them on in a way that was cruel."

"Erik, do you have something else to tell Glory?" I wanted him to spit it out.

He took a deep breath. "I won the competition after Johnny disappeared. It was a fifty-thousand-dollar prize. Betsy was Johnny's dance partner and she would never believe I had nothing to do with his disappearance. The authorities believed he was sick and fell over the railing while vomiting. Food poisoning or something of that nature. As you can understand, the cruise line was happy to bury the whole thing as quickly as possible."

"Sick, eh?" Glory knew how to add two and two. "Maybe poisoned?"

"Not by me," Erik said.

"You have to admit you have the medical knowledge to make someone very, very sick or even kill them." Glory posed her statement as a mild observation, but it went deeper than that.

"I do admit it. And I've been a hardheaded fool not to heed your advice about an alibi. I see how guilty I look on circumstantial evidence. But don't forget Snaith is equally capable of manipulating herbs and plants for a toxic outcome. Most everyone in these parts knows about castor plants, the spotted water hemlock, and a variety of other dangerous plants that grow like weeds around here."

"Was Snaith on the cruise line? Is there some secret dance society on cruise lines filled with Lucedale residents?" Glory didn't hide her sarcasm.

"He wasn't there," Erik said.

Glory nodded. "But Cosmo would know about those deadly plants, too, wouldn't he?" She waved to Reynolds, who seemed to be waiting to talk to her. "Erik, the evidence points most clearly at you, but Snaith and Cosmo are still viable suspects."

"Cosmo wasn't aboard the ship either. He isn't a violent man." Yet again, Erik defended him.

Reynolds, who'd joined us, spoke up. "I would have said the same thing a week ago, but Cosmo seemed to slip his grip on reality in the past few months. He threatened me with violence if I expanded the Holy Land another inch."

"When was this?" Glory asked, her pen already scratching across her pad.

"Yesterday, late afternoon. We had a disagreement out by the Mediterranean Sea. Cosmo just came out of nowhere and was furious because he'd seen the blocks and cement I'd moved to the west boundary of my property. He said I was violating nature and he meant to stop it."

"Are you violating nature?" Glory asked Reynolds.

"Of course not. Nothing I do harms the environment. You can see that for yourself. Cosmo really hated the people coming here to tour the Holy Land and the gardens. It wasn't what I was building or planting, but the traffic. He's a recluse. The idea that strangers were near his place drove him crazy. Literally."

"Did you know he was on your property last night or early this morning?" Glory asked. To me, it was clear she had moved Daniel Reynolds onto the suspect list. At least as far as Cosmo's assault went. "You've been here, at the scene of all four body dumps. Why here? Why not Chalk Gully or down a million dirt roads into timberland?"

"I didn't know Cosmo was on my premises or I would have reported him for trespassing. And I have no idea why some sicko would dump bodies or injure people in a scale model of the Holy Land. That's someone really, really sick." Reynolds was a little affronted at the accusation in her question. "I'm not a man who resorts to violence, for any reason. Now if you don't have any more questions, I have work to do."

"I'll be in touch," Glory said.

Reynolds whistled up Brutus and the two of them headed back into the woods.

"Reynolds wouldn't hurt anyone," Erik said. "And neither would Cosmo. But someone is trying hard to hurt a lot of people."

Glory motioned me over to the side. "Do you think this Gertrude Strom somehow knew you were coming here and set all of this up?"

With Gertrude, I'd learned that anything was possible. But to be able to dig so deeply into the lives of several Lucedale residents to uncover competitions, bitterness, and murderous impulses was extreme, even for her. "I don't think so, but don't rule it out. She wants to kill me bad enough to go to all kinds of trouble to get the job done."

"You might consider going home, Sarah Booth. Tell Sheriff Peters about all of this."

It wasn't a bad suggestion. "I want to find the person responsible for these acts. I can't do that if I leave."

"Then let's get some evidence that either convicts Erik or clears him so we can move on to the next suspect. This needs to end right now."

26

Tinkie and I stopped in at the Coffeepot Café for some caffeine. I'd delayed calling Coleman last night, so I stepped outside the café and made a quick call. I was incredibly relieved to get Coleman's voice mail. I hated fudging the truth to him. "Tinkie and I are fine. We've had more attempted murders. It's a long story. I think Glory could use your help down here. Call me tonight."

In my mind I included the assaults on Tinkie and me in the blanket statement about "more assaults" so at least I hadn't lied about that. But I hoped he wouldn't ask for details before I got home. "I love you," I said a little breathlessly. The words came easily, more easily than I'd ever anticipated. With Coleman, my love was connected to who I'd once been and to who I wanted to be. He'd known me during the worst thing that had ever happened to me. He'd been there, on the periphery, during the loss of my parents. He was the friend who'd taken a teenage girl nearly crushed by loss for canoe trips along the slow-moving rivers of the Delta, to bonfires to celebrate Beltane with other young people. He'd been a friend when I'd been unable to accept anything more than friendship. He'd given me the room to grow up. Now he was the person who loomed large in my future.

As I reentered the café, Tinkie asked, "Do you think it's too early for maternity pants? I swear I think these slacks are going to damage my pancreas or something else vital."

"Maybe just go with bigger pants and suspenders. I can see you in a pair of knee britches and lederhosen held up by festive braces. That's a great look for you."

She rolled her eyes. "When you get pregnant, I'm in charge of your wardrobe."

"We have to talk to Betsy and Cosmo, but we should go with Snaith, first. Give the docs a chance to finish up with Betsy and Cosmo."

"I couldn't agree more. Let's do it." She hopped to her feet.

We paid the bill and left a tip. It was a short drive to Snaith's apothecary, and when we got there, we were surprised to see that the front door was ajar.

"This doesn't look good," Tinkie whispered. "We should call the law."

"Sheriff Glory and her deputies are at the hospital," I reminded her. "Let's just check this out before we jump to the worst conclusions." Too late, I'd pretty much frog-hopped to the lily pad of breaking and entering, possibly murder. Though I listened intently at the door, I couldn't hear anything inside. Only silence. Snaith was not my favorite resident of Lucedale, but I sure didn't want to walk into another scene of carnage.

"The door is open . . ." I hesitated with my hand on the knob.

"It's still breaking and entering," Tinkie said.

"The place is wrecked." Through the crack, I could see broken bottles of elixir, pills scattered around the floor, and general chaos. Either Snaith had pitched one helluva temper tantrum or someone had maliciously destroyed his home. In my heart of hearts, I knew it was the latter.

"Snaith!" I called out. "Snaith! Are you okay?"

There was no answer, which was ominous in the still heat of the day. I reached for my phone. We had no option but to call Glory. Tinkie stilled me. "Hush. There's someone in there."

I heard it then, the sound of someone shuffling in one of the back rooms. If the attacker was still in the house, we had to move right away. We couldn't wait.

Since the apothecary was in an old Victorian house, we entered cautiously. There was no central hallway so we had to go through a series of rooms—and anyone could be hiding in one of them. Even Gertrude. A chill touched my neck like an icy hand. Was it possible that Gertrude was behind all of this death and tragedy? I'd disavowed that idea to Glory, but I'd learned never to underestimate crazy when it came to Gertrude Strom.

Beneath the fear Gertrude's erratic behavior elicited was a growing anger. It infuriated me that my mother was unjustly accused—and that Gertrude was so insane that she'd almost killed someone I loved and had put my friends and lover in danger. I started forward.

"Stop. Let me get the gun." Tinkie's grip on my arm held me in place. "Is it still in the trunk?"

I nodded. Tinkie was the better shot and the trunk to my car wasn't locked. She took off at high speed and I listened to more muffled sounds coming from the back. My impulse was to rush into the back rooms and confront whoever it was. But I waited.

Tinkie was back in a flash, the gun at her side. "Let me go first," I whispered.

She stepped ahead of me. She was pregnant, but she was also brave. "If I have the gun, I can't be second. I might shoot you in the back. Stay close."

We crept through another room filled with bottles of medicinal treatments, bins of flax seed, hemp hearts, some bottles of essential oils, and pills that I didn't recognize at all. The calming scent of lavender came from one area of a back room. At last we came to a small, well-lit room where a laboratory had been set up. Beakers bubbled over Bunsen burners, and I could see a back door standing wide open. Whoever had been in the house had likely left.

Tinkie moved forward and I was her second skin. When we rounded the edge of a table, I saw Snaith. He was on the floor. Fully conscious but bound and gagged, he watched me with wide eyes. He couldn't say anything, but he cut his eyes toward the door, indicating that whoever had tied him up had departed.

"What the hell?" I knelt beside him and removed the duct tape that had silenced him.

"Ouch! Dammit! You tore half my face off."

He wasn't lying. That handlebar mustache he was so proud of had mostly gone with the duct tape. I ignored his complaint and went to find something to cut the binding around his wrists and feet. Tinkie was moving outside, gun at the ready in case the attacker was lurking about.

"Who did this?" I asked him.

"I never saw. He came up from behind and knocked me out. When I came to, I was here, trussed up like a hog. I could hear him wrecking my apothecary. It sounded like he broke everything." He shook out his hands and wrists when I freed them. In a moment I had his feet unbound, too.

"You don't have a clue who did this?"

"Of course I do. It was Erik Ward."

I didn't say a word, but this time I hoped to goodness Erik had kept his word and had gone to the pharmacy.

"When did the attack happen?" I asked.

"I've been here for hours. It's a wonder I can still use my limbs. I'm going to sue Erik."

I smiled. "It wasn't Erik. He was with me."

"But—" Snaith sputtered into silence. "If it wasn't Erik, who was it? He's been creeping around here. I showed the sheriff the video proof."

"The yard is clear," Tinkie said when she reentered the house. She already had her phone out and was calling Glory. I answered Snaith's question.

"I don't know who did this to you, but I know it wasn't Erik. Or Cosmo. Maybe put your thinking cap on and figure it out so it doesn't happen again. Was there anything in your shop that someone might want to steal?"

Snaith jumped to his feet so quickly he almost bowled me over. "The tonic. Was the tonic still on the counter?"

I had no clue what he meant, but I followed him to the front of his shop. He went straight to the counter where a big, brass cash register was still in use. The top of the counter was coated in some kind of oil that dripped onto the floor.

"No!" Snaith was stricken. "This is wrong. Call the sheriff."

Glory was already on her way. "What's wrong?"

"The tonic I had on the counter was not for human or animal use. There were two bottles of it. One has been broken, but the other is missing."

"What was it used for?" I asked.

"It was for me."

"You're not human?" I took a little pleasure in the gig.

"I wasn't going to drink it, you incompetent fool." He slapped at my hand when I reached toward the counter. "And don't touch it."

"What is it?" It stank to high heaven.

"It's something for Cosmo."

"You want to be more specific?"

"Cosmo paid for it. Ask him."

This was getting better and better. "Have you seen Cosmo?"

"He was supposed to come by this morning early, which was why I was here working. He was a no-show." He got a roll of paper towels and started wiping down the counter.

"I'd leave that alone." This wasn't my crime scene, but I felt compelled to say what Glory would say if she were here.

"Why?" he asked.

Sheriff Glory had come in the back way and she

entered the room and answered his question. "Because you're destroying evidence."

"Of what?" Snaith was either trying to play stupid or he was dumb as a rock.

"The way I heard it was that someone broke in here, knocked you out, wrecked your store, and stole a bottle of some toxic tonic. Is that correct?"

"Maybe." Snaith suddenly had clamshells for lips, and they had snapped shut.

"I'll know more about what's going on when I have that substance tested." Glory used an evidence kit to scoop up some of the stinky goo. "And, trust me, I will have it tested by the best labs around."

Snaith dropped the wad of paper towels. "Be my guest. You clean it up. I'll tell you it's an herbicide to take care of some invasive plants that Cosmo wants to get rid of. It's perfectly legal."

I would have put my money on the fact Cosmo was going to poison Dr. Reynolds's plants in the gardens. "Why didn't he just buy an herbicide at the feed and seed if this is so legal and aboveboard?"

"He wanted something that would stick to the individual leaf. The commercial products wash off and then get transferred into the soil. He was trying to be environmentally conscious."

The tonic Snaith had whipped up was plenty viscous. It didn't really drip from the edge of the counter as much as it hung there. Glory was still trying to get it off the little container she'd filled, but the container stuck to her hand. At last she wrestled the sample into a plastic evidence bag and quickly sealed it.

"That stuff isn't alive, is it?" she asked Snaith.

"Don't be ridiculous." He threw a roll of paper towels into the center of the puddle. If he was hoping the paper towels would absorb the mess, he was headed for disappointment. The paper seemed to float in the gooey liquid.

"So what will that stuff kill?" Glory asked. She leaned in a little closer. "You know it's eating into the wood of your countertop." She looked down to where some had finally made it to the floor. "And the floor."

"Damn." Snaith reached beneath the counter and picked up some hazmat gloves. "You'd better get that sample you collected to a lab fast," he told Glory, nodding at the plastic evidence bag she'd put on a shelf. The plastic was beginning to smoke a little.

Glory grabbed the evidence bag and Snaith's upper arm. "You're coming with me. Sarah Booth, Tinkie, please keep an eye on the place until I can send Deputy Mixon. Shouldn't be long."

"Sure thing," we sang. This would give us a rare opportunity to poke around in Snaith's business, and I suspected he had plenty of monkey business to keep us occupied.

We separated and went through Snaith's wonderland of "cures" and hyped promises. He was claiming to cure everything from warts to baldness. It became clear to me that vanity medicine probably paid a lot more than curing real diseases—and was a lot less litigious. I mean if a wart didn't disappear as promised, no jury was going to give big monetary awards for that. More likely, a jury would laugh at the gullibility of the person complaining.

"Do you see anything that might shed light on who attacked Snaith?" I asked.

Tinkie just rolled her eyes. "Nicolas Cage could

have found the treasure map in here and we'd never know."

"Tinkie, we need to figure out who went after Snaith. It couldn't have been Erik or Cosmo. There's another player in this." I'd racked my brain and come up with nothing. Betsy Dell was a vengeful person, but she was also down for the count. Dr. Reynolds was at the gardens. Who else would want to attack Snaith and steal an herbicide?

"You have to take into account that Snaith likely has a lot of people he's pissed off," Tinkie said. "It might not be related to our case."

She was right, but my gut told me otherwise.

While we had the time we searched for any evidence. The back door had been forced open, so the attacker had come in that way. "Snaith has some video cameras." He'd captured Erik sneaking around his place.

We found the cameras and some medical gloves so that we didn't destroy any potential prints and played back the footage from that day. I wasn't even surprised when I discovered that someone had erased everything from eight in the morning up until just before Tinkie and I had arrived. I put the cameras on a table so Deputy Mixon could take them in and fingerprint them.

"If the person who broke in came to steal something, we'll never be able to figure it out," I said. Tinkie was right about that. Unless Snaith broke down and told us who had attacked him, we were likely not going to get any answers.

I snapped a bunch of photos, wishing Cece were still with us. She was the best photographer. But she was on her way to a new part-time career, and I was happy for that. "I'll check out back," I told Tinkie. "Why don't you check the front porch?"

"Sure thing."

The house was built off the ground with a crawl space beneath—not my favorite place to examine— but I ducked under and used my cell phone to light up the area. Snaith had bricked around the bottom of the house so that possums and raccoons couldn't get under the house to pull out insulation, wiring, or pipes. I found an entrance with a wire grate that I removed and crawled in on my hands and knees. I didn't have to go far. Just inside the opening, I found several containers of gasoline and an area where a large amount of gas had spilled. Two of the containers were empty.

The horror of what I'd found made me freeze for a moment. I backed out of the crawl space, but not before I found a credit card that looked to have been dropped in the dirt. I examined it and let out a big sigh. It was Erik's card. It looked to me like someone had planned to burn down Snaith's Apothecary, with Snaith in it. And Erik had been set up to take the fall.

When I found Tinkie out front, she, too, had come upon a pharmacist's smock with Best Buy Drugs embroidered on the pocket. I told her about the gasoline. Before we could decide what to do with the evidence we'd found, the deputy had arrived. We had no choice but to turn everything over to him and show him where we'd found everything.

"I'll take the gas containers in for prints," Deputy Mixon said. "This doesn't look good for Erik Ward."

"Someone is framing Erik," I told him.

"Maybe. Maybe not," the deputy said. "I'm sure Sheriff

Glory will be in touch when she returns." He turned away from us, letting us know we were dismissed.

"We can believe Erik now," I said to Tinkie. "And I think Glory will, too."

"If it isn't Snaith or Cosmo, who's trying to frame Erik?" Tinkie asked.

27

The sheriff wasn't at the courthouse, so our first stop after leaving Snaith's was the coroner's office, where we met a wall of resistance. The coroner was nobody's fool.

"I'm not authorized to give copies of my report to out-of-town snoops," she said. There was no censure in her statement, just facts, as she saw them. She glanced at her watch. "Ladies, I've got an appointment. I have to go. You should go home."

"Is there a reason you want us to leave?" Tinkie asked with a bit of a snap.

"Since you two came to town, we've had a shooting on Main Street, a shooting at everyone's favorite swimming hole, two people killed, and two people attacked.

Seems to me that you've brought a lot of trouble to Lucedale with you." She didn't mince words.

"Or maybe the trouble was here before we arrived," I said. "As soon as we conclude our case, we'll be glad to leave."

"Look, I don't mean to sound so harsh, but Sheriff Glory is coming up for election soon. As am I. We need to settle this business and have a big success with catching the bad people. I don't think you two are helping her do that."

"We want nothing more than to resolve this case," Tinkie said in a calmer tone. "I'm pregnant and ready to go home."

"Okay, I'm going to give you the reports because I do want you to leave town. And just so you know, Glory told me to give them to you." She grinned. "I don't always do what she says, but this time, she made a good call." She went to several filing cabinets and pulled out folders. In no time she had the reports copied and handed to us. I read one and Tinkie read the other. Perry Slay had been poisoned by spotted water hemlock and Patrice Pepperdine had been poisoned with a very strong herbicide. We already knew both of these facts. The coroner's ruling in both instances was murder. The time of death was around midnight in each case. Both Slay and Pepperdine had been killed somewhere else and the bodies taken to the dump site. From what I knew from Glory, the original crime scene hadn't been discovered for either body. There wasn't really anything in the reports that we didn't already know.

"Does anyone know where that spotted water hemlock came from?" I asked. "Like, a specific place where it grows . . ."

She pursed her lips. "It grows wild around here. And you'd have to eat it, meaning touching it wouldn't poison you. It has to be ingested. But only a tiny amount can kill, and as you can tell from Slay's body, it's not a pretty or easy death."

"Would he have tasted the poison?"

The coroner shrugged. "I went searching for the plant around the gardens and found some down in a swampy area. I dug it up. The root is the deadliest part, and it smells kind of like carrots or parsnip. It might be palatable, but I'm not going to test that. I know a few people I could volunteer for the service." She held up a hand. "I know, I know. Poor taste, and I was just kidding."

"Yeah." I was thinking specifically of Gertrude Strom. She'd make a great toxin tester. "What about Pepperdine? How was the herbicide administered?"

"Could have been ingested or inhaled."

"How small a dose?"

"Taken orally, maybe a quarter teaspoon. Inhalation is just as toxic but it takes longer to have an effect. Generally it's cancer that kills the person. Long, drawn-out process. But from what the medical examiner said, Patrice's liver was gone. Again, not a pretty death."

"Any idea how the herbicide was delivered?" Tinkie's nose was wrinkled.

"It could have been in a pill or hidden in spicy food."

"Which means the murderer would have to be friendly with Patrice," I said.

"Glory's working that angle. Patrice wasn't exactly a social butterfly. She was bitter. But there had been a visitor to her place in recent weeks."

"An identified visitor?"

"Glory will give you the details, but the woman was

not from Lucedale. She had an argument with Patrice a week or so ago."

"Thanks." I had a few more questions. "Have you heard any updates on Cosmo Constantine or Betsy Dell?"

"Word around the streets is that Dell was also poisoned with spotted water hemlock, but Erik Ward and his two PIs—that would be you guys—saved her life." She pointed a fore- and middle finger at us. "You were asking where Glory is, and you should go if you want to catch her before she leaves her farm."

Glory Howard's horses were beautiful. Along with the stunt-rodeo horse, Raylee, she had a dressage horse, a hunter jumper, and a walking horse.

"A horse for all seasons," she said as she finished feeding. "Great job on finding that gasoline," she said. "Whoever left it there probably intended to set the place on fire with Snaith in it."

I told her about the surveillance videos being erased.

"So whoever is behind this knows what they're doing."

"Snaith could have erased the tapes and left the gasoline if he really wanted to frame Erik," I pointed out. Tinkie and I had discussed this exact angle. "The whole thing could be a setup by Snaith to point the finger of blame at Erik."

Glory nodded. "It's possible. But you don't believe that completely," she said, watching us closely.

"I think we have to consider the fact that there's someone else involved in these murders. Someone we haven't identified yet." Tinkie and I had discussed a theory. I decided to try it out. "Snaith was attacked but not killed. His business was ransacked and an herbicide stolen. Gasoline was spilled, or poured, under his house. If someone had lit that fire, Snaith would have burned to death and the implication would be that a poisoner was at fault. The suspicion would have gone back on Erik."

"That's true. But Erik was with you."

"Yes."

"Do you have another suspect in mind?"

"No." At first the coil of the mystery seemed to revolve around Erik, Snaith, Cosmo, and the miniature Holy Land. Snaith's attack changed that.

Glory's phone rang. She answered and I watched the emotions play across her face. Disbelief bled into anger. "I don't have the manpower to track down an escaped hospital patient. Has Ward turned himself in yet?" She listened again. "Call down to the drugstore. Make sure Erik is there and tell him his time is up."

She hung up and faced us.

"Who skipped out?" I asked.

"Cosmo left the hospital against doctor's orders. I don't have a clue where he went. He didn't have a vehicle and the hospital says he didn't call anyone. He didn't have a cell phone, as far as I know. Of course he was within walking distance of Erik's house or business." She gave me the suspect eye.

I wondered if he was holed up at Erik's drugstore, but I didn't offer a comment. I'd learned not to defend our client when it was possible he was doing something that wasn't all that smart.

"I have to go," Glory said.

I glanced at my partner, who'd grown suddenly quiet. "Are you okay, Tinkie?"

"I'm going to take a seat over there in the shade," Tinkie said. "My feet are killing me and I'm feeling a little light-headed."

Tinkie's feet were swollen, but there was no need to point out the obvious. She also looked a little green.

"There's a drink machine in the gazebo. Maybe a soda would help her stomach," Glory said. "I'm going back to town. If Cosmo is wandering the streets I need to nab him."

"We're right behind you," I told her.

I headed to a large screened-in gazebo where a soda machine blinked neon at me as I opened the door and entered. I'd first assumed I was alone, and it took me aback to see a woman in a plain gray dress—stifling from the look of the long skirt, long sleeves, and what had to be flannel material. She wore a hat to cover her hair and a large red A on her chest. I knew her instantly. Hester Prynne.

"I'm not in the mood, Jitty." I fed some quarters into the machine and got a diet drink for me and a fully loaded cherry Coke for Tinkie. I absolutely didn't want to deal with a fictional character who so willingly bore the blame and the shame and the public censure of an illegitimate child while that scoundrel Dimmesdale had gone free. "Take the damn A off your dress and skedaddle back to fiction land." If I had to deal with fictional characters, I much preferred the clear-eyed courage of Jean Louise Finch, who stood with her daddy against the racism and cowardice of a mob.

"Not all moments in time require the same action." Hester stepped closer to me.

"Stay away from me. You're the creation of a male

writer who found it acceptable to blame the woman." I'd almost been thrown out of my college literature class when I had a hissy fit about the professor's misogynistic reading of "the Edenic myth" and how Hester Prynne was synonymous with Eve and the snake in the garden. She was the temptress that had cost Dimmesdale his innocence, just as Eve was to blame for the fall of man.

"I could have said no," she said.

That really burned my bacon. "Yeah, and Dimmesdale could have kept it in his pants." I held out an imaginary apple. "Take a bite, Adam," I mocked her. "Just a tiny little bite. It's so delicious. A special treat for a handsome man like you." I did my best Marilyn Monroe impression and stopped—Jitty had also appeared as Marilyn Monroe. What was going on with her?

"Why are you here as Hester?" I asked.

"You need to consider that to bear the shame, without naming Dimmesdale, is a different kind of courage."

She had me there. I couldn't deny it, even though it smacked of inequality, unfairness, and a woeful lack of responsibility and spine on Dimmesdale's part. He could have spoken up instead of keeping silent. "*He* should have spoken up and claimed the child. You shouldn't have had to rat him out."

"In a perfect world." Jitty was fading in and out of Hester's form. Finally Hester was gone and Jitty stood in front of me, a sadder version than normal. "We share a lot with Hester, Sarah Booth. You lost your parents when you needed them most. Your Aunt Loulane gave up her life to take care of you. None of that was fair. My life wasn't fair. I had no freedom. I lost my man in a war that meant nothing to us."

"And yet you stayed with Grandma Alice. You took care of her."

"We took care of each other. The lives we were born into were not of our choosing. Not either of us. But the bond between us was stronger than circumstances. Stronger than fair or unfair, just or unjust. We survived because of that. Neither of us alone would have made it."

Jitty's perspective gave me plenty to think about. I understood her point about Hester Prynne. Hester had acted in a way appropriate to her time, to her place in history. As we all must. She had displayed courage I'd never appreciated. I'd viewed her as weak because she hadn't named names. Perhaps she'd had a different kind of courage to remain silent.

"Why are you here?" I asked.

"The past points to the future."

I started to ask another question, but then I thought. Was she telling me that someone remained silent with details because they wanted to be strong? Or was she saying that someone innocent would be blamed? "Jitty, I—"

Her cloak whipped around her and she was gone in a whirl of gray.

"Are you bringing me a drink or are you having a conversation with nobody out here?" Tinkie asked. She'd sneaked up on me.

"Both," I said, holding out the drink I'd bought her.

"Who do you talk to, Sarah Booth?"

"My subconscious." It wasn't a lie.

"One day I'm going to find out the truth. Until then"— she popped the top on her soda—"let's head over to the inn. I need the internet. We have a lot of work to do on

Johnny Braun's background. He fell overboard and his body was never recovered. What if he isn't dead? What if he's the person behind all of this mayhem because he hates Erik?"

She had opened a door I'd never even seen.

28

I was ready to pull out of the drive to Glory's farm when my phone rang. Ed Oakes was calling. I put the phone on speaker.

"Where the hell is Cece? You said she was coming back to Zinnia."

"She left at daybreak." I checked my watch. She should have been back in Zinnia by now. "Have you checked with Coleman so he can find out if there's been any road trouble?" I tried to hold on to logical explanations.

"No accidents along the highway she would have taken. When did she leave?"

"She was gone when we got up. She headed north with Hans O'Shea trailing her. He was going on to

Memphis so they probably took Highway 55." Cece would have peeled off for Zinnia somewhere around Grenada and Hans would have gone straight up 55 to Tennessee.

"Did she seem okay?" He sounded worried and aggravated.

"We didn't see her this morning before she left, but she was fine the night before. We were dancing and having a good time."

"She's not answering her phone."

That was bad news. Cece was a phone junkie. She never let a call slip past her if she could help it. She had a nose for news and loved her job. "Keep calling. We will, too. There are dead spots along the highway." A few, but not many. I was grasping at straws.

"I'll check with Coleman again. There've been no reports of traffic accidents that I've heard." Ed was over his anger. "This isn't like her. She knows Millie and I are counting on her. She wouldn't muck this up."

"No, she wouldn't. We'll see what we can find from our end." Glory would have good relationships with the adjoining county law officers. That was the best place to start. If something had happened on the highways, they'd know.

"Ed, please let us know if she shows up," Tinkie said.

"She'd better be in serious trouble because if she's not, I'm going to kill her."

His threat was empty, but his sentiment was shared by me and Tinkie. "We'll help you."

I hung up and glanced at Tinkie. "Do you think this is serious, or do you think maybe she and Hans came up with a story idea and decided to take a little detour to get some video footage?"

"I don't think Cece would do that." Tinkie was deadly serious. "She's taken with the opportunity Hans has offered her, but she wouldn't put that ahead of her commitment to Ed, Millie, and the newspaper."

"You're right." I turned into the B&B. "So where is she?"

"We're both really worried about the same thing, aren't we?" Tinkie didn't look at me.

I said what we were both thinking. "We're afraid Gertrude has somehow gotten her hands on Cece."

She nodded. "We have to call Coleman."

She was right about that. "Let's check with Donna before we do anything. Maybe Cece told her something about her plans."

We dashed inside to find Donna in the kitchen making a praline cheesecake. "When Cece left this morning, did she mention anything about stopping anywhere on the way home?" Tinkie asked.

Donna thought a moment. "Not really. She said she had a new celebrity column coming out Sunday and she was eager to get back to Zinnia to make sure the launch went off without a hitch."

"Did Hans say anything?" I asked.

"No, only that Cece had done some incredible interviews and he was eager to get into a studio to edit the footage and prepare some shows. They seemed focused on their work."

"They left together?" Tinkie asked.

"In separate cars, but at the same time. Why?"

"Cece never made it home to Zinnia. Her boss says she never showed up at the newspaper offices and he's worried about her." I had to ask. "Did she seem okay when she left?"

Donna frowned. "The only thing out of the ordinary was that she didn't eat anything, and I have come to understand that you Zinnia girls can pack away the grub. She didn't even want to take coffee."

That didn't sound like Cece. Donna was a terrific cook, and even if they could grab something on the road, she would have taken one of Donna's biscuits to eat along the way. Tinkie and I exchanged worried glances. "And Cece seemed okay. Not upset or agitated?"

"She was fine," Donna said. "Or at least she didn't say anything to the contrary. She was in a really big hurry to get on the road."

"Have you noticed any strange cars around?" I asked. I didn't want to think that Gertrude might have struck again, but I had to ask.

"There was a woman here yesterday. Older lady. Very polite and knew a lot about gardening. She said she was driving through, saw the road sign to the inn, and she wanted to tour the gardens. She said she used to have a B and B."

Tinkie couldn't suppress the gasp that escaped. I know I went pale because Donna looked immediately distressed. "What is it?"

"Did she say anything else, this woman?"

"No. She was very pleasant. She seemed to be touring around the South visiting gardens and such. I told her about the Garden of Bones, and she said she'd been there already."

That much we'd suspected, but the implications were ominous.

"We have to call Coleman," I said. I should have done it the minute I knew Gertrude was around this area.

"Can I get anything for you?" Donna asked.

"May we look through Cece's room?" Tinkie asked.

"I haven't cleaned it yet so help yourself," Donna said.

We hurried to the suite Cece had used and stopped inside the doorway. The bed was unmade but that was the only disarray in the room. There wasn't a trace of her luggage or belongings. Not a tube of lipstick left in the bathroom. No evidence that my friend had ever been there. And nothing left for us that might indicate she was leaving under duress.

"If Gertrude has her, she took her after she left here," Tinkie said.

"Cece is too smart to let Gertrude pull her over."

"Maybe Hans would, if he thought she was an older woman in distress." Tinkie was biting her lip to keep from crying. Pregnancy made her hungry *and* emotional.

"If Hans stopped to assist an old woman broken down on the side of the road, Cece would go back to help him." That was just how our friend was. She'd never leave Hans in the clutches of a madwoman.

Tinkie was too right. But if that was the case, it was likely a car had been left somewhere along the highway headed north. I called Glory and put our problem to her.

"I'll check with dispatch and see what the other counties nearby report."

She was as good as her word and not five minutes later she called back. "No accidents. There've been no reports of foul play at any of the area sheriffs' offices. We'll keep looking. There are a lot of little roads into the woods. I don't want to alarm you, but it could take some time to find a car if it was hidden."

"Thank you." I was disheartened.

"We've positively identified the shooter as Gertrude Strom, as you suspected. I sent a photo of her over to the car rental place in Mobile, and the leasing agent positively identified her." There was a pause. "Why is she so determined to harm you?"

I gave her a quick rundown of the events, as I understood them. "She blames my mother for a past sin that never happened."

"Mrs. Reynolds told me she was the nicest old lady anyone would want to meet." She laughed. "Sociopaths can be such tricksters."

"I wish she'd disappear and leave me alone."

"I hear you. We'll be on the lookout and we'll find your friend if she's had car trouble."

"Thanks, Glory." I hung up. Tinkie had followed the conversation without any need for a speakerphone.

"Something bad has happened, hasn't it?"

"Maybe not." I put as much heart into it as I could.

"Bullshit, Sarah Booth. Gertrude is in town and has been bird-dogging us everywhere we go. Cece is missing and no one has a clue where she is. Cosmo is out of the hospital and gone. Something bad has happened. We can't pretend it hasn't."

I feared she was right, but I wasn't going to feed her fear. "Let's see what Glory can turn up on Cece. I have to call Coleman. I have to tell him about getting shot at and about Gertrude. I'm sorry, Tinkie, but I think you should tell Oscar."

She nodded. "You're right. I'll do that now."

While she was calling Oscar, I bit the bullet and called Coleman. When he answered it was all I could do not to sob. I managed restraint. "I should have told you yesterday. Gertrude Strom has been in Lucedale. She tried to kill me and Tinkie twice. I didn't tell you because Tinkie knew Oscar would make her come home. I'm sorry."

"They say confession is good for the soul." Coleman's tone was droll.

Where was the fire? Where was the fury? Something was not right in this conversation. "What's wrong with you? Didn't you hear me? Why aren't you more upset?"

"I already knew."

Sheriff Glory had called him. The brotherhood of brown! They'd stuck together as sheriffs. "Why didn't you tell me?"

"I had a secret of my own, Sarah Booth."

This did not sound good. "Okay." I hesitated. Sometimes it was best not to know secrets. They could be hurtful. And dangerous. "What is it?"

"I knew Gertrude was around. That's why I didn't come down to visit the other day. I had a report that Gertrude had been seen in Zinnia, and the deputies and I were trying to set a trap."

"Has anyone been hurt? Are the animals okay?"

"Everything is fine. She's just on the loose. I thought for sure we had her with a roadblock but she got by the Leflore County officers."

The mix of emotions I felt weren't easy to sort through. Mostly, though, there was relief. Coleman wasn't mad at me. Maybe disappointed, but not mad. And he'd withheld info from me as well. I had to admit, no matter how good his reason, and it was as good as mine, it didn't feel great.

"She shot at me and Tinkie. Twice. She went to an elaborate scheme to lure us out into the woods so we'd be sitting ducks. Do you think she has Cece?"

"What do you mean 'has Cece'?"

I closed my eyes for a moment. "Cece left this morning with Hans O'Shea, the TV documentary and entertainment filmmaker. She should have been home by now. She's not in Zinnia and she's not here."

"Cece is too smart to fall into Gertrude's trap."

"But Hans isn't. And Cece wouldn't have left Hans."

"Look, why don't you and Tinkie come home, where you're safe. Oscar will take care of Tinkie and I'll look out for you. We'll put our heads together and find Cece pronto."

"And what about Erik Ward? Who'll look out for him?" I didn't want to argue this point. I wanted nothing more than to turn the car to Zinnia and never look back. "What if Cece is still here in George County? Maybe a prisoner or something?"

"If Gertrude has her, don't you think you would have heard by now? Gertrude would do whatever she could to extract the maximum amount of pain."

He was right about that, though the reality of what he said was pretty harsh. My phone beeped, and I saw I had a call from Sheriff Glory. I told Coleman that I'd call him back.

"Sheriff Glory?" I said.

"We found your friend's car."

"Where? Was there an accident?"

"No accident. The car was pulled down a wooded

trail on Sixteenth Section Land here in George County. There wasn't any sign of a struggle, but the car was definitely hidden."

"And Cece?"

"No trace of your friend."

"What about Hans O'Shea?"

"There's no evidence he was ever there," she said. "Is it possible they could have split up? Maybe he went on to Memphis?"

"It's possible." At this point, I didn't have any clue as to what might have occurred. "Can you call KDT Studio in Memphis? He was looking to lease some Memphis office space. I think he's worked with KDT in the past, and they may know more about his whereabouts." I checked my watch. It was possible he hadn't had time to drive all that way.

"I'll check and get back to you. Where are you and Tinkie?"

"At the B and B."

"Stay there. I'm sending Deputy Mixon to keep a lookout."

"Thanks." We couldn't just sit at the B&B. If that was all we were good for, we might as well go home. I needed some time to put together the things that had happened. Somewhere, there had to be a clue to Cece's whereabouts. "Where is Cece's car?"

"I had it towed to the sheriff's office. It's right outside my window."

"Please let me know if you track down Hans. Otherwise we may have two missing people, not to mention Cosmo."

"Will do."

"Any word on how Betsy Dell is doing?" If I could

focus on my case, I wouldn't go nuts with worry. "If Betsy was talking, she might have information that would help me."

"She's improving. She came very close to dying, and she said she didn't see who attacked her, only that they approached her from behind, grabbed her around the throat, and forced something into her mouth. She said she struggled and her attacker hit her in the head and knocked her unconscious. Ironically, that may have saved her life because she didn't ingest the full dose of poison."

"What was Betsy Dell doing out in the gardens?"

"She refuses to say. But she'll come around. They always do."

"Thanks, Glory." I hung up and called Coleman back. After I'd given him the updates, he had one for me.

"Hans never made it to Memphis. He should have been there by now."

"I have a terrible feeling Gertrude has them both."

"You can't know that, Sarah Booth."

I couldn't. And I didn't. But it was what I feared. "If you find out anything, Coleman, call me."

"I'll be down there as quickly as I can, Sarah Booth. You have my word."

29

Tinkie drank the hot tea that Donna prepared for her and nibbled at some cranberry scones. I had Jack on the rocks. I was frustrated, anxious, and ready to take action. Only there wasn't any action I could take. My common sense—and everybody in authority—had told Tinkie and me to stay here at the B&B. A deputy was patrolling the grounds.

After I finished my drink, I claimed a headache and went to my room. My plan was to slip out and drive to the hospital. Betsy Dell owed me an explanation. And I wanted to also check Cece's car at the sheriff's office, when it was dark. It wasn't that I didn't trust Glory to do a great job, but I knew Cece better than almost anyone else. I might see something others overlooked.

I waited until I thought Tinkie, exhausted by the activities and the emotional trauma of the day, had likely gone to lie down, and I slipped out the door of my room. Only to find Tinkie sitting on the floor in the hallway.

"Going somewhere?" she asked.

"I was trying to."

"Without me?"

"I thought my pregnant partner might need a nap."

She held out her hand and I pulled her to her feet. "Where are we going?"

It was pointless to argue. Tinkie would never let me leave without her. And I couldn't really blame her. We tiptoed past the dining room. Donna was in the kitchen cooking something that smelled heavenly and talking to the deputy that Glory had sent over to protect us. We slipped right past them both and out the door. Luckily I'd parked the Roadster fifty yards away under a tree for shade.

We hustled to the car and moments later I pulled out onto the road without attracting any notice. I drove straight to the hospital. Sheriff Glory had relayed Betsy's recounting of her attack, but I had some basic questions. Like how tall was her attacker? Or did he smell of anything? Surely she would have some clue as to who'd tried to kill her.

The hospital was busy, which meant our entrance didn't draw too much attention. I had a cover story ready, but a young nurse gave me Betsy's room number without blinking.

Tinkie and I walked in and closed the door. I had to admit, Betsy looked a lot better than she had at our last meeting. She was no longer green and struggling to breathe. Her color was better, but she looked terrified when she saw us.

"Don't kill me!" She held up her hands and was about to set up an ear-splitting screech before I clapped a hand over her mouth.

"We aren't going to hurt you," I said harshly in her ear. "Unless you make us. Will you shut up?"

She nodded vigorously and I removed my hand.

"We're the people who found you, almost dead," Tinkie told her. "Erik Ward saved your life and we helped."

"Fat chance of that." Betsy's mouth drew down in an ugly line. "He's not a nice man. Not at all. He pretends to be all fun and charming, but he's a bad man."

"I don't think he killed Johnny Braun," I told her. "The police reports said Braun's disappearance was an accident."

"The cruise line made them say that. They didn't want the bad publicity. And Erik went right on to dance in the competition and win. They should have canceled the competition. By all rights, that crown and the prize money belonged to me and Johnny."

This was a refrain that would grow old very quickly. "Do you know who attacked you, Betsy?"

"I don't know. I didn't see the person."

"Someone tried to poison you and you didn't see who it was?"

"He clamped his arm around my throat and then forced something into my mouth. I didn't swallow it. I bit his finger and spit most of it out. That's when he hit me hard with a flashlight."

"He? So it was a man?"

"Had to be. He was strong. And tall."

"Any distinctive smell to him?" I asked.

"Yeah, he smelled like a pharmacist. Like Erik Ward," she said. "Or maybe I should say he smelled like a skunk, because that's what Erik is."

"It couldn't have been Erik," Tinkie said. "When you were attacked, he was with us."

She rolled her eyes. "Yeah, well I'm not convinced. That's what I told the sheriff."

"You said you bit his finger? Hard?"

"I chomped down on it pretty good."

"Erik has all of his digits in working order," Tinkie said. "He didn't try to harm you."

"Tell it to someone who cares," Betsy said.

She seemed willing to ruin a man without any evidence because she carried a grudge. "Why do you hate Erik so much?" I asked. "Surely it isn't just a dance crown and some money."

"No. It's a lot more than a dance competition and some money. He paralyzed my best friend."

Tinkie looked at me and blinked. "What?" she said.

"Ask him. I told you about Claudia Brooks, but you didn't bother looking for her. Erik was her dance partner and he dropped her. She landed wrong. She was paralyzed from the waist down."

Tinkie and I didn't say a word. Betsy had mentioned another dancer when I first interviewed her. But she'd never mentioned an injury or that Erik was involved. And Erik was clever at omitting pertinent facts, but it seemed he would have said something about this.

"You don't believe me," Betsy said, turning away to face the wall. "I don't care. It's true and I know it."

"Do you really think Erik would deliberately drop someone?" I asked.

"He pushed her into performing that lift. She didn't

want to do it. She wasn't confident, but he told her they had to have that lift to win. And he really wanted to win. Claudia wanted Erik to have whatever he wanted. She could never say no to him."

"Where is Claudia now?" Tinkie asked. "Stop stalling and tell us the truth. If she's pertinent to what's going on here now, we need to talk to her today."

"She left Mobile. She went to live with a family member. She was only in her twenties and the rest of her life she'll be in a wheelchair." Betsy was crying now, hard and ugly. "I've tried to find her but she's disappeared. And it's Erik's fault."

I handed her the box of tissues. "I'm sorry for what happened to your friend."

"He took her future. That's why I hate him and why I'm going to see he's punished, however I have to do it."

I looked at Tinkie and I realized we were likely thinking the same thing. Friendship taken to this extreme was bordering on psychotic. Was Betsy Dell someone who could kill innocent people just to frame a man she hated? She was tall and athletic, and she could have faked the attack on herself.

"Can you tell us anything else about your attacker?" Tinkie asked.

"He was smooth-shaven. Like Erik. Short hair, unless he had it tied back. He meant to kill me for sure."

"Why were you in the gardens?" I asked.

"I got a call from someone who said they knew about the ad I wanted to run in the local paper. The caller was male and he said he had evidence to prove Erik was guilty of killing Johnny. I knew Erik would never be punished for what he did to Claudia, but I wanted that evidence that showed he murdered Johnny. I took a risk."

"And you almost died."

"And I'll do it again if I have to. Erik Ward is going to pay for what he did to my best friend. Claudia believed in me when I went out to Hollywood. She was the only person who ever believed in me."

"We're going to look for Claudia. If we find her, we'll tell her to get in touch with you." Tinkie was far more compassionate than I was.

"Good luck with that."

Betsy was so bitter, I just stared at her. "You know where Claudia is. Tell us."

"She's dead. She killed herself a month or so ago. In Dubuque, Iowa, where she was living."

Tinkie shook her head. "I'm sorry, Betsy. I am. But you can't blame Erik for something that happened in the past and was an accident."

"Check into it. See if you can look me in the eye and say it was an accident once you know the details." She rolled over to face the wall.

It turned out a search of Cece's Prius was futile. Tinkie and I combed over it, while Sheriff Glory looked out the window watching us. We found zip. About the time we finished examining the car, Deputy Mixon showed up, only a little annoyed that we'd given him the slip at the B&B. We apologized, and he shook his head and walked inside, grumbling. When we were finished, Glory came out the door and called us inside.

"I thought you might want to take a look at her cell phone," she said.

"You could have told us you had it," Tinkie said.

"You could have come in here and asked," Glory said, unwilling to take the blame for Tinkie's pique.

I thought Tinkie would stamp her foot, but instead she burst into a full-blown laugh. "You're right, Glory. We should have done that. And mea culpa to Deputy Mixon for sneaking off."

"May I see the phone?" I asked.

"Do you know her password?" Glory held up the phone. "I've called a state expert, but he won't get here until late today."

"I do." Tinkie, Cece, Millie, and I had all exchanged phone passwords and other critical online data. I took the phone and opened it, going straight to the camera roll. "Can you track where the phone has been?" I asked.

"I don't think so. We just don't have the capability," Glory said.

I opened the photo file and stopped. There were a dozen pictures of the interior of Cece's car, of the ground, around the area, and of Hans, in the passenger seat looking very upset.

"Where in the heck could Cece and Hans be?" I asked. I hated to do it in front of Tinkie, but the photos, with the crazy camera angles and the photos of the car's headliner and other nonsensical things, made me think the two of them had been swarmed and attacked. Surely one older woman—old enough to be my mama—couldn't have taken both Hans and Cece alone.

"There was no blood or any indication of anyone being wounded," Glory said. "No one has seen Gertrude Strom in this area since the shootings yesterday. Coleman believes she may be headed back to Sunflower County in preparation for your return."

"Coleman believes Gertrude has Cece, doesn't he?"

"He does, and he thinks she means to make an example of her, to draw you out, to bring you home and within her reach."

Tinkie stepped to my side. "Maybe we should go home."

I nodded. It was time to do that. I'd never walked away from a case—and neither had Tinkie. This, though, was circumstances beyond my control. I filled Glory in on what I'd learned from Betsy Dell about Erik's dance past and the sad story of his former partner Claudia Brooks.

"Let me check that." Glory went to a database. "There were no criminal charges filed against Erik in a dance accident. If it happened the way Betsy said it did, it seems this Claudia would have filed charges or at least a civil suit."

She was right about that. "Check the obits in Dubuque, if you don't mind."

She went through some clicks and clacks and turned the computer screen for us to view. It was a death notice for Claudia Brooks. She'd died in January. Glory checked another database. "The death was ruled accidental, but the elements of suicide were there. Looks like an overdose. Could have been accidental."

"This only gives notice of her death. Could you check and see if there are any relatives? Maybe we can call a family member and get more information."

"Sure. She has a brother who was a teacher at a local high school, and I'll make the call," Glory said. "Folks will talk to a lawman quicker than a PI."

She was right about that. In a moment she was talking to the principal at the school where Charles Brooks taught. The conversation wasn't long or in depth. She hung up. "Charles Brooks quit teaching several years ago to care for his sister full-time. The school doesn't have any contact information on him."

"Charles would have a very good reason to hate Erik, if he believes the same thing Betsy believes—that Erik was responsible for her accident. The death of his sister could have been a trigger."

"You're right about that," Glory said. "I'll see if I can't track him down. It couldn't hurt to at least check in with him. Thanks for the lead. Now you two, if you're going to Zinnia, you should get on the road."

30

We were still standing on the courthouse steps when my phone rang. It was Jaytee, Cece's fiancé. Dread overtook me at the thought of telling him what had happened.

"Coleman and Ed have already told him Cece's missing," Tinkie said, reading me perfectly. "Talk to him or give me the phone."

She shamed me into answering. "I'm so sorry, Jaytee."

"I know. It isn't your fault, Sarah Booth."

"Yeah, it is. Gertrude is after me."

"Not because of anything you did. She's insane. That's no one's fault. Not really even hers."

Jaytee was just that kind of person. He didn't cast blame. I wasn't nearly that forgiving. I wanted to get my hands on Gertrude and rip her head off her shoulders.

"Tinkie and I are heading home soon. I swear to you, I won't rest until we find her."

"Could you hold off on coming home? At least until tomorrow?"

I was confused. "Hold on, let me put this phone on speaker so Tinkie can hear, too." I clicked the appropriate buttons. "Okay, tell us why we shouldn't come home yet?"

Jaytee didn't hesitate. "I got a really weird message from Cece. I haven't been able to make any sense of it, but I thought maybe you could. I think she's still down in George County. I think she's being held there. I don't want you to leave her. She has to know you're looking for her." His voice broke and Tinkie blinked away tears.

"Sure, we'll stay here and keep looking. Coleman has Sunflower County sewn up and he doesn't need our help. The sheriff here is great and she's looking for Cece, too." I wanted to give Jaytee as much comfort as I could.

"Cece told me a story when I last talked to her. She'd been researching with that TV guy, Hans, and she said there was something else about the gardens and why they're called the Devil's Bones." Jaytee was trying hard to be factual and not emotional. I could hear the strain in his voice.

"What did she say?"

"According to the local lore, Devil's Bones is a nickname because of the spotted water hemlock growing there. But there's more to it. Cece said it was supposed to be a cemetery for Confederate soldiers. Ultimately, only two soldiers were buried there, but they were Union. It seems the fellows were executed by a mob and buried out in the woods to hide the murders. Rumors grew up around the graves, which no one could ever find again. The local folks said the cemetery contained only devil's bones."

I'd heard the Garden of Bones referenced as the Devil's Bones, but I hadn't dug into the folklore of it. "Okay." I still didn't see where this was going to help us find Cece. "Why is this helpful?" I asked Jaytee.

"Cece sent me a text just before she disappeared."

My pulse increased, and Tinkie's eyes widened. "Tell us!"

"It's cryptic, and that's not like Cece. She's pretty plainspoken," Jaytee said, and he was correct. Cece didn't mince her words.

"Tell us." I was going to have to jump through the phone line and pull the words out of his mouth.

"She said that we'd all been dancing with the devil's bones."

That was cryptic as hell. Tinkie shook her head. "That's the whole message?"

"There's one more line of it. She said she needed to explore the source and to never forget how to salsa."

"Jaytee, that doesn't make any sense."

"I know, but it makes more sense down there than it does up here. At least you know where the devil's bones might be located."

The Garden of Bones probably covered sixty acres. And I seriously doubted a grave site of two Union soldiers would be marked, if it even existed in the first place. "We'll look."

"Maybe ask that historian fellow who runs the gardens. Cece said he was really smart."

"It couldn't hurt. We're on it." My plans to head home had been blown to smithereens.

Jaytee chuckled and it was good to hear it. "Coleman's going to be mad, but I'll smooth it over because you're doing me a favor. Do you think I should come down?"

"No. Stay there in case Cece shows up. We've got it handled down here."

"Thank you, Sarah Booth and Tinkie." Jaytee's voice broke again, and I knew the strain he was under.

"We're on it."

We hung up and Tinkie nudged me in the ribs. "Let's get out to the gardens. If Daniel Reynolds knows anything about the grave of two Union soldiers, he's going to tell us. And while we're there, maybe we can track that Cosmo down. Somehow, I have a feeling he's in all this up to his eyebrows."

"Why?" I asked.

"He's been out in the gardens every time a body was dumped there. He's known everyone who was killed. He's supposed to be Erik's friend, but I haven't seen him show any real concern for what's going on with Erik."

She was right on all counts. "What if he has Cece out there tied to a tree somewhere? Think about those photos on Cece's phone. Didn't it look like she was struggling with someone?"

Tinkie had a point.

Jaytee had done the dirty work of letting Coleman know that I wasn't heading home. Tinkie managed a chat with Oscar, and whatever she told him—likely that we'd been ordered to stay in Lucedale—persuaded him not to press her to come home.

"All good?" I asked.

"Not totally good, but Oscar isn't mad at me. He's worried. To be honest, so am I. Every time we go to the Garden of Bones, we find someone dead or injured. I'm almost afraid to go there."

To be on the safe side, I called the Best Buy Drugs on Main Street. Erik answered. "I'm right where I'm supposed to be. Never fear. I spoke with the sheriff. She relented about locking me up, and I swear I won't go anywhere without an alibi. If I go over to the Coffeepot Café for a cup of java, I'll take someone with me. I swear it."

At least the need to protect himself had penetrated Erik's skull. "Thank you. Erik, we need to talk to you about your dance partner. Tinkie and I are stopping by the drugstore right now."

"Sure. See you in ten."

We left the Roadster at the courthouse and walked down to the pharmacy. Erik was behind the back counter, again with a gaggle of young women hanging on to his every word.

"He seems to have the magic touch," I said to Tinkie. "I wish I knew what that was. I could bottle it and sell it."

She laughed. "He can dance, Sarah Booth. Every woman alive wants a dance partner who can make her shine. Erik can do that. Hans, too. I'm surprised both of them are still single."

We waited at the soda fountain with another Coke float for Tinkie until Erik's posse of hot young women had disbanded before we went back to talk to him. "Tell us about Claudia Brooks." I watched his reaction closely.

"That was such a tragedy," he said. "I still feel terrible about what happened."

"Did you drop her on purpose?"

He was pouring some liquid into a smaller bottle and he stopped. "I've thought about that moment ever since it happened. Everything that led up to that lift haunts me. I still have nightmares about it."

"What happened?" Tinkie asked.

"I did urge Claudia to do the lift. She was like a golden butterfly. She seemed to defy gravity when she danced." He looked away and swallowed. Then he continued. "It was the big Christmas competition on the cruise line. Claudia was my first professionally trained dance partner. It was . . . incredible, the way she could move, her frame, her footwork. And she was such a nice person. She came from a family of dancers from somewhere in the Midwest. I think her folks had a dance studio."

"How did she end up in Mobile?" I asked.

"She was working as a nurse at the state docks in Mobile, and she won a free ticket on the cruise line that leaves from the Mobile port. I'd been hired to put on a dance show every night of the cruise and also to dance with the customers. The dance boys, as they called us, were big draws for women who had non-dancing husbands, and for a few who were looking for a little action off the dance floor." He shrugged. "That was never for me, but some of the dance boys saved up enough over a summer to pay the full ride to college or a down payment for their first home."

"Those were some busy boys," Tinkie said under her breath. Normally Tinkie was always stomping my foot or poking my ribs for ill-timed or inappropriate remarks. This time I pinched her at the waist just above her left hip and was gratified when she jumped a little.

"Anyway, I met Claudia. I discovered that she and Betsy had long been friends. I think they met in nursing school, but I'm not certain."

The history lesson was great, but I wanted to know if he'd dropped the woman with malicious intent. Still, I'd learned that letting a suspect or witness wind down in his own way was often the quickest way to an answer.

"The first time I danced with Claudia, I knew she was the real deal. She could take on an international competition. She was that good. But she was insecure. I don't know what happened to make her doubt her ability, but she was always too cautious. I wanted to help her get over that, even if she ultimately left me behind. After all, I had a life and a business. I couldn't globe-trot to all the big ballroom competitions. But she could. She had it, that magical quality where she seemed to express the music with her body. People couldn't take their eyes off her."

It was clear Erik still mourned what had happened to her. I wondered if he knew she was dead.

"Anyway, sorry for getting lost in the past. It was a simple lift. I don't know what happened. I think her ankle twisted at the very last minute before she took the leap. She was off balance, and I did everything I could to take her down easy. I didn't drop her. Not exactly. It's more like she fell . . . It was one of the worst evenings of my life."

"Was she instantly paralyzed?" Tinkie asked.

"That's the weird part. She wasn't. The ship's doctor said she'd bruised her spine somewhere in mid-back. He recommended a course of strong anti-inflammatory drugs, traction, and rest."

"The cruise line offered to get a helicopter to take her

back to the mainland, but she refused to go. She said she wanted to finish the cruise even if she couldn't dance. That's when I met Johnny Braun. He was dancing with Patrice."

"When the cruise was done, I went home to Lucedale and Claudia's brother was visiting her. The next thing I knew, she was in a Mobile hospital and was paralyzed."

"I'm so sorry." I'd come to believe Erik didn't lie, and if his account of this story were true, I didn't see how Betsy Dell could hold him responsible for Claudia's fate. "I hate to tell you, Erik, but Claudia died earlier this year."

"What?" He put his hands on the counter for balance. The news hit him hard. "I didn't know."

I paused, then with a rueful face, said, "Suicide, by the looks of it."

"I lost touch with her. I did try. I called and wrote but she stopped answering the phone and my letters were returned unopened. I figured she blamed me for the paralysis, and so I let it go. I didn't want to cause her any more distress."

"I'm sorry for both of you," Tinkie said. "Do you know if she followed the doctor's orders?"

"I don't. I honestly thought she was fine. She was in Mobile, and I had to come back to Lucedale and get busy. I have to be here, at the pharmacy. That's what people expect, and if I'm gone, my business suffers. I assumed she was healing, until I called and her phone had been disconnected. Then I started looking for her and Patrice told me she'd been paralyzed. I was stunned. Claudia's family had come to get her, and they told Patrice that they never wanted to hear from me again, that I had destroyed their daughter's life."

"She never even let you know?"

He shook his head. "I can be selfish and self-centered sometimes, but I would never have ignored her. I liked Claudia. I wish I'd persisted in trying to stay in contact. I wish I could change a lot of things."

31

We'd just stepped out of the drugstore when Tinkie gripped my arm. "We need to talk to that Ana Arguello dancer woman. No matter which way this case turns, it always comes back to dancing."

"Sheriff Glory was going to talk to her, but I don't think she ever made it. She's had her hands full with Snaith and Betsy and Cosmo." I'd forgotten about Erik's other dance partner, but Tinkie, per usual, was right. And I still had Ana's phone number. "Let's give her a call."

The phone rang and rang, never going to voice mail, which was pretty strange. I didn't know how to turn my voice mail off. I had a vast collection of voicemail robo-calls from solicitors I'd've liked to stop.

Tinkie checked her watch. "Look, let's just run over there. It's not twenty minutes from here to that part of Mobile County. We have time to go there and get back."

"Let's roll."

We went back to the courthouse and I actually left a note for Sheriff Glory outlining our plans and telling her about the strange text Cece had sent Jaytee. Why not cooperate with someone who was trying to keep us safe? It was kind of a novel idea.

Mobile really was within spitting distance, and the GPS on my phone took us right to Ana Arguello's door. The hot-stuff Latin dancer didn't open the door when Tinkie pounded.

"You knock," Tinkie said. "Your hands are bigger than mine and make more noise."

"Okay." I pounded hard on the door, then turned the knob. To my surprise, it creaked open. We were looking right into Ana's foyer. The house had an eerie quality of emptiness.

The neighborhood was upper middle class with perfectly manicured lawns and brick structures with high ceilings, dark shingle roofs, and a big energy footprint.

"Ana!" Tinkie and I called in unison. "Ana Arguello!"

Her name bounced off the beautiful tile floors and echoed. Empty. The house sounded empty.

"Do you think she'd care if I used her bathroom?" Tinkie was literally crossing her legs as she stood beside me.

"Go. We can beg forgiveness later if we find her."

Tinkie found a bathroom under the stairs that led to the upper floor and I drifted into the den area, which was furnished in vibrant colors and materials that reflected a love of the Southwest. I appreciated Ana's taste. In a glass cabinet in a corner were dozens of dance trophies. I paused to look at them. I was only a little creeped out by stumbling around a woman's home when we hadn't been invited in.

I heard the toilet flush and went back to the front door to wait for Tinkie. Ana wasn't home. We'd made a trip for nothing. When Tinkie didn't appear, I called her name.

"Just a minute." Her voice came from upstairs. "While I'm here I'm poking—Oh no! Sarah Booth, get up here, fast."

I took the stairs two at a time until I found her in a narrow hallway. She was leaning against the wall and breathing heavily. "What? What happened?"

She pointed into a room. I eased past her and walked into what looked like an office/study. The smell hit me first. Then I saw a woman's legs extending beyond the base of a big desk. I didn't have to look, but I did, while I was pulling out the phone to call Sheriff Glory.

There was a reason Ana Arguello hadn't answered her phone or the door. She was dead, and had been for a day or two, if the color of the corpse and the buzzing flies were any indication.

Tinkie took the phone from my hand and called Sheriff Glory. "You aren't going to believe this, but Sarah Booth and I are in Mobile. We've found another body."

By the time the Mobile, Alabama, police detective finished taking our statements, we were close to being suspects in the murder. If Sheriff Glory hadn't showed up to speak for us, we might have gone straight to the po-

lice department to cool our heels while our statements
were verified.

After dealing with the police, Glory followed us out
to the car. What we'd learned was that Ana had also
been poisoned, and the estimated time of death was
during a span of hours when Erik didn't have an alibi.
Glory leaned against the Roadster. "Every death goes
back to Erik's dancing career. Even your friend Cece's
disappearance has dancing involved. 'Dancing with the
Devil's bones' was in her note," Glory said. "I'm going
to pick Erik up. I don't have a choice. I'm charged with
protecting the citizens, and right now he's looking like
a serial killer."

"Oh for heaven's sake. Erik is no serial killer."

"I have two dead bodies in George County and one in
Alabama that all relate to Erik. Two attacks on people
that also are connected to Erik."

"I do believe Erik is being framed," Tinkie said.
"There's not even a motive for him to kill Ana Arguello.
The only thing he said to me about her was that she was
a firecracker of a dancer. As far as I know they were
planning on doing the solstice competition on the cruise
line. Why would he kill his partner who could help him
win a fifty-thousand-dollar purse?"

"Your logic is infallible," Glory said. "But serial killers are driven by compulsion and deviant behavior, not
logic."

I felt like a two-hundred-pound weight had been put
on my shoulders.

It was just coming on six when we crossed the state
line back into Mississippi. Tinkie called Donna to let
her know we'd be back for the night, and we decided

to go straight to the Garden of Bones to see if we could find Cosmo—in the hope he could identify his attacker. Betsy Dell could only say her attacker was a tall smooth-shaven man. I hoped Cosmo could add more detail, and the gardens were the logical place to look for Cosmo. Tinkie and I would soon qualify to be tour guides of the gardens if we spent much more time there.

The sign for the slain Perry Slay was still blinking purple, green, and gold when we passed. By the time we pulled up in the parking area, it was completely empty. Reynolds wasn't in his office. We backtracked and went to Cosmo's house, which was also empty.

"Maybe the aliens sucked everyone up into the mothership," Tinkie said. "This is weird."

We got flashlights and a gun out of the trunk and doused ourselves with mosquito repellant just in case. My partner did look tired and done in, but she didn't complain.

As we walked toward the miniature Holy Land, I put in a call to Coleman, hoping against hope that Cece had turned up. When he answered, I knew from his voice that he didn't have happy news.

"Jaytee is worried. So are Ed and Millie." Coleman sounded lower than the bottom of a well. "This is my fault. I should have caught Gertrude by now. How is it possible she escapes every trap I set?"

"It's not your fault." I so desperately wanted to be with Coleman, to give him comfort and to also take the comfort he offered me. Worry bored into my brain like an earwig. "Hans hasn't shown up in Memphis?"

"No, and no word from him. Have you had any indication Gertrude is still in your area?"

"Glory only has one deputy, but she has a lot of community support. No one has reported any sightings. She's gone to ground." With my friend and the TV producer/star with her.

"How's your case?" Coleman asked.

I told him about Ana Arguello's murder. "Glory is going to arrest Erik and hold him. That may be for the best. If he'd been in jail this whole time, he could have avoided a lot of trouble."

"She doesn't have a choice," Coleman said. "She has to do it."

"I know." I couldn't help that I sounded defeated. "This should have been a simple case. The problem is that the person behind all of this, the person who concocted the frame for Erik, is plenty smart. And completely relentless. I don't know how anyone could hate Erik this much."

"Sane and rational thought doesn't always apply."

Coleman sounded a lot like Sheriff Glory.

Tinkie had been shifting from foot to foot and now she signaled she needed a word. "Hold on, Coleman."

"I have to pee. I'm about to pop. I'm going back to the restroom at the parking lot. I'll be back in a jiffy."

"Should I come with you?"

"I have the gun," Tinkie reminded me.

"Keep your eyes open."

She disappeared down the trail and I returned to Coleman. I was just about to tell him how much I loved and missed him when he said, "I'll call you back, Sarah Booth. Someone may have sighted Gertrude."

"Call me," I said before he hung up.

32

Pacing around in the woods as the sunlight faded, I looked down the trail for Tinkie and saw someone approaching. This was not my petite friend, but someone taller, but just as elegantly turned out. This woman wore a sleek blond bob and a fitted white suit with a perky little fascinator on her head. Definitely British.

"Remember, if you find someone to love in your life, then hang on to that love."

"Princess Di." I knew it was Jitty. She'd come to haunt me in the guise of one of England's most beloved royals, and the one woman that Millie Roberts from the café in Zinnia would never hear a bad word about. Millie adored Diana, Princess of Wales. And Elvis. To her, they could do no wrong. I, on the other hand, was a little apprehensive. Diana had lived a sad, and to me, lonely life. Since I was consumed with worry about Cece, again, I didn't want to wallow in sad and lonely. "What can I do for you?"

"Your friends are your family, Sarah Booth, and family is everything."

I knew the paraphrased quote, one Di was famous for. But what did this mean? Cece was my family, and she was missing. I didn't even know where to look for her. "Do you know where Gertrude is?" I asked.

"I'm not allowed to tell you factual things."

The rules of the Great Beyond were more than frustrating. "Cece is at risk. Couldn't you bend the rules just this once?"

"Is that really what you want?"

Jitty was good at throwing my questions back at me. If she broke the rules, she might be gone from me forever. Did I want to know something more than I wanted Jitty to continue in my life? "Can you tell me if she's safe?"

"Think, Sarah Booth. You have to shake it all up and look at the picture anew. I gave the British people a different kind of monarch to look at, a different focus on war crimes and the horror of children suffering under brutal regimes. Because I showed the world those pictures with love instead of judgment, the world looked at them and responded. You just have to reimagine the way you're looking at what's happening around you."

"Shake what up? We don't even have any real clues as to where she might be."

"Only do what your heart tells you." Another famous Di quote—and one I would gladly throttle Jitty for, if I could get my hands on her. Too bad she was beginning to fade.

"My heart tells me to find Cece," I yelled at her as she vaporized.

There was a cackle of laughter and Princess Di disappeared to be replaced by Jitty. "Exactly," she said. "Di sure knows how to make her points. Quit lollygagging and find your friend."

With a little pop, like a champagne cork, she was gone, leaving the trees and velvet black sky glittering with stars. Only a few clouds floated high above. Tinkie came up the hill. Thank goodness Tinkie hadn't heard me talking to Jitty. My *escapades* were getting harder and harder to explain away.

"I feel a lot better," Tinkie said. "It's terrible, but the urge just comes on me and it's all I can do to run to the closest bathroom. If this is what old age is going to be like, I'm going to invest in adult diapers."

"It's just because you're pregnant." I tried to be comforting, but my thoughts were on the puzzle Jitty had left for me. Shake it all up and look at the pieces anew. "Help me think where Cece might be," I asked.

"In the trunk of Gertrude's car." Tinkie had quickly gone to the dark side. She wasn't being sarcastic, but she was that afraid. She was about to burst into tears.

"I think she's still here in George County." I wasn't certain that's what Princess Di's visit was all about, but that's what my heart told me.

"Why do you think that?"

I couldn't tell her it was because of Jitty/Princess Di. "Remember what Jaytee said. She'd sent him a text about dancing with the devil's bones. It has to be a clue. We just haven't put the puzzle pieces together properly. Let's review. She didn't eat breakfast." I held up one finger.

"That isn't like Cece at all. She eats like a house on fire."

"She left without saying goodbye. Her car was found only a few miles from the B and B. Hans's car was never found and hasn't been seen." Three more fingers popped up.

"Do you think the killer here has both of them?"

"That's exactly what I think. We've been focusing our search on the highway between Lucedale and Zinnia. We've wasted time. She's here."

"Where here?" Tinkie leaned against a tree and shucked off one shoe to give her foot a break.

"Remember about the legend of the Devil's Bones. Supposedly the bodies of two murdered Union soldiers are buried right around here."

"That's right. That's why this place didn't become a cemetery, but a garden instead. I don't see how that points to Cece's and Hans's whereabouts."

"What if Cece and Hans are here. What if they came here looking for the soldiers' graves? You have to admit it's a whale of a human-interest story. What if they ran up on the killer?"

"Gertrude Strom?" Tinkie guessed.

"I'm not sure. Coleman said he had a sighting of Gertrude north of here. He's on that lead right now."

"Then who is the killer? We have to figure that out. Now."

Tinkie was right about that. "I think Cosmo may know more than he's let on. It's possible that he fled the hospital because he felt threatened."

"If he saw the person who attacked him, he could be in real danger."

"And he could also be a really big help, *if* he saw his

attacker. I thought he ran out of the hospital because
he was dodging Sheriff Glory. Now, I'm beginning to
wonder."

"Why would the killer come back here?" Tinkie
asked.

"The same reason he came here in the first place."

"Which is?" Tinkie had her shoe back on and was
impatiently tapping her foot.

"I'll tell you when I figure it out."

Before we went any deeper into the gardens, I decided
to call Daniel Reynolds and alert him to the fact that we
were traipsing about. With the things that had gone on
in the last week, Reynolds might be inclined to shoot
first and ask questions later if he caught a trespasser. I
didn't believe he'd object to us searching for Cosmo and
Cece—and I hoped he might even come help us. Or at
least send Brutus. I'd gotten so used to Sweetie Pie and
Chablis, and even Pluto, helping with our cases, that I
felt naked without an animal along.

The phone rang and rang and neither Daniel nor his
wife answered.

"Maybe they went into town for a meal or something.
He works hard all the time." Tinkie nudged my arm. "Do
you have any snacks in your purse?"

"I don't carry snacks in my purse. If I had anything it
would be cigarettes and I don't have any of those either."

"I could use some nabs or chips or even pork rinds."
Her face lit up. "Hot and spicy pork rinds. I want some."

"I am never getting pregnant. Never. I will not become some kind of bottomless pit of hunger. And the
things you want to eat! Good grief, Tinkie."

She shrugged. "I've never had a greater appreciation
for the pleasures of food. The crunch, the poof of each

little puff of rind, the smoky sweet. You don't know what you're missing."

"Oh, yeah I do. About fifty pounds. Girl, I'm going to have to start wheeling you around in a cart if you keep this up."

Tinkie only laughed. "I'm going to have the healthiest, finest baby ever. Who cares if I blow up like a Macy's parade balloon?"

I had to laugh. "I sure don't as long as you're healthy and happy. Now let's start looking for those soldiers' graves. Any ideas?"

"We've been to the boundary of the property on the north and west. Let's go south or east."

"I'm not so great at navigating by the stars." I didn't know one constellation from the next.

"That's why I have a compass app on my phone." She held it up and pointed down the trail. "That's south. This will take us into the area where the spotted water hemlock grows. I also have a topography map app and I checked it yesterday. We have to be careful. There are natural springs in the area, so there'll be water. And maybe snakes. I don't have a lot of love for moccasins."

"Me either."

"Watch where you step. If those soldiers are buried anywhere, I'd be willing to bet it's in this area."

As I was stepping from root to root in the boggy area that ultimately fed the River Jordan and the Dead Sea, I pondered how so many of the dead—or assaulted—people in our case were tied to dance competitions. But not Snaith or the original corpse, Slay.

"Do you still have the number to the hospital?" I asked Tinkie. She always had the number to everywhere.

"Sure."

"Would you call Betsy Dell's room? Ask her if Perry Slay was ever involved with Claudia Brooks."

"Good question." Tinkie dialed and put the phone on speaker. "Betsy, do you know if Claudia Brooks was ever involved with Perry Slay?"

"She wouldn't have anything to do with that billboard lawyer!" Betsy was indignant.

"Not romantically, but legally. You said she was dropped on a cruise. Did she sue the cruise line?"

There was a long hesitation. "Yes, she did, but it was a huge secret. She never wanted Erik to know. After she was paralyzed, she wanted Erik totally out of her life."

"But Slay represented her in the suit?" I pressed.

"He sold himself as being able to handle that kind of suit, but he really couldn't. He said he could pick the jury that would give her the biggest award. It was all just total bullshit. He couldn't lawyer his way out of a paper sack."

"Why didn't he win the suit?" Tinkie asked.

"The jury said it wasn't the cruise line's fault. They said Claudia was up and walking when she left this area. They claimed it was the treatment she took, against the cruise ship doctor's advice, that left her paralyzed. And she also signed a release for the cruise line."

"What was the treatment?" I knew it in my bones. This was the final twist of the knife, but I had to hear it from Betsy. "Did Erik provide her with painkillers or some kind of drugs?"

"Heavens no. Erik is by the book on that prescription stuff. It was Snaith. He told Claudia to do rigorous exercise and take some of his pills and tinctures."

"What happened?"

"The combination of the aggravated muscles, swelling, and then the exercise, along with whatever he gave her that caused more swelling, well, her spinal cord was pinched between two vertebrae and it was severed."

Tinkie and I found a fallen tree to sit on. It was like all the air had been let out of us. "Why would she go to Snaith for medical care and not a licensed doctor or physical therapist?" I asked.

"She wanted to dance in another competition. She didn't want to take the time the orthopedic said she needed to heal from the fall."

"Then it wasn't Erik's fault at all."

"You can't say that. She wouldn't have been seeking Snaith's help if Erik hadn't dropped her." Her words rang hollow, and I knew reality was dawning, even on her.

Tinkie chimed in. "Claudia's accident is the link," she said. "That's what ties Slay, Erik, and Snaith all together. And Patrice Pepperdine, too. She replaced Claudia as Erik's dance partner."

"And Ana Arguello, too." I added. This wasn't information we needed to be giving Betsy Dell, but I had a few more questions for her.

"You were Claudia's friend and you've tried to make Erik pay for what happened to her. Why would a killer, if he or she is seeking retribution for what happened to Claudia, attack you?"

"I'm the person who suggested Claudia go to Snaith." Her voice was thick, and I knew she was crying.

"You were trying to help her."

"I have to quit blaming Erik and accept the part I played in what happened. After she was paralyzed, she moved away. I tried to stay in touch, but I felt so guilty. I just let the weeks pass. I was a terrible friend."

"Who would want to avenge Claudia's death? Do you know?"

"I don't know."

"If you think of anyone, please call us."

"I have to go." The line went dead.

In the pale starlight, Tinkie and I sat on our log in silence. We'd linked the attacks and the murders, all except for Cosmo, who I believed I could eventually prove was in the wrong place at the wrong time. But we were no closer to finding the actual killer. Nor our friend.

33

When Tinkie finally stood up, she squared her shoulders. "I have to pee again."

I snorted a laugh. It was such an unexpected comment. "Here Cece is missing—again—and your bladder takes center stage."

"We're going to have a talk with Cece. She can't keep this up. It wasn't a month ago we were worried sick about her, and now, here we are again."

Her little bit of humor gave me the courage to stand up and start to work. "Let's find that grave site."

"Should we call Snaith and warn him? He's been attacked once. If our theory that the attacks go back to Claudia Brooks and her injury are correct, Snaith might consider leaving town until the killer is found," Tinkie said.

It was a consideration. I didn't care for the snake-oil salesman, but I also didn't want his death on my head. "Call him, but hurry."

She was about to press call when the sound of an animal either in pain or in anger stopped us in our tracks. "What was that?" Tinkie asked.

"I don't know." The woods around us had turned very quiet, as if even the animals were reluctant to move or make a noise. The cry came again. "I think it's something small, like a rabbit," I said. "Predators are out at night. Owls and foxes and things."

Tinkie shuddered. "I hate the cruelty of nature sometimes."

I'd stepped off the path and as I turned to face Tinkie, I saw something glint in the moonlight. "What's that?"

We worked our way across the little spring and found ourselves on a road. Not exactly a road, but a woodland trail. Someone had driven down it recently. The tire impressions in the soft earth were still visible. I looked down the trail and saw the glint of light again. We hurried forward and stopped when we realized what we'd been seeing was moonlight reflecting off of Hans O'Shea's car. It was pulled to the side of the road, sitting like some abandoned ship.

"What the hell?" Tinkie started forward and I was hot on her heels. "Where is Hans? And where is Cece?"

Good questions without answers. "Look in the car."

She tugged on the door handle, and the ding, ding, ding from the open door sounded loudly. I reached in and removed the key from the ignition, careful not to touch anything else. The car quieted. That's when I realized the interior was blotted in blood. It was mostly contained in the passenger seat. There had been no evidence of foul play in Cece's Prius when I'd examined it at the sheriff's office. Someone had been injured, though. This car was a definite crime scene. Blood had collected around the console.

I didn't have to tell Tinkie to call Sheriff Glory. She was already on it. "Glory, please hurry. Someone's been hurt and we don't know where they are. And call an ambulance. We're going to need it."

I searched the car as thoroughly as I could in the pale overhead light. The most important thing was not to mess up any evidence. Tinkie was shifting from foot to foot. She really had to go to the bathroom.

"I'll walk you back to the office area," I said.

"No, I'm good. While I'm gone, search around here for Cece. I'll be right back. And I do have the gun."

I hesitated. This sounded like a bad idea. "Can't you just squat in the woods?"

Tinkie put her hands on her hips. "I may be pregnant and getting fat, but I am not going to cop a squat in the woods."

Tinkie was the Queen Bee of the Daddy's Girls, and I was the tomboy who'd gone on camping trips and horseback rides where toilets didn't exist. "Okay. Hurry. Maybe Reynolds is home by now and he can help us look."

I watched her disappear in the shadows along the path. It was a direct shot down the trail where Hans's car was parked and back to the office, if my calculations were correct. We weren't far, and this way Tinkie wouldn't have to cross the marshy wetlands.

I left the car and moved to the edge of the woods, searching for evidence that Cece had gone that way, or that a body had been dragged. Hans was a tall, solid man. Whoever had moved him had to be pretty strong. Cece was slender, but she was also tall and well-muscled. I thought I could rule out a woman as the prime suspect, which narrowed the field of suspects, but not in any way that really helped me. Who would want to frame Erik and kill people involved in his dance past?

The logical answer would be a jilted lover or another dance partner—or a competitor. That was an angle we hadn't explored. When I got back to my laptop, I'd look up the most recent winners in the cruise line competition and share the list with Sheriff Glory. Right now, though, Cece was on my mind.

I started a methodical grid search of the woods, moving away from the car. The terrain was filled with hardwoods and pines, shrubs and brambles, and deadfall that could be a real ankle breaker. I found an area of disturbed vegetation and pine straw raked into a lump, as if someone had pulled something through the area. Like maybe the heels of an unconscious woman.

I tried not to use the flashlight, but I had to. The woods had grown deeper and the thick trees blocked out even the minimal moonlight. It was as if I'd entered a room without windows or doors. I kept slowly working my grid, but my hopes were drying up. The land had begun to slope downhill, and I worried that soon I'd be in another situation with natural springs, boggy ground, and snakes. My foot hung in a tangle of limbs and I almost went sprawling. When my cell phone rang, I answered it with a degree of relief.

"You have to get up here, Sarah Booth."

It was Tinkie. "What's up?"

"I found Brutus. I think he's been drugged."

"Is there any sign of Daniel and his wife?"

"The house is locked—I've already tried the doors. Their car is in the garage. I'm worried."

"I'll be there as quickly as I can. Just stay put." The crackle of a branch about twenty yards away made the hair on my neck stand on end.

"Hurry, Sarah Booth. I think I heard someone in the woods behind their house."

"You have a gun. Use it."

"What if it's just Cosmo poking around?"

"Try not to kill him, but don't take a risk, Tinkie. Shoot him in the leg or something. We don't know his involvement in this."

The rustling in the darkness seemed to have moved closer. "I'm on the way." I began to back out of the woods. If I could get to the trail without breaking my neck, I had the keys to Hans's car in my pocket. I could drive back to the office where Tinkie waited. And I would run over anyone who tried to get between me and my friend.

The sound of movement in the underbrush came from the darkness.

I froze in place. I wanted to call out to see if Cece would answer, but hesitated. I listened for a long moment. "Cece?" I called into the night.

The woods were completely silent. Not even the sawing cry of a cicada or the hoot of a barn owl. Only silence.

I edged back toward the trail, moving slowly and deliberately. I had to find Cece, but I couldn't risk falling for a trick. Cece, Tinkie, and I would all be lost if I jumped into the middle of a trap.

Feeling the ground with my foot before I put weight down, I was almost to the road when something crashed through the woods toward me. Pulling the car keys from my pocket, I ran to Hans's car, jumped in, hit the lock, and turned the ignition. I did my best to avoid disturbing the blood that was mostly centered on the passenger side and console. To my ultimate relief, the car started. I had visions of chain saws in the woods, a stalled car, and old leather face coming after me. Slamming the Lexus in reverse, I hit the gas and backed down the trail.

In the glare of the headlights, I saw something run across the road. It was hunched over. I couldn't be certain if it was man or beast, but it moved with preternatural quickness. What if our killer wasn't even human?

That thought, as ridiculous as it was, put my heart into overdrive. I'd already made a fool of myself once for thinking a robotic machine fitted up to resemble a dead woman was a zombie. I'd actually shot it in the head. Now I had to "man up" and not allow fear to rule me. As I made my way, driving in reverse along the trail, I calmed. Supernatural killers didn't use poison. They used fangs and nails or hollow teeth. Whatever I'd seen, it was human or animal. And it possibly had been Cece and Hans in the woods with it.

"I'll be back," I whispered under my breath as I found a place to turn around. I didn't hesitate to floor the gas pedal. Careening down the trail, I drove to the main office of the gardens where Tinkie and a wobbling

Brutus stood waiting for me under a "booger light" that had drawn a swarm of moths and insects.

I gave Brutus a quick check over. He seemed fine, just a bit lethargic. The pup didn't object when I tried to force the door to the Reynoldses' house. I didn't like the idea of breaking in, but I did it anyway. Tinkie was right on my heels, gun out and ready to blow a hole in anyone who threatened us.

"Glory is on her way," Tinkie whispered as we searched the house, room by room. At the end of the hall was the master bedroom. A slight thumping came from there. I signaled to Tinkie that I would push the door open and if anyone came at us, she should shoot them. She nodded.

The thudding came again. Soft and muted.

"What the hell?" Tinkie asked.

I shook my head and put a finger to my lips as I turned the knob slowly and then threw the door wide with a quick motion. Tinkie stepped in front of me, gun at the ready. In the beam of my flashlight I saw Daniel Reynolds and his wife tied back to back, sitting on the floor. They were gagged with what looked like socks. Daniel was thudding the floor with his heels.

"Damn." Tinkie and I rushed to help them, removing the gags and their bonds. "Who did this?" I asked.

"Cosmo." Daniel was hopping mad. "He came over and I told him the sheriff and everyone else was looking for him. He agreed to turn himself in, after a cup of tea. Paulette made the tea and, while we weren't looking, he must have put something in it. We both got woozy and passed out and woke up like this."

"Are you okay?" The knots weren't that thoroughly tied and I had them both free in a matter of minutes. I helped Paulette to her feet. She was steaming mad.

"Cosmo has to go," she said. "I've had all I can take. We've tried to be decent people and good neighbors to a man who does nothing but harass us. We've turned the other cheek a hundred times. But enough is enough. I'm going to press charges against him and maybe some time in prison will teach him the lessons he needs to learn."

Daniel put his arm around his wife's shoulders. "It's okay, honey. We're going to let the sheriff sort this out." He faced me, eyes widening. "Is Brutus okay? I just realized he isn't in the house. Cosmo hates him and Brutus returns the favor."

"He's fine. He was drugged but he's coming out of it now. He's outside, waiting for you," Tinkie said. "Shall I let him in?"

"Please." Daniel didn't seem to want to let go of his wife. The episode with Cosmo had really unsettled them.

In a minute Brutus came bounding into the bedroom and jumped up on the Reynoldses. He was tall enough, standing on his hind legs, to lick Daniel's face. The family was reunited. And we had other work to do. "Where did Cosmo go?"

Daniel shook his head. "He didn't say. He came by pretending to need our help. It was just a ruse to give us whatever he put in the tea to knock us out."

"Why would he do that?" Tinkie asked.

"I think he was afraid we'd call the sheriff on him. He was running around the gardens and Daniel saw him. Instead of shooting him, which is what I would have done, Daniel invited him in for some tea," Paulette said. "Daniel always wants to turn the other cheek, but I've never trusted him, because he's not trustworthy. I don't know why Erik Ward defends him. He said Erik was coming out here and—"

"Erik is here on the grounds?" He was supposed to have been picked up by Sheriff Glory.

"I haven't seen him, but Cosmo insisted Erik was coming to get him, to help him hide somewhere else." Daniel spoke with a lot of regret. "I should have called the sheriff, and I think that's what Cosmo was afraid of. That I'd bring in the law the minute he was out of the house."

If Erik was truly intending to hide Cosmo from Sheriff Glory, I was going to bust his chops. So now we had Cosmo, potentially Erik, possibly Hans, Cece, and the killer all running around the miniature Holy Land. If Gertrude Strom was in the mix, too, then it was a gathering of fools and devils. It was one of those moments that called for some smiting.

"If you two are okay, we have to go." I motioned Tinkie to come with me. "Sheriff Glory is on her way. Our friends Cece and Hans are missing and we found his car down the path that goes behind the Dead Sea. Please tell Glory that's where we are when she arrives. Tell her to check Hans's car in the parking lot. There's blood. Too much blood."

"What can I do to help?" Daniel asked.

"Don't you dare think you're leaving me," Paulette said, and I didn't blame her.

"Daniel, please stay here. Direct the sheriff to us. Be ready to call an ambulance." I had to believe Cece and Hans were still alive. They might be hurt, but they had to be alive. "If you see Erik, tell him he'd better find us pronto and to answer his phone."

"Take Brutus. He can help you."

I wanted to take the dog, but he was still a bit under the influence. He'd climbed up on the bed and fallen fast asleep, snoring like a freight train. At the mention of his name, he looked up at us, then gave a sloppy "woof" before he put his head down and continued snoring.

34

As Tinkie and I drove to the place where we'd found Hans's car—there was really no need to walk through the dark woods when we could drive the Roadster—I filled Tinkie in on the conclusions I'd come to.

"The murder victims are all connected to what happened to Claudia Brooks," Tinkie said. "That's brilliant work. But who is the killer, and why are they trying to frame Erik? I mean if he's part of this dance conspiracy that crippled a young woman and drove her to kill herself, why not kill Erik, too? Why kill all the others to frame him?"

"Maybe this person has some weird crush on him? Maybe the killer feels being framed for murder is worse than being murdered." It didn't fit exactly, but it was the best I could do to reimagine the puzzle, as I'd been instructed to do. "That makes perfect sense, kind of. I saw something in the woods over that way." I pointed as we got out of the Roadster. "But who would care enough about dancing to do all of this?"

We looked at each other. "Someone who cared about Claudia Brooks!" We said it together, as we often did when our brains clicked.

"She had a brother," I said. "He quit his teaching job to take care of her."

"Listen!" Tinkie held up her hand. "Did you hear that?"

"I saw someone in the woods here earlier. Or something." I recalled the figure speeding across the path in the faint glimmer of moonlight. "It could have been an animal."

"Like a bear?"

"No, it was smaller. Quicker. Probably a coyote." I didn't want to spook Tinkie or myself. We had plenty of work to do. The idea of some feral creature shuffling in the underbrush made my body prickle with fear.

"Werewolf!" Tinkie jumped to the worst conclusion possible.

"Hush up and listen. I hear something."

"What is that?" Tinkie moved a little closer to my side, even though she was the one with a gun.

Something moved about in the underbrush. I could identify the sounds: the crackle of a stick, the shush of leaves being moved or crushed, and what sounded like a soft grunt. I couldn't say what was making them. Whatever it was put no effort into being quiet. The sounds moved steadily closer to us.

"We should run," Tinkie said.

I put a steadying hand on her shoulder. "Let's give it a minute."

Now the sounds were moving away, deeper into the woods.

"What if that's Cece trying to signal us? We should follow the noise." We stepped off the road and into the woods.

Tinkie and I were both unnerved. I tried to put up a front of bravery as we stepped into briars and deadfall. Tinkie stumbled and almost went down. I caught her elbow in time.

"I don't hear anything anymore," Tinkie said. We both shut our pieholes and listened. There was nothing. "Maybe we should go back to the office and wait for more help."

"Sheriff Glory can find the answers to our questions much more quickly than we can. We have to find Claudia's brother or at least someone who might feel Claudia was cheated out of her life." I was about to talk myself into going back. Tinkie was correct. The noises had stopped and as it was, we were sitting ducks if anyone had a nightscope or any tactical equipment and malice in his heart. The more I worked as a PI, the more situations I encountered where people had really great killing devices. Maybe Santa would bring me some night-vision goggles for Christmas, but as it stood now, Tinkie and I couldn't see more than five feet in front of us.

I stepped sideways to prepare to retreat and tapped Tinkie on the shoulder to signal her to follow. Suddenly, the bush in front of us exploded as a human form burst out of it.

"Help me! Please help me. He has Cece!" Hans

O'Shea, disheveled and covered in dirt and leaves, grabbed me by the shoulders and all but shook me.

"Where's Cece?" I wrenched myself loose from him. "Where is she?" I had to find my friend. "Is she hurt?"

"She was bleeding and he was going to do something with her. He was dragging her away when I saw my chance to escape. She's back that way!" He pointed vaguely north.

"Are you hurt?" Tinkie asked him, reaching up to a spot on his shirt that looked to be soaked in blood.

"He cut me. He was going to slit my throat, but Cece stopped him. That's when he turned on her. He knocked her out and he said he was going to gut her."

"Who is this man?" I demanded.

Hans shook his head. "I don't know. He was hiding in the backseat of my car. I've never seen him before. I don't think Cece knew him either. He kept talking about making Erik Ward pay for what he'd done."

"What, exactly, has Erik done?" I asked.

"I don't know," Hans said. "I don't have a clue what's going on or why any of it is happening. We just have to find Cece. She was bleeding a lot. He said he was going to gut her. Please, please find her."

"Tinkie, take Hans back to the office. You can take the car." I was worried he wouldn't make it if he was walking. "Let him out and ask the Reynoldses to help him, then come back to help me look for Cece. She's somewhere in these woods."

"Got it," Tinkie said. We both helped Hans into the front seat of the Roadster, and Tinkie hauled boogey. I was alone in the woods again.

There'd been so much commotion that I abandoned all attempts to be silent. "Cece! Cece!" I called out to my friend hoping that if she were conscious, she would answer.

I searched the area where I'd first heard noises and found nothing. About twenty minutes had passed and I went back to the road. Tinkie was nowhere in sight. Panic surged, but I fought it back. Tinkie could easily be treating Hans's wounds, or helping the Reynoldses, or gathering Sheriff Glory and the locals she'd likely deputized to help search.

I called Sheriff Glory and was shuttled to voice mail. I left a message, telling her everything and asking for a call back. The Reynoldses had said she was on the way. Where was she? Then I called Coleman, because I was growing more and more afraid that both of my friends were now in trouble. When my call to Coleman went to voice mail, I had to fight back panic. What if Gertrude had him? What if everyone I loved and cared about was in jeopardy right this minute? As a person who'd lost both parents at an early age, I knew that fate could be cruel and relentless. Fate did not believe in fair or just.

I had to rein in my thoughts or I would render myself a victim of whoever was in the woods. Help was on the way, but I was the person on scene right now. It was up to me to find Cece, and possibly Tinkie, and put things to right. And when I found this person, whoever it was, I was not bound by the laws that prevented Coleman or Sheriff Glory from beating the thunderation out of him. I was going to inflict the maximum damage.

"Cece!" I screamed her name as loudly as I could. I was at the end of my tether. Even the small creatures of the night had stopped shifting and hiding. My fear and anguish seemed to have frozen them in place.

"Cece? Tinkie?"

No one answered. There wasn't even the snap of a twig. Flashlight in hand, I plunged into the woods. Tinkie had been gone over half an hour. The night was getting chilly, and the beautiful moon, now waning, was high overhead. I would track down the slope to the wetlands and back up in a pattern. I had to move, to search, to do *something* to find my friends. I would believe that Tinkie was caught up in helping Hans at the Reynoldses' office or home. I would believe that Hans was being treated and would mend. I would believe that Cece was alive and I would find her before it was too late.

My cell phone buzzed in my pocket and my heart lifted. I prayed it would be Tinkie or Cece. I answered in a whisper.

"Sarah Booth," Sheriff Glory said, "I'm on the way. There's something you should know. The fingerprints we lifted in Cece's car were a match for the prints we took off the gasoline cans under Snaith's house."

The person who'd attacked Snaith and planned to burn him alive in his shop had also been in Cece's car. "Who do they belong to?" My heart was hammering so loud I almost couldn't hear her answer.

"No one in the system."

"You checked with Coleman?" He had Gertrude's prints on file. He could match them.

"I did. No match."

"The killer has Cece." There was no other conclusion.

"You and Tinkie stay safe. I'm on the way."

"See if you can find anything on Claudia Brooks's brother. I believe he's our killer."

"We're already searching for him."

"Hurry, Sheriff Glory. I think Tinkie may be in big trouble, too."

The sound of a dog howling came to me, and I thought I recognized Brutus's voice far in the distance. Was something bad happening up at the office? I was having zero results trying to search the woods in the darkness. If Cece were gagged or unconscious, she couldn't answer me, and I didn't believe I would be lucky enough to just stumble upon her. I needed powerful lights and volunteers to truly do a grid search. In the darkness, with a flashlight fading to weak, it was possible I'd been ten yards from her and missed her. It was time to accept that my efforts here were useless.

I started back to the road at a trot. I had to find Tinkie, to make sure she and Hans were okay. I could see the sandy trail through the last of the trees. I was almost there. My brain was going a thousand miles a minute as I shifted pieces of the puzzle, trying to make a solution fit, trying to look at the evidence anew. I stopped abruptly. We were looking for Claudia's brother as a possible suspect. The memory of Hans dancing with Cece and Tinkie was like a physical slap. Hans said he came from a dance family. Hans, the journalist, had the perfect opportunity to ask questions about everyone. Fear surged through me. I'd just sent my best friend off with the killer.

A noise in the underbrush told me someone was following me. I clicked the flashlight off and suddenly, something swung out from the darkness and hit my forearm with enough force to knock the flashlight into the underbrush.

"What the hell?" I turned and ducked simultaneously, and a good thing. Hans O'Shea stood panting beside a big maple, a tree limb in his hand. He swung it again at my head. By some miracle, I avoided the blow and dove clear of the underbrush and into the sandy road. I rolled as he came after me, thwacking the ground with brute force as he tried to hit my head.

"Hans! Stop it. It's over. The law is on the way."

"He's going to pay." He struck at me again and missed my head by an inch. I felt the breeze of the tree limb. He was trying to beat me with a stick, but he had a pistol in the waistband of his pants. If I had half a chance, I'd get it. As if he could hear my thoughts, his hand went to the gun and brought it out.

I'd watched a few Westerns back in my day, and it was always the bad guy who pulled this move, but I didn't care. I grabbed a handful of sand, jumped to my feet, and threw it into his eyes. He cried out in rage and came at me blindly. I tripped him with my foot and grabbed the tree limb from his hand as he had to use his arms to break his fall.

When he was down on both knees, I swung the limb with all of my might, making a solid connection with his ribs. Hans sent the gun flying into the woods, and he sank into the dirt in a moaning heap. I took one more swing with the tree limb, and Hans went down. He was whimpering so I knew he was alive, and he was conscious.

I put my foot on the ribs I'd just broken and pressed. "Where is Cece? And if you've hurt Tinkie, I will flay you alive."

"I'll deal with Tinkie and the Reynoldses when I'm done with you. Cece, though, is just another floater,"

Hans gasped. He tried to laugh. "A floater in the Dead Sea. That really appeals to me." He collapsed in the road. I tried to roll him but he grabbed my wrist. He'd been playing possum. I twisted free and this time I brought the tree limb home on his left temple.

"Lights out, asshat."

I wanted to kick him repeatedly, but instead checked the trunk for something to tie him with. I didn't find anything, but when I examined him, he was out cold. When I next saw Coleman Peters he was going to give me a set of handcuffs. And a Taser. And a baton. Next time, I would be equipped. My flashlight was completely dead, and I spent valuable minutes searching in the dark for the gun Hans had lost. He'd thrown it into the undergrowth and I couldn't find it. Deviled by images of Cece slowly drowning in the Dead Sea, I gave up the search.

I bolted up the path toward the Dead Sea.

35

The night was cool and I ran up and down the hills, praying my sense of direction was accurate. I didn't even have a flashlight, and in hindsight I worried that I should have searched harder for the gun. Sure, Hans was unconscious, but that didn't mean he was permanently disabled. Besides, I didn't know who else I might run into.

I thought of all the time we'd spent with Hans. He'd been so charming and interesting we'd never seen it. He'd all but served it up to us on a silver platter with his dancing and sticking to us like glue. And we hadn't even realized it.

It was almost perfect. Erik had once been investigated for poisoning a dance competitor, Johnny Braun.

Time had passed, and suddenly Betsy Dell turned up trying to buy an ad in the local paper accusing Erik of murder. Betsy had undoubtedly been manipulated into trying to place that ad, which was intended to bring up the past and cast Erik in a bad light. With his former dance associates dropping like flies, Erik would look completely guilty to a jury. I had to hand it to Hans, he'd spun a delicate web that had snared Erik time after time until my client was completely cocooned in deceit. Hans was perfectly willing to put his burgeoning career on the chopping block to get this done. Hans had what it took to be a network personality. He was a travel reporter with an internet viewership that was skyrocketing. He'd trashed his whole life to frame Erik.

In the distance I heard the wild baying of Brutus. He was ahead of me, and I hoped that somehow Daniel Reynolds was with the dog. If Cece were in the Dead Sea, I might need help with CPR. She couldn't be dead. She couldn't. It was unthinkable. I had wheedled Cece into taking a little time away from work to come with us. I'd thought I could keep her safe. How wrong I was. Even Tinkie could be in risk. Hans said he hadn't hurt her, and he really hadn't had time to do much—he was back in the woods with me in a flash. But I didn't trust him at all. Were the Reynoldses okay? My mind was a whirligig of dire scenarios.

At least Brutus was out and running in the woods. I could hear him ahead of me. That gave me hope.

I chugged up the last hill, panting and with a stitch in my side. The Dead Sea was not far now. Any minute I'd be able to see the ripple of the water in the moonlight. And Cece would not be there drifting about in a dead man's float. She wouldn't.

At last I came to the little path to the lake. I pressed through the low shrub branches to the edge of the lake. My heart almost stopped when Brutus joined me, staring intently out at the water. He began to bark, running in and out of the lake, almost demanding that I follow.

"What?" I asked him, wishing he could talk. With his keener senses, he knew something I didn't. Hampered by the dark night, I didn't see anything in the water. The moon had shifted behind a cloud and the horizon was merely black.

"Cece!" I called. "Cece, where are you?"

"Give it up, Sarah Booth. You can't save her. She's gone."

Hans stood behind me with the gun I should've looked harder to find. It was pointed at my chest.

"Rookie mistake to leave the gun." He was gloating.

My aggravation level rocketed to red alert. "What are you, freaking Jason? Somebody kills you and you pop right back to life? You were out cold. I hit you really, really hard. You should be in the hospital with a brain bleed. I know I broke your ribs."

"I'm not as fragile as my sister."

As much as I wanted to do something dastardly to Hans, my focus was on the lake as the moon broke through and the silvery light illuminated the water perfectly. Hans was between me and dry land. I would have to figure a way to get around him if I intended to escape. I was a strong swimmer, but not faster than a speeding bullet. In the water there was no cover.

"I figured it all out, Hans. You blame Erik for dropping your sister during a dance and causing her paralysis. She killed herself recently and that was the trigger that sent you on a killing spree." I waved a hand at him.

"That's pretty standard psychological profiling 101 trigger stuff. Not very original, you know." I hoped to provoke him so he might rush at me and at least I'd have a chance at knocking the gun from his hand.

His features were visible as the moonlight slipped through the branches of a tree, and I saw the anger building. Yet he was too smart to come at me directly. "My sister was everything to me. She didn't deserve to have her life stolen from her. I had to change my name, create Hans out of thin air. A big weight loss, a little nip and tuck, and I was a whole new person with a chance to avenge my sister."

"Do you think Erik really meant to drop her? Did your sister believe Erik was negligent or deliberately failed to lift her properly? Did Claudia blame Erik or herself? Erik said they were both to blame. He told me that Claudia went into the lift with bad footing and was off balance. She overbalanced him and they both fell. It was an accident."

"He pushed her to do that lift. She was hesitant, but he kept pushing. You can't shame a person into doing something they're afraid of and then pretend you're not responsible for the consequences. She'd be alive and happy today if he hadn't made her feel like a coward about that lift. She didn't blame him, but she should have."

I couldn't speak to what had happened to his sister. Unless he was there, neither could he. Now probably wasn't the time to make that point. "Tragedies don't always have logical explanations." I was speaking from personal experience. "Bad things happen." My parents died in a one-car accident on a straight road through cotton fields. There was no explanation for the wreck that had killed them both when I was only twelve. I had a crazy woman chasing after me with one desire—to put me and the people I cared about in an early grave. There was no logical reason for Gertrude to hate me so much, but she did.

"You don't know how Claudia suffered. You have no idea what losing the use of her legs did to her. My sister was so beautiful and alive. When she danced people couldn't look away. She was in love with the world. The day they put her in that wheelchair she began to die. She just curled into herself and stopped living until, in the end, she was only a dried little husk of the person she'd once been. It was a long and cruel death."

"You went after Erik because you blame him for the accident. And Slay let you down in the lawsuit. Snaith you blame for giving her bad medical advice. But why Patrice and Ana Arguello and Betsy?"

"Patrice and Ana made it clear they were ready to step on Claudia to get what they wanted. She felt she didn't have time to heal properly, that she had to dance even when she should have rested and recovered because they were ready to push her aside."

There was no point in arguing with Hans that Claudia always had the right to say no. That she could have insisted on self-care instead of pushing too hard. It was a predicament a lot of athletes faced. "And Betsy? She was on your side. She wanted to punish Erik."

"At first. But she was losing her nerve. I sent her the ad copy and the money to have it printed. She was about to fold and tell the sheriff."

"Betsy knew you were Claudia's brother?"

He shook his head. "No, I sent her the material anonymously. With a little extra cash for her trouble. She was only too happy to do it. But you and your part-

ner and the sheriff would have figured it out. You were getting closer and closer every day."

"You left Snaith alive. Why didn't you finish the job?"

"That moron Cosmo showed up to get something Snaith was concocting for him. I spooked him out of the apothecary, but I was afraid he got a look at me. That's why I lured him over to the Reynoldses' shed."

"I know you're hurting from the loss of your sister, but will any of this help? Erik can't undo anything that happened. He never meant for any harm to come to your sister, but he can't change any of it. I honestly believe he would if he could."

"You *believe*." He mocked me. "Give Erik the benefit of the doubt. Maybe he didn't mean for it to happen." He swung the gun around. "No! I'm not giving him anything. My sister was destroyed and now she's dead. That's on him. He dropped her. She didn't weigh more than ninety pounds, and he dropped her. That's on him!"

Clearly this wasn't the topic to debate. The more he talked, the angrier he became. I had to calm him down. I shifted closer to the lake, and the ground trembled. The slight, rhythmic rumbling of . . . a running horse. I knew of only one person who might be riding her horse in a miniature Holy Land at midnight. Sheriff Glory was on the way. I had to alert her that Hans had a gun. He could easily shoot her as she rode up. He had nothing to lose, and he knew it.

Brutus, who'd been so quiet, suddenly erupted into barking and growling. He stood at the edge of the lake bouncing up and down, barking at the rippling moon-glow that a soft wind had kicked up. The dog was laser focused on something floating about halfway across the surface of the big lake.

"Cece!" I started into the water. "Cece!"

"You're too late. She's been floating out there for too long now. She was too sedated to swim. Stop or I'll shoot you in the back. I don't have anything to lose."

"Why? What did Cece ever do to you?"

"She found the herbicide I used on Patrice. When we were doing some stories for my cable show, she went out to the car to get something. She found the herbicide in the backseat and she put it together, just the way you did. I told her if she didn't leave with me I'd kill you and Tinkie."

Brutus gave one desperate volley of barking, and far in the distance I heard an answering bay. I listened again. It wasn't possible, but I knew that voice! It was Sweetie Pie Delaney, my very own red tick hound. If Sweetie Pie was here, so was Coleman. If I'd ever needed his protection, now was the time.

"Sarah Booth, don't try anything stupid. Get back up here," Hans ordered.

"Come and get me." I waded deeper, expecting a bullet in the back at any minute, but I had to take the risk. The farther away from him I stood, the better my chances.

The beat of a horse traveling hard and fast was now clear even to Hans. "I'll shoot her, too," he said. "I like Sheriff Glory, but I'll shoot her just the same."

"You don't have to take this further. Hans, does the revenge taste as sweet as you anticipated? It never does."

"It's not about sweetness. It's about justice. My sister is dead because of Erik. It's only fitting that Erik should be punished. And he will be. I'll see to that."

He cocked the gun just as Raylee burst into sight. The horse was running wide open, but he was riderless.

"Where the hell is Sheriff Glory?" Hans noticed the empty saddle and he started to laugh. "She's fallen off her own horse. Some trick rider she is! Now, Sarah Booth, this is your last chance, get your ass out of that lake. Now!"

The appearance of the riderless horse disconcerted me. I'd been counting heavily on Glory's help to save Cece. Now it looked like only half the cavalry was coming to the rescue.

"Glory! He has a gun." I didn't know if she'd dismounted down the trail or if the horse had gotten away from her, but I had to try to warn her. And I wanted a distraction. As soon as he looked toward the horse, I hurled myself into the cold water.

Hans whipped back to me. "Shut up." He fired.

I came up for air and dove back into the deeper water, and the chill was such a shock I couldn't tell if I'd been hit. Brutus had reached whatever was floating in the water and he had grabbed it and was pulling it toward shore. I could only pray it wasn't Cece, or if it was her, that she wasn't dead.

I came up for air and saw that Raylee had passed Hans, turned around, and was coming at the killer again. When Raylee circled sideways to reverse, I had a clear view of Glory hanging on the offside of the horse, biding her time to jump Hans. With his superior weight and power, she'd need the element of surprise if she meant to take him. I saw her plan, and I rushed toward the shore and Hans. I would divert him to give her a chance.

"Hans! I'm going to kill you!" I hurled the threat at

him as I plowed out of the water and onto dry land. My teeth were chattering and I felt like my joints were frozen.

Hans took the bait, but only for a split second. He shot once at me and then fired the gun up in the air to divert the horse, but Raylee kept coming. When Hans pointed the weapon at the horse, I screamed out. Taking another wild shot at me, Hans failed to notice the form that suddenly appeared in the saddle with a lariat. Glory swung the rope and neatly captured his gun arm. She jerked the rope tight and when Raylee hit the end of the slack, Hans was jerked slam out of his shoes. I was surprised his arm wasn't ripped off by the force of the galloping horse. His scream was sweet music.

I began swimming toward the body that Brutus was dragging back. There was a splash behind me and Sweetie Pie was also in the water speeding toward us. In a moment she had hold of Cece's clothes and the two dogs and I worked as a team to bring Cece to shore, for it was indeed my friend.

All I wanted was my friends to be safe and a quiet corner to sit down in and stop the ridiculous shivering that made me feel like the protagonist in some creepy Victorian novel.

I put all of my thoughts and focus into getting Cece to shore, and I swam with the dogs. I could clearly see the edge of the lake and the horse and rider as Glory dragged Hans to the place where I'd been standing. A tall, broad-shouldered man jogged up. When he looked out to the water and saw us coming with Cece, he threw off his hat and gun, did a shallow racer's dive, and came after us. Coleman was a terrific swimmer—something I hadn't realized.

He was at my side in record time. "Are you okay?"

"I am. It's Cece. I don't think she's breathing."

He didn't try to verify my worst fear, he merely put his effort into helping the dogs get her to shore.

36

Cece's skin was flawless white porcelain, a color not seen on a person with pumping blood. Water dripped down her cheeks as we pulled her up on the bank. Her mouth was open slightly, but I couldn't tell if she was breathing. She'd been floating on her back, but I didn't know if that was a good sign or happenstance.

"Cece! Cece!" I knelt beside her and chafed her cold hands. The water temperature was frigid. That's what had stolen the blush from her cheeks. That had to be it. My friend was alive. "Cece, don't leave us."

Brutus had withdrawn into a guard stance beside Hans O'Shea, who lay facedown in the sandy path. Sweetie Pie hovered over Cece and licked her face as if she were drying her tears.

"Call the paramedics," Coleman said.

I had to get the phone out of his pocket because mine was drenched. My trembling hands didn't help matters. "Is she alive?" I asked, terrified of the answer.

"Her pulse is really weak," Coleman said as he began chest compressions. "She's still with us, but I don't know if she's inhaled water or if she's been drugged."

"She's been drugged." I told him what I'd learned from Hans. If Coleman needed more information I'd get it out of Hans one way or the other. He was conscious on the path. I could see the gleam of his eyes in the moonlight. Oh, I would welcome the chance to make him sing.

The dispatcher answered and I gave her the information. She assured me an ambulance had already been called for my location and was on the way.

Kneeling beside Cece, I gave two rescue breaths for every thirty chest compressions Coleman performed. Whenever I glanced at Hans, it gave me great pleasure to see Brutus hovering, saliva dripping from jaws that could almost contain Hans's entire head. Anytime Hans tried to move, Brutus sat on him, crushing the air out of his lungs, which I thought was a fine and fitting thing to do.

"Tinkie!" I had to trust Cece to Coleman and Glory. Tinkie was still AWOL.

"Where is Tinkie?" Coleman asked, his question coming in a short, breathless gasp as he worked to keep Cece's heart pumping.

"Calm down, Sarah Booth. She's keeping an eye on the Reynoldses," Glory answered. "I'm still not certain what their role is in this, but when I arrived I found them all trussed up. I cut Tinkie loose and left her to guard them."

"You swear Tinkie is okay?"

Glory nodded. "She's doing what I asked her."

"You think the Reynoldses have a role?" I asked. I would plot some very delicious revenge for them, too, if they were involved in my friend's situation.

"Not in the murders," Glory said, "but something is going on with Cosmo. They definitely know something about that, and they're going to spill everything before this night is over."

"We should call Erik," I said.

"Tinkie did," Glory said. "He's rounding up Betsy Dell to bring her out here."

"Why?" I asked.

"Betsy has something she needs to tell Hans. Something he's going to want to hear. She's going to tell him in front of Erik," Glory said.

I heard the sirens wailing through the woods, and in five minutes a team of paramedics arrived with a stretcher. We cleared back and let them work on Cece. Glory and Coleman moved over to Hans. They untied him, cuffed him, and Glory tied his cuffed hands to a rope and then to her saddle horn and began to ride Raylee back to the office of the Garden of Bones. I hoped she'd get out of sight and put the horse in a fast trot so Hans had to run to keep up or be dragged.

I walked up to Hans and got in his face. "Justice rides a slow horse, Hans. Now you're going to see what it feels like to be behind that horse." I slapped Raylee's rump and he and Glory took off at a trot. When the slack went out of the rope, Hans was jerked forward at a brisk jog. Glory wouldn't hurt him, but she would put him through his paces.

* * *

After we got everyone back to the main office area of the gardens, Tinkie and I stood, arms around each other's waists, as the paramedics set up fluids, blood pressure checks, and all the things necessary to stabilize Cece. She was alive, and her color was returning as they tucked warm blankets around her. The paramedics were re-assuring us that she would fully recover once her body temperature was brought back to normal. Whatever drug she'd ingested was not going to be fatal.

Erik and Betsy arrived just as the ambulance left. Once Cece was on her way to the hospital, Erik literally pushed Betsy forward to stand in front of Hans. "Tell him." Erik's voice cracked with anger. "You'd better tell him right now."

Betsy looked around. If she was hoping for help from any of us, she was sadly mistaken.

"Do you have something to add to the case?" Glory asked.

Betsy started to cry. "I can't say it to Charlie."

"You can and you'd better start now." Erik pushed her even closer to Hans.

"What?" Hans's voice was ironhard, and it snapped Betsy's face up so that she stared into his eyes.

"I put soap on Claudia's shoe bottoms that night. I wanted to win the competition. I wanted to be the star just for that one night, to be the center of attention. I knew Erik and Claudia had the talent and were going to win, but I thought if maybe she slipped in one of the dances, I would have a chance. I didn't know she was going to do the lift. I swear it. I only wanted her to slip on the dance floor, not on the way into a lift."

"She was your best friend. She loved you like a sister."

Hans was colder than anyone I'd ever heard. "Her death is on you, Betsy. You killed your best friend."

"I know," she sobbed. "Don't you think I know that? Why else would I agree to help you with this crazy revenge scheme? I knew it was you who sent me the ad to put in the paper. I knew you were hurting people. I knew you were the one who attacked me and tried to poison me. But I didn't say anything, because guilt has been eating at me."

"People are dead," Tinkie said to her. "My friend almost died here tonight. You're as guilty of murder as Hans."

"I hated Perry Slay. He did screw over Claudia. I didn't care what you did to him. I didn't like Patrice, but she didn't deserve to die. But Ana? She wasn't even on the scene when all of this started. You shouldn't have killed her."

"No, you're right about that," Hans said. He leaned into Betsy's face. "I should have killed you. And if I get a chance to, I will."

Glory looked over at Coleman. "Consider yourself deputized in George County. Cuff her and put her in the back of my pickup."

"Is that legal?" Tinkie asked.

I shook my head. "I don't know and I don't care. Glory can sort it out at her office."

When both prisoners were in the bed of the pickup and Raylee had been loaded into his trailer, Glory asked us all to stop by the sheriff's office before we left town.

"What about Cosmo?" I asked. "He's still missing. He may be in trouble."

"I know where he is," Daniel Reynolds said. "He's not hurt. He's just . . . out of trouble for the time being."

"Where is he?" Glory asked. "Don't beat around the bush. Spill it."

"I'm not telling where he is. He was going to poison the plants around the springs that feed the Dead Sea and River Jordan. He was going nuclear on total destruction. Snaith had cooked up something for him that would have left this area completely barren for years." He looked at me and Tinkie. "We fixed him so he can't do anything bad."

"Get Cosmo and bring him here," Glory said. "Now. And bring the poison."

"Go on with the horse and your prisoners," Coleman offered. "I'll find him and bring him along to you. Since I'm deputized, it shouldn't be a problem." He grinned at her.

"Thanks," Glory said. "I'm glad this case is wrapped up." She looked around at us. "I'll need statements from everyone. Now I have a hungry horse to feed." She climbed in the truck and took off.

Tinkie and I had done everything we could do. There were loose ends that needed sorting, but all could wait until daylight.

Tinkie put her arm around my waist. "I'm going inside to talk to the Reynoldses. Seems to me you and Coleman might have a few things to say to each other."

Coleman and I found a private moment, and I was in his arms in a flash. I'd never been gladder to see anyone in recent memory. For the hundredth time I realized what a haven his arms were, how the feel of his chest pressed against mine was a comfort I craved as much as I needed air and water. Only a few weeks earlier, I'd come so very close to losing him. Doc Sawyer, the sawbones in Zinnia who'd spent his career patching Coleman, Tinkie, Cece, and me up from our misadventures, refused to say how Coleman had survived a gunshot wound that should have killed him. Magic elixir, extraordinary constitution, or just a plain miracle, the only thing Doc would say was, "Don't look a gift horse in the mouth, Sarah Booth. Take your miracle and say your thanks." And I did, every single day.

"Thank God you're here," I whispered against the damp cotton of his uniform shirt. Saving Cece had left him a little soggy, but so was I.

"I've been worried about you and your posse," he said, forcing a lightness into his voice. I appreciated the effort it took for him not to give in to the sweeping emotion—generally aggravation at being so afraid— that always followed relief. He held me back from him so we could stare into each other's eyes. "I couldn't come down here, Sarah Booth, because of Gertrude. I knew she was in Sunflower County. She was spotted and I thought twice that I had her in a trap. I meant to have her behind bars as my welcome home gift to you."

"Did you catch her?" I was afraid to hope.

"No. The day you and Tinkie were shot at, I had a roadblock out for her. A reliable source reported the car and an older woman driving it. I knew it was her." He sighed and tightened his arms around me a little. "We did stop a Chinese-red Roadster of the same vintage as yours, and there was an older red-haired woman driving it. When we pulled her over, she confessed she'd been paid to drive the car along a particular route. She had a map. Someone, namely Gertrude, had given her very good instructions for showing up and then disappearing. While I was distracted by that, Gertrude was down here trying to kill you."

"She's getting crazier and crazier." It was a fact. To go to such extraordinary lengths to harm me and my friends—it was psycho. "Do you have any idea where she might be now?"

"The last report was Memphis. The city cops there found another antique Roadster, Chinese red, dove interior, abandoned in a parking garage. I don't know where she's finding these cars, but it can't be cheap. She was registered under an alias at the Peabody. She's living life large."

"She is." The true horror of Gertrude was that she would disappear for weeks and then show up when my guard was down.

"When the officers staked out the hotel room, she never appeared. The only evidence there was the Roadster, which was a rental. The paperwork at the rental agency listed the car in the name of Libby Delaney, your mother."

I was going to kill Gertrude. To use my mother's name to terrorize me. That was the final straw. It was all-out war now, and I would kill her if I got the chance. "But no one has a clue where she is?"

"No one. And the better question, Sarah Booth, is who is funding this. Renting those antique cars, and there were four of them counting the one down here— we arrested a second driver, same story—the cost of hiring actors, the cost of Gertrude running around the state and keeping tabs on you enough to be able to pinpoint where you'll be, this is expensive."

"She sold the B and B. She has that money."

"Not enough for all of this elaborate scheming. This

little operation of diverting me and a number of law officers up in the Delta while she was running amok in Lucedale—that's costing someone big bucks."

I gave it some consideration and he was right. "If we can find who is funding her, we can find her."

"Exactly. And why they're funding her. Why would someone have it in for you?" Coleman's hands moved from my shoulders to my waist. The look in his eyes changed, too, from cool anger to hot anticipation. "Enough about that for now." He drew me toward him.

When he kissed me, I stopped fretting and worrying and fuming—I simply gave myself to the kiss. He was a master at it, and I loved the way his lips could bring me to a place outside the worries of the world. The heat that followed was swift and completely inappropriate in the parking lot of a miniature Holy Land. The rumors that the garden had once been called the Devil's Bones made me smile as we eased back from each other before the heat consumed us. Another few seconds and we would have burned past the point of return. Coleman just had that effect on me.

He gave a weak chuckle. "Sarah Booth, I swear. You go off for a girlfriends' weekend and you get in more trouble than an egg-sucking hound dog. I guess I'm going to have to put you on a leash and keep a tight hold on the end of it."

"I wouldn't try that!" Even when my body was trying to rebel and jump on him, I had to defend my independence. Speaking of hounds, Sweetie Pie sat at our feet and gave her little yodel of affection. She made it clear she liked Coleman, but she loved me. "Good girl." I broke away from Coleman to kneel beside her and give her the praise she deserved—and to give me a chance to gather my wits.

"She's a good dog," Coleman said.

"The best." Sweetie Pie and Brutus had helped me get Cece to land before Coleman stepped in. My respite of doggie kisses had given me enough time to gather my self-restraint. Coleman and I couldn't go at it like wild monkeys in the parking lot. Well, we could, but it would be bad form. And I didn't trust Tinkie not to make a video to use for blackmail purposes at a later date.

When I stood up, Coleman laced his fingers through mine. "Let's get Tinkie and make sure Cece is going to be okay. The paramedics seemed to think hypothermia was the worst of it. Then maybe you could show me your room at this B and B I've been hearing so much about."

"Sounds terrific."

"We have to find Cosmo first." Erik Ward stepped out of the shadows not the least bit embarrassed that he'd likely been spying on our little passion session.

"Cosmo is your problem, Erik." Of all the times I'd needed Erik to stay close so he had an alibi, now, when the case was over, he chose to stick to me like lint on Velcro. Cosmo was not my worry. I'd been hired to prove Erik innocent. Tinkie and I had done so. Now, I needed some time with my man. Alone time. "And don't you even think about coming to my room at the B and B and sneaking in the window again."

Erik cleared his throat and I realized Coleman was giving me a long stare. "It isn't what it sounds like."

"I should hope not."

Coleman was not a jealous man and he had no reason

to be. "I thought the Reynoldses knew where Cosmo was," he said.

"They won't tell me." Erik was annoyed. "I've been accused of every heinous crime in Lucedale for the past twenty years. Now that I'm proven innocent, I just want to find my friend and make sure he's safe."

Coleman waved me toward the office where everyone was gathered. "Go talk to the Reynoldses. See what's what. I'd like a word here with Erik."

Now that was a conversation I'd like to be a fly on the wall to hear. The lawman and the dancer. It could be a romantic comedy. I was grinning when I went into the office where Tinkie sat with Daniel and Paulette Reynolds. There wasn't any tension in the room, but so far no one had given up the whereabouts of Cosmo. Tinkie arched her eyebrows when I walked in, a signal that she was still on the job.

"Any sign of Cosmo?" I asked, directing my question to everyone.

"He's somewhere on the grounds," Tinkie said. "I just have to either figure out where or maybe Daniel or Paulette will tell me."

The married couple remained silent. They wouldn't even look at us or at each other. Something was definitely going on.

"I already know that Cosmo was going to poison the plants on this property," I said. "He had Snaith mix up the herbicide he was going to use. You said you had 'fixed him.' Now I need to find him and Glory needs to charge him with whatever laws he's broken."

Silence. Tinkie only rolled her eyes.

"Would you care for some hot tea?" Paulette asked. I'd never really met her but she was a pretty woman with upturned lips and beautiful, glossy hair. "You look a little damp and a lot done in. Tea would warm you up."

Something hot would have been lovely, but I preferred my heat packaged in a brown sheriff's uniform and in a candlelit room. "Please, just tell me where to find Cosmo so I can put an end to this bloody night."

Her lips shut and she said nothing else. I looked at Daniel, who was petting Brutus. Sweetie Pie had followed me in and she gave Brutus a come-hither look and a soft little yodel of temptation. My dog had fallen in love! Brutus, with his pirate look, was indeed a handsome rascal.

Daniel and Paulette could remain close-lipped, but I had a secret weapon. "Sweetie Pie, Brutus, let's go." The dogs were instantly out the door. Sweetie Pie could track Cosmo. She had a nose on her that could run to ground even the most delicate scent.

Tinkie stood up. "Last chance. If you've done something with him, you're going to be in a lot of trouble. Helping us find him might make it easier for you."

"The man was going to poison these gardens I've worked on for most of my life," Daniel said. "He had to be stopped."

For the first time a glimmer of real concern for Cosmo swept over me. Surely the Reynoldses had not harmed him. They were religious people. They weren't killers, unless I'd sadly misjudged them.

Tinkie nudged me. "We need to find him, and fast."

Tinkie and I followed the dogs out the door. Daniel and Paulette stepped into the night that would never end. Coleman and Erik were sitting companionably on the tailgate of his truck. "Did you find Cosmo?"

"They won't tell us, but Sweetie Pie will find him. We

need to get something for her to sniff from his cottage. We'll find him eventually."

Coleman slapped the tailgate of the truck and Sweetie Pie and Brutus jumped in. They were obviously a team, like me and Coleman. Erik, Tinkie, and I climbed in after them. "Erik can direct you to Cosmo's house through the woods. Save some time."

"Wait!" Daniel came forward. "I left him on a little island in the middle of the springs."

Tinkie and I had plowed through there. The water wasn't deeper than our knees. He could leave whenever he wanted. So why hadn't he wanted to leave? "What did you do to him?" I asked.

Paulette came forward. "We lied to him. We told him the concoction he was going to dump was already in the water. He'd have to wade through it to get away. He's just sitting there, because that stuff was obviously so toxic that he's afraid it'll kill him."

"But you didn't put the poison in the water?" Tinkie wanted to be sure and I didn't blame her. The Reynoldses could be facing charges of attempted murder if they'd actually put Cosmo on a hillock surrounded by deadly poisoned water.

"We did not. We would never do that. Heaven forbid, we wouldn't poison our own property and that stuff he had would have laid this land barren for at least three generations. We just wanted to teach him a lesson."

And they'd done a masterful job of that. "Let's go get him. Glory will want him down at the jail. Attempted environmental poisoning surely is some kind of felony."

"Good luck convincing him to step into that water." Daniel chuckled and his wife started to laugh. "Smote by his own hand." They both laughed harder, and I couldn't help it, I joined in.

"I'll get him." Erik was still shaking his head as he jogged off to find his friend.

It didn't take long for Erik to return with a chagrined Cosmo. He went directly to the Reynoldses. "I'm sorry for what I almost did. You should know that I would never have forgiven myself. I love this land. Thank you for stopping me."

"If Cosmo will agree to simply live and let live, we can work this out," Daniel said. "He loves this land as much as I do. To be pushed to the extreme of poisoning it—he had to be in complete emotional distress. I think we can find common ground. I don't want to press charges."

I didn't know what to say, but Coleman did. "You'll have to sort that with Sheriff Glory. Perhaps Cosmo can agree to counseling or some community work here at the gardens. If he understands what this place is, maybe he will treat it with respect and love."

"Great idea," Reynolds said. "Cosmo and I have a lot more in common as friends than we do as enemies. And that's what the good book teaches. Forgive."

"We should head out," Tinkie said. She'd taken a seat on a bench and she did look exhausted. "I'm buying a new wardrobe and new shoes when I get back to Zinnia," she said. "Vanity be damned." She made a face and turned to the Reynoldses. "Apologies for the cursing."

"No apologies necessary. A dark cloud of evil came over us here, and you've chased it away. We owe you thanks."

"Put Cosmo in the back of the truck," Coleman pointed out.

"You guys go to the B and B," Erik said. "I'll take Cosmo to the sheriff's office and sort it out with Sheriff Glory. I'll tell Sheriff Glory what the Reynoldses have offered. I'm pretty sure she'll release him to come home, so I'll return him here."

"I do thank you," Cosmo said to Daniel and Paulette. "I almost did a terrible thing. It made me realize how easy it is to step into the shadow of evil. I'd be happy to work here to help you with the miniature Holy Land and the gardens, if you'll have me. I need to change myself and this is a good place to start."

"No need for Erik to bring you back, Cosmo," Daniel said. "I want to speak on Cosmo's behalf. If the sheriff listens to me, I'll bring him home."

Coleman opened the truck door. "Let's load up and get moving. I have some business that is pressing urgent." He winked at me as I put Sweetie Pie in the backseat and made room for Tinkie in the front. Our duties were done for the night.

Donna insisted on making a round of martinis for us and bringing it into the garden where the fairy lights twinkled and a magnificent moon commanded the sky. I only wanted to leap into Coleman's arms and renew our passion. But first Cece.

"Coleman, have you had any word on Cece?" I knew Sheriff Glory, though she seemed genuinely fond of Tinkie and me, would share more fully with another law officer.

"She's doing fine. Glory said the doctor would release her in the morning to go home."

That news cheered me immensely.

"Glory wanted it clearly understood that you three are to head home immediately, as soon as Cece is released. They have her car down at the sheriff's office, and Glory had a mechanic check it over. It's fine." He grinned. "She said it would take her the next two years to rejuvenate Lucedale's reputation as the safest small city in the nation."

"That wasn't exactly our fault," I told Coleman. "We had nothing to do with Hans O'Shea's, aka Charles Brooks's, obsession with revenge."

"Nor that same obsession coming from our local fruitcake Gertrude Strom," Tinkie said with some vehemence.

"Don't talk bad about fruitcake. Sarah Booth makes a pretty good one." Coleman put his arm around me.

"Any word on Gertrude?" I asked. I was hoping they'd somehow run her to ground in Memphis.

"She vanished into thin air." Coleman was a little grim, even as he thanked Donna for another drink.

"Is she even alive?" I had to ask it. Gertrude, with each attempt she made to hurt me, was becoming more and more mythic. "I mean she seems to be more Ringwraith than human."

"True that," Tinkie said. She was sipping a very tall sweet tea and sighing with pleasure. "But she's going to slip up, Sarah Booth. And then we'll have her and Coleman will lock her up and throw away the key."

"I will." He picked up my hand and rubbed the back of it with his thumb. "If I don't get her, old age will soon." We laughed, but deep in my heart, I wasn't laughing at all. Gertrude had to be stopped. She was going to hurt or kill someone I loved, and I couldn't continue with that hanging over me. Once I had Tinkie and Cece safely back in Zinnia, I intended to hunt for Gertrude. The prey would become the hunter. I'd been willing to leave her alone, hoping she'd grow tired of trying to kill me. That wasn't going to happen. Whatever wires had short-circuited in her brain, time wasn't going to un-cross them.

Coleman leaned over to me. "You aren't in this alone."

"I know that. It's what worries me the most."

He kissed the back of my hand. "Why don't you call Jaytee and let him know that Cece will likely be home tomorrow. I've kept him updated, but I'm sure he'd like to hear it from you that she's fine."

"Good idea." Coleman always remembered the things that slipped past me. I reached into my back jeans pocket for my phone to find it gone. Then I remembered it was waterlogged. "Can I borrow yours?"

"It's in the truck. I'll get it for you."

"No." I pushed him back into his seat. "The trunk is around the corner, not fifty yards from here. I can walk over there and get it. I need to move and I need a mo-ment to myself."

"Bring some more snacks," he said. "That Donna knows how to put together a good nosh. I'll bet she and Harold could roll out some finger foods at a party."

"No doubt." I kissed his lips lightly, just a promise of what was to come as I left to find his phone. "Make our excuses and meet me in my room," I whispered.

"I'll give you ten minutes, then I'm coming after you." There was an edge to his voice that sent a blaze of heat through me.

I took off at a trot so I would have enough time to answer all of Jaytee's questions and still meet Coleman within the time frame. I'd just rounded the corner of the inn when I stopped in my tracks. A beautiful woman was reaching up to pick an apple from a laden tree. A naked woman. Both the woman and the apple tree had magically appeared. She seemed to have no sense of her nakedness. She was childlike in her innocence.

"Who are you?" I asked, realizing as the words left my mouth that I should have known better. It had to be Jitty. She was the only haint who could appear in such magnificent beauty in the middle of a garden where anyone, at any moment, could walk around the corner and see her.

"Do you believe knowledge should be forbidden?" she asked.

I wasn't going to get caught in this trap. "Sometimes I do, and sometimes I don't. Humans do a lot of terrible things with knowledge, like building atomic weapons and learning how to maim and kill vast numbers of people. We'd be better without that knowledge."

"Is that your answer?" she asked. Her fingertips caressed the apple, and I knew who Jitty was portraying. Eve. According to the good book, her desire for knowledge was what got her and Adam booted out of the Garden of Eden.

"No. Because science has also cured a lot of diseases and given sick people a chance to stay alive."

"Is that your answer?" she asked.

I shook my head. "I don't have an answer. It would be marvelous to be innocent all of our days, wouldn't it?" I thought back to the years when my world was so much easier to navigate. Right and wrong were simple. No shades of gray. No struggling to pick the least bad path. Life had an order and a purpose back then that I'd somehow lost.

"Ignorance is bliss," Jitty said. From somewhere she'd gotten some fig leaves to cover her nakedness. How she kept them in place I couldn't say. And I wasn't going to ask. She wouldn't tell me anyway. "You don't have any responsibility to choose good over evil if you're ignorant."

I was seeing more and more benefits to the innocent aspect.

She sighed and the last vestiges of the biblical Eve slipped away, leaving full-bore Jitty. "If you were so innocent, you wouldn't have a smokin' man waiting for you in a big comfy bed."

"Oh." She had a point. Truly innocent meant no sexual pleasures.

Jitty grinned wickedly. "'Oh.' Is that all you can say?"

"I can say goodbye. Goodbye." I tried to brush past her but she called my name.

"You're just here to torment me, Jitty. I'm tired. Coleman is waiting on me. I would have thought you'd be pushing me in a wheelbarrow to that bedroom."

"Life isn't fair, Sarah Booth."

There was such sadness in her voice that I faced her and inhaled. "What's wrong?"

"Nothing. Yet."

"Please, just tell me."

"I can't."

This was old ground. We'd covered it a thousand times since I'd come home to Dahlia House to find my ancestral home haunted by Jitty. "We've solved the case. Hans is arrested. Cece is okay. Tinkie is pregnant and while we're driving home, we'll talk about religions and belief systems, magic and ghosts—all the things she wants to either tell or hide from her baby when it comes."

"Tinkie is a traditionalist. She'll go with Episcopal."

I couldn't help smiling. Jitty was dead-on. That was the church Tinkie had been raised in, and that's where her little bundle of joy would also go. But Tinkie would be sure to expose her baby to all the wonders of the great teachers of other religions, too. This baby would have choices. And choice was all about knowledge. I had my answer for Jitty. "Reach up and grab that apple and take a bite," I said. "We can't make good choices without knowledge, and losing our innocence is the price of knowledge."

Jitty pulled one apple and the tree vanished. Still, she held the fruit in her hand. "Are you sure?"

"Positively."

"Better get that phone. I'll wait right here for you."

That was weird. Jitty generally disappeared with a pop and a sizzle. Now she was lingering. Frowning, I went to the truck and opened the passenger door. His phone must have come out of his pocket when I was jammed up against him. The memory made me realize I was ready for some full-body contact sports.

I saw the phone and reached for it and a note fluttered onto the floorboard. Curious, I picked it up.

The note read: *It's not over, Sarah Booth. Not by a long shot.*

I looked over to see Jitty waiting for me with a worried expression. She'd seen Gertrude slip up here. It wasn't over. It wouldn't be over until either I was dead or Gertrude was locked away. That knowledge sank into me all the way to the bone.

I folded the note and put it in my pocket and made

the quick call to Jaytee, who was in between sets at Playin' the Bones. His joy at Cece's safety and return home was the real deal.

When I looked back at Jitty, she was gone. A single apple sat on the side of the fountain, which had replaced the apple tree. When I walked by, I picked up the apple, polished it on my shirt, and took a big bite. I could handle the truth. And I would handle Gertrude Strom. Coleman would help me.

At the thought of Coleman waiting for me, I picked up my pace until I was running over the gravel and up the stairs. I didn't stop until I was in the bedroom. Coleman was under the covers in bed. "I choose you," I said to him.

I stepped out of my clothes and slid up against him.

"Are you okay?" he asked.

"I am." I could tell him about the note tomorrow. "I'm so glad you're here."

"Not as glad as I am! Let me show you."

I reached over and turned out the light.

Acknowledgments

When I was in grammar school in Lucedale, Mississippi, the Easter trip to Palestine Gardens (formerly Palestinian Gardens) was one of the high points of the year. On Good Friday, my class would take a school bus to the western edge of the county where we would tour the miniature Holy Land created by a Presbyterian minister with a love of history and geography. As Reverend Harvell Jackson led the tour, Bible stories came to life.

Following the tour, we'd have an Easter egg hunt in the open fields and woods around the gardens. Our classroom mothers provided the dyed eggs, candy, and prizes. While we toured the miniature Holy Land, they would be busy hiding eggs. Following the egg hunt, there would be sandwiches or burgers and ice cream—another treat provided by the classroom mothers. It was a day of adventure, learning, and fun. It is one of my favorite and most carefree memories.

While the miniature Holy Land in my fictional story is based on the real place, none of the events portrayed in the book ever happened. To my knowledge, a dead body has never been found among the holy cities.

Reverend Jackson and his wife began creating the miniature Holy Land in 1960 and gave year-round tours to anyone who stopped and showed an interest. There was never a charge. You could donate if you wished to support the project. As the years passed, the cities and towns of the Middle East sprang to life, the project growing and covering more land.

Reverend Jackson retired and sold the gardens to Don Bradley and his wife, who now manage the property and give tours, still maintaining and building on. If you're ever in the area, it's just off Highway 98 west of Lucedale. And if you'd like to look into it, here's an article from Atlas Obscura: www.atlasobscura.com/places/palestine-gardens.

So many things go into writing a book—not just the writing but the sharing of ideas and thoughts, the editing, the typesetting, and the cover design. So many people work hard, not just the writer. I want to thank Jennifer Haines Williamson, Diana Hobby, Gloria Howard, Susan Y. Tanner, and Don Bradley, who helped me recapture the wonder of these magical gardens.

Many thanks to my terrific "team" at St. Martin's: Hannah Braaten, Nettie Finn, Lisa Davis, and John Morrone. Thanks also go to the art department's David Rotstein. A special thank-you to my agent, Marian Young.

As always, a thank-you to the wonderful readers and booksellers.

Another Sarah Booth adventure comes to a close, but there are more cases to be solved. Hope to see you in the future for the next *Bones* puzzle to solve.